# THE  VERMONT MYTH

PALMA HARCOURT

# *The Vermont Myth*

HarperCollins*Publishers*

This book is fiction. Any relationship between the characters in this novel and any person who exists in reality, including persons who may hold or have held official appointments mentioned in it, is purely coincidental.

HarperCollins*Publishers*
77–85 Fulham Palace Road,
Hammersmith, London W6 8JB

Published by HarperCollins*Publishers* 1994
1 3 5 7 9 8 6 4 2

Copyright © Palma Harcourt 1994

The Author asserts the moral right to
be identified as the author of this work

A catalogue record for this book is
available from the British Library

ISBN 0 00 224528 0

Set in Plantin

Printed in Great Britain by
HarperCollinsManufacturing Glasgow

# CONTENTS

# The Letters

*1993*

'It was your late father's request that a year to the day after his death, or as near as possible to that date, I should hand this envelope over to you personally. So – here it is.'

Charles Drew, now the senior partner of Drew, Drew & Watson, solicitors of Maiden Lane, London, smiled wryly as he slid a buff-coloured envelope across his desk. His firm had dealt with the Vermonts' affairs for many years, and he liked Peter Vermont, though their relationship was not close. Peter picked up the envelope, which had his name on it in his father's recognizable handwriting.

'Thank you. Do you know what's in it?'

'No. As you can see, it's sealed and, on this occasion, your father gave me no explanation.'

Peter nodded his understanding. He fingered the envelope, which was slim except that in one corner there was a small hard object. He didn't try to guess what it might be.

The older man studied him, wondering if he should make a suggestion. It was not really his business and, if anyone were capable of making his own decisions, it was surely Peter Vermont, at present in his mid-forties and a highly successful barrister. Nevertheless –

'Although, as I said, I have no idea what is in the envelope, your father assured me that its contents could have no possible bearing on his estate, and thus have no effect on the probate of his will. I took him at his word and have kept the matter entirely confidential, and I believe it might be wise if, until you are sure of his wishes, you behaved with similar circumspection. I need not add that I shall always be ready to help if and when you should consider it necessary.'

'I know. I'm grateful, and I shall certainly take your advice.' Peter gave the solicitor an amused glance and slipped the envelope into the inner pocket of his jacket. 'There was nothing else – no message?'

9

'No, but it may interest you to know that the envelope, together with the instructions concerning it, was delivered to me by a special courier from Switzerland some months before your father died.'

'Dad would have known he hadn't much longer to live. He'd already had one massive coronary.'

'So he told me when we last spoke on the phone. I was sorry to hear it. He was a fine man, Sir Simon Vermont. It was a great pity he had to retire early.'

'Yes. He would have liked to be Foreign Secretary.' Peter pushed back his chair and stood up. 'I must be off. Thank you once again.'

Charles Drew saw Peter Vermont to the lift where the two men shook hands and said goodbye. A cruising taxi took Peter to his chambers. It was lunch time and he hadn't eaten, but he was too curious about the contents of the envelope in his pocket to care about food.

He sat at his desk, pulled out the envelope and stared at it. To his surprise he suddenly felt apprehensive. He put this down to the solicitor's unexpected warning about the possible need for secrecy, and dismissed his forebodings. He reached for his letter-opener.

Peter Vermont was a tall, lean, attractive man to whom everything had come easily throughout his life. Educated, like his father and grandfather before him, at Eton and Christ Church, Oxford, where he had read law, he had accepted his good fortune without question. But he had worked hard, taken silk and became one of the most sought-after barristers in London. He had married for love the daughter of an impoverished farmer, and it was a good marriage. As a result, in middle age he was happy, contented, and perhaps inevitably a little too self-satisfied.

He slit open the envelope. It contained, in addition to the small hard object he had felt – which proved to be a key – a brief letter, undated, the heading that of the villa on the north shore of Lac Léman where his parents had lived. He read it through twice.

Dear Peter,

Sorry to be so mysterious, but the matter is highly confidential as you will appreciate later. Enclosed you will find the key to a safe-deposit box in the Geneva office of the Banque St-Pierre de Genève. The bank holds a second key; both are required to gain access to the box. Go there as soon as is convenient *without telling anyone* – not even Julia – of the purpose of your visit. Ask for Monsieur Le Rossignol. You will be expected. The contents of the box will, I hope, clarify the situation for you, and until that has been done you must accept that it would be most unwise to confide in *anyone*.

My apologies for imposing this task on you. I know you will deal with it as you believe best. I'm lucky to have had you for a son. I wish I could have been a better father.

Much love,

There was no signature, but only a squiggle of initials that could have been anything.

Peter blinked away a rush of emotion. He had loved his father. What was more, he had enjoyed his company and admired him as a man. Since he had become an adult, married and had children of his own, their relationship had become more that of friends, even brothers. But each had respected the other's privacy, and Peter had no clue as to the letter's meaning, though it appeared that after all Charles Drew had been right about the need for secrecy.

Then it occurred to Peter that possibly what his father wanted of him was to arrange some provision for an ex-mistress or an illegitimate offspring that needed care. Simon Vermont might have preferred to make no mention of such a thing in his will, which would in due course become public, and would also explain why he had not used his regular Swiss bank. However, if this were the case, he seemed to have made heavy weather of the procedure. Why, for instance, shouldn't Julia be told, and why the delay of a year from his death?

Peter sighed. His not to reason why. He would have to do as he had been asked, and the sooner the better in order to satisfy his own curiosity and assuage the slight anxiety that he found he still could not completely suppress.

He pulled his engagement diary towards him. As he would be going to a bank the weekends were out, and he was extremely busy at present, being forced to turn down briefs that he would have been pleased to accept had he been free. Frowning, he turned the pages of the diary. On Monday he was due to start the defence at the Old Bailey of the son of a peer accused of attempted murder. It promised to be a lengthy and complicated case which would ensure a lot of publicity, so that he would have to play his full part and leave the minimum to his junior. He certainly wouldn't be able to take a day off until it was over. His father's commission would have to wait and he would have to curb his personal feelings. It wasn't going to be an easy time.

In the event, six weeks passed before Peter had a chance to go to Switzerland. He had won the attempted murder case, and a grateful peer, in addition to the prompt payment of the huge fee for legal services, had sent him a dozen bottles of vintage claret. With other less well-publicized briefs, he had been fully occupied. He had also accepted a new brief for what looked like a long battle over an inheritance which would come to court in a fortnight. But now there was a short lull.

'Darling,' he said one night as he got into bed beside Julia, 'I have to go to Geneva next Thursday. Fly back Friday night with luck. Sunday at the latest. I'll phone before I leave.'

'Not this coming weekend, Peter!'

'Why not?' He was startled by her response.

'It's Antonia's birthday. Her party's on Saturday. We'll all be in the country. Surely you remembered that?'

Peter swore. He had forgotten. He reproached himself. How could he? He was proud of his two sons, both teenagers, but Antonia, who had been conceived during a holiday in Italy after he and Julia had given up hope of having a daughter, was his darling. Named after her great-grandmother, she was six, with wide brown eyes and curly brown hair – very like her mother – a solemn, dreamy child.

'She'll be dreadfully disappointed if you're not there.' Julia looked searchingly at her husband. 'Peter, is something wrong? You've been so – so distrait lately.'

For a moment he was tempted to tell her the whole story, but his father had been definite about the requirement for secrecy. 'No. Nothing's wrong. On the contrary. I'm just a bit tired.'

'Then why dash off to Geneva? Do you have to go? Why?'

'Yes.' He hated lying to her, but there was no option. 'I have to interview a potential witness before I decide whether or not to accept a brief.'

'I see.' She didn't sound convinced, but she didn't argue.

'Darling, I'll do my utmost to be home on Friday night, I promise

– even if it means having to go back to Switzerland later.' He drew Julia to him and kissed her. 'Forget it for now. I want to make love to you.'

Peter sank into his first-class seat with a sigh of relief. He was the last passenger to board the flight. In fact at one point he had despaired of catching it. The traffic on the way to Heathrow had been appalling that Thursday evening, and only the determination of Gussey, his chauffeur, had got him there in time.

The aircraft doors clunked shut. He fastened his safety belt and, as the plane took off, reached its required height and levelled off, he made himself relax. He accepted the proffered champagne and drank a silent toast to his father. He was looking forward to his meeting with Monsieur Le Rossignol of the Banque St-Pierre which he had arranged over the phone for ten o'clock the next morning. He would be glad to have the mystery inherent in his father's letter resolved.

He arrived at the bank at five minutes to ten, having first done some shopping and, precisely on the hour, after providing identification he was shown into an elegant room which, apart from a large semi-circular desk, in no way resembled an office. The carpet was deep, the furniture modern but obviously comfortable and custom-made, and among the paintings on the walls Peter recognized several Klees. He didn't doubt that they were originals.

Monsieur Le Rossignol, hand outstretched, came forward to welcome him. The banker was a tall, thin man – not unlike Peter, but slightly stooped. He had silver-grey hair, very thick and by English standards unfashionably long, a pointed nose and bright blue eyes. He wore morning dress, striped trousers, black jacket, a pearl pin in his wide grey silk tie. In impeccable English he offered Peter commiserations on his father's death.

'I would like to think that Sir Simon and I had been friends, Mr Vermont. It would certainly be fair to say that we had a nice appreciation of each other.'

Peter bowed his head in acknowledgement of this rather curious remark, and murmured his thanks. It wasn't often that he felt at a loss for an appropriate reply. He considered himself a good judge of men, but he didn't know what to make of this banker. However, the

niceties over for the moment, Monsieur Le Rossignol became businesslike.

'You wish to visit the safe-deposit box. You have your key?
Good. I suggest you take your briefcase with you as you may wish to
remove something, but that you leave your shopping here. It will be
quite safe.'

'I'm sure it will.' Peter placed the parcel he was carrying on a side
table that the banker had indicated. 'It's a small cuckoo clock.'

'A cuckoo clock?' The blue eyes widened in amazement. 'A
present for your wife?'

'No.' Peter laughed. 'For my daughter. Tomorrow is her birthday and she'll be six, as yet too young to appreciate one of your fine
Swiss watches.'

'Of course! Of course! A cuckoo clock. How delightful. It's the
sort of gift that your dear father would have thought of for a child,
Mr Vermont. You too, I see, are a family man, as indeed I would
have expected. Now shall we go down to the vaults?'

Down was the operative word, Peter thought, as the lift
descended further and further. When finally they arrived and the
gates opened, they were greeted by an armed guard. Monsieur Le
Rossignol signed a book. Then they went through two electrically-
operated doors, past another guard and eventually into a small
room, obviously one of several similar rooms. Its walls were lined
with numbered metal doors, each with its own keyhole in the
front. The only furniture was a table and two chairs. The banker
inserted his key into one of the locks and, when Peter followed his
example, slid out a surprisingly large deposit box and placed it on
the table.

'Here you are, Mr Vermont. I'll leave you alone for a few minutes
to examine the contents. The door of the vault can stay open. This
place is air-conditioned, but some of our clients find it claustropho-
bic. I'll be within call.'

'Thanks,' said Peter absently.

Peter sat himself at the table and opened the deposit box. It
contained a slim envelope – another letter? – and a heavy jiffy bag.
There was also a small leather chamois bag with a drawstring
opening.

Peter's guess was correct. It was another letter, also undated and
from the Lac Léman address. It read:

14

Dear Peter,

The typescript in the jiffy bag is self-explanatory. I have written the story in the form of a book for simplicity of reading and understanding. However, to the best of my knowledge it represents a true account of what happened and, I believe, is of some importance, even today. I asked Charles Drew to delay delivering the original letter to you for a year, until you were free of any commitments arising from my death, and could give your full attention to the tale.

It is right that you should know and understand it. The past has an unpleasant habit of suddenly blowing apart the present, as I've found to my cost. I hope the story will not come as too much of a shock, and that you won't judge me too harshly. I've tried to be fair and not to plead my own case. When you have read the typescript you will appreciate the situation. Take a deep breath, and decide to do whatever you think best. I have every faith in your judgement.

My love – and I mean it more deeply than I can express – to you and all the family.

The identical squiggle of initials followed.

The thought crossed Peter's mind that in his old age his father had suffered from some mental disorder, but he dismissed it at once. The letter had been handwritten, and the writing was firm, legible, grammatical. Only its content was inexplicable and absurdly melodramatic. He glanced in the jiffy bag. There were, he thought, at least three hundred pages of typescript. Impossible to read them now. A discreet cough outside the door reminded him of Monsieur Le Rossignol.

But there was still the little chamois leather bag. Peter emptied it into his hand. He didn't know what he had expected. Uncut diamonds? Gold sovereigns? What he had not expected was a large, ugly, gunmetal pocket watch, as unlike the Patek Philippe he was wearing as it could be. Absurdly he felt disappointed. He rebagged the watch, and hastily stuffed it into his briefcase with the type-script. He slid the deposit box back into its place and called to Monsieur Le Rossignol.

He would have liked to refuse the banker's invitation to coffee, but felt it important to remain on amicable terms with him. However, as soon as possible, having remembered to collect

15

Antonia's cuckoo clock, he was on his way to the Hôtel d'Estève by the Parc de la Grange, where he was staying, not for the first time.

He phoned Swissair. Yes, there was a midday flight to London. If he left at once he should get to Cointrin airport in time to catch it. He flung his clothes into his weekend bag, called down to Madame Fleurie at the desk to say he was leaving immediately and needed his bill and a taxi. Then he phoned his secretary in London and arranged for Gussey to meet him at Heathrow later that afternoon. He would be there for the whole of Antonia's birthday and would devote the weekend to the family; he admitted to himself that pressure of work had forced him to neglect them shamefully in recent weeks.

His father's 'book' would have to wait.

In fact it was not until Tuesday evening that Peter got around to the typescript. Alone in their town house in a square behind Knightsbridge – Julia was spending the week in the country – and having made himself a light supper, Peter sat in a comfortable chair in his study, coffee and brandy on a table beside him. He was relaxed. The vague fear he had experienced earlier had passed. By now he had glanced through the opening paragraphs of his father's book and had realized that it had been written as a novel, whatever facts the fiction might disguise.

Nevertheless, when Peter started to read the typescript in earnest, for his father's sake and because it was natural to him, he gave it the serious attention he would have given an important brief.

# THE BOOK

# Part One

*1944–46*

# CHAPTER ONE

There was a moon, but it was a sickly affair, much of the time obscured by scudding cloud, and the wind had risen, blowing across the field where the aircraft was to land. I wondered if it would come and what I would do if it didn't; I had no wish to spend another night in that barn among the rats, though I had been glad of the shelter. It was early autumn but none too warm at night. I shivered as I huddled under the hedge in my thin clothes.

The year was 1944. The Allies had invaded Europe a few months previously, but were meeting stiff resistance. The fighting fluctuated and there was no clear front line, so that there was considerable confusion, and that hadn't helped me. I had already been shot at once by a 'friendly' British soldier when I had stupidly panicked and run. But this time it was more than a year since I had been parachuted into Europe – too long a period to live in constant fear of capture, torture and death. I was feeling the strain. Nevertheless, I hadn't asked to be lifted. It was the powers-that-be who had ordered it, and the decision had seemed too good to be true. Perhaps it was. There was no sign of the plane.

I shifted my position on the hard ground, and winced as a sharp branch of the hedge pierced the skin of my neck. I was used to discomfort, but at twenty-four I reckoned I was getting too old for this sort of game. I thought how pleasant a cosy office job would be. I hoped they wouldn't send me back to France again after a bath and a debriefing. If they did I doubted I would survive unless the war ended very quickly. So far I had been lucky, but even a cat has only nine lives.

Still no sign of the plane – almost certainly a Lysander – which was badly overdue. I decided to count slowly to five hundred and, if it hadn't appeared by then, to salvage the radio transceiver that I had buried with some other gear in a nearby ditch, and then trek off somewhere. I would have to lie up until I could contact HQ and get fresh orders. Where I could lie up, I didn't know.

I had reached three hundred when I heard the sound of an aircraft engine. But it was too far to the west, off course. I stopped counting and strained my ears. The sound got louder. The damned plane seemed to be circling, doubtless alerting every German for miles around. Dare I risk placing the lights? I crawled out from under the hedge as the clouds parted and in the glow of the feeble moon I saw it.

The plane was closer than I had thought, and I rapidly placed my three torches in an L-shape with the point of the L at the upwind end of the meadow. By this time in the war we had got past the stage of attempting to light a flare path, especially when the lift was to be an agent operating without back-up. The pilot and his navigator were supposed to identify the site almost by instinct and the torch beams; it was a pity the moon was not brighter.

The small Lysander was suddenly coming in fast and low, too fast and too low. The pilot was never going to make it. Unless he realized his position and his danger and climbed and tried again he would hit the belt of trees at the side of the field to the right of me. For a long minute I watched in agony. There was nothing I could do.

And seemingly nothing the pilot could do either, for he made no attempt to gain height. The plane flew straight into the trees, then slewed sideways until it rested at an angle. There was the noise of splintering wood and metal and crashing branches as it settled, one wing pointing up into the air and the other crushed into the ground. The earth shook beneath me. The engines cut out. Silence, so heavy I could feel it. I started to run.

In the small short-take-off-and-landing aircraft used for these clandestine operations there were unlikely to be more than three or four people – pilot, navigator and perhaps an agent who was meant to take my place – but the chance that anyone had survived the crash was minute. Nevertheless, I had seen a body thrown clear, and I had to make sure that the poor bugger wasn't still alive. Strange things can happen in accidents, and aircraft crashes, as everyone knows, are no exception.

I reached the man and knelt beside him. One glance assured me he was dead, his head half severed from his body. In a way this was a relief, because if he had been alive I had no idea what I could have done for him. I had to think of myself, and the first thing was to get clear of this area before the Germans arrived.

But I had waited too long. I should have gone as soon as I saw the crash because, as I stood up, there was a dull boom and the aircraft burst into flames. The blast from the explosion knocked me off my feet, and I fell on top of the dead airman and lay there, cowering, while bits of metal hurtled through the air. I was not aware of being hit, not until I tried to stand and my left leg crumpled beneath me with an agonizing pain.

I was now in desperate straits. I had no chance of escaping. The most I could hope to do was crawl away from the trees before the plane, which was now well alight, collapsed on top of me. But the fire was illuminating the night sky, putting the moon to shame, and the Germans would be here any minute. It was surprising that they hadn't already been alerted.

The Germans were not fools. They would read the scenario laid out for them correctly – the wrecked light aircraft, the wounded man in civilian clothes with French papers, when no respectable Frenchman would be abroad after curfew. It wouldn't take a genius to guess that I was an enemy agent, a spy, who had expected either to be landed in France that night or to be lifted away. And they didn't like spies. They wouldn't treat me kindly before they shot me. They had no reason to show me mercy. I wasn't protected by any Geneva Convention.

While these thoughts skittered through my mind I was already beginning to act on them. Kneeling up, I took off the airman's helmet, removed his identity discs and, with a great effort, his padded jacket and his RAF battledress blouse; the two light blue rings on his battledress blouse showed he was a Flight Lieutenant. I noted his name and number, but I didn't have the strength to cope with his trousers, and luckily those I was wearing were a bluish grey and my shirt was a similar colour. His clothes were covered in blood, but I didn't care; the airman and I were much the same build and his garments fitted well. I changed quickly.

I threw my jacket with its false papers and francs into the blaze, but kept my gunmetal watch. At the last moment I added my cheap foreign-looking shoes which would have been a dead giveaway and, as a final gesture, slipped the airman's signet ring onto my little finger.

Then, dragging my injured leg, I started to crawl across the field. It was hard going, but I don't remember the pain and think my leg must have become numb. I didn't go too far, just far enough to be safe from the blazing aircraft and the trees surrounding it, some of which had been set alight. I had scarcely reached what I hoped was a suitable distance when two things happened: the wing and part of the burning fuselage collapsed, hiding, I was sure, the body of the airman I had stripped, and a lorryload of Germans arrived.

In fact, five of them plus an officer spilled out of the canvas-covered vehicle. They made straight for the remains of the burning plane and I wondered if they had seen me; I didn't want to be left with my wounded leg, possibly to bleed to death. I raised an arm and called out, but they were grouped in front of the plane and, intent on the fire, their backs turned to me, they paid my signals no attention.

One of them darted into the flames as if to retrieve something but retreated hurriedly, driven back by the heat and the flying sparks. I prayed that they hadn't spotted some tell-tale clue that might cause them to suspect that I was other than I seemed, a member of the Royal Air Force.

Then the German officer started giving orders. I couldn't hear what he said, but it was obvious they were going to retreat. At present there was nothing his men could do about the fire, which was in any case beginning to burn itself out. Already it was much less fierce than twenty minutes ago, and it was starting to rain. Clearly, they would leave someone on guard, and return in the morning to sift through the ashes, but that was no cause for anxiety; by that time the bodies would be indistinguishable, unidentifiable, merely charred remains, and, with any luck, I would be a prisoner-of-war, which was vastly superior to being a captured enemy agent.

I propped myself up on an elbow, waved and shouted, 'Help! Help!' The officer barked an order and two of his men, pistols in hand, approached me carefully, one from the left and the other from the right, as if they feared some kind of trap. '*Nein! Nein!*' I said anxiously. 'Don't shoot! Don't shoot! I'm injured,' I added in English, as if *nein* was the limit of my German, which in fact I spoke fluently.

The taller of the two soldiers frisked me to make sure I had no weapon and stood back to allow the officer to inspect me. He was young, not much older than me, with a thin pointed face. He didn't look like a professional soldier, and I guessed he had been some kind of academic in civvy street – a schoolmaster, perhaps. This guess was given credence when he spoke in correct, over-correct, English, but with a pretty fair accent.

'You are an American airman?' He sounded dispassionate, but he tut-tutted when he examined my leg.

'British!' I corrected him. 'Royal Air Force. Officer.' I knew my rank and my name and number, which was all that was necessary. I had had no opportunity to discover any more about the officer I was impersonating.

'Ah, yes. And you flew that aeroplane from England to France and into the trees. Bad show!'

When I didn't speak, he smiled, and I remember thinking that in different circumstances we might have become friends.

'Now, name!' I gave it and the number from the identity discs.

He asked me what I had been doing, if I had been dropping an agent or picking one up, and a few more questions, but he didn't expect answers. He knew the rules as well as I did. Name, rank and number. Then he instructed two of his men to give me a fireman's lift to their truck, and himself saw to it that I was made reasonably comfortable.

'You are now a prisoner of the German Reich, Englishman,' he said, not unkindly. 'The war is over for you, and soon it will be over for all of us. It cannot go on much longer.' Then he added in his own language and half under his breath so that I only just heard him, 'Though God knows who will be victorious in the end.'

He went around to the front of the lorry to sit beside the driver, and I never saw him again. I hope he survived, but I doubt it. The other four men climbed into the back and we started across the field. Lying on the floor, I felt every bump in the ground, however small, and fierce pain from my leg shot up into my body, so that I had to dig my nails into the palms of my hands to stop myself from crying out.

It was no better when we left the field and, with a heart-stopping lurch, crossed what I assumed was a ditch and reached a lane, for the lane had been rutted by farm carts. The van humped and bumped its way along. The noise of the engine and the rain beating on the canvas roof were the only sounds. The soldiers squatting around me made no effort to speak. They were mere youths – conscripts – and I think they were tired.

The journey seemed to me to be endless, but it can't have lasted more than twenty minutes or so before the van stopped abruptly, causing one of the soldiers inadvertently to kick my leg. I screamed with pain, but I didn't lose consciousness and, as the pain subsided,

I listened hard to the argument that was going on up front between the officer and the driver.

It was not difficult to follow. The driver had taken a wrong turning; these French lanes can be very confusing. And we were lost. If I had known where they wanted to go I could probably have directed them, but as they debated whether to go on, to turn back or to take what they hoped might be a short cut, I didn't volunteer.

I'm not sure what decision they finally arrived at, but whatever it was, it was the wrong one, for five minutes later we ran into a hail of gunfire. The canvas roof of our vehicle was no protection, and I was glad to be lying on the floor. At least a couple of the soldiers with me were shot, and the driver must have been hit too because without warning our van slewed sideways, seemed to climb up a bank and then fall – fall . . .

Or that is how I remember it. But, I admit, my memory is probably unreliable, at any rate about what happened after we left the scene of the crashed aircraft. Up until then, however, my memory is clear; I would swear to the events I have described. Afterwards, no. I have no idea what happened to the Germans. I don't even know what happened to me.

# CHAPTER TWO

I have a very hazy recollection of the days that followed, and no memory at all of some of them. I was to learn later that I had been found by an American reconnaissance team who had lighted by chance upon the Germans I was with and had wreaked havoc on the van. The Americans had been surprised to discover, among the corpses beside a stream at the bottom of an embankment, a British Royal Air Force officer, badly hurt but alive. They had taken me to their field hospital, and I owe a lot to the doctors there, one especially.

It was due to him that I didn't spend the rest of my life looking like some kind of monster. But I'm getting too far ahead of my story. The Americans passed me on to the British and finally I regained consciousness in a French hospital that had been taken over by the Allies.

Consciousness, however, was a relative term in my case. I was aware of lying in a narrow bed, but I seemed to be immobilized. I couldn't move my head, and when I tried to lift an arm to touch my face which felt stiff and strange, a small cold hand at once prevented me. There were tubes, too, attached to various parts of my body, and they helped to hinder any movement.

Not that I cared. I was content to lie in my semi-conscious state while people – doctors and nurses, I assumed – came and went, cared for me and murmured over me. I was so heavily sedated that I had almost no pain and my drug-induced dreams were not unpleasant. Time passed, but I had no sense of its passage.

Then, one day, for no reason apparent to me, I had the impression of change – of being 'with it' again, part of the real and everyday world. And the world started to take an added interest in me. Because I couldn't move my head, I could see little more than straight in front of me, which meant that my vision had been largely restricted to hands and medical instruments. But now a face bent close to mine.

It was a pretty face, and she was a nice girl, blue-eyed and earnest, devoid of make-up and with a silly white cap pinned to her hair, denoting that she was a nurse. She looked anxious.

'Sir, you must *not* try to speak or move your head! Do you understand? It's very important. You must *not* try to speak or move your head.' She took my left hand from underneath the bedclothes and laid it flat on the army blanket that served as a coverlet. 'Tap with your fingers once if you've followed what I've said, twice if you haven't.'

I tapped once firmly, and saw the relief on her face before she withdrew. I was relieved too. After what seemed a very long time I had at last made some human contact. I was no longer an inanimate object. I could communicate.

'That's splendid, Flight Lieutenant, sir.'

She sounded genuinely pleased, and I was touched. That she had got my service and rank quite wrong was unimportant. I couldn't cope with that problem at the moment; it would have to be sorted out later.

What was important was that she had reminded me of what I had been doing in France – and of my gunmetal watch. It had been in my trouser pocket when the Germans removed me from the vicinity of the burning Lysander. Since then I was not aware of having seen it, but the chances that it had been stolen were not great. The signet ring, which would have appeared far more attractive to any would-be thief, was still on my little finger. However, the watch could have been taken by a medic or a nurse, put aside, lost. I had to know.

The difficulty was framing the question. Without thinking, I found myself tapping frantically on the blanket. The girl understood immediately.

'Something wrong, sir? You want something?'

I tapped once in affirmation, but was then at a loss. The newly acquired skill of communication, for which I had been so thankful a few moments ago, now seemed completely inadequate and frustrating. I yearned to speak but, notwithstanding the apparently serious order that I was not to try, I was far from sure that I could. On one occasion when I had sensed I was alone, I had managed surreptitiously to touch my face and I knew that I was heavily bandaged, my head held in some kind of vice.

I tapped again impatiently and turned my wrist to suggest that I

26

was looking for a watch. The girl was sympathetic. She did her best to grasp what I was trying to convey.

'You want to know the time?'

I signalled 'yes', followed by a quick 'no'. Again I showed my non-existent watch, and made an effort to point towards myself. And she understood.

'Your watch? Your other possessions? Of course. They're right beside you. You can't see it, I know, but there's a little cupboard next to your bed, and your things are in it. I'll show you.'

I heard a door creak as she got out a small canvas bag. She held it in front of my eyes, so that I could see it before she opened it for me and removed the contents. There wasn't much. After all, RAF officers about to fly over enemy territory were not encouraged to take a lot of personal possessions with them. Nevertheless, few kept strictly to the rules.

'Your wallet,' she said. 'I've peeped in. Some English money, and some francs. In case you landed in France, I suppose. A piece of white heather – for luck – and you have been lucky, sir. And a couple of photographs. I'll hold them up so that you can see they're quite safe.'

I made my hand express pleasure by playing a trill on my imaginary keyboard, though I couldn't have cared less about the photographs. They meant nothing to me. One was of a handsome sheep dog; had he been alive forty-five years later he could have doubled for that appealing animal in the television commercials for a well-known brand of house paint. He sat, looking as if he had just had a bath, if not a full beauty treatment, in front of a pleasant country house, the size of which it was impossible to estimate from the snapshot. Anyway, as I said, I was not interested.

The second photograph was of a girl. She was of medium height with a neat figure and a long, serious face. She looked intelligent but rather distant, and she did nothing for me. Not that the most glamorous blonde could have done much for me at that moment.

'Imogen,' my nurse said. 'A pretty name. Is she your wife, sir?'

Impatiently I tapped twice. The girl was beginning to annoy me. She was curious about the photographs, but they were not what I wanted.

'Your girlfriend?'

'Yes,' I signalled, willing her to show me what else was in the bag.

'And this is your home? It looks a lovely place.' She sounded wistful. 'And your dog? What's his name? "Rory" it says on the back of the photo. I've always wanted a dog, but we lived in a flat and it wasn't possible.'

I flapped my hand in a gesture that she probably took for sympathy, but she produced the other objects that had been on me when I was found – a fine cambric handkerchief, a comb in a leather sheath, an expensive cigarette lighter, a gold pencil, and finally my gunmetal watch, incongruous among the rest of the superior and obviously costly items. But if the nurse wondered why the watch was so different in quality from my other possessions, she didn't comment, and I closed my eyes in relief.

She patted my hand. 'That's fine, sir. You must rest now. The doctor will be coming to talk to you later.'


I slept. The effort of trying to communicate with the nurse had exhausted me. I hadn't realized how weak I was. I woke and slept again. I had no sense of time. My tunnel vision, which I now knew was restricted by my bandages as well as by the need not to move my head, didn't help. I had no idea whether it was night or day. There was always a light on, always the murmur of voices, soft footsteps, an occasional groan or cry of pain. From this and other sounds I deduced that my small kingdom was a curtained enclave at the end of a ward, perhaps allowing me greater privacy than the other patients. Perhaps they had thought I would die. If so, I had fooled them.

When I woke again the doctor, as promised or threatened – I wasn't sure which – had come to speak to me. He drew up a chair and sat beside the bed. I couldn't see him, so I had no idea how old he was, but he sounded incredibly tired. He started by introducing himself. My attempt at a response was immediately halted by a sharp command.

'Sorry about that,' he said. 'I didn't mean to bark at you, but you must keep your face as still as possible. I realize it's frustrating, but it's essential if you're ever to regain your former good looks – if you ever had any, that is,' he added jocularly.

He was doing his best to be kind and considerate, to show he was interested and cared, but somehow I sensed that he resented having to make the effort. This could have been because he was desperately in need of sleep himself, but it annoyed me. What did the man want?

'Nurse tells me you hear and understand what's being said to you,' he continued. 'Do you know how you got to this hospital, in what is once more free France?'

'No,' I tapped.

So he explained about the Americans who had inadvertently saved me from the Germans. 'You were badly smashed up,' he said, 'they did a wonderful job on you, considering the limited resources of a field hospital. You don't remember it at all?'

'No.'

'You remember crashing your aircraft?'

'No.'

'You don't?' He was vaguely puzzled. 'Well, you remember being briefed before you set off from the UK? Oh, yes, we've been on to the Air Ministry – not that they were very forthcoming – but I gather that your unit was delighted to hear you were alive.'

'No.'

'You don't remember your briefing? None of it?' The questioning was no longer casual. 'At any rate you remember your girlfriend, Imogen? You had her photograph in your wallet.'

'No!' I tapped hard, bored with these irrelevant questions which I had answered truthfully. 'No!' I repeated.

'All right, Flight Lieutenant Vermont. Don't get excited, please. You've been concussed and obviously you've lost your memory. It'll come back. There's nothing to be worried about.' His chair squeaked on the floor as he stood up. 'Anyway, I came to bring you some good news. You're going home, back to England, in a day or two. The powers that be are sending over a special evacuation aircraft to fetch you. What it is to be one of the privileged, eh?'

So that was why he resented me, I thought. He believed I was privileged. What a laugh! Anyone who imagined that I, Nigel Hawker, was or had ever been privileged was out of his mind. But then he didn't know that I was neither an officer nor a gentleman; in those days the first was meant to equate with the second, though it was not always the case.

I had been a thoroughly bored lance corporal in an infantry regiment when the request appeared in daily orders for linguists to volunteer for special duties. My French and German (especially my French) were more than fluent, so I applied. This resulted in a trip to London and an interview at the War Office. By this time I had some inkling of what it was all about, and I was hopeful. I wasn't without ambition and I was sure I would have got a commission, except that I was fool enough to correct my interviewer's French; this was not well received.

Nevertheless, after training, I was seconded to a nameless outfit as an acting sergeant, though I never got around to putting up the stripes. The unit was a mixed bunch, including a peer of the realm and an ex-convict. No one ever wore uniform and rank wasn't all-important, though there were some stuffed shirts among us, like my immediate boss, an army Major called Adrian Sherry-Box. I'm sure that by this time you can guess the sort of unit I'm writing about – a part of SOE, the so-called Special Operations Executive.

I made several drops into France, to organize cells and report on which of the groups were worth further support and which were worthless. Mostly I worked on my own and as things turned out I found myself stranded on the Continent during the invasion, with no clear role.

I suppose the alternative would have been to be fighting my way across Europe, that is if I hadn't been killed in the D-Day landings. But I definitely would not have been in this hospital in my present appalling state, masquerading – not by design, but by accident – as an RAF officer called Vermont. I wondered idly what people supposed had become of Sergeant Nigel Hawker – it would have been too soon for him to have been reported missing, believed killed – and I wished I could see Sherry-Box's face when he learnt the truth about what had happened to me. I was not to have that pleasure, but when we did next meet, I was able to imagine how he would have reacted.

Sorry! I digress. The doctor had said a day or two, but the following morning the nurse whose voice I knew so well by now came to tell me that my plane was on its way, and I would be home in a few hours. I didn't really believe it. I was sure fate would intervene again. With my run of luck, the Lysander crashing, a piece slicing my leg when the aircraft exploded, and the American attack on the Germans who had captured me – in which I had been an accidental victim – I was fully prepared for the air ambulance to be shot down into the sea.

At least I would know nothing about it. I would have none of the sensations that a drowning man was meant to experience. The girl had assured me that I would be heavily sedated for the journey.

'And when you wake up tomorrow, sir, you'll be back in the UK.

30

I envy you. So, I expect, do a lot of people here. You're very fortunate. What it is to be a general's son.'

She had spoken without any of the resentment that the doctor had implied when he had said I was privileged, but she had explained his attitude. A general's son! Of course! I should have realized. I should have recognized the name, but somehow I hadn't associated Flight Lieutenant Vermont, the airman whose identity I had borrowed in order to deceive the Germans, with Lieutenant-General Sir Patrick Vermont, retired, a friend and advisor of Churchill, and a famed, much decorated soldier.

Perhaps it was stupid of me, but at the time my one thought had been to save my skin, and afterwards everything had been taken out of my hands. I didn't regret what I had done. In the circumstances, since Vermont was dead, it had been the most sensible course. I only hoped that the General and his family would see it in that light. But I had an unpleasant premonition that perhaps they wouldn't.

This was not, however, an immediate problem, and I had little time to contemplate it. The doctor arrived. There was some jovial banter between him and the nurse, but directed at me – the man who would soon be home, the lucky and privileged man, whose family would do everything possible to return him to health.

I felt the jab of a needle in my arm and, as I slowly sank into a deep sleep, I thought how different reality was from their suppositions.

# CHAPTER THREE

The first thing I was aware of was a different smell. It was not the unpleasant odour of disinfectant that had been characteristic of the hospital in France, but the scent of new-mown grass. I was in the country. Slowly I opened my eyes.

Directly in front of me was a window, its curtains blowing in a gentle breeze, the paintwork beside it coloured cream, and the blanket covering me was thick and soft. I sensed that I was not alone – I realized later that a nurse was watching over me – but neither was I in a ward. This was a private room.

Otherwise, little had changed. My face was still heavily bandaged, my head still held immovable in some kind of vice. My left leg was in a cradle. I could feel it through the bedclothes and was thankful that this was so; at one point I had been afraid that they might cut it off without consulting me. With great care I took a deep breath, and immediately regretted it; my ribs were clearly no better. And I was still attached to innumerable tubes.

Nevertheless, we hadn't been shot down over the Channel, and I had survived the journey, though I doubted if it had done me much good. But I was home, back in England, and the very idea should have made me happy. In fact, I felt terrible.

I must have dozed because what I next remember is a man's voice – authoritative but pleasant. It was a voice with which I was to become very familiar. It belonged, I learned eventually, to an army medical officer – a Lieutenant Colonel, Dr Michael Davidson – who was to oversee my treatment and recovery.

'Any sign, nurse?' he asked now.

'Yes, sir. The patient's becoming restless. I think he'll be fully conscious before too long.'

'Right. I've got to look in on another chap, but I'll be back in a few minutes.'

I expect he was as good as his word, but I don't know. It wasn't until the next morning that I made real contact with him. He lent over my bed and showed me his face, which was round and red-cheeked, capped with dark, almost black, hair. He introduced himself, and I took an immediate liking to him.

'We're going to be seeing a lot of each other,' he said, 'because I shall be supervising all your activities. I'll tell you about them in a minute. First, I've had a detailed report on you from France, so I know you can hear me, and reply with your hand. Okay?'

I signalled yes.

'Right. Now, Simon – I propose to call you Simon; I'm sure you won't mind. You can't call me anything at the moment, but you will. Meanwhile, think of me as Mike and don't curse me too much, though I expect you'll want to. Life is not going to be easy for you in the next weeks, months. However, I promise you I'll make it as painless as I can, and you're going to have absolutely top-flight specialists taking care of you, surgeons and – '

He stopped. He must have seen my hand make an involuntary fist at the mention of surgeons. I suppose it was stupid of me, but in my confused state I had thought in terms of needing to be put together, like Humpty-Dumpty, rather than to be carved up. My poor body cringed at the idea of surgery – or perhaps it was my mind. At any rate, Mike Davidson responded.

'Simon, you're going to be okay. I give you my word. You won't be one hundred per cent as you were before. The chances are that you'll have a limp, but according to Mr Tandy, who's to operate on your leg, it shouldn't be severe, so you could be a lot worse off.'

He gave me a moment to accept what he had said, and I appreciated that he was talking sense. I had never been an athletic type, and a slight limp shouldn't inconvenience me too much – if it really was slight. And somehow I trusted Mike Davidson. I lifted my hand and pointed in what I hoped was the direction of my face.

'Yes, your face, Simon. As I'm sure you've realized, you've smashed it up pretty badly, at least the lower part. Fortunately your sight hasn't been affected, nor your hearing, and you weren't burned. It's your bone structure that has suffered, and your teeth. However, Sir Hugh Glendon, the plastic surgeon, examined you when you arrived here; X-rays were taken and he consulted with colleagues. He's confident he can rebuild your face so that no one in the street would give you a second glance. You'll look perfectly normal, though you may have an odd scar. And, believe me, Simon, Sir Hugh is a wizard. I've seen some of his work. When he's finished with you, you won't look exactly as you did before – we've got photographs from your father – but it'll be a fair likeness of your former self.'

My former self? What did he mean by that? I was Nigel Hawker and I was – I had been – a good-looking young man, or so I had always been given to understand. Now I was to be something of a physical wreck, lame, scarred. It was not a happy prospect, and I moved my hand in what was an instinctive gesture of protest.

'No, there's nothing else, nothing serious. A couple of cracked ribs, some bruising and pulled muscles, and your right wrist has a hair-line fracture, but none of that's important. Nor is your loss of memory. It often follows concussion, and Dick Curzon, who's an expert on the subject, will be seeing you. There's no need for you to worry, Simon. You'll be all right. Now I expect you want to know where you are.'

I tapped once.

'Well, you're in an extremely well-equipped military hospital in the Home Counties – just outside Reading, in fact. It's convenient for our civilian consultants visiting from London, and it's used for people needing specialized treatment – like you.'

'Dr Davidson!'

A nurse had entered the room, and I heard the urgency in her summons; someone needed him more than I did. He rose at once, but before he left he bent over me and said cheerfully, 'Have to go now, Simon, but I'll be in later.' Crises, I suppose, were part of his life.

The door shut behind him and I was alone, though there was a bell-push pinned to the blanket within easy reach of my hand. I lay, silently cursing myself. If only I hadn't dashed across that field towards the crashed plane and Simon Vermont, if only I had ignored the body lying on the ground, if only . . . There had been a lot of 'if onlys' in my life, but none that had affected me more than this one was likely to.


My mind had begun to reel at the implications of what had happened, but on this occasion I didn't have long for regrets or self-recriminations. No more than five or ten minutes can have passed before the door opened again and someone came into the room and approached the bed. Of course, I couldn't see who it was and I didn't at once recognize the voice, for he spoke in a whisper.

'Are you awake, Flight Lieutenant? They warned me at the reception desk that you couldn't speak but you could signal with your hand.'

I acknowledged his remark and wondered who he was, if he might be one of the specialists whom Mike Davidson had mentioned. I wished he would tell me. But when he did, I was horrified.

'Flight Lieutenant, you don't know me, but my name's Adrian Sherry-Box. Major Sherry-Box actually, from the War Office. I'm sorry to bother you when you must be feeling like hell, but it is most dreadfully important, or we think it might be. It's about the chap you went to pick up in France – not much of a chap really, in my opinion, not worth the price of a Lysander, quite apart from the death of your navigator and knocking you up like this.'

I was astounded, first by the presence of Sherry-Box in my hospital room, and then by what he was saying. Even if I had been able to speak, I don't believe that at this point I could have made a sensible reply. I knew that Sherry-Box had never liked me. He was an utter snob, which was rare in our unusual outfit, and he resented the fact that, though I had never been to a public school or a university, my knowledge of colloquial French and German – and my accents – were vastly superior to his own. Such attitudes may seem ridiculous now, in the 1990s, but you must remember that I am writing about a period nearly fifty years ago.

'Mind you, Vermont, the Sergeant was a clever bugger, but not nearly as clever as he thought he was. Like most bright people of his class he had pretensions and an extremely inflated idea of his own importance.'

I banged my hand on the blanket in anger. How dare this man patronize me? He had never been to Europe except on holidays with family and friends before the war. He hadn't survived for months in occupied France, living in fear of his life every minute, not knowing whom he could trust, wondering if he would ever see England again, not daring to ask what would happen to him if the Germans caught him. I was consumed with rage.

It wasn't until much later that I realized his fatuous remarks about Nigel Hawker were partly due to nervousness. He had been so shocked by the appearance of the supposed Flight Lieutenant he had come to question – after all he and Simon Vermont, son of

General Sir Patrick Vermont, were entitled to the same old school tie – that he had wasted time by spewing forth his true feelings, perhaps even his envy.

He ignored my furious hand and continued. 'This chap, Hawker, you went to pick up – and what I'm going to tell you is very much in confidence – had told us he was on to something big, which is why we wanted to pull him out. Of course it could have been a lie, an excuse to get back to the UK. I wouldn't put it past him. At any rate, we've not heard hide nor hair of him since the night your aircraft pranged, and we hoped you might have some info. It just might – might – be vital. For instance, did you see him in the field? Did he signal to you? Or did you by any chance hit the blighter as you landed?'

Even had I wished, I couldn't have answered three questions at the same time, and I was astounded that Sherry-Box would be so candid with a mere Flight Lieutenant, who should have known no details of the outfit's operations. In any case, by now my frantic hand had found the bell-push. I pumped it furiously. My one desire was to get rid of Sherry-Box. And the hospital authorities didn't fail me. There was the sound of running footsteps, and I didn't need to see in order to know that the door had been flung open. My room seemed suddenly filled with people.

'Who the hell are you? Get out of here!' That was Mike Davidson.

'It's all right, sir. It's all right.' The nurse released my fingers from the bell-push.

'Leave me alone! I'm Major Sherry-Box from the War Office. It's of tremendous importance. I've every right –'

'You've no rights, no rights whatsoever, not in this hospital.' Mike Davidson bit off each word. 'And I don't care a damn if you're the Archangel Gabriel from Heaven. Get out!'

'Come along, Major!' This was a voice strange to me. I guessed it belonged to an orderly.

There was a shuffling of feet, another attempt at protest from Sherry-Box and a click as my door shut. The nurse was still holding my hand; I found it oddly comforting.

'He's gone, sir. Not to worry. I'm sorry about that. He should never have got in here to annoy you, but we had a bit of a crisis earlier. One of Dr Davidson's patients started to haemorrhage suddenly and everyone on the floor was busy. Not that that's an excuse. Your unwelcome visitor ought to have been stopped at the main gate or certainly at reception.'

She was chatting to distract me, and I let the words flow over me. My anger was gradually subsiding. I knew Sherry-Box's attitude was not typical of my outfit, but I found little joy in the knowledge.

The trouble was that in a sense he was right. I did have pretensions, though I would have preferred to call them ambitions. Not that many of these had ever been realized.

Mike Davidson returned to add his apologies and to explain that there had been some confusion at the gate and the reception desk. Both had been told that Flight Lieutenant Vermont was to be allowed a visitor, and had assumed it was Sherry-Box, who had given the impression that he was expected.

'We didn't tell you before that you were to have a visitor, in case after all your father was unable to come and you were disappointed. As you know, he's extraordinarily busy, but he has indicated that he has every hope of spending a short time with you this afternoon.'

My father? For half a minute I thought the doctor meant my real father, for whom I had little affection. He was a self-opinionated man, who was confident that he always knew best. Even when my former headmaster urged him to let me stay at the grammar school, to which I had won a scholarship, so that in due course I might go to a university, he refused. He said that at sixteen it was high time I went to work and he needed me to help him in the shop. My mother did her best to dissuade him, but nothing would change his obstinate mind, and in the two years before I went into the army in 1938 he made my life absolute hell, which was why I joined up a year before the war started.

But of course Mike Davidson was not referring to Thomas Hawker, grocer. To him, my father was Lieutenant-General Sir Patrick Vermont.


This time I was warned of the approaching visitor. The nurse came to inform me that the General had arrived and was talking to Dr Davidson. He would be coming to see me very soon.

I steeled myself. Patrick Vermont was not altogether unfamiliar to me. I had seen his photograph in various newspapers, and had on one occasion heard him speak on the wireless, but I had never met him in person – there was no reason on earth why I should have.

37

And I had no idea what his relationship with his son might be. I was soon to learn.

In the meantime, would he accept me? As far as I could recall, Simon Vermont and I had much the same build – at least his battle-dress blouse had fitted me. His colouring I had only seen vaguely in the light of the moon and the burning aircraft, but it seemed to me that it was not unlike mine. What was more, the fact that I couldn't speak and that my face was so heavily bandaged was in my favour. I had no intention of continuing with this ridiculous impersonation for longer than I had to, but as far as I could see there was little I could do to remedy the situation at the moment. I couldn't speak; I couldn't write; I certainly couldn't describe the circumstances by tapping on the bed – even in Morse code. The whole thing was too complicated. I had no choice. I had to play along and see what happened.

The door opened, and a figure came close to the bed and lent over it so that I could see his face and he could see me. 'My dear boy,' he said. 'My dear boy.' And his voice broke as he took my hand. I breathed a sigh of relief. At least my eyes – which were about all of me that was visible – resembled his son's. I wasn't going to be faced with an immediate dreadful scene.

General Vermont was exactly like his pictures in the newspapers. He was, or had been, a handsome man, though his forehead was now creased with lines of worry and he looked weary. It was obvious that he loved his son very much and I envied Simon Vermont. I couldn't imagine that my own father would have been similarly affected; he would have been worried in case I was going to be a burden when I left hospital. At this point I must have made some inarticulate sound; perhaps, in spite of everything, it was an involuntary attempt to tell the General the truth. At any rate, he immediately hushed me, and pulled up a chair beside the bed.

'Don't try to speak, Simon. It's important you shouldn't. I'll do my best to tell you what I think you want to know, but I'm only allowed a short time with you – even less than it might have been because of that bastard Sherry-Box. I gather he's been bothering you with questions about that probably useless agent you were picking up. I'll be having words with his masters. They're fully aware of the situation, and although they'll want to have a chat with you eventually, they know they'll have to wait.'

Those words – 'that probably useless agent' – riled me. They were, implicitly, a repetition of what Sherry-Box had said of me – that I hadn't been worth the crippling of Simon Vermont, the death of the navigator or even the loss of a Lysander. Their effective repetition dissipated at least temporarily the sympathy I had felt for General Sir Patrick Vermont.

'First,' he continued, 'your mother and all the family send their love. Everyone is thankful you're back in England – and safe. Imogen, needless to say, is delighted. So you're not to worry, dear boy. All we want now is to get you home where we can look after you. Meanwhile I've been promised that you'll have the best possible care here. And you're going to be fine, Simon. You may be a bit lame, but Hugh Glendon assures us he can make a good job of your face, so that's no problem. Nor is anything else – and that includes your present loss of memory. It will return in due course. There's no hurry.'

He paused as if for thought. 'What more is there? Oh yes, the war's going pretty well. It'll be over soon, thank God, and, you know, your mother and I have been saying how fortunate we've been to have all the family safe – especially you and Martin. We feel so sorry for the Diaments, losing Alan. I'm afraid there's no longer any hope for him. Incidentally, Simon, they send you their best wishes.'

'General Vermont, sir!'

'Yes, nurse. I'm coming. I'm being kicked out, Simon.' He squeezed my hand. 'Goodbye for now, dear boy. God bless.'


I was thankful to be alone at last. I felt exhausted. I lay, trying to make my mind a blank, but it wasn't possible. Too much had happened that day.

I thought of Sir Hugh Glendon, and wondered if he were as brilliant a surgeon as he was cracked up to be. I thought of myself with a scarred face, and lame. I thought with residual anger of Adrian Sherry-Box, and the anger carried over to General Vermont who, without knowing any of the circumstances, had dismissed Nigel Hawker as 'a probably useless agent'.

I thought of Alan Diament, who I guessed – rightly, I was to discover – had been the navigator of that crashed Lysander, and of Simon Vermont, whose place I had taken temporarily. I wondered if it was a crime for an acting sergeant to pose as an officer and a gentleman, not to mention the son of a general, and I decided I didn't care a damn; I could always fall back on pleading loss of memory. And it was at that moment that I resolved to gain what benefits I could from the situation. After all, if I hadn't tried to help Simon Vermont I wouldn't have been here in my present appalling condition.

So my thoughts came full circle. It had been quite a day.

# CHAPTER FOUR

Mike Davidson told me that my operations were to start on Friday – the day after next. My leg was to be done first. Mr Tandy would drop in tomorrow evening to say hello and to explain how he planned to repair my thigh. The anaesthetist would also look in. The operation was expected to take four or five hours and, all being well, would enable me to walk. It was a slightly tricky bit of surgery, but Tandy didn't expect any problems.

Until then I was to rest, relax and not worry. The last instruction wasn't easy to follow, especially when I was given what was meant to be the encouraging news that my mother was to be allowed a brief visit the next afternoon. I had no desire to be visited by Lady Vermont.

In the event the visit was painless. Antonia Vermont produced no surprises. She followed the same routine as her husband, leaning over to see what she could of my face, and taking the opportunity to plant a gentle kiss on my forehead. I realized when I saw her that she was, and always had been, a beautiful woman. Then, like her husband, she pulled a chair up beside the bed and began to talk.

She sounded as I had imagined she would sound, calm and composed, her emotions if anything more in control than the General's. I, her supposed son, must have looked an awful sight, but she took the situation in her stride. She called me 'darling' and patted my hand consolingly, but there were no tears in her voice.

She stayed, I would guess for about seven or eight minutes, certainly less than ten, but during that time I learnt quite a lot about the Vermonts. They had always been an army family. Martin intended to make it his career, like his father. He had just been promoted to captain and his CO spoke highly of him.

There was a warmth in Lady Vermont's voice as she spoke of Martin that left me in no doubt that he was her favourite son. I did not need her to add that of course even as a small boy I had preferred to make model aeroplanes than to play with toy soldiers like Martin.

She laughed when she was, as she thought, reminding me of this, but she also unwittingly made it clear that the whole family had considered it a very odd preference.

As an only son, indeed an only child, I had never had cause to be jealous of other siblings or to resent them. But, on Simon Vermont's behalf, I objected to the implied disparagement. I felt a sudden, unexpected sympathy for the dead Flight Lieutenant. Why shouldn't he have liked model aeroplanes more than toy soldiers? Personally, I had had neither. When I wasn't in school, I was doing my homework, helping in the shop or delivering special orders on my bicycle. It was a different way of life.

My mother, too, was as different from Lady Vermont as the proverbial chalk and cheese. Maria Hawker, née Huber, had been born in Alsace, her mother French, her father German – hence my fluency in these languages. She had lost both her parents in the First World War, but had found an English lover, Corporal Hawker, who had kept his promise and returned to marry her as soon as hostilities ended. She was not a happy woman. She never really liked England, though she was to spend most of her life there. Better educated than almost all her neighbours, who despised her for her funny foreign ways, she had always been something of a misfit, and inevitably their attitudes to her rubbed off on me.

'And did your father tell you?' Lady Vermont continued. 'Susan has her commission, which is such a relief. She came across some very rough types among the other ranks, but now she's been posted to Bletchley Park and we've arranged for her to stay with the Diaments in Buckingham. They're glad to have her. I think they hoped that she and poor Alan . . . but it was not to be. Imogen's been more fortunate and – surprise, darling! – she's outside, waiting to visit you for a few minutes, so I shall have to leave.'

I made a vague gesture of farewell, and she said goodbye, squeezing my hand. I had survived Lady Vermont, and that word 'survived' describes how I felt. But now I had to meet this Imogen. Imogen who? I didn't even know her surname. Was she a Diament? It didn't matter. But Simon Vermont had carried her photograph in his wallet, even when he was flying on a mission, and Lady Vermont had more or less suggested that she and Simon were engaged, or likely to become so. The degree of commitment wasn't important at the moment, but I hoped she wouldn't be too emotional at this reunion with someone who might or might not be her fiancé.

I needn't have worried. She was certainly warm and friendly, but more like a sister than a lover, and she satisfied some of my curiosity about the Vermonts.

'Aunt Antonia will have told you all the news about Martin and Susan,' she said. 'Between you and me, Simon, I don't believe Susan was ever serious about Alan Diament, but now – ' It was easy to visualize the shrug of her shoulders. 'Poor Susan! She thought of the ATS as freedom after boarding school, but she was soon disillusioned. Anyway, I'm jolly glad I never went into any of the services, in spite of pressure from the family. I've been much happier and, in my opinion, doing at least as worthwhile a job in the local hospital.'

She chatted about herself for a few more minutes, then said she must go as her time with me was rationed. She said they would all be thinking and praying for me the next day when Mr Tandy was to operate on my leg. And before she went she took my hand, turned it over and implanted a light kiss on my palm, which confirmed my belief that neither she nor Lady Vermont had the least suspicion that I was other than Simon Vermont.


The same evening the anaesthetist came in to see me. He was a hearty young man who examined me briefly and assured me that my premedication would make me at least half asleep before my bed was wheeled to the theatre. I wouldn't regain consciousness until I was safely back in my own room with a 'brand new leg' and a nurse watching over me.

He was followed shortly by Mr Tandy. To judge from the bustle and rustle that heralded his appearance, he had come with a small entourage. Among it was Dr Davidson, who introduced him.

'Ah, Flight Lieutenant!' boomed Mr Tandy. 'We've met before, but on the last occasion you were in no position to recognize me. However, I examined you and we took X-rays, so I've a pretty good idea what I have to do for you.' He went on to explain in more detail than I understood, and concluded, 'It's not going to be easy, but we'll manage, and you'll be glad to hear I have every hope of a successful outcome.'

Unfortunately he was not as confident as he wished me to think, and his booming voice carried. He had stopped outside my door to unburden his doubts on Mike Davidson, and I couldn't help but hear what he said.

'We must hope for the best, but I don't like it. I don't like it one bit. He's not strong enough yet for five hours of surgery. I'd much rather postpone it, but Glendon wants to get going on his face and it makes sense to do the leg first.'

So I lay and wondered if I was going to die, if all the reassurances I had been given were phoney, if no one, not even Mike Davidson, was to be trusted. It was absurd, but I was scared – absurd because I had accepted the possibility, even the likelihood, of death every day I was in France, and that wouldn't have been a pleasant death, not like a continuation of the long sleep the anaesthetist had promised me. The Germans didn't take kindly to spies, and who can blame them? If they had caught me I would probably have been thankful when at last the Gestapo got around to shooting me.

The thought of France and the Germans reminded me of the gunmetal watch that had been Nigel Hawker's great acquisition. Of course I should have given it to Sherry-Box, my immediate superior, but while he was with me his stupid babbling had so annoyed me that it had never crossed my mind. And, in any case, Sherry-Box had come to see me as Simon Vermont, and some complex excuse about how Simon came into possession of Hawker's watch was beyond me, especially without the power of speech. So now what could I do? It was still all too difficult.

Then the irony of the situation struck me. If I were to die on the operating table, no one would ever know the truth of what had happened. I would be buried as Simon Vermont in the Vermont family grave, if they had such a thing. Nigel Hawker's disappearance would remain a mystery. And the watch, for which men had fought and died? Perhaps Imogen would in the end treasure it in memory of Simon, or perhaps she would discard it; she would probably have other, superior, keepsakes.

Somehow the thought of such a sequence of events amused me, and illogically I felt more cheerful. Having come so far and escaped so much, I was damned if I was going to die here.


Of course I didn't die. I was tougher than Mr Tandy thought. I survived the operation well, so well that the great Sir Hugh Glendon decided to start work on my face the following Monday. He was a type of man quite different from Tandy. In spite of the fact that everyone seemed to speak of him with awe, he seemed modest and appeared in my room without any fuss and accompanied only by Mike Davidson. Nor did he pull any punches.

'You're in for a rough ride, Flight Lieutenant,' he said. 'We can't do more than a little at a time, so it means a series of operations. You'll find this frustrating, especially as I refuse to let you see yourself until I've finished the job – and that goes for your family, too. Even after the bandages come off, we'll put you in a gauze mask for visits as we progress. It's best that way, believe me. And you'll have to get used to your new face. It won't *feel* the same. It's strange how one knows one's own body, and for a while the face you experience won't feel like your old one. Do you understand?'

I made a vague affirmative gesture, though I was far from sure just what he meant. Mike Davidson had assured me that I would look perfectly human, and, if I were honest, I guessed that this was all I could hope for.

'You'll be glad to hear, Simon, that Sir Hugh has already been busy on your behalf,' said Davidson.

'I have indeed,' said Glendon, 'and so have others. We have a model of your face as it would seem to have been, and I've been playing with that, and planning the steps I shall take. Incidentally, you'll need a completely new set of teeth, and we'll have a temporary set as soon as your gums are ready for them.'

He talked on for a while, punctuated by encouraging remarks from Mike Davidson, but I was no longer listening. I was thinking about my home and my father's false teeth. We mostly occupied one all-purpose room behind the shop. Kept scrupulously clean by my mother, like the rest of the house, it served as kitchen, laundry – clothes would steam on a horse in front of the fire in the winter, though in summer they would hang out in the yard behind – and living room. Here my mother knitted and read, my father did his accounts and, with the wireless turned low, I did my homework when it was too cold to be upstairs in my bedroom.

There were two bedrooms upstairs, but no bathroom. We each had a bath once a week in a zinc bath in the scullery, off which led a lavatory, so that the loo couldn't be described as 'outdoor'. Our daily ablutions were performed in the sink in a corner of the kitchen where the washing-up was done, and every night my father left his false teeth in a glass beside this sink. They had fascinated and revolted me for as long as I could remember.

Now I too was about to have false teeth, and I had a vision of my tooth glass sitting side by side with his. It was a horrible prospect. But I wouldn't be able to stay in the hospital for ever. When everything was sorted out and the Army let me go, what was I to do, where to live? I doubted that the invalidity pension of an acting sergeant would amount to much, and it wouldn't be easy to get a job. I saw myself, minus any qualifications, money or influence, having to choose between queuing up at the Labour Exchange or returning to life in the 'family business', as my father liked to call it.

I shut my eyes, as if that would make the picture I had conjured up disappear, and heard Mike Davidson say, 'I'm afraid he's gone to sleep, Sir Hugh. It's all this sedation. Sometimes he seems quite bright, but at others – '

'Poor lad! It's not surprising after what he's been through. How I hate war. Thank God this one will soon be over.'


So the weeks and months passed in a haze of pre-operative anxiety and post-operative exhaustion. Often I wasn't sure if I was awake or asleep. I would dream I was lying in the operating theatre, and wake to find myself in my own bed. There was a certain amount of pain and a great deal of discomfort. Christmas came and went; I was not interested.

But I was making progress, however slowly, and everyone assured me they were pleased. My ribs no longer hurt, nor did my wrist, and there were red-letter days, such as the one on which I was allowed out of bed for the first time.

Some of my tubes were temporarily removed. My head was relaxed from the vice that held it in position except when my face was undergoing its ordeals, and I was warned to keep it as still as I could. Then very carefully I was helped to sit up, to slide my legs over the edge of the bed and to stand. I was as weak as a kitten. But the object of the exercise was to try out my new leg, or as I thought of it my 'game' leg, and with help I managed to take half a dozen drunken steps.

'Splendid! Splendid!' boomed Mr Tandy, who was watching the proceedings. 'Wait till you get your shoes and you'll be galloping down the corridor.'

This forecast was not precisely accurate, but the shoes did make an enormous difference. They were handmade to fit me, beautiful suede shoes, the left one cleverly built up so as to mitigate my disablement. They looked and, I am sure, were expensive. I hated to think what would happen when they wore out and I had to replace them; the Army would see to the cost, but I guessed the replacements would be less comfortable than these. That, however, was a worry for the future, and I dismissed it.

Meanwhile, I was growing stronger, both in spite of the operations on my face and because of them. To some extent they sapped my strength, but soon they enabled me to feed myself by mouth, pappy foods such as babies eat, but nourishing. Then, as if by magic, I had teeth. I was encouraged to use them. Those damned tubes had gone, and the wretched vice. I could speak, though with difficulty, as my face didn't seem to belong to me, and the voice I produced was low and hoarse. I was getting up daily, and walking further and further; Tandy hadn't been so far off the mark. But everything was a tremendous effort. I had my good days, but also my bad ones, and after one of the latter I would sink into a black mood when I wondered why I was going through all this; it would have been simpler to die.

During this period, especially when I was depressed, Mike Davidson and Dr Curzon, the psychiatrist who came to see me regularly, were great supports. Davidson must have been working at least fourteen hours a day, but he always found time to chat to me about my progress, about the war, even about his wife and two small children whom he rarely saw. He didn't understand my reluctance to have visitors, but since I was only allowed family he was prepared to humour me, and did his best to discourage them.

Fortunately, the Vermonts, though they certainly didn't neglect me, had problems of their own. The General was busier than ever, now planning for the peace which was soon to come. Martin had been wounded, though not seriously, and Lady Vermont was giving him priority for the moment.

Susan and Imogen were both working hard. There was also the difficulty of travel because of petrol rationing and the uncertainty of trains and buses. A trip to see me meant the expenditure of time and effort for very little reward, for visitors still tired me quickly. Nevertheless, they did come, and were delighted to see me sitting up, and hear from Mike Davidson how well I was doing. Sir Hugh continued to insist that my face below the eyes should be concealed behind gauze until the process of healing was complete – he now gave the danger of infection as his excuse, but I suspected that it was a kind of professional pride that made him reluctant to demonstrate his handiwork to the world until it was finished.

And so winter passed and spring came. Once more there was the smell of new-mown grass, and talk of my going 'home' for the week-end. My voice was still weak and hoarse, and I made no attempt to explain the strange situation in which I found myself. Soon enough, when Sir Hugh Glendon had finished with my face, it would become obvious that I was not Simon Vermont, and then I would plead loss of memory. Meanwhile I was content to let things slide.

# CHAPTER FIVE

At last came the great day, the day on which I would be allowed to see the result of Sir Hugh Glendon's work. I was nervous. He had warned me not to hope for too much; there was still some 'tidying up' to be done, and the scars would take time to fade.

And of course I had another reason to be nervous, apart from my appearance, which I feared might be at best unattractive, at worst hideous. Once my whole face was exposed I had to expect the first member of the Vermont family to visit me to be shocked and to announce that, whoever I was, I was certainly not Flight Lieutenant Simon Vermont.

So far I had told no direct lies. I had covered myself by maintaining that I could remember nothing and becoming agitated when put under pressure, either by Imogen's gentle probing or Mr Curzon's attempts to make me recall my childhood, so that Mike Davidson had finally been forced to intervene and order that I must not be stressed and to reiterate to me that I was not to worry about my loss of memory. I had qualms about deceiving him, but I seemed to have no alternative.

However, once it was discovered that I was not Simon Vermont, it wouldn't need a Sherlock Holmes to figure out that I might be Nigel Hawker, the agent Vermont was to have lifted from France. And then I would have to be very, very careful. I wanted no blame, no court martial, for a chain of events which had been triggered off by what I shall always believe was the right and sensible action for me to have taken in those extraordinary circumstances.

My favourite nurse, a comfortable middle-aged woman who had two sons in the army, had helped me to get up, and I sat in an armchair and waited for Glendon and Davidson. I was wearing the pyjamas and dressing gown that Imogen had brought me on one of her visits. They were loose on my body, but that was to be expected; anyone who had suffered as I had would have lost weight.

Glendon and Mike, a file tucked under his arm, arrived with a nurse carrying a large mirror. They greeted me cheerfully and after some small talk Glendon drew up a chair in front of me, straddled it and gestured to Mike to pass me a photograph from the file. It was a studio colour print of Simon Vermont's face, obviously obtained from the family.

Glendon said, 'This is what you looked like originally; I'm told it's a good likeness. Now, you'll be different but, Simon, when you see yourself, it will be the worst you'll ever look. After this, as the scars fade, your appearance can only improve, so don't be too worried.'

My heart sank. Sir Hugh had never called me Simon before and this familiarity, added to his warning, I took as a bad omen. I had to tense myself as he carefully removed the light gauze mask I was wearing and held the mirror up in front of me.

I stared – at the image in the mirror and at the photograph. I couldn't believe what I saw. If I had been capable, I might have screamed a denial. Or would I? And, if I had, how would it have been interpreted? God alone knows.

Once again I looked from the photograph to the mirror. In fact, and within his brief, Sir Hugh Glendon had done a wonderful job. He had not recreated Simon Vermont's face; that would probably have been impossible. But the face in the mirror could have been that of Simon's twin brother, if he had had one. There was the long straight nose and the slightly turned down mouth, which perfectly reflected the haughty expression in the print. I had not known a lot of twins in my life, but I am sure many would have looked less alike.

Suddenly I realized that Glendon was speaking, explaining that the cheekbones he had built had somehow altered the shape of the eyes. He was wrong, of course. The eyes were mine, but they were not unlike Simon's, as I had realized since I had first met the General and his wife and the other Vermonts and they had made no comment.

There was no doubt that Simon and I had been similar types – same colouring, same general build. But that was not to say that before all this plastic surgery we would ever have been mistaken for each other, not even at a cursory glance. What Sir Hugh Glendon had created was a kind of composite of Simon Vermont and Nigel Hawker. It was no wonder that I was appalled.

'You've not said anything, Simon,' Mike Davidson encouraged, 'but you must agree you look amazingly good, very reasonably like your photograph.'

'Yes.' I realized he was prompting me to thank Glendon and say what a great job he had done – which indeed was true from everyone's point of view, except mine. But at that precise moment of crisis I couldn't speak; there were so many vital decisions to be made, though this was no time to make them.

Glendon saved me. He laughed. 'Poor man! It's shock, I know. I've been through this with other patients, Mike. They can't believe it. It's not their face – not exactly them. It doesn't feel right. They want to deny it.'

Sir Hugh stood up, and added, 'But I assure you, Simon, as you get used to it you'll come to terms with it, until it becomes more familiar than your former face, and when the scars have faded you'll be quite a good-looking chap again.'

'I'm sorry,' were the only words I managed to stutter.

I didn't know why I was apologizing. I continued to stare into the mirror, as if by willpower I might metamorphose what I saw. I hadn't expected to look like my old self, but neither had I expected to look so much like Simon Vermont, or rather his photograph, which is what the surgeon had used as a guide. None of the doctors had ever seen him in the flesh, and I had caught only the briefest glimpse of his face in the light of the burning Lysander as I took off his identity discs and his outer clothing; I couldn't have described him. But now, for the rest of my life, I was to look like his twin.

Bitterly I thought that this was rough justice. Once I could speak, however poorly, once I could write, I should have made a bald statement that my name was Nigel Hawker, and let the authorities take it from there. Why hadn't I done so? What were my excuses? I could think of several, but I knew that my real reason was that I wanted to enjoy for as long as possible the benefits and privileges of being Flight Lieutenant Simon Vermont, son of General Sir Patrick and Lady Vermont. And how would *they* react when they saw this clone of their dead son?

It was too much for me. I was still weak. Tears welled in my eyes and trickled down my cheeks. I lowered my head. I wept.

Everyone was very kind, very understanding. Mike Davidson blamed himself. I was helped back to bed, given a sedative, urged to rest and, to my surprise, I fell asleep almost immediately.

★

I woke some hours later to be told that Miss Vermont had arrived unexpectedly at the hospital. Imogen! I had learnt several weeks ago that Imogen was a Vermont, the only child of a cousin of the General. Her father had been killed with his wife in a car accident when Imogen was twelve, and she had been brought up with Simon. But it was too soon. There was no way I could cope with her, or the other Vermonts – not yet.

'No, nurse! No! I don't want to see her. I can't see her.'

'Flight Lieutenant, you're going to have to see her – let her see you – some time. Why not now? Get it over.' It was said gently.

'Because – ' I changed my mind. 'No, you're right, nurse. I might as well get it over.'

But it was not as I expected. In a way it was an almost trivial meeting. Imogen showed no hesitation. She put down the small suitcase she had brought with her, sat on the bed, held me lightly by the shoulders and studied me, her own long, serious face aglow with happiness.

'Simon, it's wonderful! Oh, dearest Simon, I'm so glad! I was afraid, for your sake and the family's – not for mine. I wouldn't have cared what you looked like. But there's no need to worry any more now. You've some terrible scars, but most of them will disappear in time, and anyway they're honourable wounds.'

She buried her head in my chest and began to cry. I held her close and felt her tears soaking through my pyjama jacket. There was nothing else I could have done. Fortunately, she recovered quite quickly. She sat up, wiped her eyes and grinned at me. The best I could say for her was that she was a nice girl, whom I liked. I didn't want to hurt her, but – I reminded myself that I was meant to be suffering from loss of memory. It was she who must realize I was not Simon Vermont; there was no way I could tell her the truth.

The problem was that I was not in control of the situation. Suddenly I found that I had started pulling my ear lobes, first one, then the other. I had done this since my childhood in moments of great stress, but I thought I had rid myself of the habit. It seemed I hadn't.

I made one effort. 'Imogen, look at me! I'm not – not really Simon, am I?'

'Of course you are! Simon, you've been awfully brave through all these operations. Don't be silly about your face now.' She bent and kissed me, on each cheek and then on the mouth. 'I've brought you a few casual clothes that may fit. We'll have to do something about your wardrobe once you come home for good. You've got so thin most of your things won't do any more. Still, I expect you'll get extra clothing coupons when you leave the RAF, and you'll be able to go on a buying spree.'

She chattered on, taking everything for granted, imagining a clear, bright future, and I didn't disillusion her. At that point I stupidly assumed she was fooling herself, that she had been so much in love with Simon Vermont that she was willing him to be alive, to be this 'wounded hero', to be her Simon, whether in fact he was or not.

I couldn't have been more wrong. I underestimated Imogen, but I was always to do that. She truly believed that I was Simon Vermont. And, amazingly, so did the rest of the family when they visited me – the General, Lady Vermont, Martin and Susan.

In retrospect, I can appreciate that it was not as amazing as I thought at the time. They had all been deeply grieved when they heard that Simon's aircraft had not returned to base and he was believed to be dead, or possibly a prisoner-of-war. Then had come the good news that he was alive, though seriously wounded, in a hospital in France. No one had questioned the identity of the man found wearing a Flight Lieutenant's battledress blouse, Simon Vermont's identity discs and signet ring and, it transpired, with a photograph of Imogen Vermont in his wallet. I had thought that once I had a recognizable face they would see through the deception at once. Instead, Glendon's work had merely confirmed their belief in my identity.

Of course there were discrepancies. My face was not quite right. Neither were my voice or the length of my legs, though the former point was easily accounted for by the change in the shape of my face, and the latter by my new limp. What was more, subconsciously they all wanted to accept me; it was only natural, after all these weeks and months, when I had feigned loss of memory and done nothing to discourage them.

Nevertheless, at that time I didn't visualize that taking Simon Vermont's place for ever was a realistic possibility.

I thought of Easter as the watershed. Encouraged by Mr Curzon, who was hopeful that being in familiar surroundings would

53

stimulate my reluctant memory, I was going 'home' for a long weekend. In a way I was looking forward to it. This reaction may seem strange, but after so much personal contact with the Vermonts I was curious to see how they lived. Besides, the hospital, magnificent though it was, had begun to irk me. Short walks in the grounds were not enough. They merely increased my desire to return to normal living, a desire growing, almost against my will, as I grew physically stronger.

Not that a weekend with the Vermonts could be described as normal living, at least by me, but it would be a change from hospital routine and I knew I would be assured of every comfort and consideration. And what was the alternative? There was none for Simon Vermont, and personally I had no wish to return to the small cramped bedroom over the grocer's shop while I was still a semi-invalid.

Moreover, I was sure that if by some chance I betrayed my identity to the Vermonts while I was staying with them, they wouldn't treat me badly. However great a shock the revelation would be for them, and even if they suspected I had deliberately deceived them, they would do what they considered right. They would do their best to understand my dilemma. I suppose it was the arrogance of youth, but I felt I knew the family well.

Then, before Easter, two incidents occurred which were to have a considerable influence on me, since they showed how differently Simon Vermont and Nigel Hawker were assessed. Mike Davidson informed me that Brigadier Mark Bashford and Squadron Leader Stephen Segar were each eager to have a talk with me. I had never heard of the Squadron Leader, but I had met Brigadier Bashford on one occasion. It was he who had interviewed me at the War Office before assigning me to the outfit that had subsequently sent me to France. I had always blamed him for the fact that, because I had corrected his French, I had not been offered a commission.

'They did ask before, Simon, but we put them off, said you weren't up to it, but there's no reason why you shouldn't see them now, is there?'

'I suppose not. Do you know what either of them wants?'

'No, but I can guess.' Davidson grinned. 'Segar was your Squadron Leader and I suspect the Brigadier's connected with that chap who upset you so much before – Sherry – Sherry-Box! Funny name,' he added ruminatively.

'Do they know I don't remember much?'

'Yes. They've been warned. Don't let them worry you, Simon. We'll put a bell close to hand so you can always summon help to get rid of them.'

'Thanks.'

I laughed, though I didn't feel like laughing. I didn't mind Segar. I expected him to be friendly, and not to press me too hard. The Brigadier was a different matter. He wasn't likely to be unpleasant to the presumed son of a General, but that was not the point. What was I going to tell him? It was my duty to give him the gunmetal watch, to explain its significance and how I came by it. But I couldn't visualize him as a sympathetic listener. The alternative was to produce some lie to explain how it had come into my possession, but, try as I might, I couldn't think of one that was even remotely plausible. And, as it turned out, Bashford wouldn't have been interested.

Squadron Leader Stephen Segar arrived next morning. I was up and dressed, and he greeted me warmly, without any formality.

'Glad to see you on your feet, Simon, and looking great.'

I thanked him. He was a short, square, purposeful man with a row of decorations, and it soon became clear that not only was he a friend of Simon, but that he also knew the family. He mentioned spending an enjoyable weekend at Aubyn House, which I gathered was the Vermonts' Cotswold home.

He went on to talk about several members of his squadron, none of whom I'd ever heard of except for Alan Diament. We agreed it was sad about 'poor old Alan' and Segar gave me a curious glance. Perhaps I hadn't sounded sufficiently sorrowful. I should perhaps point out that throughout the conversation he showed no sign of doubting who I was.

'The two of you were very close. His death must be a blow to you, Simon.'

'Yes, indeed – and to sister Susan.'

'Poor Susan! I imagine she's terribly upset. At least Imogen's lucky to have you safe.'

I remembered what Imogen had told me about Susan's relationship with Alan Diament, but I didn't comment. Subconsciously I was gleaning information. It seemed to be accepted among Simon's friends and acquaintances that as he and Imogen made a pair, so had Susan and Alan Diament.

'Simon . . . ' Segar paused to cover the silence that had fallen between us. 'This is meant to be an official visit, so do you mind if I ask you some questions? It's just for the record. I know you probably won't be able to answer them, but – do you remember anything at all about the night you pranged the Lysander?'

Because I liked him and thought it wouldn't hurt to set some of the record at least vaguely straight, I said, 'Not really. I have vague flashes of memory, but I wouldn't like to swear to them.'

Segar nodded understandingly. 'Tell me.'

So I described the crash (inserting a reference to being thrown clear by chance), the burning plane, and the explosion. I concluded: 'I remember my leg being hit and trying to crawl away from the fire.'

'Alan?' he queried.

'He didn't have a chance.'

'You're sure? Since you turned up so miraculously it's made his parents hope.'

I shook my head. 'They're wrong. I'm quite, quite sure he's dead! He was still in the plane when the tanks exploded.'

I spoke with such vehemence that he looked surprised. Talking about it had brought it all back to me too vividly. I shut my eyes. Suddenly I felt very tired, and luckily Segar took the hint. Without being asked, he stood up, preparing to leave.

'That's fine, Simon. We won't bother you any more for the moment. There'll be an inquiry, of course, and you'll have to appear. But it'll be pretty informal. And I've some good news. Someone heard by chance that the chap you were meant to be picking up was going to be recommended for an MM when he got back, if he'd done a good job. So we thought why shouldn't you have a gong? After all, this was your fourth trip. You're going to get a DFC, Simon. Congratulations.'

Such, I thought when he had gone, was British justice. Flight Lieutenant Vermont would receive a Distinguished Flying Cross. Acting Sergeant Hawker would have got (might get) a mere Military Medal. Rank apart, the difference between the two awards was ludicrous when one considered for what they were being given. Can you wonder that I felt bitter?

\*

General Vermont had made an official complaint about Sherry-Box, which probably accounted for the arrival the following day of Brigadier Bashford, rather than an officer of less importance. Unfortunately I was no more impressed by his approach on this occasion than when we first met.

As expected, he wanted to know if I had any information about Nigel Hawker, who had not been heard of since that fateful night. I described the crash as I had to Segar, because I didn't want to appear uncooperative.

'What do you think has happened to this chap Hawker, sir?' I asked. I saw no reason why I shouldn't be curious. 'Major Sherry-Box said he had something special for you.'

'So he gave us to understand, but it may have been an excuse to get himself back to England. At any rate, special or not, it doesn't matter now. The war in Europe will be over in a week or two. As to what happened to him, I'd guess he was caught. The burning aircraft would have been a beacon to the Germans.'

Bashford shrugged; obviously he couldn't have cared less about Hawker. 'Of course, you never know,' he added, giving a loud laugh. 'He may have changed his mind, shacked up with some French girl and decided not to come home at all. He was an odd type.'

I rang the bell. I had to get rid of the damned man quickly before I lost my temper and told him what Nigel Hawker thought of him, and where he could stuff his MM.

# CHAPTER SIX

On Good Friday the General picked me up in his staff car, and we were driven at a steady pace along the main roads and then through leafy Cotswold lanes to Colombury, a small market town, and beyond to Aubyn House. It was a part of England I didn't know, but even the most ordinary things – buses, bicycles, traffic lights, for example – seemed strange to me, as they do if one has been ill or out of the country for a long time.

It was a pleasant drive and I enjoyed it. The weather was good, sunny and surprisingly warm for spring, and the General didn't burden me with conversation. He must have been tired for I saw his head droop and for a while he dozed. But he woke up as we drove through Colombury and grinned at me sheepishly.

'Sorry. I've had too many late nights, burning the candle at both ends.'

He was a pleasant and agreeable man and I liked him. I wished I really had been his son. As it was, I had to resist a temptation to call him 'Sir'.

'It's a lovely day,' I said tentatively.

'Yes.' He paused, then went on, 'Simon – we're hoping that being in familiar surroundings will help to bring back your memory, but don't try to force it, and don't pretend. We hope to have a small drinks party before lunch on Sunday, after church, to celebrate yours and Martin's safe return, but otherwise it'll just be family. Entertaining's not easy these days when almost everything's rationed, though we don't do too badly in the country. People in towns are much worse off.'

'Are you growing much yourself? Digging for victory?'

'Not personally, of course. But your mother gardens, as you know, and so does Imogen when she has time, and we still have old Crosby and his lad, who's a bit soft in the head. Do you remember them, Simon?'

'No. I'm afraid not.'

'What about Nanny Pettigrew? You children used to call her Nanny Petticoat. No? She's the only help we have in the house now, except for a woman who comes in once a week to do the laundry. All the village girls have been called up, or they're working in a munitions factory over towards Cirencester. Making a fortune, some of them, I gather.'

With growing doubts I listened as he continued. It was not going to be quite the simple weekend I had visualized. I had known that General and Lady Vermont, Martin and Imogen would be there, and Susan was coming on Saturday night, but they were all people whom I had met and who had accepted me. It had occurred to me that a neighbour might drop in, perhaps the parson after the Easter Sunday service. But I hadn't thought of old retainers. Stupid of me. After all, I had read in books how 'the County' lived.

'Here we are!' said the General as the car turned into a short drive and swung in front of the imposing main door of Aubyn House. He patted me on the knee. 'Don't worry, my boy. Everything will be fine now you're home.'

Hoping he would be proved right, I climbed carefully out of the car and stood leaning on my stick while the driver got our bags out of the boot. The General went over to give him some instructions. This gave me a minute or two to take a good look at the Vermonts' house.

Aubyn House was long and low. Built around 1800 of that lovely creamy-coloured Cotswold stone that mellows so well, it was a beautiful simple building. The woodwork, I noticed, could do with some paint, but I was sure that was due to the problem of getting workmen in wartime, rather than lack of money. It was a house that in my wildest dreams I would never have hoped to own.

Lady Vermont must have heard the car, for the front door opened and she came out to greet us. She was wearing slacks and a man's shirt, and her hair was windblown. This made her look somewhat more human than when she had visited me in hospital, but she was still elegant.

'Hello, my dears,' she said at once. 'You're just in time for tea. Imogen's not back from her hospital yet, but Martin's arrived, so we're beginning to gather. There'll be some tea for you in the kitchen, Johnson, before you return to London,' she added to the driver.

'Thank you, my lady,' he said.

And, as he carried in our bags I saw the stripes on his sleeve. I had been so occupied with the General and my own thoughts that previously I had paid the man scant attention. Now I realized that he was a corporal – the equivalent of my own substantive rank. It was ironic. I wanted to laugh, but Lady Vermont, having given me a peck on the cheek, was insisting on helping me up three shallow steps to the front door.

My first impression of the interior of the house was vague and confused; I had found the drive down more tiring than I had expected. As we moved into the hall a small, dark-haired woman, wearing a neat black dress with white collar and cuffs, appeared from the rear. With her pointed nose she reminded me of a magpie.

'Nanny Pettigrew,' the General murmured to me, just in case I hadn't guessed.

'Mr Simon,' she said. 'How very good to have you home again.'

'Thank you, Nanny.'

Without thinking I bent and kissed her, and was relieved to see the General nod his approval. I had done the right thing. Then Martin came running down the stairs, while Nanny disappeared, presumably to fetch the tea.

'Simon! How are you, old boy?'

Martin Vermont must have resembled his brother closely. He had the same slightly supercilious expression. But somehow the general impression he gave was different. I could only judge from Simon's photograph, but while I considered Martin to be the better-looking of the two according to conventional standards, I thought his face was rather weak – even effeminate. I was glad that if I had to look like either of them it was Simon's appearance I was to take on. Nevertheless, on the occasions Martin had visited me in hospital I had found him pleasant enough.

'I'm all right. A bit exhausted after that drive, I have to admit. What about you, Martin?'

'Fine. In fact I'm rejoining my regiment next week. Mine was only a superficial wound. You made the wrong choice. The Army's much safer than the RAF.'

I didn't correct him, but I thought how easily I might have been the one who was dead, for indeed, during my last year in France I had been at greater risk than Simon had. However, it was I who had survived – and here I was in his place.

The General took me to a cloakroom, then to what he called the morning room, which was comfortably furnished in a modern style, but with some good-looking old pieces, which I took to be antiques. It was three times the size of the living room behind the shop to which I had been accustomed, and looked out on to a large lawn.

'We'll use the drawing room on Sunday,' Lady Vermont said. 'It'll do it good to be aired for once. Really, it's been quite impossible to heat it over the winter with the little fuel we're allowed. Let's hope that by this time next year the war will be over and all this wretched rationing will end.'

'The war will almost certainly be over, at least in Europe, but I suspect that rationing will continue, my dear,' said the General. 'That may go on for years.'

The conversation continued over tea – scones and jam, both homemade – and since Mike Davidson had taken to bringing me a daily newspaper and the odd magazine I had some idea of current affairs and was able to take part without too much effort. It was an enjoyable meal. I appreciated the silver tea service and the fine china. But I felt my head begin to nod.

'My poor Simon, you're half asleep. You must go to bed, and I think you'd better have supper in your room and an early night.' Lady Vermont was firm.

'Yes, come along. I'll take you up,' Martin said at once.

They brushed aside my apologies and Martin led me upstairs and into what was obviously a bedsitting room. There was a collection of framed photographs on the walls, and I was surprised to see three model aircraft hanging from the ceiling. Martin took the cover off the divan and folded it over one of the armchairs. He asked me if I needed help to undress, but I shook my head and he pointed to a second door.

'Our bathroom and loo. My room's on the other side. All your stuff's been sent over from your airbase. Simon – doesn't any of this seem familiar to you?'

'No, I'm afraid not, Martin.'

'Oh, Lord! No matter. Maybe you'll suddenly remember.'

Someone – presumably Nanny Pettigrew – had unpacked the bag I had brought. Martin produced pyjamas and dressing gown and regarded me doubtfully as I sat on the divan and took off my shoes.

'Are you sure you're all right, Simon?'

'Quite sure, thanks. Just tired.'

He was genuinely concerned for me, and I was touched, but I was glad when he left. I finished undressing, put on Simon's pyjamas, inspected the bathroom cursorily and got into bed. I was asleep almost at once. There would be plenty of time to examine the room and Simon's possessions later.


In a couple of hours a knock on the door woke me, and I propped myself up as Imogen came in preceded by a large shaggy dog, who made straight for my divan. 'Rory!' I said without thinking as he snuffled at my hand.

'Simon, that's wonderful!'

'What?'

'You remembered Rory's name. No one had told you, had they?'

'No. No one had told me.'

That was the truth, but she was so pleased that my memory had shown some sign of recovery that I hadn't the heart to mention the photograph found in Simon's wallet. And Rory, who must instinctively have known that I wasn't his former master, was responding to my caresses as if to confirm my acceptance in the household. He was a lovable old thing and, though he might have regretted Simon, would have welcomed anyone. I wondered what I would have done if he had growled and tried to bite me.

Imogen sat on the side of the bed and kissed me lightly. I was sure she wanted me to make love to her a little, but when I didn't respond she didn't persist. She assumed I was too tired. She repeated how pleased she was that I'd remembered Rory's name and promised that the following day, when luckily she wouldn't be on duty at the hospital, she would show me round the house and gardens. She was sure a tour would bring back all kinds of memories.

Nanny interrupted us with my supper – vegetable soup, roast pork, roast potatoes, beans and a fruit compôte. Everything, she assured me, had come from the garden, except for the pork, and that was a gift from a neighbouring farmer. There was also a glass of wine. It was an excellent meal, better cooked than the hospital food, but then my appetite was returning and if Nanny – I was beginning to think of her as that – who said I was woefully thin, wanted to spoil me, I wasn't going to object. It was clear that the Vermonts didn't do too badly, rationing or not, and I didn't feel guilty about cashing in on their good fortune.

Imogen had left me to my supper, taking Rory with her, but she came to collect my tray and kiss me goodnight. When she had gone I got up and went again to the bathroom I was to share with Martin. With its blue tiles and big fluffy towels it was luxury to me, accustomed as I was to the spartan hospital facilities, and before that . . . I didn't want to remember.

Purposefully I set out to examine Simon Vermont's bedsitter, not that he would have dreamt of calling it that. It was a comfortable but dull room and, given Simon's resources, I wouldn't have chosen it. The furniture consisted of the divan, two small armchairs, a desk with a swivel chair under the window, a table on which were a couple of model planes, and a bookcase. The clothes cupboard, hanging space and shelves were built in. There were no pictures on the walls, only a large poster of a Spitfire and the photographs.

Although it was infinitely superior to any room I had owned, somehow I didn't envy it. But I did envy Simon his possessions, the gramophone with its stack of records – we both liked jazz – the camera, the binoculars, the wireless, the golf clubs and *two* tennis rackets – not that I had ever played either game – and his clothes! Most of them must have been pre-war, but they were of the best quality, little worn while he was in uniform, and they had lasted. There were piles of shirts and sweaters, underclothes, a row of suits, a dinner jacket, casual wear. Of course they were all symbolic of his way of life, and I knew that was what I really envied; it was very far removed from what I had had.

I learnt a lot about Simon Vermont from his room and his possessions. The photographs were informative. Simon and Martin had both been at Eton, where they had played a variety of games and presumably done a certain amount of academic work, but Simon had not been a scholar at Oxford; one print showed him in his commoner's gown, and from his books and what appeared to be notes for an essay in unformed, rather childish handwriting, it was clear that he had read French. But generally I got the impression that he wasn't much of a student.

And I thought what a chance wasted, and how much I would have liked to have gone to Eton and Oxford. For that matter, how much I would have liked to have had all Simon Vermont's advantages, and to have them now and for always. Resentfully I went to bed, leaving the rest of my examination till the next day.


My breakfast arrived at eight o'clock: coffee, two eggs, two rashers of crispy bacon, toast and marmalade. It was delicious. I waited until Nanny had collected the tray and then got up slowly. This was the life! Never had I been so spoilt. I bathed and was dressing when Martin poked his head in and said hello.

'Come down when you like. No hurry. I'm going to beat the bounds, as it were, with Dad. We have to keep an eye on old Crosby these days. He's getting dreadfully forgetful.'

'The gardener?'

'Yes. That's right. You remembered, Simon. That's great! Imogen told us about Rory. Your memory is coming back.'

It had been an involuntary remark. I hadn't meant to deceive him, but I didn't comment. However, I did warn myself to keep a watch on my tongue. If I weren't careful I'd be calling General Vermont 'Sir' and referring to him as 'the General'. So far, unable to bring myself to call him 'Dad', or Lady Vermont 'Mother', I had called them nothing.

Martin gone, I sat at the desk and went through the drawers. I found a copy of Simon's birth certificate; Nigel Hawker was the younger by two months. I studied Simon's bank statements: he had over a thousand pounds on deposit, and in 1945 that was a large sum for a young man to have spare. I read a few letters which he seemed to have kept at random, but they weren't interesting, except perhaps a brief note from 'Aunt Isobel' complaining that he hadn't thanked her for a present she had sent him. I wondered who Aunt Isobel was. There was nothing else of importance, and I went to look at the books in the hope of finding something to read. I had only glanced at them the night before.

I pulled out an Aldous Huxley and saw that another book had slipped behind. Automatically I attempted to right it and, curious to find it covered in brown paper, opened it. To my amusement it was a fairly elementary exposition on sex, with lurid illustrations. I was laughing when there was a knock on the door and Imogen came in. Hurriedly I thrust the book back where it had been hidden, behind the others. It was not a book I would need. I had not been a virgin when I was first dropped into France and I had had a lot of experience there. Since my return to England, of course, I hadn't been interested.

'Good morning, Simon. Ready to have a look around?'

'Sure, Imogen. Let's go.'

I picked up my stick and followed her. Going down the stairs she held my arm, but otherwise she wasn't possessive, and accompanied by Rory we went slowly around the house. Needless to say, I was impressed. For one thing the drawing room, its floor covered by a huge Chinese carpet, its walls hung with oil paintings that seemed to me worthy of an art gallery, was forty feet long, and the fact that Nanny and Lady Vermont herself were busy dusting and polishing in preparation for the party on Sunday didn't detract from my admiration. And the grounds were impressive, too. I learnt later that there were about six acres, including a large fruit and vegetable garden and a hen house, which between them accounted for much of the food the Vermonts ate. On this tour I saw only a fraction of them.

I was getting tired and by the time we returned to the house I was genuinely exhausted and feeling slightly unwell. Lady Vermont was furious. She vented her anger on Imogen.

'You should know better. For heaven's sake, you work in a hospital. Have you no sense, girl? The poor boy can scarcely stand up.'

I had an awful vision of being undressed and tucked up in bed by Lady Vermont, but Nanny took charge and I didn't mind Nanny. She helped me up to my room and ordered me to stay there for the remainder of the day. I must rest. She would bring me meals, as indeed she did. She was authoritative, but wonderfully comforting. I dozed, read the Huxley, listened to the wireless and even played a couple of records. I relaxed, thinking casually about Simon's relationship with Imogen. It was very like being in hospital, only much, much better.

During the evening each of the Vermonts paid me a visit. They asked how I was and if I wanted anything and Susan, when she arrived, proudly showed off her ATS officer's uniform and told me about the Diaments, with whom she was living, and something of her work at Bletchley Park. I was one of the family.


The rest of the weekend passed easily and pleasantly. Even the drinks party before lunch on Easter Sunday was not the ordeal I had feared. The dozen or so guests, obviously warned of my loss of memory, went out of their way to appear casual and incurious, treating me like Martin, glad to see us both safe.

And by Monday when Corporal Johnson arrived to collect the General and myself I knew that if I wished and if I were lucky and careful, I could spend the rest of my life as Simon Vermont, with all the advantages and privileges that went with being the Vermonts' elder son. It was a tremendous temptation.

# CHAPTER SEVEN

VE Day, 8th May, the date that brought the end of the war in Europe, also saw me discharged from hospital. In a little over three months I would be twenty-five, but before that I would be celebrating Simon Vermont's birthday as my own.

I had made up my mind after another weekend at Aubyn House. It seemed to me that I had everything to gain and nothing to lose by becoming Simon Vermont. If I was cheating the family, taking from them what was not rightly mine, I was returning something to them too. In a sense, chance and circumstances were forcing me to replace son, brother and, probably, fiancé.

It was this last point – my relationship with Imogen – that I found the most difficult to face. It was Imogen who took me shopping in Oxford on her day off, Imogen who managed to persuade an Oxford tailor to alter my uniforms and a few suits to fit me again – the remainder could wait for the attentions of the General's – and my – tailor in London. It was Imogen who nagged the General, busy as he was, to organize additional pairs of my special shoes: 'He can't possibly go around in suedes all the time!'.

But I was not in the least in love with Imogen and, though she was far from demanding, it was an effort to behave as if I were; in particular, I could hardly ask her about her relationship with Simon – had they been lovers, for instance? Somehow I didn't think so, though once or twice I noticed her giving me questioning glances, but she said nothing and I was content to let things drift. After all, I was still a semi-invalid.

The end of the war in Europe had made little immediate difference to the Vermonts' lifestyle. The General seemed busier than ever and spent most of his time in London. Lady Vermont, with Nanny's help, continued to run Aubyn House and play her part in various local affairs. Imogen was still working at her hospital, and Susan was still at the communications centre at Bletchley Park. Martin, fully recovered from his wound, had been posted to the

War Office. Inevitably I was left to myself a great deal. Why not? I couldn't expect to be treated as a guest. After all, I was a member of the family.

I didn't mind being on my own. I wandered around the house and garden. I took one of the bicycles from the old stables at the back of the house and, errand boy that I had once been what now seemed aeons ago, I had no trouble riding it in spite of my game leg. I went into the village and around the countryside. I even ventured as far as Colombury, and everywhere I was accepted as Simon Vermont. At that time there were a lot of young men coming home, wounded and scarred; I was merely one of them, to be pitied for his loss of memory and his other disabilities, but I was also the son of General Sir Patrick Vermont, and to some extent this put me in a privileged position. No one was about to question my identity or my integrity.

During this quiet period, this lull, I did my utmost to adapt myself to being Simon Vermont. I spent a lot of time in my room, playing records, listening to the wireless, reading and resting. Also, when I was sure of not being interrupted I practised copying Simon's signature – he had put his name in several of his books – and his handwriting. It was not a difficult exercise, and I was soon prepared to trust my ability to forge his hand.

In the end, I wrote myself a cheque. I thought it unlikely it would be challenged but, to be certain, I phoned the bank manager in Oxford to explain why nothing had been heard of me for so long. He greeted me with enthusiasm and assured me that he was aware of the situation, and there would be no difficulty, and said how pleased he was that I had escaped from the plane crash with my life. Then I got Imogen to drive me to the city and successfully cashed the cheque. The next time I went to Colombury I bought drinks all round at the local, the Windrush Arms, to celebrate my return; I felt that to carry this off successfully was an achievement.

Further, I went to Matins every Sunday with Lady Vermont, whom I occasionally brought myself to call 'Mother'. Imogen came too, when she was free from duty. I attended the church fête. I picked lettuces for Nanny's salads. Both she and old Crosby liked to gossip, and I learnt a lot from them. Rory became devoted to me. I was at home.

But one thing I couldn't stand were those damned aeroplanes hanging from my room's ceiling and standing on the table, or the poster of the Spitfire on the wall. I didn't want to be constantly reminded of Simon's obsession with flying or of the night he had died. I said I wanted to be rid of them, and surprisingly everyone was understanding, or behaved as if they were. At any rate the wretched objects were removed. Other changes to the room would have to wait. I couldn't make my moves too fast.

My confidence was growing in all respects, and in spite of my doubts about Imogen I began not only to appreciate but to enjoy my life as Simon Vermont.


In due course I was summoned to London to face a Medical Board which would sanction my official discharge from the RAF and decide on the amount of the invalidity pension I should receive. Imogen drove me to the station at Colombury and I went up by train. I had a first-class travel warrant and a porter found me a corner seat so that I could stare out at the passing countryside and ignore the pitying glances of the two middle-aged women sitting opposite me.

I was feeling uncomfortable enough without strangers taking an interest in me. I had put on weight, thanks to Nanny's cooking, and Simon's uniform had been altered so as to fit me not too badly, but this was the first time I had worn it and I wasn't at home in it. Besides, I was a bit dubious about the medical; there was a possibility that Simon had had some distinguishing mark on his body which had been recorded. A tactful question to Nanny had produced the information that his appendix had not been taken out and neither, luckily, had mine, but even so –

However, I need not have worried. The medical was something of a farce. The Board had received letters from Mike Davidson, Mr Tandy, Mr Curzon and, not least, Sir Hugh Glendon, and the result was a foregone conclusion. But they were kind.

One of them asked me if I would like to have psychiatric help. I wasn't sure if this was because of my supposed loss of memory – a memory which I was allowing to return by slow stages – or a supposed loss of confidence on account of my scarred face and my limp. Anyway, I refused. I had had enough of doctors for a while.

Another said, as I was told I could go, 'You've done well in the Air Force, Flight Lieutenant. You're just twenty-five. You've a great many years ahead of you, and we believe that you'll do equally well in civilian life. We offer you our best wishes.'

'Thank you, sir. I certainly intend to do my best.'

Whether it was the reference to my age, when in fact I wouldn't be twenty-five for another three weeks, or the remarks about my future, I don't know. Perhaps it was a combination of both that provided an unintentional reminder that I was not Simon Vermont. At any rate, after I had had lunch with Martin at one of the War Office messes and he had put me in a taxi for Paddington and the train to Colombury, I suddenly changed my mind and told the driver to take me to a street in Islington.

I was paying off the taxi when I saw my mother. She had come out of the Post Office and was heading straight towards me. I forced myself not to turn away and she passed close to me. I could see the little mole beside her mouth. She was wearing a green summer suit with a matching straw hat that I hadn't seen before, with beige-coloured shoes, gloves and handbag; in the shop she always wore a white coat like a doctor's, but when she went out, even if it was only around the corner, she always dressed up and today, as usual, she appeared over-smart.

I stumbled as she went by and she gave me a startled glance, but it held no hint of recognition, and she didn't turn around, as would have been natural if something about me had suddenly struck her as familiar. I suppose it was my changed appearance, the uniform and her conviction that I was dead. As for me, my main feeling was relief, tinged with more than a little sadness. I had been very fond of my mother, who, unlike my father, had done her best for me, but I realized that, given my decision about my future life, I must put such sentiments behind me.

The sensible course was to leave the district – which meant nothing to me any more – but I had an irresistible impulse to see Tom Hawker just one more time. It was, I suppose, an act of bravado, but I limped along the street to the shop. It was a lovely day and the door was wide open. I went in. My father was serving Mrs Pulent, a neighbour; I had been at school with her son Jim.

'And I gather you've had no more news of your Nige, Tom,' she remarked.

'No, 'fraid not, Martha,' he said, 'and to be frank, we don't expect any after all this time. But we're not the only ones to have lost a son. We must be philosophical about it. Life must go on.' He sounded as if he was tired of having to answer a too often repeated question.

He turned to me. 'What can I do for you, sir?'

I looked him in the eye and thought how much I had hated him – and still did. No, I thought after a moment; that was too strong a word. After all, he was my father; perhaps 'dislike' would be more appropriate.

Tom Hawker had grown fatter in the last few years, and the bloodvessels in his nose were more obvious. Otherwise he hadn't changed. I would have bet that the only regret he had felt at my presumed death was the fact that there was no hope of having me as his underpaid assistant in the business, doing more and more of the hard and dull work while he served his favourite customers, did the accounts, and generally took it easy.

As an excuse for my presence I asked the way to Balmoral Gardens and, given directions by both my father and Mrs Pulent, I thanked them and limped out of the shop. I could feel their eyes on my back as I departed, and could imagine their comments on my face. But I didn't care. I wondered vaguely what had happened to Jim Pulent, who had always disliked me and, unsure of my mother's true nationality, had called me alternatively 'Kraut' or 'Frog', but I didn't expect to see him again – or my natural parents, or any of the people from my past life.

Eager to get away, I walked as rapidly as I could down to the main road by the Angel pub, and managed to hail a passing cab. I told the driver to take me to Paddington. I was going home.


I returned to face a family crisis. Imogen and Susan were having a violent argument. They stopped abruptly as I came into the morning room, and both turned to glare at me.

'What's the matter?' I asked.

Susan spoke first. 'I confided something to Imogen because I thought she would help, but all she's done is preach at me and insist that everyone must be told.'

'Not everyone, Susan,' said Imogen.

Susan ignored the protest. 'Right! I'll start with Simon then, and we'll see how he reacts to the happy news. I'm pregnant, Simon. Three months gone with child, as they say.'

'Oh dear!'

'Oh dear!' she mimicked me sarcastically, but she was near to tears.

I thought for a moment. Then, 'I need details, Susan, before I can make any useful comment. Does the man know? Do you love him? Do you want to marry him? Does he want to marry you? Do you want to keep his baby?'

'The answer to your first question is yes, but to the others, no. He's already married, with a small child.'

'In that case I would suggest you don't have the baby. I know it's illegal, but I expect you could arrange to have an abortion, a proper one, not some backstreet affair.'

'I know I can. There's a girl I work with. She had an abortion last year. She's married, but her husband's a POW, and she didn't think she could have a baby without him knowing about it, even if she got it adopted immediately. But it's a question of money. Her operation cost two hundred pounds and I don't have anything like that, and Imogen won't lend it to me.'

'No, I won't! Not for that. I know it's 1945. I know the war's made a difference to everyone's moral standards, but it's still wicked to kill anyone, quite apart from an innocent unborn baby. You must have it and get it adopted. Of course, Aunt Antonia won't be pleased, but that's too bad. You should have thought of that before you – you – Why couldn't you have been more careful?'

'Before anyone tells Mother,' I said, 'don't you think it would be sensible if Susan made sure that she *was* pregnant?'

The three of us had been standing, and to control her temper Imogen had walked over to the window and was staring out at the garden. As Susan opened her mouth to say she was quite sure, I put my fingers to my lips and nodded at her vigorously.

Susan was a bright girl, as well as promising to be a beauty like her mother, and she understood what I was trying to signal. Her eyes widened and she gave me a brilliant smile.

Imogen turned back to us. 'Aren't you sure, Susan? You said – '

'I've missed two periods, that's all, so I suppose there is some hope.'

'You'd better make sure, then.' Imogen was taut; she hadn't liked me taking Susan's side. 'Go to a doctor in Buckingham or Bletchley as soon as you get back there. You can't go to our man. Meanwhile, I agree with Simon. We'll say nothing about it. There's no point in upsetting Aunt Antonia unnecessarily.'

'When do you go back to Bletchley?' I asked.

'Tomorrow after lunch. I must be there by four. I'm on the evening shift.'

72

I retreated to my room to change out of uniform. I practised Simon's signature a few times before I wrote another cheque. I went along to Susan's room and gave it to her. She flung her arms around me and hugged me.

'Dearest Simon, thank you very, very much. I'll pay you back as soon as I possibly can.'

'No need. Think of all the money I got paid for lying in bed in hospital.'

'You mean that?'

'I do.'

For a moment she looked at me as if puzzled. 'I didn't expect you to be so understanding and generous. You didn't used to be. Everything about you has changed, even your attitude. I'd have sworn you'd have agreed with Imogen.'

'I've had plenty of time to think about life – and death. It tends to make one less dogmatic, less critical of others.'

'Yes. Poor old Simon! Anyway, I couldn't be more grateful, and if ever you're in a hole and I can help dig you out of it, you've only to ask. I'll do it, whatever it is, and I won't ask questions, I promise.'

'Thank you.' I grinned at her.

'I'm serious, Simon, so don't forget. Whatever it is.'

'I won't forget.'

It was to be many years before I recalled her offer and took her up on it, but luckily for me she hadn't forgotten either and she kept her promise.


Meanwhile everyone learnt of the horrors of the extermination camps in Germany. General Vermont, who visited Belsen with an official party from the War Office, was made physically sick by the appalling scenes he witnessed and couldn't eat for several days afterwards. The war in the East continued until Hiroshima and, as if that wasn't enough, Nagasaki – the price of peace in the Far East. We had entered the atomic age.

I continued to live quietly at Aubyn House until, by the late autumn, I was as strong and fit as I would ever be. Although I still limped I didn't really need a stick any more, but I had got used to the support and was lost without it. The limp was now a part of me, as were my other infirmities. Even my scarred face had become famil-iar, though the scars were fading noticeably. And, strangely enough, my life as a gentleman of leisure was beginning to pall, not that this period was without incident.

There was a small party of family and friends to celebrate the Vermonts' thirtieth wedding anniversary. The difficulty of a suitable present was solved by Martin. He had discovered that a London club in financial straits was selling off part of its wine cellar, and the sum required, divided by four, was reasonable. The bottles made an excellent gift. It was on this occasion that I first met the Diaments, my late navigator's parents, who had brought Susan, looking pale and still recovering from what was claimed to be a minor operation. It was an embarrassing meeting; Mrs Diament, embracing me, nearly broke down.

The next occasion was also somewhat embarrassing as I was expected to show signs of a grief which of course I failed to feel. Aunt Isobel, whose letter I had found in Simon's desk, reproaching him for not having thanked her for a present she had sent, had died in the United States. Aunt Isobel, the widow of one Duncan Malwood II, whom she had married after the demise of her first husband, was Antonia Vermont's eldest sister. She had been cremated in the States, but the ashes were flown home and buried in the local graveyard after a brief service. She had left Susan some jewellery and Martin a small painting – a Constable – but I, who it appeared was her godson, was to inherit her house behind Knightsbridge, at present rented. This was a munificent legacy and I certainly had reason to be grateful, but it was not easy to fake sorrow at the death of an old woman whom I had never met.

And then there was the investiture at Buckingham Palace. I was so overwhelmed at the thought of the imposture I was undertaking that my memory of the occasion is a little blurred. I know that the General and Lady Vermont and Imogen accompanied me to the Palace, though I was separated from them at an early stage in the proceedings, when those of us who were to receive awards were taken to one side. The routine was, in fact, highly organized and we were fully briefed with precise instructions: Do not speak unless spoken to, but if there is any conversation address the King as 'Your Majesty' the first time and then as 'Sir'. As you leave the presence, take three steps backwards before bowing and turning away.

I heard my name – the name of Flight Lieutenant Simon Vermont – called and I went from the ante-chamber into the main room where everyone was assembled. The King was a smaller man than he appeared from cinema newsreels and still photographs, and he looked tired and ill. An aide passed him my medal on a cushion. He murmured something about having heard that I had had a bad time, and hoped that I was making a good recovery. He sounded as if he really meant it. Then he pinned on my DFC, shook hands and smiled as he said, 'Your family seem to make a habit of earning decorations, Flight Lieutenant.'

I am no Royalist but I was impressed. What's more, I felt on reflection over lunch with the Vermonts and Imogen at the Army and Navy Club on the corner of St James's Square, on the site of the former home of Nell Gwynn, that somehow the King had by his words granted me the right to be Simon Vermont, and to have all that went with this, both the advantages and the obligations.

# CHAPTER EIGHT

I was reminded of my obligations at the beginning of December. Imogen, who had a headache, had gone to bed early after dinner and Lady Vermont had tactfully departed to telephone a friend. The General and I sat in the library, a comfortable room with big leather chairs, drinking port.

'Simon,' the General said, 'I think it's about time we had a talk about your future, don't you?'

I wasn't surprised. I had had some warning, having overheard part of a conversation between the Vermonts in which Lady Vermont had seemed to be pressing her husband to speak to me, though he had wanted to leave the matter until after Christmas. It wasn't hard to guess the subject she had in mind.

'Yes, I'm sure it is,' I agreed readily, 'but it's quite a problem.'

'Have you thought of going back to Oxford and taking an Honours degree in place of that war degree they gave you? There would be no difficulty.'

'It's too late. I'm too old.'

'Nonsense! There'll be a lot of men coming out of the services and returning to their universities. You might get more from it than you did before. You're not an academic, I know. You were much keener on sport, but –'

'No.' I added, 'Dad.'

I spoke positively. Of course I had already given my future some thought. The idea of Oxford was attractive, but I had meant it when I said it was too late. If I had been eighteen I would have leapt at the chance, but now it no longer appealed to me. I was indeed too old, not only in age, but also in experience; I was too battered physically, and there was an added complication. I was damned sure that, given the opportunity, I could have got a First Class degree. But how to explain Simon's sudden brilliance? My lameness would cover my inability to play any game, and I could always fake a spectator's interest. But it would be much more difficult to fake my work and I could easily finish up with a poor Third. In any case, what was the point?

'The war's taken up so many years,' I said. 'Oh, I'm not complaining. It's been the same for everyone, but Oxford would mean yet more delay, unless I really wanted an academic career – and I can't see myself as a don, or even a master in a minor public school.'

The General sighed. 'I see your point,' he said. 'But do you have any idea what you'd like to go in for?'

'I've considered journalism. There are going to be a great many changes in Europe and here in England as a result of the war: economic changes, social changes, moral changes, changes in relations between countries. It would be fascinating to see what happens, and perhaps have a part in it.'

'Yes, I agree with you, Simon, but journalism – '

Obviously the idea didn't appeal to him and I wasn't wildly keen on it myself, but I had not been able to think of any other occupation I would be capable of doing. Indeed, I wasn't too sure that I'd make much of a journalist.

'Have you any other suggestions, Dad?' I asked meekly. 'After all, I've no qualifications apart from the so-called war degree, which is pretty worthless, and no particular aptitudes.'

'Come, Simon, don't sell yourself short.' The General was annoyed. 'And yes, I do have another suggestion. The Foreign Office. I know it means taking an exam, but I'm told by a reliable source that they're eager to have chaps like you with good backgrounds and war records, so they're prepared to be lenient. How does the idea appeal to you?'

I thought of Paris, Rome, Washington; but there were ghastly posts too. I hesitated. Then I said, 'It – it sounds as if it might be an excellent idea.'

I knew it was not what I really wanted – not in the long term. I couldn't visualize myself as a diplomat in knee breeches and a cocked hat. Nevertheless, the Foreign Office could become a good springboard for whatever I ultimately decided upon. It was then that the thought came to me that I might go in for politics – a career to which I would be much better suited and which I would enjoy more. I had met the local MP, an old chap in his late sixties, who had said he probably wouldn't stand in the next election. This would leave a safe Conservative seat going begging right here on my doorstep –

surely a distinct possibility. I made up my mind to consider it very carefully. The Labour Party, to many people's surprise, had just won the post-war election in July, so there would be plenty of time to arrange matters.

'Well, that's settled then, Simon. I'll make inquiries, find out exactly what you have to do. You'll need sponsors, I have no doubt, but that will be no problem. Nor, I'm sure, will the exam. And you'll have that house in Knightsbridge that poor Isobel left you, which will be most convenient.'

'Yes, thank you,' I said, thinking that it would be equally convenient for the House of Commons.

I knew I was being organized, but I didn't object; it was meant for my benefit and, if I made a different decision, as Simon had done when he went into the RAF rather than the Army, no one would stand in my way. There were, however, some other obligations which could not be disregarded, and I guessed what was coming when the General cleared his throat a little hesitantly.

'Er – ' he said. 'I don't want to interfere in your private life, Simon. You're not a child any longer. But oughtn't you and Imogen to be making your engagement official and setting a wedding date? She won't wait for ever, you know.'

'No, I wouldn't expect her to do that. The trouble is I'm such an awful crock. She could do so much better than me and – '

'Nonsense!'

I tried to argue, but he wouldn't listen. Nor would Imogen, who brushed aside my protestations when I tackled the subject with her the next day. I knew I was committed. In the circumstances I would have been a fool to make a major issue of it. Imogen was an attractive girl, who would make an efficient and caring wife; an added bonus was that she had a private income of almost a thousand a year, which was riches in 1945. Of course it would be a marriage of convenience. She wasn't what you would call exciting, and I wasn't in love with her, but then I wasn't in love with anyone and, I told myself, if it didn't work there was such a thing as divorce.


Our engagement was announced in *The Times* and the *Telegraph* the following week and we decided to marry in the spring. Another Christmas came and went. I attended a couple of interviews at the Foreign Office and I sat the exam, which was not difficult. The papers were very wide-ranging and anyone with a good grammar school education who had read the newspapers against a fair background of general knowledge and current affairs would have had no problems. I took oral exams in French and German, and was congratulated on my accent and fluency; I blessed my mother for insisting that I should speak both these languages from childhood. In due course I was informed that I might have the privilege of working in the Foreign Office for such a pittance of a salary that I was tempted to tell them to go to hell.

Meanwhile preparations for the wedding intensified, and I must have been one of the most compliant bridegrooms-to-be. I raised no objections whatsoever to any proposals. When consulted, I merely agreed – the village church, a simple white wedding, family and close friends only, a reception at Aubyn House afterwards, a brief honeymoon in Devon. Needless to say, the reality bore little relation to these plans.

The church in the village, dating back to the days when almost everybody worshipped in it as a matter of course, was surprisingly large. For the wedding it was packed with people whom I had never seen before, or so it appeared to me as I stood nervously beside Martin, my best man, waiting for Imogen to walk down the aisle. Martin grinned at me encouragingly as at last the organ swelled into the opening chords of 'Here Comes the Bride' and, amid murmurs of appreciation, Imogen came slowly towards me on the General's arm, followed by Susan and a trail of bridesmaids.

Imogen looked calm, composed and rather lovely in a wedding dress that had belonged to her mother and a Honiton lace veil that was a Vermont heirloom. The ceremony went smoothly; we kissed and signed the register in the vestry; we were man and wife, though I must admit that I didn't feel like a married man until our first son, Peter, was born the following year.

For me, the reception was a blur of champagne, congratulations, kisses, speeches and cutting a three-tiered cake made by Nanny from carefully hoarded rations. Then it was over and – irony of ironies – we were driven away by ex-corporal Johnson who, having been demobbed, was now employed by the General in a civilian capacity as chauffeur and general handyman.

However, he did not drive us to the railway station in Colombury to catch a train for Devon. We were to spend the night in London in Brown's Hotel and the next morning go on to Switzerland.

Switzerland? We were being lent a villa, complete with servants, on the shore of Lac Léman, quite close to the city of Geneva, by friends of Lady Vermont who were going to New York on business. They had also arranged for us to receive a sum of money in Swiss francs, which we could repay when they next visited England. This was to prove extremely useful, since at that time strict exchange control regulations prohibited us from taking more than a small amount of sterling out of the country. I didn't care if we were breaking the rules by this form of exchange, but it amused me that the Vermonts were prepared to bend the law like this when it suited them.

Our wedding night was happier than I had expected. I had assumed that, in spite of the book on sex that Simon had kept hidden in his room, Imogen would be a virgin; she was not the kind of girl to take lovemaking lightly, and I doubted if Simon would have pressed her. I was wrong, though she was very far from experienced. For my part, not having had a woman for ages, I came almost as soon as I entered her. But, waking early, I made love to her again, this time slowly and carefully, until she was gasping with pleasure.

'You enjoyed that?' I said as I rolled off her.

'Oh, darling, yes. It was wonderful.' She laughed. 'So much better than the other time.'

'Last night, you mean?'

'No. The other time, Simon, at the end of your leave before – before you went back to your aerodrome and – and had that crash.' She frowned. 'You don't remember?'

'No. I'm sorry.'

She gave me a curious look, then kissed me as if to reassure me, though in fact she had already done that. I knew now the extent of her experience and, more importantly, I knew that we would be able to have a satisfactory sex life together.

It was, I believed, a contented couple who set off for Geneva later that morning.


Our honeymoon was extremely pleasant. If that sounds a tepid description of what ought to be, but rarely is, a cherished memory, it must be remembered that I was not in love with Imogen and she, who had known Cousin Simon all her life, could scarcely have expected him to be transformed suddenly into a dashing romantic

80

character. But, perhaps because our expectations were not high, we got on well together.

It was good to be in a bright, clean city, undamaged by war and clearly prosperous. Neither of us had ever been to Geneva before, so we had plenty to see. We strolled around the picturesque Vieille Ville. We visited the Cathédrale St-Pierre, where Calvin used to preach and, because Imogen liked picture galleries, the Musée d'Art et d'Histoire and the Petit Palais. One day we hired a car and drove out to the medieval Château de Chillon. On another day when it rained, we spent the afternoon in bed, making love and watching the famous Jet d'Eau appear by the harbour entrance and disappear in the mist. We explored antique shops and gazed with envy into the windows of the many impressive boutiques. We tried two or three restaurants, but with limited francs we mostly ate in the villa, where we were fed sumptuously. We promised ourselves that we would come back when there were no longer restrictions on the money we could bring.

Little did we think that we would come to make our home in Geneva for so many years and, in spite of everything, be happy there. Nevertheless, it was on our honeymoon that I took the first step towards it.

I had taken Imogen to a beauty parlour to have her hair done, and was therefore free for a couple of hours. I had been wondering how I might achieve this as, inevitably, we were always together. I had also made some discreet enquiries, and been given the name of a relatively small private bank based in Geneva, but with branches in Zurich and elsewhere. It was known as the Banque St-Pierre de Genève, and I had decided that it might well serve my purpose. I seized my opportunity and took a taxi to the place. I gave my name and asked to speak to a senior official. I admitted that I had no appointment, but said I was sure that wouldn't matter.

In retrospect I realize that this was absolute cheek on my part. Nigel Hawker would never have done it or, if he had tried, he would have had no success. But I was Simon Vermont, and I had acquired not only his arrogant nose but his expensive suit and a great measure of his self-assurance. He might not have been much good in bed, but he had the bland belief of his class that people, if asked nicely, would do his bidding.

And even on this occasion it worked. I was shown into a small but informal room where shortly I was joined by a Monsieur Le

Rossignol, not of course the Monsieur Le Rossignol with whom over the years I was to become friendly and who was to be such a great help to me, but his father. I stated my business; I wished to open a Swiss bank account, and also to rent a small deposit box.

I spoke in my fluent French, which impressed him. 'Of course, Monsieur,' I explained, 'I'm sure you'll appreciate that with the restrictions on taking sterling out of Great Britain, I can only pay a token sum into the account for the time being.'

When I told him what I meant by a token sum, his eyes widened and his lips twitched with amusement. But I had had difficulty in raising even this little. Some I had smuggled illegally out of England and, as for the rest, I would have to tell some lies to Imogen to explain our sudden shortage of Swiss francs – say I had stupidly lost them, perhaps.

'You have credentials, Monsieur?' The banker had regained his gravitas.

'Certainly. My passport and a letter from my bank manager in Oxford.'

I watched him as he glanced through the passport and then read the letter. The envelope had not been sealed and I knew what it contained – an excellent personal reference for me, both as a member of the distinguished Vermont family and as a former RAF officer who was recovering from terrible war wounds and was about to enter the British Foreign Office. The letter also mentioned that I was on my honeymoon, and that this was the reason for my presence in Geneva. Clearly, to protect his own interests under the exchange control rules, the Oxford manager had been careful to avoid any reference to financial matters, or to the possibility of my opening an illegal account.

'War is a dreadful thing, Monsieur, a dreadful thing,' Monsieur Le Rossignol said, returning my passport but keeping the letter. 'We have been fortunate to escape it here in Switzerland, but I have a son – still a boy, half your age – and I fear for him in the future. However, I must not be depressing. I hope you and your bride are enjoying Geneva. Where are you staying?'

'At the Villa Villetri, Monsieur. The De Vavascours are friends of my family. They're in New York at present and they've lent us the villa.'

Monsieur Le Rossignol raised an eyebrow in acknowledgement. I think that up to this moment he had intended to refuse me. He was not a sentimental man. It was clear that he had never heard of the Vermonts, but thought that perhaps I should not be dismissed out of hand. I suspect his remarks about the war and his son had been intended to make his refusal more palatable to me.

The mention of the De Vavascours changed all that. From the size of the villa, its furnishings and its staff, I had gathered they were rich, but it now seemed they were also influential. Certainly they shifted the balance in my favour.

'Monsieur, while we have been chatting of other matters,' said the banker blandly, 'I have been reflecting. Your request is unusual. You must realize that it is not our normal practice to deal in such small sums. However, today the circumstances are unusual too, and as a favour to you and your country – to which we Europeans owe a great deal – I'm prepared to agree.'

I thanked the old rogue prolifically and, as I went to meet Imogen, I walked on air, my limp unnoticed. Assured as my position seemed, I would always remain vulnerable. But at least I possessed the security of a numbered Swiss bank account – small, admittedly, though I hoped it would grow – and I had found a safe repository for my gunmetal watch.

# Interlude

*1993*

It was after two when Peter Vermont finished reading Part One of the typescript he had acquired in Switzerland and he couldn't take any more, not now, not until he had had time to think about it, to check some facts. His head ached, his eyes were sore and he felt slightly nauseated.

He found a file cover for the typescript and locked it in a desk drawer, but he had forgotten the watch. There was the little chamois bag on his desk in front of him, beside a silver-framed photograph of Julia and their three children. He took out the watch. It was an ugly gunmetal object of no intrinsic value, and there was no obvious reason why his father had treasured it.

Taking the small Swiss knife which he always carried in his pocket, Peter opened the nail file and with some difficulty prised off the back of the watch. It was a waste of effort. There was nothing to be seen except the works, which looked perfectly normal. He replaced the back, put the watch in its bag and locked it up with the typescript.

'Dear God!' he murmured aloud.

The story was incredible. He could not believe that it was true, that his father had been killed in an air crash in France. But, of course, it wouldn't have been his father. It would have been Simon Vermont, young Simon Vermont, whose place, so the script claimed, had been taken by someone called Nigel Hawker, an impostor, a crook. In that case he – Peter – was *Nigel Hawker's* son! No! His every instinct protested against the idea.

By this time Peter's head was reeling and throbbing from these fruitless cogitations. He pushed back his chair and stood up, staggering a little. The half-empty brandy decanter reproached him. He had long ago finished his coffee and, absorbed in what he was reading, had absent-mindedly continued to drink brandy. He cursed silently. He'd have a hell of a hangover in the morning, and at eleven o'clock he was up in front of Lord Justice Marrett who was a stickler for correct procedures.

Slowly he made his way upstairs, took a couple of paracetamol tablets and got ready for bed, having taken care to supplement his alarm with a request for a telephone call at seven. But he was awake before that, having scarcely slept.

As he breakfasted in the kitchen on black coffee and toast a further point occurred to him. The script had mentioned a numbered account as well as a safe-deposit box in the Banque St-Pierre de Genève, yet the banker, Le Rossignol, had made no mention of it. Surely this was odd.

He shrugged his shoulders, abandoning currently unanswerable questions and decided on some direct investigation. He went to fetch a pad and jotted notes, names of people mentioned in the type-script that could be checked. There was, of course, the possibility that they were pseudonyms, but he himself could vouch for those he knew – members of the Vermont family, Nanny Pettigrew, the Diaments – and there seemed no reason for false names to have been used for the others.

The main problem was Nigel Hawker. Then there were the service officers in the RAF and the Army, especially Stephen Segar who had been a personal friend, and the various doctors who had cared for Simon Vermont – if it had been Simon Vermont – after his return from France. Suddenly Peter gave a wan smile as he wondered if he would have the nerve to ask Aunt Susan if she really had had an abortion while she was in the ATS.


Gussey, his chauffeur, drove Peter to the Inner Temple im-mediately after breakfast. Apart from a full law library there were a certain number of reference books in his chambers and, ignoring a brief he should have been studying, Peter set to work on some private research.

He had more luck than he had expected, since anyone mentioned in the typescript, if still living, would have been at least in his seven-ties. He found the names of Stephen Segar and Adrian Sherry-Box in *Who's Who*. Segar had retired from the RAF as a Wing Commander and had gone into business; he had a flat in Marylebone. Sherry-Box had retired as a Brigadier, and was living in Hampshire. Under Glendon he found Timothy Glendon, eldest son of the late Sir Hugh Glendon, the surgeon who had recon-structed 'Simon Vermont's' face.

Peter knew that these were all individuals whose relationship to his father he could have checked simply by asking his Aunt Susan or his Uncle Martin, but they would have wanted to know why he was suddenly interested, and he couldn't possibly explain. The two letters and the first part of the 'book' he had read had infected him with the need for secrecy.

His secretary and the Chief Clerk arrived, both expressing surprise at seeing him there so early. Gradually other members of chambers drifted in. The telephone rang. There were questions to be answered. A solicitor who had sent him several important briefs wanted an urgent appointment. He was due in court at eleven and a difficulty had arisen; one of the witnesses had come down with influenza, complete with doctor's certificate. With a deliberate effort Peter shut his mind to his personal problems.

It was some hours later that, back in chambers, he had the chance to telephone the Ministry of Defence on his private line. He explained who he was and said that he wanted to make an enquiry about one Nigel Hawker, thought to have been a corporal in the Army in 1945. He murmured something about the question of a will, but no one seemed interested in the reason for his call. In due course he received the information for which he had asked. Nigel Hawker had joined the Army in 1938. In 1940 he had been transferred from the Somerset Light Infantry to the Intelligence Corps. In 1944 he had disappeared in France, and had subsequently been posted as 'missing believed killed in action'.

Peter thanked his informant and replaced the receiver. Reluctantly he accepted the hard fact. Nigel Hawker was not an invention, and his army record fitted the account in the typescript. So it was necessary to find out more about him.

Peter looked at his watch. He had an appointment at four. There wasn't time to get to St Catherine's House and order a copy of Hawker's birth certificate before that, and it would be too late afterwards because the place would be shut. After a moment's hesitation he asked his secretary to come in. Valerie Gosport – a widow in her late thirties with an invalid son – had worked for Peter for ten years and he knew she could be trusted not to gossip.

'Nigel Hawker,' he said, 'born 1920 or thereabouts. I hope you don't mind. You know the routine?'

'Of course. It'll be no trouble.'

'Thanks a lot. And make a note of the details, so that we don't have to wait till they send us the copy.' Peter hesitated, and decided not to say that it was a private matter.

As soon as she had gone, Peter telephoned Wing Commander Stephen Segar. According to *Who's Who*, Segar had been born in 1917, which made him seventy-six, but he didn't sound so old on the phone. He seemed delighted to hear from Simon Vermont's son, and suggested that if Peter were free he should come along for a drink that evening around six o'clock, an invitation that Peter accepted with alacrity. He had been afraid that Segar might be ill or too frail, or simply disinclined to see him.


In the event Stephen Segar was as warm and welcoming as he had sounded on the phone. He was a white-haired man, solid rather than fat, with an upright stance and a strutting walk. Peter took an immediate liking to him.

'This is a very pleasant surprise,' Segar said, leading Peter into a large living room overlooking Regent's Park. 'I always regretted losing touch with your father, but I was posted abroad while he was still in hospital and when I returned I was too busy, too lazy, to pick up the threads again. He was married and had children, and so did I. Different lives. It happens all the time, I suppose.'

He waved Peter to a chair, asked him what he would like to drink and poured them each a whisky. Then he continued before Peter had time to explain the reasons for his visit – reasons which he had previously rehearsed.

'I was very sorry to hear of your father's death, very sorry. There aren't so many of us left now. What about the others – Susan and Martin?'

'Both reasonably well, thank you.' Peter registered the fact that there was little wrong with Segar's memory.

Segar chuckled. 'I was half in love with Susan once. She was a great girl, lots of spirit. I must say I can't visualize her as a don's wife, but then I wouldn't have visualized Simon as Foreign Secretary, which he certainly would have become if his health hadn't broken down. I wouldn't have thought he had the brains or the ambition. When I knew him all he cared about were aeroplanes. Even your mother – they were unofficially engaged then – seemed to take second place.'

He stopped, smiling at his memories. Peter felt cold; if anything, this was further confirmation of the typescript, which had stressed that whereas Simon Vermont had been a fine athlete he had not been much of a scholar. Nigel Hawker had been the clever one.

'But here I am, rabbiting away as usual. My family say I never stop talking. It comes of living alone. I didn't do it when my dear wife was alive, but now I'm so happy to find someone who will listen that I go on and on.'

'That's really why I'm here, sir, to listen and to hear you reminisce. I've been going through my father's papers and I'm considering the possibility of writing his biography,' Peter lied.

'I see. Of course, he didn't make it quite to the top, but still – Why not? It could be interesting. However, I'm not sure I can help you much.'

'You must have been one of the last people to talk to him the night he crashed. What sort of mood was he in? Do you remember?'

'I remember that night well enough. Simon ought never to have gone on the mission. He wasn't on the roster, but he and Alan Diament were friends and, when the pilot who should have flown was taken ill, Simon volunteered. It was a tricky job, picking up this agent, and there wasn't anyone else as suitable as Simon, so I agreed.'

'This agent – Nigel Hawker.'

'Yes. That was the name. I had forgotten it. Anyway, God knows what happened to him. I don't think he was ever heard of again, poor devil.'

'Would my father have been told who he was to pick up?'

'Oh no! Just an agent. Where and when. Nothing more, except a recognition signal. The people we were working with were very cagey. Need to know, and all that, you recall – but of course you don't. The places they picked for such operations were nearly always difficult to land in, and the times were often inexact. Sometimes the bod never appeared, and it was a wasted effort. Sometimes it was a trap and the pilot flew into a welcoming committee of Germans.'

'But you recognized the name of Hawker when I mentioned it just now.'

'Yes, but the circumstances were unusual. Hawker's outfit – and I still don't know if that was his real name or a cover – made a fuss because we'd failed. He was supposed to be bringing important information. One of them tried to question your father while he was still desperately ill and there was a row. I don't remember the details.'

More confirmation of the typescript, Peter thought, as Segar went to pour them a second drink. In addition, unless the script were true, Simon Vermont had known far more about Hawker than Segar had implied. For instance, he had known that Nigel's father, Thomas Hawker had been a grocer, and that his mother's maiden name was Huber, as verified by the details noted by Valerie Gosport from Nigel's birth certificate. Even stranger, he had known that Nigel Hawker was two months younger than himself.

There was, Peter supposed, a possible – though far-fetched – explanation. Simon Vermont had been extremely ill and had suffered a great deal. During this period he might have acquired a guilt complex about the agent whom he had failed to retrieve. Later, perhaps, he had found out what he could about Hawker, until in his old age it had become an obsession, and he had come to imagine that he was Nigel Hawker.

This theory seemed not so much impossible as incredible. But the mind was a funny thing. In the course of his career as a barrister Peter had come across some apparently impossible or inexplicable behaviour patterns. The main trouble with the theory, however, was that his father had been – or had appeared to be – one of the sanest of men even up to the time of his death.

'What? I'm sorry.' Suddenly he had become aware that Segar was speaking to him again.

'I asked if you would care to stay and have supper with me. I should be delighted if you would. My housekeeper always leaves me an evening meal – something simple. There's a pheasant casserole tonight, salad and cheese. Plenty for two.'

Peter opened his mouth to say he was sorry, a previous engagement, but Stephen Segar was so obviously lonely that he hadn't the heart to refuse.

'That sounds wonderful,' he said. 'Many thanks. But might I make a phone call to Hampshire first?'

'Of course. I'll show you to my study. You can phone while I lay an extra place. Come along.'

Alone in Segar's study Peter tapped out Adrian Sherry-Box's number which he had jotted down in his diary. A woman's voice answered, and he asked if he might speak to the Brigadier.

'No, you can't. He's in bed.'

'Is he ill?'

There was a harsh laugh. 'Ill? He's dying. The doctor gives him a week. He should be in hospital. Who's that?'

'It doesn't matter. I'm very sorry, and I'm sorry to have bothered you.'

Peter put down the receiver and returned to the living room. Obviously, Sherry-Box was no use as a source of information. He told Segar what he had been doing. Segar remembered Sherry-Box.

'The trouble is, we're all so ancient,' he said. 'You'll do better when you research your father's political career.'

'Yes,' said Peter. The mention of his father's political career had reminded him unpleasantly of the rest of the typescript that remained unread and which he assumed would cover that period. It would have to wait until the following night, and he could only hope it would contain no more ghastly shocks or supposed revelations. The business of Nigel Hawker was enough.


On Thursday evening Peter Vermont returned home, tired and mentally exhausted after a hard day in court. What he would have liked to do was lounge in a comfortable chair, feet on a stool, a drink beside him, and watch a video or listen to some music, before a light supper and an early bed.

But he knew this was impossible. He had still not come to terms with the first part of his father's typescript, see-sawing between belief and disbelief, and he knew he must try to finish reading it and satisfy his curiosity before he went to bed, however late that might be. But he was hesitant to start, fearful of what he might learn. In blunt terms, he dreaded what the rest of the book might reveal.

# Part Two

*1960–61*

# CHAPTER NINE

And so the years passed. They were not uneventful for the Vermonts. Shortly after the end of the war Mother became seriously ill, and cancer was diagnosed. She lived long enough to see Peter born in 1947 and Edward in 1948, but died shortly before Noreen's birth in 1950. Martin had remained a bachelor and Susan, who had married an Oxford don a decade older than herself, had suffered a series of miscarriages. So our three – mine and Imogen's – were the only grandchildren.

Imogen had always preferred the country to London and, with Dad on his own and the children still babies, she spent more and more time at Aubyn House. So far I had managed not to be posted abroad, but when this became a real possibility I resigned from the Foreign Office. I had never intended to make it a career.

Our Member of Parliament had been as good as his word and had declared his intention not to stand again. Warmly recommended by him to Central Office I had been accepted without any difficulty by the local committee as their prospective Conservative candidate.

After all, I had everything going for me. I was young, but not too young, and personable; my facial scars had faded more than I had hoped, and the slight disfigurement that remained, added to my limp, made me a romantic figure, a war hero. Then, I was a responsible married man, and Imogen was an enormous asset; popular in her own right, she worked assiduously to nurse the constituency when I was unable to be there. But my main advantage was that I was a Vermont, whose family had lived in the district for generations, not some outsider who wouldn't understand the constituents' problems.

The other candidates didn't stand a ghost of a chance. In October 1951 I was returned to Parliament with an increased majority. It was a seat I was to hold until I resigned on health grounds and went to live in Switzerland – but of course at this point that was some years ahead.

Meanwhile, whether my Party was in power or in opposition, I worked hard, both in the House and in my constituency. I specialized in foreign affairs, and my time in the FO stood me in good stead, but I didn't neglect the problems at home. I accepted invitations to speak and to attend functions whenever they were worthwhile and went out of my way to help colleagues standing in by-elections, even if there was no chance of winning the seat. I did my best to co-operate with the media, though I was careful to avoid too much publicity. I tried not to take sides in the many petty squabbles which were rife in all parties. I wanted to be liked but to remain my own man, and I succeeded. By 1960 I was a Junior Minister with a reputation for intelligence, hard work and integrity, marked for promotion. A political career is more of a slippery slope than a ladder, but my future looked rosy.

Altogether it was a good life. I was very fortunate. I enjoyed the variety that politics offered, the cut and thrust of debate, the club-like atmosphere of the House, the opportunities to travel and meet interesting people; and, if one reached the top, there were all kinds of privileges and advantages to be gained. It was an alluring prospect.

My private life was also satisfactory. My marriage, though not exciting, was happy, and I got a lot of pleasure from the children. What is more, in my secretary, Renata Tamson, I had the ideal mistress. Renata was in her early thirties, a tall dark gypsy of a girl; her mother had been Spanish. She was a divorcée who had no intention of marrying again or desire to do so, and our arrangement suited her as much as it suited me.

Renata was completely independent. Apart from her salary as my secretary, which she earned and more, I never gave her money or contributed to the rent of her small flat behind the Roman Catholic Westminster Cathedral off Victoria Street, and she had many friends of whom I knew nothing. But I could depend on her loyalty and her discretion, and I was as much 'in love' with her as I ever was with anyone, even though by 1960 we had been together for six years. I believe she felt the same about me. It was a fine relationship. Perhaps if we had married it would have been different, but that was never on the cards, and it's useless to speculate.

Of course no life this side of heaven is worry-free, and during the Fifties I had my share of problems. As Dad grew old he became more demanding of his children and his grandchildren, and was apt to interfere in matters he didn't understand; he missed Mother desperately. There was a dreadful family row when Martin decided to leave the Army, but in fact he had no choice; it was either resign his commission or be kicked out – with the resultant scandal – for seducing a Second Lieutenant, a surprisingly innocent young man. Dad also blamed Guy Sinclair, Susan's husband, for her miscarriages, and Imogen for Noreen's poor school reports. I was the one who had to arbitrate, the one to whom they all seemed to turn.

They turned to me in every other kind of crisis, such as when Edward ran away from his preparatory school, when Peter knocked down an old lady with his bicycle, when Guy was (wrongly) accused of assaulting a policeman who had stopped him for speeding, and when Nanny had a stroke. Imogen was the comforter, the support, but it was I who took the decisions. Little by little, as Dad grew more and more frail, I assumed the mantle of head of the Vermont family.

I rarely thought of the Hawkers.


Then came 1960, my own personal crisis year. It began innocently enough with an evening spent with Renata. I had been at Aubyn House with the family for Christmas and the New Year, and had come up to London two days before the Parliamentary recess ended. As we had arranged, Renata had returned at the same time from the Highlands of Scotland, where she had been spending the holidays with friends.

I went around to her flat at six that evening. It was a cold, damp night, but it was beautifully warm in the flat, which smelt of some delicious food that she was cooking. I couldn't place what it was; Renata was an excellent cook who loved to experiment, and we always ate well.

I had brought a couple of bottles of champagne as my share of the meal, and a packet of smoked salmon, which Renata could keep in the freezer if she didn't want to use it now. We hadn't seen each other for several weeks and when we kissed she whispered, 'The casserole can wait, but I can't', and we made love at once on the sofa, quickly and fiercely.

Then I opened a bottle and we drank and chatted about our respective holidays, and what was likely to come up in the next Session of the House. Renata collected old jewellery and I had brought her an antique pendant which I had found in a shop in Colombury, and this delighted her. When the food was ready I laid the table and we ate. Afterwards we went to bed and this time made love slowly and luxuriously. It was a wonderful evening.

I left Renata's flat soon after midnight. It was even colder now and the damp air had become a fine drizzle. Head down and rain-coat collar up, I went in search of a taxi, but as always in London, the taxis seemed to have disappeared with the onset of rain, and I was out of luck.

The thugs came at me from behind. My mind was full of Renata, and my body content with lovemaking. They took me by surprise. But that's only an excuse. Although I was almost forty and my game leg had made it difficult for me to take a great deal of exercise, I had done my best to keep fit, and I was not in bad shape. Nevertheless, I couldn't possibly have coped with them even if I had had any advance warning. They were two large louts in their twenties and they knew their job; doubtless they had had plenty of practice. My resistance was minimal.

As one of them seized me by the arms, almost jerking them out of their sockets, I let myself go slack and kicked backwards at his shins, but though I landed a blow the damage I did must have been slight. In return, letting me fall, he kicked me on the base of the spine. His boots were metal-capped and I cried out with the pain. Then the other thug hit me on the head with something hard and heavy and I blacked out.

The next thing I remember was wondering where the hell I was. It was dark and raining steadily. Water purled into a nearby drain. I was aware of being very wet and uncomfortable, but I didn't have the energy to try to improve my situation. I felt sick and without warning I vomited, which didn't help.

Suddenly a cold, damp rubbery object prodded at my cheek and a rough tongue licked me. For a moment, before I realized it was a dog, I was terrified. Then I tried to push it away, expecting it to urinate over me, and a bright light shone down on me.

A woman's voice said, 'A drunk! How horrid! Come away, Pedro! At once. Bad dog! Come here at once. Leave it alone.'

I don't know if she was referring to me or my vomit and I didn't care. I wished she would either do something to help me or go away. I groaned and pushed the dog hard. I had had enough of its minis-trations.

Another voice, a man's, said, 'Are you sure he's drunk, dear? There's blood on his head. Perhaps he's hurt.'

'If he is, it's his own fault. Look! He's been sick. It's revolting. Of course he's drunk. Don't be stupid, Cyril. Pedro, come here!'

The matter was resolved, happily for me at least, by the arrival of a police patrol car. Cyril, his spouse and Pedro departed. By now I was recovering a little from the effects of the assault I had suffered at the hands of the two thugs. As a policeman bent over me I summoned all my resources.

'Officer, I am not a drunk. I'm Simon Vermont, a Member of Parliament, and I've been mugged.'

Whether he believed me or not I don't know, but my claim to be a Member of Parliament was not one likely to be made spontaneously, so I suppose he did. At any rate, I was treated with care and consideration.

I refused to be taken to Westminster Hospital, so they drove me to the police station in Rochester Row. There, after I had been offered a cup of tea and been examined by a police doctor, to whom I made light of my injuries, I gave the officer in charge such particulars of the attack as I could and signed a statement. Then I was driven home. Luckily I still had my keys, and the Constable came into the house with me to confirm my identity. As soon as I had found my credit cards and my House of Commons identity card, which luckily I had left at home that night, I got rid of him and went straight to bed.

Apart from the physical harm done to me, I had lost my wallet containing about fifty pounds, and my watch, and there was not much hope of seeing either of them again. The whole episode had been annoying, but scarcely more. I had not been badly hurt though by the next morning I still felt stiff and sore and my head ached. Anyway, I decided to ignore the advice of the police doctor who had suggested I should get a check-up from my own GP. I would, however, have an easy day.

I had counted without the media. By the time I had finished breakfast the telephone had rung three times: two newspaper reporters and someone from the BBC; as far as I could make out, there must have been some leak from the police. In any case, I suppose the sort of attack I had suffered was not so common in 1960 as it has become now, and I assume there must have been a dearth of other news.

Having dealt with these calls by making simple statements praising the kindness of the police, I thought it wise to phone Renata and Imogen to warn them not to be upset by what they might read or hear. They were both solicitous and I had difficulty in persuading Imogen that there was no need for her to drive up to London to cope; Mrs Curwen, who came in three days a week to clean, would look after me.

It never occurred to me that the incident would be of any great importance, or would mean more than a little casual publicity. I was soon to be disabused.


The doorbell rang at six o'clock. Mrs Curwen had gone home, leaving me some supper to be heated up. I was in the sitting room, reading, and I was tempted not to answer the bell; I assumed it was some wretched journalist. But I had drawn the curtains carelessly and it was obvious to whoever was standing outside that someone was in. Reluctantly I got up and went into the hall. I took the precaution of putting up the chain before opening the door.

'Mr Vermont? Good evening, sir.'

'I'm Vermont, yes. What do you want? If it's press –'

'Police, sir.'

I took down the chain and opened the door wide. As the light streamed out on to the visitor, my mouth was suddenly dry. I couldn't speak. I took a quick breath and swallowed hard. I didn't know what to do. Once I had feared a chance meeting with someone who had known Nigel Hawker well, but it hadn't happened, and over the years I had been lulled into the belief that it never would. Now here was Jim Pulent on my doorstep.

I recognized him immediately, though I hadn't seen him since we were at school together. He had put on some weight, but he had always been a short stocky boy. Otherwise he hadn't changed. There was the same gingery hair, red face and small blue eyes. He had not become an attractive man.

'What – what –' I wetted my lips. 'What do you want?'

I spoke abruptly, sharply. I knew I had been staring at him and that he might well have noticed my somewhat strange reaction. He was watching me closely, or perhaps I was imagining it. Had he recognized me? Surely not. I had certainly changed a great deal more than he had. I forced myself to smile, but simultaneously looked down my arrogant Vermont nose at him.

'Sir, I'm sorry to disturb you. I'm Chief Inspector Pulent, CID.'

The moment of mutual recognition, if there had been such a moment, was over. I had my feelings under control once more. He offered me his warrant card and, having glanced at it, I waved him into the hall.

'What can I do for you, Chief Inspector?'

'If you could spare me a few minutes, sir, to tell me about the attack last night.'

'All right, though I've already told the police what I know, which isn't much. There were two thugs, large, strong and, I would guess, in their twenties or late teens. I didn't stand a chance. That's about all I can tell you, but come along in, though I really can't see that a simple mugging warrants the attention of a senior officer.'

I led the way into the sitting room and when we were seated waited for him to speak. He seemed in no hurry, but looked around the room with interest. The inspection made me feel nervous.

At last he said, 'You are probably not aware, sir, but you are the third Member of Parliament to be attacked in the last six months. Of course this fact might be a coincidence. Most likely it is. But we considered it advisable to inquire into last night's incident, especially as you are a Minister.'

'For heaven's sake! It was a dark, rainy night. I doubt if anyone would have recognized me. I'm not particularly well known, not like the PM or members of the Cabinet. I'm only a Junior Minister.'

'At present, sir.' Pulent smiled knowingly as if he had some inside information. 'May I ask where you had been? Would anyone have been expecting you to be in the vicinity of Westminster Cathedral at that time?'

'I had had supper with my secretary, Mrs Tamson. I wanted her to do some work for me in advance of the new Session of the House.' I paused to allow his smile to become an even more knowing smirk before I added, 'No one would have known this. It was a sudden decision. Oh, that is, except for my wife to whom I happened to be speaking on the phone just before I set out.'

'I see.' He couldn't question the half-truth. 'If you were working, then you would have had a briefcase. Was it stolen? You mentioned a wallet and a watch.'

'I had left the briefcase with Mrs Tamson.'

There was silence while Pulent appeared to be ruminating. I was beginning to get angry. 'If that's all, Chief Inspector – I have various things to do.' I made to stand up, giving him no alternative but to do the same.

'That's – that's fine. Thank you for answering my questions, sir. I'm sorry to have bothered you.'

I saw him out, returned to the sitting room and poured myself a large Scotch. I gulped it down and poured another one. I was horribly shaken. Jim Pulent! After all these years, a Chief Inspector. It was unbelievably bad luck. Suddenly I realized that I was tugging at my earlobe, that old habit I had had since schooldays and which would have looked horribly familiar to Pulent. Had I been doing it while he was here? I didn't know. I couldn't remember.

I didn't sleep well that night, but by the next morning I was more composed. I told myself how unlikely it was that Pulent would have recognized me in this totally different environment. Even if he had noted a certain resemblance between me and the former Nigel Hawker he must have dismissed it as coincidental. It wasn't unusual for one person to remind you of someone quite different, and Simon Vermont, DFC, MP, was not generally known to have any connection with Hawker. There was absolutely no reason for Chief Inspector Pulent to be suspicious. I had been foolish to panic.

# CHAPTER TEN

Two, three weeks passed. I was still wary, but my fears of Jim Pulent and what he might do had abated. I was extremely busy in the House, and the work helped to concentrate my mind on affairs of State rather than any personal problems that might or might not exist. And at weekends, what with the family and constituency, there was little time for brooding either. But I suppose there was a certain frenzy about my activities, because once or twice I caught Imogen looking at me anxiously, though she made no comment. I had never been good at waiting, preferring to act rather than react, but of course this was not always possible.

I don't know when it occurred to me that I was being followed. When it did, I dismissed the idea as absurd. It was not the kind of operation that Imogen would have set in motion, however suspicious of me she might have become; she would either have accepted that I was being unfaithful, or she would have confronted me. But who else would want to put a tail on me?

Whoever my follower was, he was not a professional. A tall, gangling youth, about twenty, he wore a dark blue suit in which he looked uncomfortable as if normally he brought it out only for weddings and funerals, but was now having to make it serve a daily purpose. His hair was greasy and shoulder-length, usually loose, but sometimes tied into a kind of ponytail at the back of his neck; the style didn't go with the suit. And, even in the days of Carnaby Street, at the start of the decade when anything became acceptable, he seemed out of place loitering around the Palace of Westminster or leaning on the railings across the road from my house, pretending to be waiting for someone or something.

When he continued to pop up in unexpected places and I could no longer disregard him, I wondered what to do. He was beginning to irritate me. But, as suddenly as he had come, he disappeared, and I forgot about him – more or less.

*

Then one of my constituents, who had connections with the theatre, offered me a couple of tickets for *Beyond the Fringe*, the cult satirical revue of the moment, and Imogen decided to come up to London for the week so that we could also give a dinner party and return some hospitality. Busy as I was, I left the arrangements to her, only making sure that I would have a 'pair' with a Labour MP that evening, and wouldn't have to return to the House for the Division. But I was surprised when Renata told me that she had been invited and had accepted, even though she had occasionally visited us at the house. And briefly I wondered whether Imogen really did suspect my relationship with Renata and, unlikely as it seemed, had arranged for that strange young man to follow me.

'Why did you invite Renata?' I asked casually as Imogen and I were dressing. 'I thought this was going to be a non-political dinner party.'

Imogen shrugged. 'I wanted to invite Dennis Cartwright so I needed an extra woman and, as I'd not seen Renata for some while, I decided to ask her. You don't mind, do you? After all, she's good value.'

I wondered if she was attaching any double meaning to the term 'good value', but said, 'No, I don't mind, and I'm always glad of a chance for a chat with Dennis.' Sir Dennis Cartwright was a back-bench Member of Parliament. In his early fifties and a widower, he was highly respected, both for having a good deal of common sense and for being an entertaining guest or companion.

Cartwright was also, incidentally, one of the two other MPs whom Pulent said had been attacked in the street. In his case the assault had taken place in broad daylight and had been interrupted, so that Dennis had suffered just minor bruises, and had lost only his briefcase. Whatever he had hoped to find, the attacker had been unlucky; the briefcase had contained nothing but a copy of that day's *Times*. I had asked Dennis about the incident, and discovered that Chief Inspector Pulent had called on him too. This fact had helped further to still my doubts and fears.

Dennis Cartwright was the first of our guests to arrive, but the others followed him quite soon. We were to be twelve at table, the most that we could seat, and it was a pleasant, informal affair. We had a regular married couple who came in to cook and buttle on these occasions, leaving Imogen free to be the excellent hostess that she was.

The invitation had been for seven forty-five. Dinner was scheduled for eight-thirty and meanwhile we stood around, drinking and talking and eating titbits. It was developing into a good party when Imogen drew me aside. She was looking anxious.

'It's half past eight and Renata hasn't come yet!'

'Oh dear! Perhaps she's had trouble getting a taxi.'

'She might have allowed for that.' Imogen spoke sharply; she hated unpunctuality.

Dennis, who had overheard our conversation, said, 'A missing guest? What usually happens is that they've mistaken the day, and turn up on the following one.'

'I sincerely hope not!' Imogen was now thoroughly annoyed. 'Go and telephone her, Simon. Then at least we'll know if she's left her flat.'

I did as bidden, but there was no answer. She had to be on her way. Ten minutes later, when she had still not arrived, Imogen decided that dinner could wait no longer. By now I was worried. It was unlike Renata to be cavalier about an appointment, especially a dinner date, and I was sure she hadn't forgotten the day; she had mentioned the party that morning in the office.

Of course, she might have been taken ill, or her taxi might have been involved in an accident, but then she could have phoned or got someone to phone for her, unless – unless she was unconscious! I imagined her lying on her sitting-room floor, having suffered a sudden and improbable heart attack, or in a coma in the intensive care ward of some hospital. I found it difficult to make conversation and play the host when all I wanted to do was dash off to Victoria and assure myself that no harm had come to her.

It was a relief when shortly before midnight the last guest left, though I was still not free to do what I wanted. Imogen would have considered it most extraordinary and extravagant behaviour on my part. However, she acquiesced at once when I said I proposed to telephone Renata again.

I must have let the phone ring a dozen times before I put down the receiver. There was still no reply and I had no option but to go to bed. Imogen was tired and went to sleep quickly, but I lay awake, listening to her regular breathing and counting the strokes of our grandfather clock as each hour passed. I wondered how early in the morning I could call Renata without Imogen thinking me over-anxious, and eventually I must have slept.

The alarm woke me at seven and I went downstairs to the kitchen to make us an early morning cup of tea. Here was my chance. I plugged in the kettle and went into my study. I dialled Renata's number, praying that she would answer. Providing that she was all right, I didn't care a damn about why she hadn't come to the dinner party the evening before.

The receiver was picked up almost immediately and a man's voice barked, 'Yes. Who is that?'

It was the kind of robotic response that always annoys me. 'Who are you?' I asked coldly.

'Chief Inspector Minor, CID, New Scotland Yard,' came the reply. 'Now, please, give me your name.'

For a moment I couldn't speak. Police – in Renata's flat at this hour of the morning. Something was wrong, badly wrong. I felt chilled, sick, fearful for her.

'My name is Simon Vermont. Is Mrs Tamson there?'

'And your address, Mr Vermont?'

Obviously my name had meant nothing to him. I gave him my address and again asked for Renata.

'What's happened?' I demanded. 'Tell me! Is Mrs Tamson all right?'

Instead of answering my questions, he said, 'What do you want with Mrs Tamson? Are you a friend of hers? It's early in the day for a social call, isn't it?'

I gritted my teeth, knowing it would do no good to lose my temper. 'This is not exactly a social call, Chief Inspector. I am a Member of Parliament. Mrs Tamson is my secretary at the House of Commons. Last night she was to have had dinner with my wife and myself and a few other people at our house. She never came, and there was no answer to her telephone. Naturally we were anxious, which accounts for my early call.'

'I see, sir. That's very interesting and the information may be useful. Times, you know.' His attitude to me had changed, but only fractionally.

'No, I do not know! What has happened?'

'Mrs Tamson, I regret to tell you, sir, is dead.'

108

He went on speaking for a minute or two, and I caught the words murder or manslaughter, but I didn't take them in. I was thinking of Renata and the last time we had made love. The last time, though we hadn't known it then. I could have wept.

'. . . Are you still there, Mr Vermont?'

'Yes, I'm here, but what you've told me has been a shock, Chief Inspector. My wife and I have known Renata Tamson for many years and are fond of her.'

'I understand, sir. Perhaps when you and Mrs Vermont have had a little time to absorb the sad news I might come around and see you both. Would ten o'clock be convenient?'

I yearned to say it would not be convenient. I felt he was pressuring me. But it seemed wiser to agree and get it over.

'Just one more thing before you put down the receiver, sir,' he said. 'Would you know the address of Mrs Tamson's next of kin?'

'Not off hand, but I can find it. Hang on.'

I rummaged through my papers, not concentrating on what I was doing, until I found what he wanted. He thanked me and said good-bye, repeating that he would see me at ten o'clock.

Then I went into the kitchen, made the tea and took the tray upstairs to break the news to Imogen. This was not the moment to give way to my private grief.


Chief Inspector Minor appeared with a sergeant at ten o'clock precisely. He was a tall, dark-haired man, younger than I had expected and eager to show that he was not overawed by the house or the fact that I was an MP. I suspected that he had looked me up in *Who's Who* before he came. He was polite and chose his words with care.

When we were all seated and the sergeant had taken out his note-book I repeated that we had expected Mrs Tamson to dinner the previous evening; he questioned me closely about the times of my unanswered phone calls, explaining that they might help to fix the time of Renata's death. His sergeant also made a note of the dinner party guests.

Then Imogen asked the question that I had wanted to ask but had somehow shied away from – exactly how Renata had died. I hoped it had been quick and painless. I couldn't imagine why anyone should have wanted her dead but, apart from her work at the

House of Commons and her relationship with me, when I was forced to think about it I realized that I knew very little about her or her private life.

The Chief Inspector was surprisingly forthcoming. 'Well, we know somewhat more now than we did when I was on the phone earlier,' he began. 'As it stands at the moment, this is how I see it. Mind you, it's only a theory.'

He went on to explain. According to his theory, Mrs Tamson had left the flat in good time for her engagement, but had forgotten something, so had returned, only to surprise a burglar in her bedroom. She was a brave woman. She struggled with him. The signs were clear. A chair was broken, a small table overturned. But she was hampered by the fur jacket she was wearing, and her long skirt and high-heeled shoes, and anyhow it was a fair assumption that he would have been stronger than she was. Eventually she was knocked down or fell and hit her temple on the edge of a metal radiator.

As he paused I asked if that had killed her, but he shook his head. I could have screamed, as perhaps poor Renata had done to no avail. Would the man never get to the point?

'We won't know for sure until the post-mortem,' he said. 'That's one of the oddities of the case, sir. You see, apart from the blow to the head, which could easily have killed her, she was also strangled.'

'Oh God!' Imogen murmured. 'But why?'

'Possibly because she recognized the intruder or because he thought she might be able to identify him later, and so he needed her dead. The strangling doesn't strike me as having been a panic action.'

He let the silence last until I was forced to ask. 'You implied there were other "oddities", to use your word, Chief Inspector. What were they?'

'Well, first of all, a certain amount of powder was spilt around the place.'

'Powder? What sort of powder?'

'I shan't know till it's been analyzed, sir.'

He gave me a minute to absorb what he had said before he continued. 'Then there are indications that it was not necessarily an ordinary burglary. Very little appears to have been stolen. The intruder might have been after something special and the so-called burglary a front, merely intended to deceive. Of course, it's difficult to tell, but we had one of Mrs Tamson's neighbours look around. Actually it was she who found the body. She's a nurse. Her shift ended at midnight and when she got out of the lift on her floor – her flat is opposite Mrs Tamson's – she saw a pendant with a broken chain lying on the carpet in front of Mrs Tamson's door, which was ajar. Incidentally, Mrs Tamson collected antique jewellery, but none of it seems to have been touched. It's possible she was wearing the pendant and that it was torn off in the struggle and her assailant took it but dropped it in his hurry to get away.'

Without warning, the Chief Inspector reached in his pocket, produced the pendant, and held it up by its broken chain so that Imogen and I could see it. I was sitting beside her on the settee and I felt her tense. At once I realized she had recognized it. I had been a careless fool to buy Renata a present from a Colombury shop.

'I don't imagine it's relevant,' I said, 'but I gave Mrs Tamson that pendant as a Christmas present.'

'Really, sir. Were you in the habit of giving her expensive jewellery?'

'Don't you think that remark impertinent, Chief Inspector?' I countered.

'And anyway the pendant wasn't expensive,' said Imogen. 'We found it in an antique shop in Colombury and I was sure she would like it. It wasn't always easy to find her a suitable gift.'

'I'm sorry, sir. I didn't mean to be impertinent, but the nurse did say she had often seen a lame gentleman visiting Mrs Tamson and I assumed –'

'You assumed it was me, and I'm sure you were correct, Chief Inspector. But let me put you straight before you make any incorrect assumptions. I did not visit Mrs Tamson *often*. It happens that my office in the House of Commons, like those of most MPs, is extremely small, and Mrs Tamson did quite a lot of work at home, which meant that *occasionally* I went to her flat.'

'Yes. Yes, sir. I understand, sir.'

Glad to see that the Chief Inspector was no longer at ease, I pressed home my advantage. 'Good! Now, I think that's about all we can tell you. If you want to confirm what we've said about last night you can contact Sir Dennis Cartwright at the House of Commons, or any of our other dinner guests.'

'I'm sure that won't be necessary, sir.' He stood up. 'You might like to know I've been in touch with Mrs Tamson's parents and they will be taking care of all the necessary formalities and arrangements. So, thank you both for your co-operation, and good-day.'

He turned to go and then added, 'As you were an occasional visitor to Mrs Tamson's flat, sir, it's possible your prints could be somewhere there; cleaning ladies aren't that dependable. I wonder if you'd mind my sergeant taking a set of yours for purposes of elimination, just in case.'

I made no demur, and the sergeant, who hadn't uttered a word throughout the interview, produced an ink pad and did his stuff. Then I saw them both to the front door, saying casually, 'Are there any other oddities about the case you haven't mentioned, Chief Inspector?'

'Not really, sir, but it's interesting that Mrs Tamson believed she was being followed.'

'Followed?' I was genuinely surprised.

'My authority is the nurse again, sir. She says she happened to meet Mrs Tamson a few days ago outside their building and Mrs Tamson pointed out a long-haired young man in a dark blue suit who was lounging on the corner opposite. Mrs Tamson said he was always around.'

I shrugged. 'She never said anything to me about it, but I suppose there was no reason why she should.'

'No, sir. Goodbye. We ought not to be bothering you again.'

I shut the front door behind them and leant against it. I hoped the Chief Inspector was right and the police wouldn't be bothering me again, but it was obvious that the youth Renata believed had been following her was the same one who had been bothering me in recent weeks. There could be no question of coincidence.


I went back to the sitting room. Imogen was staring out of the window and when she heard me she turned around. She tried to smile, but there were tears in her eyes.

'Darling,' I said. 'I'm sorry, desperately sorry. Can you forgive me?'

She nodded her head. 'It was partly my fault. I left you too much alone in London and when I guessed what was happening – that you were having an affair with Renata – I did nothing about it.'

'You didn't consider having me watched?'

'Watched? By a detective? A private eye?' She laughed. 'Don't be silly! Of course not! I tried to persuade myself it wasn't true, that I was imagining it. But when the Chief Inspector produced that pendant – I'd seen it in Bethune's in Colombury when I was looking for a birthday present for Susan – I knew it was true.'

'And you lied for me.'

'Yes. It was none of that man's business. Besides – '

'Besides?'

'I love you,' she said simply. 'You don't know how much.'

'I love you too,' I said. 'I'll never hurt you again. I promise.' But I thought of the youth who had been watching me and Renata and wondered if I would be able to keep that promise. I was afraid.

# CHAPTER ELEVEN

During the following weeks, while Renata's death was still of interest to the media, I read the newspapers and listened to the radio
with more than my usual attentiveness. I saw no mention of the
mysterious powder to which Chief Inspector Minor had referred,
but a young man, answering to the description given by the nurse,
was arrested and then released. His name, given in a couple of
papers, meant nothing to me. It's possible he was the same youth
who had been tailing me, but fortunately he had abandoned that
effort.

Meanwhile I wrote a letter of condolence, on Imogen's behalf and
mine, to Renata's parents. In reply her father informed us that when
the body was released the funeral would be in Cornwall, where they
lived. This was a relief; it meant that I wouldn't be expected to
attend. So, after consultation with Imogen, I arranged to send a
cheque from us both to the Cancer Research Fund – the charity her
father had named – in Renata's memory, and thought what a cold
and unsentimental way it was to say goodbye to someone with
whom I had been in love. But for Imogen's sake, and my own, I hid
my grief and did my best to keep thoughts of Renata at the back of
my mind.

The police seemed to be making no progress with the case and it
soon ceased to be news, which helped. However, I had got into the
habit of searching for references to it in the papers and, as a result, I
came by chance upon an item which gave me an unexpected twinge
of fear, though on the face of it there was no reason why it should
have done. There was no apparent connection with Renata, and
not really with me, not any longer. Nevertheless, it made me
apprehensive.

It was a mere couple of paragraphs tucked into a corner of an
inside page of the *Telegraph* – what journalists would call a 'filler' –
but the name Hawker caught my eye and caused my pulse to
quicken. I read it through twice.

Headed 'Bobby on the Beat', it was not worth much as a news item, but there had been a certain amount of discussion in the papers recently on the subject of the service provided to the public by police officers on foot versus that by police officers in cars. Here was a small contribution on the side of those who favoured foot patrols by officers known in their districts, though it emphasized that they should always patrol in pairs.

It seemed that last Friday night a bobby walking his beat in Islington noticed what he took to be a flickering light in the accommodation above Hawker's grocery shop. He knew Tom Hawker – 'often had a pint with him in the local', he had told the reporter – and knew that the Hawkers regularly went to the cinema on a Friday night.

Bravely or rashly, according to your point of view, he tried the shop door, found it open and called out, 'Anyone at home?' There was no answer. He flashed his torch around the shop. Nothing appeared to be disturbed. The cash register was untouched. Then something fell on him. Later it was found to be a blanket and, as he struggled to free himself, he was aware of a dark figure dashing past him and out into the street. By the time he had summoned help the intruder had disappeared. Mr Hawker, commending the constable, said that thanks to his action nothing had been stolen and, if he had had assistance, the thief would have been caught.

It was farce rather than tragedy. If it had been anyone else's premises I would have laughed at the thought of the police officer struggling under the blanket. The would-be thief had been resourceful and had done no harm. Possibly he deserved to escape.

But it was not anyone else's premises. It was Tom Hawker's shop and the intruder had been upstairs in the family quarters. Why? It seemed an unlikely place to burgle, though I suppose he might have hoped that the shopkeeper would have hoarded the day's takings in the bedroom, rather than leave them in the store overnight.

I told myself that it was nothing to do with me. Nevertheless, I felt unsettled. Renata's dreadful death had shaken me more than I had realized. Imogen commented on the fact that I was tense and short-tempered, but I brushed this aside, saying that I had been working too hard – which was true – and was in need of a proper holiday, that the long summer recess couldn't come soon enough for me. Unfortunately it was still way ahead. We were only coming up to

Easter, a period I would have to devote to the constituency and the family.

Before that, however, I decided to take stock of my position. I am not by nature a superstitious man, but I had a premonition of disaster and my every instinct was to try to safeguard myself against it.

Money was not the least of my problems. And if I were to hear cynical laughter at that comment I would understand. I owned, free of any mortgages, a 'desirable residence' in London and a house in the country; to avoid death duties Dad had made Aubyn House over to me several years ago. I had investments, derived from my mother's estate, which had been divided between her three children, and which yielded me a small private income. My investment advisers had been wise and the capital had grown, but I was reluctant to touch it except in a real emergency. Imogen had her own money which had also, due to careful investment, increased over the years. I had, moreover, what would appear to be a not inconsiderable salary as a Junior Minister in the Government.

But in spite of all this, my income and expenses were usually in a state of delicate balance. Admittedly I contributed little financially to Aubyn House, but the upkeep of the town house was high and, though Martin and Susan – even Guy – used it as a hotel whenever they came to London, I was solely responsible for it. I had two sons at Eton at this time and a daughter at Benenden, which represented a fair outlay, though Imogen helped here. As for my Government salary and the perks that went with it – such as free postage and inexpensive meals in the House – it was barely adequate to cover all the demands made on it. If one hoped for advancement, certainly in Harold Macmillan's Government, to appear other than generous in offering hospitality to fellow MPs was a serious mistake, and every charity and organization in the constituency expected as of right a large contribution from the Member. Therefore, though I lived well and was far from poor, I had little spare money.

As a result, over the years I had not been able to add nearly as much as I would have wished to my Swiss account, and I suspected that it was still the smallest numbered account on the books of the Banque St-Pierre de Genève. This had not prevented Monsieur Le Rossignol, on the few occasions we had met or when we had spoken on the telephone, from treating me as an important client. And if he was amused by what he must have considered to be my financial ineptitude, he never showed his feelings.

Then, just before the Easter recess, while I was still wondering if there was any action I should be taking, I was surprised on arriving at the Ministry to be told by my new secretary that a Monsieur Le Rossignol wished me to telephone him. I had given him my office number, but he had never used it, and at once I feared bad news.

In a way I was right. Monsieur Le Rossignol, whom I respected and trusted, had had a heart attack. He said that it was not serious, but that he intended to retire. His place at the bank had been taken by his son, Jean-Paul. The change would in no way affect my affairs; the Banque St-Pierre de Genève would always be at my service, and he hoped that when I was next in Geneva I would call on Jean-Paul in order to establish a personal relationship with him.

I found this conversation vaguely disturbing, though it would have been difficult to say why, and somehow I felt less secure. Nothing seemed to be going right for me at the moment.

Chance has always played a large part in my life and it was the day after my conversation with Monsieur Le Rossignol that I ran into a man called Roy Gunther in the Strand. I would have described Roy as an acquaintance rather than a friend, though that was how he greeted me. He was one of those slightly unusual men who seem to know everyone and be accepted everywhere, but whose backgrounds – said in Gunther's case to be part European, part South African – were cloaked in mystery. He didn't seem to take his work in the City, whatever it was, too seriously, but he always had plenty of money and he was generous with it.

'Come and have lunch, Simon,' he said at once. 'I've not got a table booked, but I'm sure my favourite restaurant will oblige.'

Roy's favourite restaurant was the Connaught, and within minutes a taxi was taking us there, in spite of my protests that I hadn't time for a long lunch. Nor were his expectations unjustified. He was greeted by the maître d', who personally escorted us to a corner table from which a reserved sign had been hastily removed; either someone was going to be unlucky or this was the old trick of keeping a table in case a valued customer should arrive unexpectedly. In any case, it was clear that Roy was such a valued customer.

Once we were seated, had ordered our meal and were sipping our gins and tonics, Roy regarded me earnestly. 'You're looking jaded, Simon, old boy.'

'I work too hard.'

'Ah, overworked and underpaid.' He was fond of clichés. 'Incidentally, I was sorry to learn about that secretary of yours, Renata Tamson. A nasty business.'

'Yes, indeed. And a shock. Imogen and I had been expecting her for dinner and she never arrived.'

He nodded his understanding and sympathy. The wine waiter came, and our choice required serious discussion. We finished our gins and started on the oysters. Roy talked about the political situation in South Africa, and how the country was misunderstood by most Europeans, including the British. I listened. I was always ready to learn, but today my attention wandered and Roy noticed.

We had refused the sweet trolley and were on to the cheese when he stopped almost in mid-sentence, gave me a long, hard look, and said, 'Simon, you've got a problem. It's none of my business, I know, but if I can help I will. I owe you, remember.'

It was true that I had done him a favour some years ago. I had perjured myself on his behalf when he had sued a scandal sheet that had accused him of having been at a drag party that had ended in a near riot, with several individuals appearing in front of a magistrate the next day. In fact, I had provided his alibi for Martin's sake. It was Martin who had invited Roy to the party, and he had gone as a joke, not knowing what he might be letting himself in for.

'I had forgotten,' I said.

'Well, I damn well haven't, Simon.'

I shrugged, thinking that there was no reason why I shouldn't pick his brains. I said slowly, 'You could give me some advice, perhaps. In a few weeks I shall be celebrating my fortieth birthday and I feel a need for security. The world is in its usual mess. There's never a time when there isn't a crisis somewhere – Africa, the Middle East. Britain's doing all right at the moment under Macmillan, but will it last? Anyway, Roy, what I'd like would be a substantial nest-egg that I could keep safe and that would preferably increase in value.'

I had chosen my words with care, and I had been surprised by the clarity with which I had expressed my objective. I hadn't known before so precisely what it was, though probably I should have done.

I hoped I hadn't been stupid and exposed myself too rashly to Roy Gunther. He was looking amused.

'Simon, the answer is simple. Diamonds. Not only are they the girl's best friend; they're also the boy's best friend. Much better than gold and easier to handle. A nice little bag of uncut stones kept in a safe-deposit box in Holland or Switzerland would be just the job.' He leant across the table towards me. 'I could get them for you.'

'Are you serious?'

'Perfectly. I'm going to South Africa in ten days' time. As you're aware, the diamond market is strictly controlled, but no system is perfect, and if you know what you're doing and whom you can trust, you can buy the stones cheap and smuggle them out – to make a huge profit.'

'Isn't it risky?'

'Prison – if you're caught – but I would take care not to get caught. Simon, I've done it before for my personal benefit, and I'm prepared to do it, once, for you. As I said, I owe you, and I like to pay my debts.'

'But –'

'No. Don't answer now. Give me a phone number where I can reach you over the weekend. If you decide to do this we can arrange to meet for lunch before I go. Incidentally, I'll need your cheque for twenty grand. It's not worth doing for less. So, think about it.'


I thought about it. It was an almighty gamble. It would mean trusting Roy Gunther. But I was tempted. If I sold all my investments I could, with luck, raise twenty thousand pounds – not a mean sum in 1960. Alternatively, I could ask my bank for a loan, which of course I would have to pay back. If something went wrong, if Gunther was caught and lost the money or absconded with it, I would have to sell my securities to cover myself. Whatever happened, I was determined that I would not touch my account with the Banque St-Pierre de Genève.

Come the weekend I was still thinking about it and by Sunday evening, when I hadn't heard from Gunther, I had begun to hope that he wouldn't phone. That would solve the problem.

But as we were having a drink before dinner he did phone and, picking up the receiver, I knew what I was going to say. This was a chance that wouldn't come my way again. I had to take it.

We made the necessary arrangements, and Roy Gunther left for South Africa. Inevitably the next weeks were agonizing for me, especially towards the end of the period, when I was expecting to hear from Gunther. Every time the telephone rang my hopes rose, only to fall again. I was like some love-sick swain waiting for a call from his beloved and, when it came, the relief was overwhelming. Gunther was in Zurich and would meet me in Geneva in three days; all was well.

At the first opportunity I telephoned Monsieur Jean-Paul Le Rossignol, and arranged to call on him as his father had suggested. I also asked if he could recommend an authority I could consult on the subject of uncut diamonds. I didn't want to discover in ten or fifteen years' time that my little nest-egg was worthless. Mr Le Rossignol showed no surprise and said he would make an appointment for me with a Monsieur de Sencourt, who was completely trustworthy. And thus began what was to prove a long and satisfactory relationship with Jean-Paul.

I met Roy Gunther at the Hôtel des Bergues, and took possession of a small chamois leather bag of uncut diamonds, which didn't look to me as if they were worth even the twenty thousand pounds I had entrusted to him, let alone a great deal more. What I would do if they turned out to be worthless I didn't know. Full of doubt I went at once to Monsieur de Sencourt's office.

Monsieur de Sencourt turned out to be a man in his early forties, immaculately dressed and groomed. I would have taken him for a stockbroker or a banker, perhaps a lawyer. But if his appearance didn't correspond with my romantic idea of a diamond merchant, his evaluation was professional and the result did not disappoint me. I shouldn't have distrusted Gunther. The stones were worth approximately one hundred thousand pounds.

From the diamond merchant's I went straight to the Banque St-Pierre, to the first of many agreeable meetings with Jean-Paul Le Rossignol. Then, my nest-egg of diamonds safely stored in my deposit box with my other security, the gunmetal watch I had brought back from France, I returned to the Hôtel des Bergues and Roy Gunther. I was extremely grateful to him; he had more than repaid whatever debt he believed he owed me.

But I was to have yet another reason for gratitude. Over our aperitifs before lunch he passed me the cheque for twenty thousand pounds that I had written him before he went to South Africa.

'You can tear it up now,' he said. 'I used my own money. It was simpler. I kept back enough of the diamonds I bought to repay myself. All right?'

I shook my head in wonderment. 'More than all right. Absolutely terrific. I can't thank you enough, Roy.'

'No need. Just returning a favour, Simon. Forget it. Let's not refer to it again. Agreed?'

'Agreed.'

And indeed, on the occasions that Roy Gunther and I met during the next five years, before he was killed in a car accident, it was never mentioned between us. Nor have I ever hinted at it to anyone else, both for his sake and mine.

That evening I flew back to London. Gunther was catching a flight to Paris. I was a happy and contented man, sure that my luck had changed and that the bad patch I had been suffering through recently was over.

My good luck, however, was not to last long.

# CHAPTER TWELVE

The blow fell on the eve of my fortieth birthday, which Imogen and I planned to celebrate *à deux* with a visit to the ballet at Covent Garden, a champagne supper and some lovemaking. The family celebration was to be at Aubyn House the following weekend, which happened to correspond with the children's half-term exeat.

I had been in the country, coping with Dad and some practical problems on the estate and in the constituency, and Imogen and I had driven up to London together that Monday morning. The telephone was ringing as we let ourselves into the house. Mrs Curwen met us in the hall.

'Phone for you, sir. I said you were just coming in. Wouldn't give his name but I recognized his voice. He called earlier.'

'Right. Thanks, Mrs Curwen. I'll take it in the study.'

I sprinted along to the study and lifted the receiver. Our London phone number was unlisted, so I assumed the call would be from a friend or a colleague to whom it had been given. I had no premonition of what was to come. 'Hello,' I said. 'Simon Vermont here.'

'Good morning, Mr Vermont. This is Jim Pulent.'

I drew a deep breath and thankfully heard the click as the receiver on the other phone was replaced. At least there was now no chance that anyone would overhear my conversation with Pulent. I wondered how he had got hold of this number.

'Good morning, Chief Inspector. What can I do for you?' My voice was steady.

'Quite a lot, I would hope, Mr Vermont.' There was an unpleasant emphasis on my name. 'But it's scarcely a matter to be discussed on the phone. We must meet. Tomorrow? Perhaps I could come to your house.'

'No!' The word burst from me. 'Chief Inspector, I can tell you no more about that mugging than I told you when we met before.'

'A most fortuitous meeting, that was, Mr Vermont.'

Again there was that stress on the name – or was I imagining it? 'I'm extremely busy at present and –'

'But not too busy to spare me an hour to discuss a most important matter. Nothing to do with the mugging. Shall we say tomorrow, early evening – so you can be back in the House in time for the Division bell?'

'Impossible!' With an effort I controlled my temper. 'Chief Inspector –'

'Jim Pulent,' he reminded me – as if I could have forgotten.

'Chief Inspector,' I repeated. 'It happens that tomorrow is my birthday and my wife is in London to celebrate it with me. It is, therefore, quite impossible for me to meet you. As for the rest of the week –'

'Your birthday? Tomorrow? Congratulations. I didn't think you'd be forty for another couple of months, Mr *Vermont*.'

I gritted my teeth. The damned man knew, or he believed he knew. But could he prove anything? Surely not. Nevertheless, I was vulnerable. If Pulent merely whispered his suspicion to some investigative journalist, he could cause me a lot of trouble. Even if I sued, and won the case with substantial damages, the resulting publicity could be horrendous. It could be the end of my career in the House – politics is a funny business – and I didn't fancy being a backbencher with no prospects. And what if I lost the case? My mind raced.

'As I was saying, Chief Inspector,' I continued, ignoring his last remark, 'tomorrow is impossible. However, I can spare you an hour on Wednesday if it's really important.'

He laughed. 'Oh, it's important all right, Mr Vermont, but Wednesday will do. When and where? As your wife is in London I imagine you don't want me to come to your place.'

I thought quickly. 'No. But shall I come to your office?' I thought I might get in a crack of my own.

'No!' was the equally hasty reply. 'Somewhere neutral, shall we say?'

'All right.' I capitulated. 'The Lamb in Wigmore Street. Six-thirty.'

'I'll be there, Mr Vermont. Goodbye till then.'

I put down the receiver without replying. I was shaking. At least I hadn't committed myself. I could still try to bluff, mock at any suggestion of Pulent's that I was not Simon Vermont, son of General Sir Patrick Vermont. And possibly I could even threaten the Chief Inspector; after all, I was not without influence. But every-thing would depend on what Pulent knew and how much of it he could support. The next couple of days were going to be full of stress. It would require an effort to celebrate my birthday without showing strain.


The Lamb in Wigmore Street used to be an old-fashioned public house, uncomfortable and rather gloomy, where more beer was drunk than anything else. But two years ago the place was tarted up. Gone was the dark wood, replaced by light oak. The banquettes were pseudo red leather, like the bar stools. The tables were mock-marble, and thus simple to keep clean. There were hunting prints on the walls, and flowers around the bar.

The former clientele had disappeared, to be replaced by young or youngish men in well-cut suits and smart women, who mostly drank gin or vodka. It was not a pub that I frequented. Indeed I hadn't been there more than a couple of times and I didn't expect to meet anyone I knew, which was the reason I had chosen it.

I was the first to arrive at The Lamb that Wednesday evening. The pub was beginning to fill up. I ordered a double whisky and took it to a corner banquette where Pulent and I could have reason-able privacy. Pulent was ten minutes late and I sat still when he came in. I didn't offer to buy him a drink.

He brought his Bloody Mary over to me and said good evening. We might have been casual acquaintances, rather than old school enemies. He apologized for being late, blaming the traffic. Then he raised his glass.

'To Nige!' he said.

I kept my cool. 'A friend of yours, Chief Inspector?'

'I wouldn't say that, but I knew him well. We were at school together. He went into the Army and was killed in France, suppos-edly.'

'Poor man. By all means let's drink to your dead school chum.'

'Oh, he's not dead, Mr Vermont. On the contrary, he's alive and flourishing.'

'Really? Well, that's very interesting, but I don't understand what it's got to do with me.'

'Of course you do.' He lowered his voice so that it was no more than a whisper. 'You *are* Nigel Hawker.'

'You must be joking,' I said coldly, but I knew he wasn't, and inwardly I quailed at the assurance with which he spoke. 'I may resemble this man Hawker, but there's no more to it than that. People often resemble each other when they're not even remotely related. You're imagining things, Chief Inspector.'

Surprisingly he agreed. 'That's what I thought. I couldn't believe it. When you opened the front door of that fine house of yours my first reaction was, "Well, I'm damned – it's my old mate Nigel", and then I realized that this couldn't be true. It was, as you said, one of those odd resemblances you sometimes get. But your expression, as if you'd recognized me too – and with no joy – made me think twice. Then, when you got a bit agitated and started pulling your earlobe, the same way you used to at school when I ragged you, I was staggered.'

'Chief Inspector, this is absurd.' I interrupted him. 'I'm not going to sit here and listen to this extraordinary accusation. You must be out of your mind to bring me here on false pretences.'

'False pretences? That must have been a Freudian slip.' It was his turn to interrupt. 'I might not have been such a clever boy as Nige, but I'm not a fool and I haven't become a Chief Inspector without knowing it's not enough just to make an accusation. You've got to *prove* the accused is guilty.'

'Go on.' I did my best to sound bored.

Pulent shrugged. 'I did nothing immediately. My suspicion still seemed incredible, but I'm a curious man, and after a while I decided to look into Simon Vermont; after all, as a senior police officer, I had the facilities at my disposal. And, the deeper I dug, the less incredible the matter appeared. Vermont crashed in France at approximately the same time as Hawker disappeared. Hawker's body was never identified. Then there were all those operations to rebuild Vermont's face, and his convenient loss of memory. It would have taken nerve, of course, but Nige was never short on nerve.'

'So it seems that Jim Pulent is capable of some excellent research.' I was sarcastic. 'But do you seriously believe, Chief Inspector, that Hawker or anyone else could have deceived Vermont's parents, his fiancée, his brother and sister?'

'Yes! Why not? They expected him to be – they wanted him to be – Simon Vermont, and because of his physical condition he was able to play the part until it became second nature. A nice theory, you

125

might say, but it's more than a theory. It's what happened. It's fact.' Suddenly he shot out his hand and picked up my empty glass. 'Here, let me get us the other half while you think about what I've been saying. I know, Nige, and I can prove it.'

By now the pub had filled up. There was a crowd at the bar and it was going to take Pulent some time to get served. I knew I could have walked out, but I felt rooted to my seat on the pseudo red leather banquette. Jim Pulent might know, but I couldn't believe he could prove his suspicions, not after so many years. He had to be bluffing. Nevertheless, it was necessary to hear what he'd got to say.

'Here we are,' he said, putting our drinks on the table in front of us and once more seating himself beside me. 'I made yours a double. I thought you might need it.'

'Thanks,' I said shortly.

'Now, where were we?' Pulent seemed completely relaxed, as if he knew he had the upper hand. 'Ah yes, proof. What would a police officer think of but fingerprints? Yours and Nige's are identical.'

Years ago I had of course thought of fingerprints myself, but after all this time the possibility of their use had quite faded from my mind. I was shocked, but I continued to play my hand.

'You expect me to believe that? Where would you get these prints, mine and those of a man who's been dead for years?'

Pulent reached in his inner pocket and handed me an envelope. 'Don't open it now. I'll tell you what it contains. Inside that envelope are photocopies of two sets of prints, one which belonged to Nigel Hawker and the other belonging to you. You can study them later on, but I assure you that they're identical. For one thing, the little scar on your thumb is obvious to the naked eye.'

By this time my confidence was almost completely undermined, but I wasn't yet prepared to give up the fight. It was true I had a scar on my right thumb, the result of trying to save myself from being pushed through a window at school, and Pulent would know about the incident; it was he who had done most of the pushing. But none of this explained how he had been able to get hold of the fingerprints for comparison.

'I'm not doubting you have two separate sets of prints, but there's only your word that one of them belongs to Hawker and that the other is mine. I suspect you'll have some difficulty in proving that.' I glanced at my watch as if I were preparing to leave.

Pulent shook his head. 'I'm not a fool, as I told you before. Let's take the prints in that envelope that are marked A. They are Nigel Hawker's. You ask if I can prove it. Right. They were taken from a book, a copy of *Le Grand Meaulnes* that Nige won as a school prize. I have the book. It's irrefutable evidence. I stole it from the Hawkers' house. What's more, I nearly got caught.'

'*You – you* were that burglar? The one who threw a blanket over the policeman?'

'Yes!' Pulent grinned broadly. 'I could hardly keep a straight face when old Tom Hawker told me all about it. Luckily they never missed the book, or the incident would have looked pretty odd. They might have suspected me.' He seemed to treat the whole thing as a great joke.

'And my own fingerprints? Do you expect me to give them to you? Or do you propose to take them off this whisky glass when I've left you?'

'Neither. I've already got a set.'

'How?' I thought I knew the answer, but I didn't want to believe it.

'I took them off the tooth mug labelled "His" in Mrs Tamson's bathroom. There were some on the bedside table too.'

I stared at him with loathing, as the implication of what he had said sank in. He returned my gaze quite calmly and I swallowed the bile that rose in my throat. 'Christ!' I said. 'You've got the bloody nerve to sit there and tell me you murdered Renata Tamson? For God's sake, why did you have to kill her?'

'I had no choice. I thought she'd gone out for the evening, but she came back and surprised me.'

'So – you still didn't have to kill her.'

'Oh yes I did. She recognized me. She knew who I was. I had called on her to ask if she'd noticed any louts hanging around after you'd been mugged that night. You'd given her name to the police who found you, said you'd been visiting your secretary. Then, after I suspected who you were, I had you both followed. It was a fair guess she was also your mistress, and I thought it would be safer to get your prints from her flat than trying your own house. It was just bad luck she surprised me.'

Just bad luck, I thought bitterly, Renata's bad luck and my bad luck. If I hadn't been mugged that night she'd still be alive, and I wouldn't be sitting in a pub opposite a man I detested – a man who, in spite of his admission that he had committed murder, killed a woman I had dearly loved, could still wreck my life. For, whereas I had no proof of his guilt, and he would make damn sure that I didn't get any, he had proof of mine.

'Okay, *Chief Inspector* Pulent,' I said. I was far from resigned, but I needed time to think. 'You're proposing to blackmail me. What do you want?'

'Blackmail's a nasty word. Shall we say I want you to share some of your good fortune with me? You're a rich man. I'm not. It won't hurt you to part with a few of your ill-gotten gains to an old school chum.'

'How much?'

'I won't ask an exorbitant amount. I'll settle for fifty thousand down and five thousand a year for the next ten years.'

'You're mad! I haven't got that kind of money.'

'You could raise it. Get a mortgage on that London house of yours for the down payment, and, for the rest, try economizing and think about increasing your overdraft. Tell your bank manager you're paying off a girlfriend.'

'It's not possible.'

'But it has to be, Nige. Think of the alternative. You wouldn't like it in prison, you know – and what about your wife, your boys at Eton and your girl at her posh school? It would be hell for them. And don't imagine you can threaten me with some counter-charge either, because it wouldn't stick. I'd simply deny it and you could prove nothing.'

'For heaven's sake, I can't produce that sort of money on demand. I must have time,' I protested.

'Of course. Of course. I'm a reasonable man. I'll give you till the end of the month. That's fifteen days, which should be plenty.' Pulent took out his watch and extracted a piece of paper which he handed to me. 'This is the account you must pay the money into. Fifty thousand by the end of the month, then five thousand same day next year and so on. You do that and we won't need to meet again. But don't try to play any tricks, Nige.'

I stared at the piece of paper. It read, 'To the account of E. Percival-Brown' and named a branch of Barclays Bank in the City, giving the sorting code and the account number. It was all in order. When I looked up Jim Pulent was disappearing through the doors of the pub, leaving me shattered.

# CHAPTER THIRTEEN

I lay awake a long time that night, listening to Imogen's gentle breathing and wondering what to do. The decision had to be mine alone; there was no one to whom I could turn for help or advice. On the other hand, the decision was crucial; it could affect innumerable people – not only those bearing the name of Vermont, whom I knew in my heart I had come to love, but also my constituents, those who had voted for me and those who hadn't, and my political colleagues. It was perhaps not going too far to suggest that my decision could even bring down the Government.

As far as I could see I had three possible courses of action. There was a fourth, but this was not one that I wished to contemplate, not yet, not unless I was driven to it. Or was I fooling myself? I don't know.

The first course was to agree to Jim Pulent's proposition, to buy his silence, for I was sure that as long as I kept on paying out he would stay silent. And it was a practical course, thanks to Roy Gunther; I could pay Pulent off with my diamonds. Or could I? What would happen when the supply of diamonds came to an end? Would Pulent keep his word?

Blackmailers were notorious for demanding increasing amounts, and after the first payment I would be completely at Pulent's mercy. Besides, it went against the grain to make such gifts to a man who had deliberately killed Renata, a man who as a boy had made my life a misery with his bullying and his taunts, and who was threatening to do the same again.

The thought of the diamonds reminded me that I had always visualized them as a security, a safety net – though not to pay off a blackmailer. Vaguely I had imagined that they would make me independent of the Vermonts if that ever became necessary in some kind of emergency. So I asked myself if this was not just such an emergency – a moment to disappear. I was still comparatively young. I had money. I could pick up my diamonds, take whatever else I could carry and catch a flight to South America – and yet another new persona.

But this wasn't feasible. There were too many problems. I was a Minister of the Crown and my disappearance would spark off a major investigation. More importantly, I couldn't leave Imogen and the children, Dad, Martin, Susan and Guy, to bear the brunt of the scandal that would erupt. Especially as Jim Pulent, to gain revenge for the loss of the source of money he had expected, would surely betray my secret.

The same would apply if I took my own life, even if I could manage to make my death appear accidental. And I seriously considered this as a possible way out, a fact which might surprise anyone who believed that I was a selfish shit who had grabbed a chance to 'better himself', as Pulent would have put it.

A second course was to call Pulent's bluff, but many of the arguments that applied to accepting his proposition and allowing myself to be blackmailed applied here equally. He would not just go away. Out of spite and envy, he would undoubtedly take his revenge on me and the family – if he could.

This raised the question of what positive proof he had. A close resemblance and a habit, not very pronounced now, of pulling an earlobe would amount to nothing in comparison with the unquestioned acceptance of my parents, my relations, my friends, my colleagues and constituents, who together represented my present life.

But the fingerprints were damning. Even if I could hire someone to steal Nigel Hawker's prize book – which wouldn't be easy – Pulent would only have to ask Tom Hawker for another one. If he hinted that there might be something in it for Tom or perhaps suggest that the school was making a collection of books from old boys, Tom would be happy to oblige his neighbour and drinking companion, the Chief Inspector.

The prints he had obtained from Renata's flat, which would reveal my true identity when compared with those of Nigel Hawker, were a different matter. Pulent couldn't admit to possessing them without involving himself in her murder.

Or could he? I thought more deeply about this matter. Surely Pulent merely had to say that his suspicions had been aroused when he had called on me about the mugging – after all, he had known Nigel Hawker intimately years ago. Then, when he had an opportunity to examine the prints in the police file on Renata's murder – prints taken from me in order to exclude them from others found in the flat – with those in a book of Nigel Hawker's, he had seized it and found his suspicions confirmed. Thus there would be nothing to connect him with the murder.

Whatever the authorities thought of this bit of private enterprise, they couldn't ignore its results. There would have to be an inquiry and eventually, after a lot of rumours, the Vermonts would become a meaty bone for the tabloids – and God alone knew what would happen to me.

So I was left with my third option, which if it failed would still allow me to fall back on either of the other two. I could make an attempt to counter-attack. Pulent had weaknesses, and he had made mistakes. He had given me the name and address of his bank, or rather E. Percival-Brown's bank. Was I the only individual he had tried to blackmail? It might be worth while to find out more about Chief Inspector James Pulent.

With this resolve making me a little less miserable I eventually fell into a troubled sleep. The morning came too soon.


After breakfast I closeted myself in the study, saying I had work to do, which in a way was the truth. Imogen had decided to go shopping and I could count on Mrs Curwen, busy vacuuming the bedrooms, not to interrupt me. I reached for the telephone.

I tried New Scotland Yard first, and was lucky to get hold of Chief Inspector Minor with little delay. I said that my wife and I had been wondering if the police were making any progress towards finding Renata Tamson's killer.

'Regretfully no, sir,' he admitted.

'That powder you mentioned was no help?'

'None.' He didn't volunteer what it was.

'So the case is closed?'

'Indeed no, sir. You must know that we never officially close a murder case until the villain is caught, but at the moment we appear to be at a dead end on this one. However, we only need a small bit of luck and we've got the guy.'

I thanked him, and said goodbye. I had no idea what percentage of murders remained unsolved in England each year, but I thought the Chief Inspector could not be too optimistic in this case, if all he had to rely on was 'a small bit of luck'. The call had achieved nothing.

I next tried E. Percival-Brown's bank, having thought out my story beforehand. Eventually I was connected to someone said to be an assistant manager. I explained that I had done business with Mr Percival-Brown, who had given me a cheque on their branch of Barclays for a sum he owed me. Unfortunately – and presumably by accident – he had dated it for the following year, which was most inconvenient. I needed to get in touch with him, but I had lost his address. Could the manager help?

He assured me that he could. No, he couldn't give me Mr Percival-Brown's address, but if I wrote to him care of the bank the letter would be forwarded immediately. I demurred, not because I wanted the address, which would almost certainly be an accommodation address at some sleazy shop, but because I hoped to find out more about the account.

'That's not very satisfactory,' I said. 'This way it could take ages, and I need the money. It's a question of cashflow.' I hoped I sounded agitated. 'The sum in question is over a thousand pounds, and I was fool enough to give Percival-Brown a receipt. I never imagined his cheque would be no good. Perhaps he doesn't have enough to cover it.'

'I assure you, Mr – er. You didn't give me your name.'

'Nigel Hawker!' If Pulent heard of this enquiry he would know it had come from me. There was no point in dissembling.

'Mr Hawker, I assure you that there's no need to worry. As you know, I can't discuss a client's affairs, but in the circumstances I will say this: Mr Percival-Brown's accounts with us are very healthy. You might say substantial. There's no question whatsoever that this cheque, when rightly dated, will be met. It must have been merely an unfortunate mistake.'

I thanked him, said I would write if I didn't manage to get in touch with Mr Percival-Brown by other means, and bade him good-day. I had learnt one thing; if Pulent's accounts were to any degree substantial, this was probably not his first attempt at blackmail. It might prove a useful piece of information.

But I only had fifteen days. I couldn't afford to waste time. I turned to the Yellow Pages. Much as I disliked the idea – for it meant betraying an interest in Jim Pulent – I needed a private investigator.

I didn't quite choose Mansard with a pin, but it was the next best thing. However, his office was neither too far from where Pulent lived, nor too close, and on the phone he sounded competent. I gave my name as Smith and he didn't query it. Nor did he ask for my address. Discretion seemed to be his middle name.

'Is it a divorce case, Mr Smith?' he said at once. 'Because if it is I'm afraid I won't take it. I don't touch divorce.'

'No. It's suspected corruption,' I said.

'I see,' he replied slowly. 'Okay, I'll do what I can.'

He told me his charges, which were high but not exorbitant, and I promised to put a hundred pounds in the mail to him as an advance payment. Then I gave him Pulent's name, rank and private address and said I wanted to know how he spent his time when he was not at work – and I wanted the information like yesterday. Mansard promised he would do his best by Monday, and since I could do nothing else that might prove profitable I resigned myself. I sent him his money in cash – used banknotes – enclosed in a plain brown envelope on which I had written his name and address in disguised handwriting. I posted it in the anonymity of Regent Street. I had worn gloves throughout the process. Even to me these seemed ludicrous precautions, but I was determined that enquiries into the Chief Inspector's movements should not be traced back to me.

The waiting for Mansard's report was going to be awful.

But the next few days and the weekend – my birthday weekend – were less unendurable than I had imagined. In the first place I was very fully occupied and, though this may seem strange, the weekend was revealing in that it helped to clarify my problem.

Imogen and I arrived at Aubyn House early on Friday evening. The children were already there. They had been lined up by their proud grandfather and, as we got out of the car, they sang, quite tunefully, 'Happy birthday, dear Daddy, happy birthday to you'. Only Noreen still called me Daddy – Peter called me Pa and Edward, my younger and rather pompous son, preferred Father – but it didn't matter. I was touched. I embraced all three of them, and Dad; it was a special occasion.

But Dad worried me. Seeing the old man so often, though I knew he was getting frail, I hadn't realized quite how much he had aged recently. Only when I gave him a hug did I appreciate to what a degree he had shrunk. His once upright body was stooped and lacked solidity. Indeed, he had become the proverbial bag of bones.

'I know,' Imogen said when I mentioned this to her while we were changing for dinner. 'Simon, he made me promise I wouldn't tell you, but it's a promise I'm going to break. A few weeks ago Dad had a heart attack. Oh, it wasn't a bad one, and he insisted on treating it lightly, but it was a warning. I questioned his doctor and he admits that a second attack at Dad's age would probably be fatal. I'm sure it's best you should know.'

'Of course it is! I should have been told before, when it happened.' I was upset and angry. 'Why wasn't I?'

'He didn't want you to worry about him. Besides, it was shortly after you'd been mugged and you weren't in the most – most receptive of moods, Simon. You had your own problems, I suppose.'

I nodded agreement. Imogen, I imagined, was thinking of Renata, but I was thinking of Jim Pulent. All my ill fortune seemed to have stemmed from that damned mugging and the chance meeting with Pulent. But I refused to let my mind dwell on Pulent now.

Imogen and I went downstairs and there were more greetings. Susan and Guy had arrived from Oxford and Martin had returned from a tennis party. With Martin was a small blonde girl in her middle twenties whom he introduced as Audrey Dreisland; from her clothes it was clear she had been one of the tennis party. I had never heard of her before.

'Do you play tennis, Mr Vermont?' she asked me.

'No, I don't play any games,' I said. I didn't use a stick in the house and she hadn't noticed my limp.

Noreen, who had been passing around nuts and olives, glared at her. 'Daddy was too badly wounded in the war to play games,' she said. 'He was in the Royal Air Force. He got a DFC.'

Poor Audrey went crimson and muttered an apology. Soon afterwards she said she must go – she had her own car – and Martin went upstairs to change. Peter carefully poured me a whisky and soda, and a sherry for Imogen.

'Who's this Audrey Dreisland?' I asked. 'I don't remember anyone mentioning her before.'

Guy answered. 'She's one of my post-graduate students. Martin met her through Susan and me and they've become very friendly. Her father's a businessman, something to do with boat-building, I believe.'

'A pretty girl,' Imogen said. 'You didn't have to squash her quite so hard, Noreen dear. It wasn't kind.'

'And anyway what's so great about the RAF? I'm going into the Army like Granddad and Uncle Martin,' Edward declared.

'More fool you,' Peter said. 'I'm going to be a barrister, a very rich and very successful barrister.'

'And I shall be a famous author.' Noreen was not to be outdone.

It was a typical family scene. A little later, when we were joined by Martin and Dad, who was looking less tired after his rest, the children continued to elaborate on their futures. I was to remember the occasion, if only because each one of them, Peter, Edward and Noreen – Imogen's offspring and mine – were all to a greater or lesser degree to achieve their ambitions.


It was to be brought home to me over the weekend how dependent on me all the Vermonts were, and how much I had come to love them.

Martin was the first. The children had gone to bed and the others had made up a foursome for bridge. Martin and I were at the further end of the drawing room, chatting quietly so as not to disturb the card players, who were taking their game very seriously.

'What did you think of Audrey?' Martin asked suddenly.

'Attractive to look at. Clever, as she's one of Guy's post-graduate students. Pleasant. But that's a very superficial impression, Martin. I only met her briefly.'

'She wants to marry me.'

I was startled. 'Would that be a good idea?'

'I don't know. It would please Dad. He's always nagging at me to get married, to get a job, to settle down. He's never forgiven me for quitting the Army when I should have been aspiring to high rank – or that's how he sees it. And Audrey would solve the problem. She's an only child. She has expectations. Meanwhile her father would provide me with a living in the boat-building industry, and she could go on with her academic work.'

'It sounds jolly!' I grinned at him. 'Don't do it, Martin. It wouldn't work and you wouldn't be happy – either of you.'

'That's what I wanted to ask you. You don't believe I could make it work?'

'I don't believe you could make it work, and I don't believe you should try, Martin. It wouldn't be fair to you or to Audrey. Have you slept with her?'

'No. I keep on making excuses.' He smiled ruefully.

'Well, there's your answer. And if the marriage ended in a scandal it would be worse for Dad.'

Martin and I both knew what we were talking about. It must be remembered that in the early Sixties attitudes towards homosexuals were very different from those current now.

I went on, 'A job, however, is another matter. What would you like to do?'

'There's a little hotel – a dozen rooms – not more than an inn, really, near Avignon. It's owned by a close friend of mine and his mother, but his mother's over seventy and would like to retire. I'd buy her half-share if I could raise the cash, but I'm about ten thousand short. I don't know where the money goes.'

'Surely there's something you could sell. What about the painting that Aunt Isobel left you? I know you're attached to it, but –'

'The Constable? Oh, I couldn't possibly get rid of that, Simon. Dad would notice, and he'd be furious.'

'I see your point. And you'd be happy in France?'

'Yes. I love the place. It's a civilized country, France. The French aren't so easily shocked by people like me as the English are.'

'When do you have to decide?'

'By the end of the year.'

'Right. I won't promise. I'll let you know definitely next month. You'll have to wait till then. But I hope to be able to let you have the money.'

He was surprised. 'That would be terrific, but can you manage it? God knows when I could pay you back, Simon.'

'If all goes well and a deal I'm planning comes off, you won't have to. It'll be a gift, and I don't want thanks. You'd do the same for me. But it will be strictly between the two of us. You understand?'

Martin nodded dumbly, overwhelmed with gratitude, and, getting up to stretch my bad leg, I patted him on the shoulder. I couldn't tell him how much I owed him. If I hadn't usurped Simon Vermont's place he himself would have been the owner of Aubyn House, and would only have had to share the money his mother had left with Susan. That probably he would have dealt incompetently with the house and almost certainly squandered the money was unimportant. Both the property and the money should have been his, not mine.

Susan was the next to confide in me; she cornered me in the study. Thank Heaven she didn't want money. Nevertheless, I couldn't accede to her request immediately, as I would have wished. Like Martin, she would have to wait. She wanted me to take on a responsibility, to make a promise, and at the moment I couldn't honestly do it. Nor was I prepared to lie to her.

'It's about Natalie,' she began. 'Guy's niece.'

'Yes? What about her?' I asked.

I had a lot on my mind and I was slow to remember. It was not a happy story. Natalie's father, a farmer, had killed himself by accidentally overturning his tractor a month before Natalie was born. Natalie's mother had never fully recovered from the shock and had been ill on and off ever since. She hadn't come to Susan's wedding to Guy, and I had never met her.

'Guy and I want to adopt Natalie legally,' Susan said. 'It would be next best to having a child of our own, which I know now is impossible.'

'Does her mother agree?'

'Yes. She's in a hospice at present. She isn't expected to last the year. She's got leukaemia. But she's perfectly *compos mentis*, and she thinks it would be an ideal solution. Natalie's living with her grandparents, but they're in their seventies and can't cope with a six-year-old.'

'I see,' I said slowly. 'It sounds a good arrangement. What's the difficulty?'

'Guy and I can give her more security than she has ever had before, but it's important she's accepted by all of us, all the Vermonts, and not allowed to feel an outsider. I want her to be one of the family, to be free to come to Aubyn House when she wants, as if – as if she was my daughter and you and Martin really were her uncles. Do you understand, Simon?'

'Yes, I understand.'

'And there's another thing. I want you to promise that if something happened to Guy and me you'd look after her, treat her as your own. Will you promise that, Simon?'

'Does Guy know you've asked me this?'

'No.' She was clearly disappointed by my response.

'Then don't tell him, please. Susan dear, I can't explain, but at the moment I can't give you that promise. I'm having difficulties of my own, and until they're resolved –'

'You're not thinking of leaving Imogen for someone else? She hasn't seemed very happy lately.'

'Good God, no! What an idea! I'd never leave Imogen.'

'That's all right then.' Susan was relieved. 'I'm sorry. I thought that might be the trouble.'

'No it isn't. Susan, please trust me. I'll let you know definitely about Natalie next month, and if it's possible I'll certainly agree.'

'Thank you. And remember, Simon, if there's anything I can do to help you've only got to ask. I've not forgotten how you helped me years ago when I needed to have that abortion. It's ironic that now I can't carry a baby, isn't it?'


And then there was Dad. He didn't want anything from me, but as we were walking slowly around the garden together, he said, 'You know, Simon, of my three children I expected the least of you. I was wrong. You have a fine career. You're a good husband and father. You're the only one who's given me grandchildren. What's more, I can depend on you to keep the family together and take care of them – the weak, like Martin, as well as the strong. Thank God you managed to survive the war.'

I bent down to pick a deadhead off a rosebush in order that he shouldn't see my face. I had to fight back my tears. But there and then I swore to myself that I would kill Jim Pulent rather than let him destroy me, and through me the Vermonts.

# CHAPTER FOURTEEN

I had arranged with Mansard, the private investigator, that I would call him at noon on Monday, and I was pleased when he answered the phone himself. He began by thanking me for the advance payment I had sent him, making no comment on its anonymity. He sounded as competent as before, and said he had a report ready. As he had no address for me, he assumed I would want to have the gist of it over the phone. He warned me not to expect too much; time had been short.

I don't really know what I had expected – a miracle that would free me from Jim Pulent's clutches, perhaps. If so, I was disappointed. The report was detailed; Mansard had done his stuff and, if he hadn't produced a miracle, he did provide me with some useful information.

I learnt that Pulent had a desk job in the Yard at present, or at least a regular nine-to-five duty. I knew what number bus he caught to work, and which one brought him home in the evening; he usually lunched in the staff canteen. The location and description of his house didn't interest me. I had been in it often enough in the past, and there wasn't much he could have done to it except add a bathroom at the back. Nor did I care about his frequent visits to the local, also patronized by his neighbours, the grocer and his wife.

'You mentioned corruption, sir,' Mansard said, 'but if he's a bent copper I saw no sign of it, though there seems to be a joke in the pub about the expensive holidays he takes each year. Evidently he went to the States last summer and on a cruise the summer before that. Otherwise he seems to live very modestly. Mind you, you only gave me a few days.' He excused himself. 'If I had a bit longer – '

'Of course,' I agreed. 'You've done splendidly. Anything else? What about sex? He's not married, is he?'

'No, but he has a regular woman friend, a Mrs Wade.'

Though he didn't realize it, Mansard had left the most important detail until last. Moira Wade was a widow. She had had a brief marriage to a Major Wade, who had been killed in 1944, the results of the union being a nice little pension and Steve, a teenage lout of a son, who lived off his mother. I guessed that this was the youth who had tailed me and watched Renata for Pulent.

It was generally believed that Jim Pulent and Moira Wade didn't marry because it would mean that she would lose her pension, and she liked her independence, but they were accepted as a couple in the neighbourhood. However, although Pulent spent several evenings a week at her house, which was five minutes' walk from his own, he never stayed overnight, as a rule returning home between midnight and one. This rather unusual behaviour was again ascribed by the neighbours to Mrs Wade's fears for her pension if she were to be considered Pulent's common-law wife.

I thanked Mansard for his efforts on my behalf, but said I didn't think he could do any more for me. I gave him to understand that from what he had learnt it would seem I had been mistaken in my suspicion of Chief Inspector Pulent. I asked him how much I owed him and, when he named a large but not unreasonable sum, said I would put the money in the post to him that day. This I did, taking the same precautions as on the last occasion, and happy in the knowledge that all he knew of me was as a voice over the telephone.


Now I could get down to some real planning. Pulent would not be the first man I had killed. Admittedly the other killings had been during the war, but this did not mean that I had dropped a bomb on Dresden or fired a torpedo at the *Scharnhorst,* or even stuck a bayonet through a soldier in the heat of battle in the Ardennes. Except by the individuals who suffered, these might be considered honourable actions. My own war was much more personal. But I plead my case in advance.

No, I had killed in cold blood, in one or other of the ways I had been taught to do by an extremely efficient sergeant in the British Intelligence Corps, and I was responsible for only three deaths, two Frenchmen and a Polish woman, all traitors to the resistance groups to which they belonged. I have never regretted them, and I didn't expect to regret Jim Pulent. It would be justice of a kind; after all, he had killed Renata.

The problem of course was how to do the job without paying the penalty for my action. I needed both means and opportunity. I didn't have a gun, and I didn't want to go through the lengthy and devious process of getting one, so I couldn't shoot him. I had no poison, and even if I had, finding an opportunity to administer it would be virtually impossible. To hit him on the head with the so-called 'blunt instrument' was too uncertain. He might survive, for I wasn't prepared to beat his brains out – much too messy a business. It would be best for him to have 'a nasty accident', but if I suddenly appeared behind him in the bus queue some morning, he would be instantly suspicious and on his guard; what was more, an accident would be no guarantee of his death. Again, he might survive to accuse me.

What was wanted was a means that would cause a sure and certain death, one that would preferably be quick and clean, and one that would leave no clues leading back to me. There was an answer, and for it I would have to go back to my wartime training. The garrotte. Not a very British instrument, perhaps, but that was probably to the good. The garrotte had every advantage. It was easy to make from readily obtained materials, impossible to trace, quite clean, and silent. But it was ages since I had used one.

I was now forty years old. I was not in such good physical shape as I had been. My game leg meant that I was far from agile. And if I tried to kill him and failed, Pulent certainly wouldn't allow me a second chance. Nevertheless, I was going to try. I had no doubt of that.

The immediate requirement was reconnaissance. I had gathered from the media that the district where Pulent and I had been brought up, and where he still lived, had changed considerably since the war, although it retained something of its village character – London, like Paris and many other large cities, is really a collection of villages – and I didn't expect to be familiar with it any more. I had been back only once, and that had been a long time ago. I needed to refresh my memory.

This, however, presented a problem. A stranger, especially one with a limp, would be conspicuous, and I didn't want to be remembered when the police came to make inquiries. So I couldn't go there by public transport, which was the obvious course to take. I needed a car, but neither my chauffeur-driven official Rover nor my own Jaguar was suitable if I wished to be unnoticed, and I disliked the idea of hiring a car, which would be smart and clean, especially as I would need it for my next, more important visit to the area.

Then I thought of Susan. Guy, who liked automobiles, had bought a Mercedes for their family use, but Susan had a Mini in which she ran around Oxford, shopping or meetings friends and supposedly doing her good works. It was four years old, and had suffered various bumps and scratches during that period. Indeed, Susan had been thinking of changing it. I was glad she hadn't; it would be ideal for my purpose as it was.

I telephoned the Sinclairs' at six o'clock that evening in the hope that Guy would be in college working or teaching so that I could speak freely to Susan. I was thankful when she answered. There were not so many days left until the end of the month that I could afford to waste any of them.

'Susan, are you alone? Guy's not there, is he?'

'No.' She was surprised by the question. 'He's dining in Hall tonight, and before that he's got a tutorial.'

'Good. Then we can talk without you having to explain my call. Susan – when you reminded me that I'd only to ask and you'd do me a favour, I didn't expect to be asking for it immediately.'

'That doesn't matter. What is it, Simon? Is it connected with the – the difficulty you spoke of when we were discussing Natalie the other day?'

'Yes. You could say that. Susan, can you come up to London tomorrow?'

'Tomorrow would be terribly inconvenient. We've got people coming to dinner. Would Wednesday be all right?'

Another day gone, I thought, but I agreed. 'What excuse can you give Guy?'

'I have a friend in St Mary's Hospital. She's just had a hysterectomy and I'd like to visit her. I really would like to, if I'm to be in London.'

'Then you shall.'

'How long will you want me to stay? Because I must be back on Friday. We're dining with the Provost.'

'I'm not sure.' I could keep the car, but might I need her presence as an alibi if one became necessary?

'Okay. I can always pretend to be ill and stay on. I'll catch the first train Wednesday morning, Simon, and come straight to the house.'

'No. Drive up.'

'In the Mini?' She didn't like driving in London. 'It's filthy.'

142

'That's what I want, a small dirty anonymous car that no one will notice.'

She asked no questions, but merely acquiesced. 'Very well. Anything else?'

'No. Except – don't mention my call to Guy.'

'I won't. I'll be with you on Wednesday, then, in time for lunch.'

'Thanks, Susan. Bless you.'


Susan was as good as her word and arrived shortly after noon. I had spent the intervening time profitably. When I wasn't in my office, attending to work which had been sadly neglected or answering questions in the House on behalf of my Secretary of State, I practised as best I could with the garrotte I had made.

This was not the traditional Spanish variety which uses rope and strangles the victim. My version used wire and had small wooden handles at each end. It would cut the victim's throat. It was a faster and more certain method, as I had learnt in France.

But this was not a subject I wished to discuss with Susan, and she was very good about not pressing questions upon me. We had a drink together and a simple lunch. Then, having promised to take her out to dinner that evening, I sent her off in a taxi to visit her friend in St Mary's Hospital, and went to find the Mini, which she had parked a couple of streets away.

It was as dirty as Susan had promised, and I was glad to see that the licence plates were almost indecipherable and that the petrol tank was nearly full. Susan must have filled up when she reached the outskirts of London; I blessed her for the thought. And, battered though the Mini looked, the engine fired immediately and the car ran well.

I drove as fast as the traffic allowed, which meant in fits and starts, but without undue haste. It took about half an hour to reach my destination, but I reminded myself that it would be a good deal quicker late at night.

As expected, the district had changed. The last time I had seen the street where the Hawkers and the Pulents had lived for so many years it had been run-down and shabby, everything badly in need of a coat of paint, typical of post-war London. Now, in the afternoon sunshine, it looked spruce and well-kept, showing every sign of the prosperity which the Prime Minister boasted that the country enjoyed. The people were better dressed, too, though my mother would still have appeared over-smart among them, and there were a lot of cars, nearly all of them sparkling clean, so that I was half ashamed of the condition of the Mini. In fact, from the variety of cars parked, I could easily have used my Jaguar without it being noticed. But, on reflection, I was glad I hadn't. Discretion was the better part of valour.

I found Mrs Wade's house easily. Like Jim Pulent's it was one of a terrace, but was in a better class street where the houses were larger and obviously superior. I decided to park nearly, but not directly, opposite for a few minutes and admire the gleaming paintwork, the white lace curtains, the shining brass knocker and letter-box of the front door. It was clear that Mrs Wade was house-proud, and suddenly I wondered what I would have done if Pulent had been married to her and had several children, all dependent on him. At least that was a problem I didn't have to face.

I drove on, wishing that I could get out of the car and go on foot, but my lameness could make me noticeable, and in fact it was simple to see what I would have to do. Unless someone was walking a dog or going for a midnight stroll there was at first sight no choice of routes from Mrs Wade's house to Pulent's place. It was a straight-forward walk, and most of it, unfortunately for my purpose, was fairly well lit.

Then I realized that there was a fifty-yard stretch where, towards the end of the war, a bomb must have landed. If only it had landed on Hawker's grocer's shop or on Pulent's house, I thought unchari-tably, I wouldn't have been in my present predicament. But it hadn't, and since then the ground had been cleared and a garage, which included a used-car lot, had sprung up on the open space, allowing for a narrow alley through to the street where Pulent lived. It was a very obvious short cut, and I was sure that on his frequent visits to the Widow Wade this was the path he would take. And it was a near-perfect place to kill him.

# CHAPTER FIFTEEN

'Simon, are you sure you want to go out to dinner tonight? We could stay at home. I could open a tin of soup, make us an omelette. There's lots of fruit and cheese.'

'Thank you, Susan dear, no. I've booked a table at L'Oiseau Bleu. You know it. We've been there before. It's an excellent little restaurant and conveniently close.'

'All right, Simon, if you're sure.'

I was sure. Indeed, it was an essential part of my plan to be seen at a fashionable restaurant where I was known and would be remembered. I couldn't guarantee that Jim Pulent would visit Moira Wade and that I would have my chance to kill him tonight, but in case this *was* the night, I wanted to bolster my alibi in advance. Dinner with my sister at L'Oiseau Bleu would give me an opportunity to do just that.

Susan and I arrived at the restaurant shortly after eight-thirty. I was greeted by the maître d', who I knew would vouch for my presence that evening – if it ever became necessary. And among the other diners already seated were the Shadow Foreign Secretary with his wife and daughters, which was a stroke of luck. I made a point of introducing Susan to them as we were escorted to our table. They would certainly remember meeting us on what I gathered was for them a family celebration.

I ate the food that was put in front of me. Each course was a surprise because by the time it came I had forgotten what I had ordered. I drank the wine, but sparingly. In view of what was to come I was inevitably somewhat distrait, but I managed to chat with Susan about the summer holidays, about Dad's failing health, about Guy's book on Herodotus which for some obscure reason his publishers were urging him to finish, and about Natalie. Susan did most of the talking.

We lingered over coffee, and it was half past ten when we left the restaurant, and a quarter to eleven when we reached the house. The timing was near perfect. I had planned to allow thirty-five minutes to drive to Islington and park in a place I had noted on the used-car lot beside the passage.

'Susan,' I said, 'I'm going out shortly. I'll be taking your Mini. Go to bed when you like, but please leave the lights on in the hall and sitting room as if we hadn't gone up yet.'

She nodded. 'What if the phone rings? It's late, but you never know.'

'The answerphone is on. We can always explain that we had been dining at L'Oiseau Bleu and forgot to turn it off when we came in.'

'I understand.' Her eyes were huge with alarm – she had turned into a beautiful woman, very like her mother – but her voice was firm. 'I take it I'm to be your alibi for something. You needn't worry, Simon. I'll happily lie for you if necessary.'

'I hope it won't be necessary. With any luck I'll be back by one-thirty, two at the latest.'

'And if you don't come back? If you're not here for breakfast?' she asked calmly.

I hesitated. I didn't want to involve her more than I had already. Nor did I want to alarm her too much, but I thought perhaps I ought to warn her.

'Susan, if everything goes wrong and I'm not here for breakfast, you'll know soon enough. The police will be on the doorstep. If that happens, you'll say you went to bed, leaving me to have a nightcap, that you didn't know I had gone out. Apart from that you tell the truth.'

'The police?'

I had surprised her. Whatever scenarios she had imagined to account for my unusual behaviour, the police hadn't played a part in them. I tried to reassure her. She was not as much in control of the situation and her feelings as I had thought.

'Don't worry, Susan dear. There's very little doubt that I'll be back long before breakfast.'

She gritted her teeth and nodded fiercely. 'It's all right. You can depend on me, Simon. But I don't think I'll be getting much sleep until you're safely home. I don't know what we'd do if anything happened to you.'


Alone in the bedroom that I shared with Imogen when she was in London, I began to wonder if I was crazy. Here I was, a supposedly respectable citizen, married, the father of three children, a Member of Parliament, a Junior Minister, planning to go out in the middle of the night to kill another supposedly respectable citizen, a police officer, a Chief Inspector, albeit also a murderer. I had to be crazy.

I believed that I had thought my problem through sensibly and logically. But had I? Had I avoided reflecting on the possible consequences of my action? If I were caught, whether I had failed or succeeded in my purpose, wouldn't I be making the situation worse? Had I allowed myself to be carried along by the desperation of my position – and my wartime experiences?

It scarcely mattered now. As I got out of my suit and put on dark slacks and a black polo-necked sweater, I knew it was impossible not to make this effort to solve my problem. I might regret it, but at least I would regret it a good deal more if at this late stage I lost my nerve and did nothing.

Thrusting my doubts to the back of my mind I finished my preparations, putting a raincoat over my rather odd garb. Susan was waiting in the hall. Sensible girl that she was, she asked no more questions, but kissed me on the cheek and wished me luck. The time was eleven twenty-five.

It was a dark night. The wind had risen and it was unusually cold for this time of year, or perhaps I was feeling chilled. There was a moon, but it gave only a sickly light. Clouds scudded across the sky, and I was reminded of that night so long ago when I had crouched in a ditch in France waiting to hear the drone of the aircraft that would take me safely back to England. Then I had cursed the weather, but now I was thankful for it. The pubs and most places of entertainment in Islington would already be closed, but anyone who had thought of giving the dog a moonlight stroll would be deterred, and those who had been out would be hurrying home, intent on their own business.

I slid behind the steering wheel of Susan's Mini and started the engine. As I had expected, the traffic was light, and I reached my destination ahead of schedule. The place I had noted on the used-car lot where I hoped to park beside the passage was fortunately still vacant. The dealer hadn't swapped his cars around.

I slid the Mini into the slot and prepared to wait, and wait, and wait, until either Jim Pulent appeared or I gave up for the night, reluctantly, because I knew I would have to try the next night, and the night after that. Mansard, the detective, had had insufficient time to establish whether Pulent visited the Widow Wade on regular evenings or at random.

It was just after a quarter to twelve. I took off the raincoat I had been wearing to give myself greater freedom of movement, laid the garrotte on the seat beside me within easy reach, and opened the car door nearest to the passage, leaving it ajar. There was nothing else to do now but watch and wait.

And it was a long wait, though not without its heart-stopping moments. A man walking his dog, in spite of the weather, passed close to the Mini. Head down, he was eager to get home, but the dog had other ideas and, perhaps sensing my presence, decided to lift his leg against the Mini's rear wheel. I turned my back and pretended to pick up something from the floor of the car and when I sat up again they had gone by. I doubted if the man had noticed me.

Almost immediately, before I had a chance to recover from the dog incident, a group of young people, six or eight of them, came laughing and singing through the passage, presumably on their way home from some party or other. Luckily they were too occupied with each other to pay any attention to the cars on the lot, and I don't believe any of them as much as glanced at the Mini.

After that there was a lengthy pause and the minutes ticked by very slowly. I stared towards the end of the passage, where a lamp threw a weak pool of light, and willed Jim Pulent to appear in it, but there was no sign of him. It seemed to me that either Pulent was not at Moira Wade's, or they were having a lengthy and, presumably, rewarding session.

At five to one I finally faced the prospect of sitting there in Susan's Mini, fearful and on edge, for a second night and even a third. The weather might improve and anyway there would be more people around late at night at the weekend. Would I be able to remain here unobserved for several nights? I doubted it.

As these thoughts crossed my mind a figure appeared at the end of the passage, lurching from side to side. But it wasn't Pulent. It was a drunk. I watched his progress as he came staggering along. He was opposite me, groping along the wall at the other side of the passage. Then, without warning, he lurched across and draped himself over the Mini. I cursed, but there was nothing I could do.

After a minute he pushed himself off and staggered on, only to fall flat on his face when he had taken ten paces. I didn't want him there. He was too close to me, a potential witness and therefore a danger, for drunks can have moments of clarity, especially in times of sudden stress. But there he lay, a dark sprawling heap, barely discernible in the night.

He had all my attention and I was cursing him, wrongly as it turned out, when something alerted me. I turned in my seat, and there in the lamplight was Jim Pulent, about to enter the passage.

I slid out of the car, and, crouching low, the garrotte clutched in my gloved hands, crawled quickly to the rear of the Mini. I was just in time. A bright beam of light shone down the passage causing the drunk to groan and bury his head in his arms. I had underestimated Pulent. I should have guessed that an experienced police officer wouldn't venture down a dark alley in the middle of the night without a powerful torch.

It was now, however, that the presence of the drunk came to my aid. Instead of flashing his torch from side to side as he might have done, Pulent shone it directly on to the prostrate man. Advancing with long strides, he passed where I crouched without a glance in my direction, and stopped about a yard from the drunk, who started to swear.

I couldn't have hoped for a better opportunity. Pulent was standing still, his back to me, his attention concentrated on the drunk. I don't believe he knew what happened. He must have sensed someone behind him because he started to turn but I had already flung the garrotte over his head. As the wire sliced through his neck he uttered a strangulated cry, dropped the torch, which luckily went out, and, when I released my hold, collapsed first to his knees and then rolled over to stare, sightless, at the sky. It was a quick, a merciful death, and almost bloodless. At least, having been behind my victim, I was free from any bloodstains. Taking care to remain so, I pushed the body between two of the parked cars. My weapon, the garrotte, I left at the scene. It was untraceable – wire and a couple of bits of wood, and it was just possible that its nature might confuse the authorities.

But none of this really concerned me at that moment. I was intent on getting out, getting away. My instinct for self-preservation had overcome all other feelings. I was in the Mini, starting the engine. I had left the ignition key in place, which was a good thing because I found I was shaking uncontrollably. Somehow I got the thing into gear and drove off, aware that the drunk was staggering down the passage in the opposite direction from mine. He could only have been aware of me, if at all, as a tall dark figure. He was no threat.

I have little or no recollection of the return journey to Knightsbridge. I remember meeting a police car, but it was too soon for Pulent's body to have been found, and the car, pursuing its own business, paid no attention to me. I suppose I obeyed traffic lights, stopping and starting, but I was mildly surprised when I found myself driving through the Hyde Park Corner underpass and real-ized that I was almost home.

I had trouble parking the Mini and consequently was faced with a longer walk than I would have liked, but I reached the house. I managed to open the door, and half fell into the hall. I was sick with relief. I felt no compunction at having killed Jim Pulent, but I never wanted to go through the last few hours again.

'Simon! Oh, Simon, thank God you're back! Are you all right?'

Susan came running down the stairs and almost threw herself at me, but I pushed her away. My stomach had revolted. I just made it to the cloakroom before I vomited. Obviously none of that excellent dinner I had eaten earlier at L'Oiseau Bleu had been digested.

Susan, as Imogen would have been, was practical. She gave me tissues to wipe my mouth, put a cold flannel on my brow and, when I had finally stopped heaving my heart out, helped me into the sitting room. I was shivering. She fetched a blanket and wrapped it around me.

'The kettle's on. Would you like tea? Or a brandy?'

'Brandy first, please. Then tea.'

Susan left me with a large glass of brandy which I sipped slowly while she went to make the tea. She returned with a tray and two cups and poured the tea for us. She regarded me anxiously, but by then I was recovering and in control of myself.

'May I ask two questions?' she said.

'You may, but I don't promise I'll answer them.'

'Did you accomplish what you wanted to do tonight, and is that the end of the matter?'

'I accomplished what I wanted to do, yes. As for it being the end of the matter, Susan, I don't know. I hope so.'

The police would be sure to search Pulent's house, and if they found the damning evidence he had acquired against me and – less likely – interpreted it correctly, they might realize that I had an excellent motive for killing their Chief Inspector. But I was probably

– almost certainly, if, as I suspected, he was a blackmailer – not the only individual with such a motive. They would hesitate to accuse me without proof, and I didn't believe they could find proof.

'We'll have to wait and see,' I said, 'but don't forget this, Susan. After we came back from L'Oiseau Bleu we were together for the rest of the evening. You went to bed leaving me to have a nightcap, but you heard me come upstairs soon after and you're positive I never left the house.'

'I'll remember, Simon,' she said soberly.

'With any luck it won't be necessary,' I said, and thought that so far in this enterprise my luck had held up. I had no regrets.

# CHAPTER SIXTEEN

The body of Chief Inspector James Pulent was found at seven-thirty the next morning by a night watchman going off duty, later than one might have expected, but the alleyway was not a particularly popular route, and the body was partially concealed. Alternatively, others might have passed by, taking Pulent's recumbent form (if they noticed it at all) for that of a sleeping drunk.

This had been Harry Goldsmith's – the night watchman was called Henry Theodore Goldsmith – first reaction too, but being a kind man he had paused to see if he could help. Bending closely over the body he had been horrified to behold the half-severed neck and the small pool of blood. He had run as fast as he could to the nearest telephone box and dialled 999.

But of course I knew nothing of this until much later in the day. I was having breakfast in the kitchen with Susan a few minutes before nine when the front door bell rang, not tentatively but firmly, and at once I thought of the police. So, I saw by her expression as we exchanged glances, did Susan.

'I'll go,' I said as Susan made to rise.

Still holding my table napkin, to indicate that I had been interrupted during breakfast on a normal morning, I went into the hall and flung open the front door. 'Good morn – ' I began.

Mrs Curwen stood on the doorstep. 'Oh, Mr Vermont, sir, I'm terribly sorry to disturb you, but I forgot my key. Mr Curwen and I went out to the pictures yesterday evening, and I moved my bits and pieces to my best handbag; then when I changed them back I must have overlooked the key.'

'That's all right, Mrs Curwen,' I said. She couldn't guess how glad I was to see her, and not two ominous figures, one possibly in uniform, their warrant cards in their hands. 'Come along in. My sister's here. We were just having breakfast.'

I led the way into the kitchen and let Mrs Curwen explain her story of the forgotten key to Susan while I had a final cup of coffee. I hoped I wasn't going to be so jittery every time the front door bell rang.

'Will you be here for lunch, Mrs Sinclair?' Mrs Curwen asked when she had finished her explanations.

'No. I'm driving back to Oxford right away.'

'And I shall be out for lunch and dinner,' I said, determined to be seen in public, behaving as if this were an ordinary day and I had not killed a man the night before. 'It's one of my mornings to be in my office in the House, Mrs Curwen. In the unlikely event anyone should want me urgently, that's where I'll be. If not, my secretary will know where to find me. Otherwise leave a message as usual. Okay?'

'Yes, Mr Vermont. Very good, sir.'


I walked with Susan to where I had parked her Mini, carrying her small suitcase. It seemed a much shorter distance than it had the previous night, perhaps because I was calmer and this morning I had my stick to help me along. I kissed her goodbye and opened the car door for her.

'My love to Guy,' I said. 'And tell him to get on with that Herodotus book of his.'

Susan laughed. 'You can tell him yourself on Sunday, Simon. We're driving over for lunch. Really, to see Dad.'

'Great.'

She got into the Mini, started the engine and wound down the window. 'You'll be all right, Simon?' She was anxious for me, and who could blame her after the inexplicable train of events in which I seemed to have involved her.

'I'll be fine. Don't worry, Susan.'

How easy to say that she shouldn't worry. As Susan drove off and I hailed a taxi to carry me to Westminster, I wished I could take the advice I had handed out to her so blithely. But I was not the innocent that she was. I was sure that she hadn't the faintest idea of how I had spent the previous night. She believed, I suspected, that in spite of my protestations, I had become involved in some sexual affair – Heaven knows the life of an MP was not conducive to marital fidelity – which could cause an unpleasant scandal, hurt Imogen and the family, perhaps destroy my political career. But she had no thought that I might have committed a serious crime – murder, for instance – and when she read about the Pulent killing there was no reason why she should connect it with me. Her worries were trivial compared with mine.

And I had to put mine behind me, at least for the moment. At eleven I was to chair a meeting on the Congo, which was in a state of total anarchy after independence – the immediate problem being whether or not we should support American intervention. Personally, I didn't care a damn about the Congo, and resented having the job thrust on me. It would take up all the morning, and then I was giving lunch to one of my constituents, a most boring man but generous to the Party – someone whom I couldn't afford to offend by turning him down at the last minute.

I had hoped to reach my office and get on with the paperwork without interruption, but it was a fond hope. Before I even reached my small, cramped room I was stopped by the Chief Whip, who wanted to know if I was prepared to speak for a candidate at a forth-coming by-election, and by a Member who needed a pair the following week. Once in the office I did my best to deal with the correspondence – people are always being told to write to their MP – answer questions on the telephone and check some facts for the meeting. I missed Renata; my present secretary was willing, but she didn't understand the niceties of her job and referred to me too much.

The meeting was difficult. In the first place, there was a certain amount of anti-American feeling, and in addition a number of doubts were expressed about our possible commitments to Cyprus and Nigeria who were to gain their independence later in the year, independence that could easily degenerate into chaos in either or both places. Eventually the meeting ended with no conclusions reached, as was only to be expected. It was by now one o'clock and as we came out of the committee room a messenger, formal in his black suit and white tie, said, 'Mr Simon Vermont, sir,' and held out a green card informing me that a visitor was waiting in the Central Lobby. This was my constituent, and after a quick visit to a cloak-room I went to collect him.

Sir Roland Mainwaring was a short stout man in his sixties, with a ruddy, broken-veined complexion, though he was, in fact, an abstemious drinker. I myself could have done with a whisky but, knowing his habits, I suggested we went straight to the Strangers' Dining Room; he acquiesced at once. On the way we met the Home

Secretary, and I was able to introduce Mainwaring, which pleased him immensely, especially as his present hobby-horse was the amount of crime in the country.

He continued with the subject as we ate our pâté and grilled sole and drank a pleasant Chablis. 'Look at this wretched Chief Inspector,' he said indignantly. 'Garrotted, if you please! Garrotted! Think of it. A horrible foreign way of disposing of anyone.'

It seemed to me that he was angrier about the *way* Pulent had been killed than the fact that a senior police officer had been done to death. Presumably, if Pulent had been shot or hit on the head with a British-made blunt instrument Mainwaring wouldn't have minded half as much. I wanted to laugh.

'There was nothing about it in my morning paper,' I said, 'and I've been tied up ever since.'

'That's because the body wasn't found till seven-thirty,' he said. 'But it was on the BBC news at noon and in the early editions of the evening papers. A ghastly story.' Ghastly or not, Mainwaring proceeded to recount it and, with salt and pepper pots and the cord from the menu, to illustrate how Pulent had been killed. His description was not very accurate, and I had a sudden urge to lean across the table and tell him that it was I who had killed the Chief Inspector and put him right about the details. Needless to say, I resisted the temptation.

'Have the police any clues yet?' I asked.

This set Mainwaring off on the inefficiency of the CID, and all I had to do was make noises of agreement. I was glad when the lunch was over and I was able to say goodbye to my guest. I returned to my office for a couple of hours, and then went home, picking up an *Evening Standard* and the other evening papers on the way. I would go back to Westminster later to listen to the debate and play my part in the Division. Before that I would read the papers, listen to the radio and watch television. I didn't share Mainwaring's low opinion of the CID, and I wanted to learn how much they knew, or at least were prepared to reveal that they knew about what was to become known as 'The Garrotte Affair'.

I was disappointed. The later editions of the papers had little more than Mainwaring had told me, apart from the surmise that, because of the nature of the killing, Spaniards might have been involved, and a carefully-worded mention of a Spanish restaurant not far from the scene of the crime. I had a suspicion that these sentences must have been closely vetted for possible libel by the papers' lawyers.

As for the police, if they had any information they were keeping it to themselves, but I was sure that they had not been idle. I knew they would be pulling out all the stops to find the killer because Jim Pulent had been 'one of their own'. I didn't blame them for this, but I hoped they wouldn't arrest the wrong man; such an action would present me with another – and very complex – dilemma, and at the moment I wasn't sure I could cope with it.

In any case, the police had issued an appeal for anyone who had been through that passage between eleven last night and three in the morning, or could help them with their inquiries in any way to phone a number reserved for communications from the public about this 'perfectly horrible crime'. I memorized the number.

However, by the next morning, Friday, the situation had worsened. It so happened that no other newsworthy events had taken place; no wars had broken out; no earthquakes had erupted; no tidal waves had submerged whole countries; not a single film star had married for the umpteenth time. As a result, Jim Pulent and his unusual death had made the headlines in both the broadsheets and the tabloids, and proceeded to usurp wireless and television time. It seemed that anyone who had a connection, however distant, with Pulent was eager to give an interview and state his or her opinion.

There were various photographs of Moira Wade, who claimed that she and 'dearest Jim' were planning to marry in the near future. Her son, Steve, appeared on television with a comforting arm around his mother, who throughout the interview dabbed her eyes with a minute handkerchief. As far as I could tell, it was Steve who had been my recent shadow. He and his mother sat together on a sofa in what was clearly their living room, a large colour photograph of Pulent on a table next to them, and Steve said that Jim had been like a father to him. The whole business was an example of telly journalism at its worst.

The Hawkers, Pulent's neighbours, who claimed to have known him since childhood, were loud in their praises of the dead man, and described him as 'a good friend of our boy who was killed in the war, and a good friend to us'. Tom Hawker added that whoever had murdered Jim Pulent deserved to hang. This sentiment was echoed by Pulent's next of kin, a distant cousin, by the publican of his local and by several other people, including his colleagues at New Scotland Yard, who were all full of plaudits for the former Chief Inspector – a murderer and a blackmailer! A good deal of this made me wonder if the Jim Pulent I had known and the one everybody was lauding were the same person.

And if I hadn't expected Jim Pulent to be so loved and admired, I hadn't expected his death and the manner of it to cause quite such a stir either. Perhaps this had been foolish of me. After all, although police officers were not infrequently shot or knifed, it was practically unheard of for one to be garrotted, at least in England, and everyone seemed to be interested in Pulent's demise. It was impossible to get away from the subject.

As it was Friday, I left Westminster early and drove myself down to Oxfordshire, and the first thing I heard on opening the front door of Aubyn House was the voice of a BBC announcer talking about 'The Garrotte Affair'. Already the term was in current use. The voice was coming from the morning room and I paused in the hall to hear what was being said.

The police were hopeful of an early arrest. The time of the assault had been narrowed down. Several people who had used the passage on Wednesday night had come forward. A Mr Bernard Crawford, who had been walking his dog, believed that someone had been hiding in a Mini near the place where the Chief Inspector had been killed, but the owner of the garage denied having had a Mini on his second-hand car lot. The police were anxious to trace this vehicle. They would also like to trace the owner of a brown leather shoe, badly scuffed, that had been found further along the passage.

The shoe meant nothing to me unless it had belonged to the drunk, but the known presence of the Mini was not good news. I cursed this Mr Crawford; he had been more observant than I had thought. And I was frowning fiercely as Imogen came out of the morning room.

'Hello, darling. I didn't hear you arrive.' She considered me anxiously. 'Are you all right? You look awfully worried.'

'Just tired.' I bent to kiss her. 'I've got to take a surgery tomorrow morning, but otherwise I hope it'll be a nice quiet weekend, family only.'

'Not this evening, I'm afraid. Audrey's here. Audrey Dreisland, Martin's girlfriend,' she added as I looked blank.

'But I thought – I thought he was going to end that.'

Imogen shrugged. 'She's a very determined young woman, and Dad keeps on urging Martin to get married. I suppose the marriage might work, though I know he doesn't really want it. He told me it was a fall-back position, whatever that means.'

I knew what it meant. If Martin couldn't do what he wanted, join his lover in France, he didn't give a damn what happened to him, and I thought that now Pulent was dead, even if I were to be accused of his murder, I could still save Martin from a life he would hate. He had said he needed ten thousand pounds to buy a share in the business near Avignon, and that evening I gave him a cheque for twelve. I have never seen a man more delighted, which as far as I was concerned was reward enough.

There was nothing I could do for Susan at present. I couldn't give her the promises she sought for the child Natalie. The situation was still much too precarious and indeed, if I was worried about the future, which inevitably I was, it was for the sake of the boys and Noreen and Imogen – and Dad, who would be more affected than the Sinclairs.

However, on Monday morning I had one less cause for worry, though in fact it was not welcome.


In spite of his age Dad was usually the first down to breakfast. Even when he was not feeling too well he refused to have a tray in his room. So, on Monday, when Martin and I had reached the bacon and egg stage and he had still not appeared, Imogen, who had only coffee and toast for breakfast, said she would go up and make sure he was all right.

Martin started to talk about France and we continued with our meal. Oddly, neither of us was unduly worried about Dad. But when Imogen, her face white, burst into the dining room, I knew at once what had happened.

Lieutenant-General Sir Patrick Vermont had died in his sleep at the age of seventy-seven, and I was now the head of the family.

# CHAPTER SEVENTEEN

Although it was some time since Dad had retired and started to live a quiet life in the country, I soon realized that his death could not be a private affair. The funeral at the end of the week was intentionally simple, but nevertheless the church was filled to overflowing with people – immediate and more distant family, close friends who had driven over for the service and others, mostly my constituents, who had known Dad and other members of the family for many years. It was not an unhappy occasion, and a few of those who attended were invited back to Aubyn House afterwards.

I suspected that the memorial service, which was planned for later in the year in London, would be much more of an effort, but it had proved impossible to avoid having one.

And the letters! They poured in, from people as disparate as Winston Churchill, General de Gaulle, and Harold Macmillan, fellow service officers, an old batman (whose spelling was shaky though his affection was obvious), and from innumerable others of whom none of the family had ever heard. There were many notes and letters of appreciation too in *The Times* and the *Telegraph* and the other serious papers, following the publication of lengthy obituaries, but thankfully most of these didn't require more than formal printed acknowledgements.

I don't think I had realized until then quite what an important person Patrick Vermont had been.

All this had the advantage of diverting my mind at least to some extent from worries about the outcome of the police inquiries into Chief Inspector Pulent's death. By now 'the Garrotte Affair' was no longer front-page news, but I knew that the search for the killer would be continuing, and it made it no easier to bear that I had to guess how close to me the dogs might be. For instance, I could only wonder if Mansard, the private investigator I had employed to gather information on Pulent, had come forward. I had been extremely careful in my dealings with Mansard, and I didn't believe

I could be traced through him, but the incident would excite curiosity and Heaven knew where that might lead.

More important, as far as I was concerned, was the residual apprehension about what might be found in Pulent's house. Nigel Hawker's old school prize would by itself mean nothing to a police detective, but if with it were two sets of identical fingerprints labelled Nigel Hawker and Simon Vermont, I would be in deep trouble. The prints by themselves were not proof that I had been responsible for Pulent's death, but in the mind of any reasonably imaginative officer they would certainly point to a motive. Nevertheless, I didn't believe that Pulent would have left such obvious evidence, however cunningly hidden, so I had every hope that, whatever a thorough police search might uncover, its significance would not be easily apparent. And as the days passed and I was not approached, my confidence grew.

Then Charles Albert Montgomery Smith was arrested in connection with Pulent's murder. He was not charged, not yet, but was 'helping the police with their inquiries'. Mr Smith was the drunk I had seen in the passage. He was, it appeared, fifty-seven, a confirmed alcoholic, unemployed, a derelict, but a member of an aristocratic family which had disowned him. Smith was not his real name.

I learnt all this from the Sunday papers, two weeks after Dad had died. I was at Aubyn House, now a quiet and subdued place that missed the old man, metaphorically an empty building. Susan and Guy had gone up to Scotland; Natalie's mother was not expected to live for more than a few days. The children had gone back to school. They had genuinely loved their grandfather, and they grieved for him. Of the family, only Martin and Imogen and I remained.

I read about Mr Smith with horror. At first he had denied being in the vicinity of the murder. Then, confronted with the shoe he had lost, he said he had been drunk and could remember nothing. Later he gave a jumbled account of a tall man leaping out of the shadows and bringing down another man on top of him. He said he had been scared and had fled. To judge from the photographs of him in the papers this wasn't difficult to believe; he looked a pathetic character. A few days in prison wouldn't hurt him – it wouldn't be his first time – but if he were convicted of garrotting Chief Inspector Pulent he would get a stiff sentence, and I couldn't allow that to happen.

Martin interrupted me as I mused over the problem. 'Simon, will it be all right if I go to France in about ten days? They're getting busy now at the inn, and they could do with my help.'

'Yes, that would be fine, if it's what you want.'

'It certainly is. And, incidentally, since Dad's gone, I won't need your cheque for that twelve thousand.'

'Why on earth not?'

I was surprised. I knew what was in Dad's will. It had been no secret. What money he left was to be divided between his three grandchildren. His possessions were also to be divided among them. Peter would inherit his jewellery, signet ring, studs, cufflinks, watch. Edward would receive his medals and military insignia, Noreen would get de Laszlo's painting of Antonia that had hung in Dad's bedroom. It was a fair distribution.

'Martin, I don't understand. You won't inherit anything from Dad.'

'I know, Simon, but now I can sell the Constable that Aunt Isobel left me. As you know, I couldn't before because Dad would have missed it.'

'But you love that painting. You mustn't sell it. I told you that cheque was a gift. I can easily afford it.'

This was a lie. I would be worse off since Dad's death. He had spent a lot on the upkeep of Aubyn House, and now the brunt of this expenditure would fall on me. But I was determined that Martin should go to France, where at least he would be happy, and I think that at the back of my mind was the idea that if the worst came to the worst his presence there would provide a base where Imogen and the children could go and join him.

'Are you sure?' Martin was doubtful.

'Absolutely certain.'

'Okay, Simon. I can't thank you enough. I'll go and phone Jean-Marie right away.'

And Martin departed, whistling cheerfully, leaving me to my worries about the drunken Charles Albert Montgomery Smith.

In the event, however, I need not have bothered. Smith was released the following Tuesday. It was on the news at breakfast time on Wednesday, with the additional detail that he had been collected by his sister. I went off to Westminster considerably cheered.

★

Wednesday was to be a good day. Coming out of the library around noon I bumped into my old friend, Dennis Cartwright, who seized me by the arm.

'Just the man I want to see. Come and have a drink, Simon.'

I had planned to have sandwiches and coffee at my desk and do some of my neglected work, but there was no way I could refuse Dennis. I guessed from his tone of voice that he had something important to impart. Nevertheless, when we had made ourselves comfortable in a corner of the bar with our drinks, he startled me with his opening remark.

'Simon, what I want to know is whether the police have been bothering you about this garrotting business?'

Deliberately I sipped my gin. 'No. Why should they?'

'Well, you know this chap, Chief Inspector Pulent. You told me he called on you after you'd been mugged that time. He was meant to be inquiring into attacks on MPs.'

'Indeed, yes. I remember. But that was a while ago, and surely has no connection with the man's death.'

'No, no!' Surprisingly Dennis looked embarrassed. 'But I wondered – Simon, look, what I have to say is in strict confidence. The police informed me that a small book was found in Pulent's house. I haven't seen it, but I gather that it was a sort of account book, listing money apparently paid to Pulent by various people, whose initials were at the top of each page.'

I frowned at him. 'Dennis, are you suggesting that Pulent was a blackmailer of some kind?'

'It would seem a possible interpretation. Unfortunately, one set of initials corresponded with mine, which is why I was questioned – quite severely I might add, damn them.'

I shook my head. 'Poor Dennis! You've clearly been unlucky with your initials, and I've been lucky, because they haven't been near me. Did the police mention any of the others?'

'Only one, in which they are particularly interested because it was the last page, and it was empty – except for the initials in the heading. What does that suggest to you?'

'That his latest victim had refused to pay up, perhaps.'

'That seems to be exactly how the police view it. What's more, they think that, instead of paying up, this chap might have chosen to rid himself of Pulent. Or if he hadn't, I or one of the others might have.'

'Come, Dennis. They can't really have suspected you.'

'Why not? Personally I believe a blackmailer is fair game. However, in this case I'm as pure as the driven snow and I damn well told them so.'

I laughed. 'As a matter of interest, what were the initials of the non-payer?'

'NH. They mean absolutely nothing to me. I thought of old Neville Henderson, but of course he's long dead and the Yard chappies were not amused by my suggestion.'

'No, I imagine not.'

I forced myself to laugh. Inwardly, I felt cold and I uttered a silent prayer of thanksgiving that Pulent had chosen to head the page of his disgusting little book with the initials of Nigel Hawker and not those of Simon Vermont. I had had a narrow escape. The police didn't realize how close they had come to solving the case.

But as I got over my first shock I realized I had been doubly lucky. Not only would the initials tend to muddy the inquiry, but now I knew that no evidence incriminating me had been found in the search of Pulent's house. If it had been, the authorities would certainly have been questioning me by this time.

'I suppose I hope they catch whoever did it,' Dennis said, 'but I've no sympathy with a blackmailer. Your secretary's death, Simon – that was a different matter. Poor woman! Why the devil did the man have to kill her? It was so unnecessary.'

'Absolutely. Poor Renata!' I agreed, and thought how wrong Dennis was.

Renata had recognized Pulent, as he had admitted to me, and therefore given him no choice if he were to save himself. I heaved a sigh and Dennis, misinterpreting it, kind man that he was, patted me on the shoulder.

'You were fond of Renata, I know, Simon,' he said, causing me to wonder how much he did know and how much he guessed, and what his reaction would be if I told him the truth – not that I had any intention of confiding in him.

The conversation turned to the Congo, and soon afterwards I made an excuse and returned to my office, my problems there, and some sandwiches. But old Dennis had given me an idea.

★

163

The Metropolitan Police Force, like any other police force, hate a bent copper and the bad publicity that results for the entire service when one is discovered in their midst. Knowing this, and knowing now that the Yard must suspect Chief Inspector Pulent of having been a blackmailer, I decided to ratify these suspicions and make them public. My purpose in doing this was to concentrate the attention of the police on the list of possible victims that they must have, and also to encourage them to be less enthusiastic about pursuing the killer of 'one of their own'.

Later in the day, therefore, I went out to a public call box and phoned the special number the public had been given if they wished to volunteer any information about 'The Garrotte Affair'. I said that the police would find it advantageous if they inquired into the bank accounts of E. Percival-Brown, alias Chief Inspector Pulent, and I gave quick, brief details. I knew they would look into it.

They would have no option. I saw to that. As soon as I had hung up on them I phoned the news editors of two newspapers, offering them the same information and mentioning Pulent's account book, now in police possession. I said I was one of the blackmailees, but refused to give my name. There was no doubt that they were hooked. They would certainly start a little 'investigative reporting', and Pulent would be further discredited.

But as soon as I put down the receiver I remembered the assistant manager – or whoever he was – at Barclays, to whom I had told that phoney story of a misdated cheque. In a moment of bravado I had said my name was Nigel Hawker. Would he remember? And if he did, would it matter? Probably not, I decided. Nevertheless, I had been foolish. I couldn't afford silly mistakes.

As it turned out, my luck held. I had forgotten that Jim Pulent's neighbour, Tom Hawker, had been christened Nigel Thomas Hawker. Questioned by the police, who may have suspected he was involved in Pulent's illegal deals, Tom sought the support of the Press, vehemently denying that he was either a blackmailer, or being blackmailed. The result was a lot more confusion and publicity, which cannot have helped the police inquiry. Whether it was to my advantage or not, I can't say, but at any rate, I was never approached about Jim Pulent's death.

And I remember the weeks following as a good period in which I grew more and more confident. Although Parliament had started its summer recess, I still had work to do at my Ministry, but I spent as much time as I could with the children at Aubyn House. The 'season' had begun, and there was Wimbledon, followed by Ascot, a garden party at Buckingham Palace and other social events, including our local Conservative fête.

We all missed Dad – and Martin, who had happily departed to his lover near Avignon. But Natalie's mother had died, and she had come to live permanently with the Sinclairs, who had commenced adoption procedures, and the three of them spent a lot of time at Aubyn House. I had given Susan the promises she had asked for, pointing out that there was no such thing as complete security, but she had been content. Luckily Natalie, though a rather quiet and subdued child, had settled down well among us, and was made especially welcome by Noreen.

We were a very different family from the Vermonts of 1944, but we had much in common with them. Aubyn House was home. And God help me, as long as I had anything to do with it, I intended that this should remain so.

# CHAPTER EIGHTEEN

In January of the next year Imogen and I, along with the two boys and Noreen, went to Switzerland, they to ski and skate, me to amuse myself otherwise. In the past we had usually spent our winter holiday alternating between French and Austrian ski resorts, but as I was unable to take part in any of the physical activities because of my leg and because *après-ski* entertainment held no attraction for me, I found these holidays boring and only went for the sake of being with the children. This year I was determined things would be different.

I declared that we should go to Geneva. We would take my big Jaguar and we would stay at the Hôtel des Bergues, which represents the height of comfort among Swiss hotels – and hotels come no better anywhere in Europe than in that country. I would spend the day poking around the city, visiting some old acquaintances and having a quiet, peaceful time. The others could drive to Villars, a popular ski resort at the far end of Lac Léman, between the Vaudois Alps and the Villais, and no great distance.

The boys complained. Of course it was not so convenient as coming out of your hotel straight on to the ski slopes. I appreciated that. But I pointed out that it was my holiday as well as theirs, and Imogen, who would have to do the driving, supported me. The grumbling ceased as soon as we had settled in and they had enjoyed their first day of skiing.

For them it was a good holiday, I am sure, and for Noreen and Imogen. For me it was a disaster, though it began well. On the first full day in Geneva I went for a short walk, did some window shopping, sat in the residents' lounge and read. I telephoned the de Vavascours, who had lent Imogen and me their house for our honeymoon – which now seemed a long time ago. They had aged considerably over the years, they said, and had moved from Villa Villetri to an apartment, but they were glad to hear from me, and when I explained about Imogen and the children, invited me to lunch.

I called on Jean-Paul Le Rossignol at the Banque St-Pierre de Genève and, after we had exchanged pleasantries and dealt with our business, he asked me if I would care to have Sunday lunch with him and his family. This was a surprise. I had had the odd meal with him over the years in the Bank's dining room and, returning his hospitality, in restaurants, but I had never visited him in his house, and I accepted the invitation with great pleasure, knowing that the Swiss are slow to ask other than relations and close friends to their homes.

It was on my return from the Bank, as I was crossing the hotel foyer in order to reach the lifts that I had a slight accident. I was passing a sofa on which sat an elderly, silver-haired man when without warning he stuck out a leg and tripped me up. My stick flew sideways and I fell heavily. Luckily the carpet was thick. Nevertheless it was quite a heavy fall, and for the moment I was winded.

The elderly man was on his feet instantly, bending over me, helping me to stand, pouring forth apologies. The doorman ran to pick up my stick and return it to me. The concierge came from behind his desk to enquire if I was all right. A couple of passing hotel guests looked sympathetic.

In fact I was unhurt, though perhaps a little shaken, and merely irritated by what had happened and resentful of the fuss. As if to make amends, the character who had caused the accident pressed me to allow him to buy me a drink at the nearby bar and I agreed. It would have been churlish to refuse.

When we were seated and the waiter had brought our drinks, he said, 'May I introduce myself? I am Claude Petitjean.'

I gave him my name and he said he had seen me the evening before with my charming family. He was fulsome in his praise of the children and their behaviour. Alas, he had none; he had never married. He was beginning to amuse me and I explained about the skiing and asked him if he too was on holiday. He said not; he was in Geneva on important business. But he did not elaborate and I didn't question him. Then he complimented me on my French; we had been speaking in that language, and my easy familiarity with it was obvious.

'Perhaps your mother is French, Monsieur Vermont?'

'No, but I read Modern Languages at Oxford and I visit France frequently.'

167

'You were there in the war, in the Army?'

'No. I was in the Royal Air Force.'

'How thankful your family must have been that you were fortunate enough to come through it, if not unscathed, at least able to start a new life.'

It was casual conversation, and I paid scant attention to the slight emphasis he had placed on the word 'new'. I refused a second drink, thanked Monsieur Petitjean, assured him once again that I was unharmed and retreated to my room. I didn't expect to meet the man again. But that evening, as we were coming out of the dining room, we bumped into him and it was impossible to avoid introducing him to Imogen and the family. He bowed deeply, kissed Imogen's hand and almost brushed Noreen's with his lips.

'I trust you have quite recovered from your fall, Monsieur Vermont,' he said to me.

'What fall?' Imogen demanded.

I hadn't mentioned the incident to her; sometimes she fussed too much over me, and it hadn't been important. 'A trifling accident,' I said.

For the benefit of my family, Monsieur Petitjean explained in English. He had tripped me up. The blame was his. He was deeply apologetic, but he suffered from cramp and sometimes when he had been sitting for too long his leg would jerk involuntarily. His English was stilted and he had an old-fashioned turn of phrase, but we all listened, Imogen politely, the boys with scarcely concealed amusement, Noreen with wide-eyed wonder. She had never met anyone like Monsieur Claude Petitjean before.

For that matter, neither had I.


The following day was a Saturday and, as I had promised the children, I went to Villars with them. I drove, which was a relief to Imogen, who disliked the eight kilometres of hairpin bends that form the steep climb from Ollon. Having parked the car, I helped them to unpack their skis and left them to make their way to the rack railway, while I went off to the ski train which was already announcing, with a fanfare of air-horns, its departure for the restaurant on the peak at Bretaye.

The restaurant was almost empty when I got there. It was a lovely, sunny day, not too cold, and most people were out on the slopes. I found a table by one of the big windows, and there I sat, alternately admiring the colourful scene, sipping cups of coffee and reading the book I had sensibly brought with me, until the family arrived, full of their exploits, their cheeks rosy, their eyes bright with health, and we all had lunch together.

Later I drove them back to the Hôtel des Bergues, their enthusiasm and happiness my reward for a dull day. From my personal point of view, Sunday was far more enjoyable. I had a most delightful lunch with Jean-Paul Le Rossignol and his wife Marie-Louise in their house on the rue de Haut, across the Rhône, near the Cathédrale St-Pierre. It was an old house with uneven floors, low-beamed ceilings, two staircases and a cobbled courtyard. It had been modernized, with an extra bathroom and a fine kitchen, but had lost none of its character. I was introduced to their two children, still babies – Jean-Paul himself was ten years younger than I – who were then whisked away by their nanny before we settled down to a long, civilized meal, such as I didn't often enough enjoy in England, with excellent food and intelligent and interesting discussion of a wide range of subjects.

Although I was frequently to visit the Le Rossignols in their home in later years, I remember this first occasion because it seemed to me to mark the beginning of a new relationship with Jean-Paul. I felt, rightly as it was to be proved, that we were now more than banker and client, and that I could trust him completely.

So the weekend passed by. I had not seen Monsieur Claude Petitjean around the hotel, and I had almost forgotten his existence.


He reappeared on Monday. There he was, sitting on the sofa in the same place that I had originally seen him. I was tired. I had walked further than I had intended. I was looking forward to a drink and a quiet lunch, but he buttonholed me. He suggested we should lunch together and I had to lie in order to get away from him, pretending that I had to make an important telephone call.

'Tomorrow, then, Monsieur Vermont? It would give me great satisfaction.'

I was not in the business of satisfying Petitjean, and declined, pleading a previous engagement. This was a nuisance. It meant that I couldn't very well lunch in the hotel. And it was a waste of effort. Petitjean was persistent.

'Please, Monsieur Vermont. We must talk before you go back to England. I have a proposition to put to you which I believe you will find interesting.'

'Monsieur, I don't think you understand.' I wanted no part of any proposition he might offer. 'I am not a businessman. I am a politician, a Member of Parliament.'

'Oh, but I do understand, Monsieur. I understand perfectly. Until Wednesday then. We meet here at twelve-thirty. Yes.'

It was a statement – almost a command – certainly not a question, and, with a wave of his hand, he left me to regret my refusal to lunch with him the next day. Now I would have to wait forty-eight hours before I knew what he wanted of me. I told myself it couldn't be important, that there were a hundred and one reasons why this Swiss or Frenchman, whichever he was, might hope to buy a favour from a British politician. I was sure he couldn't know anything about James Pulent and his blackmailing activities. But I didn't like Petitjean's persistence. In fact, I didn't like the man at all. I no longer found him in the least amusing.

Giving the excuse that I had a migraine, I spent most of Tuesday in my room, having lunch sent up to me, but I had to appear to have recovered by the evening, or Imogen and the children would have worried. Petitjean came into the dining room as we were finishing our meal, but he merely bowed low and didn't come across to us. I congratulated myself on having avoided him all day. He was probably, I thought, just a lonely old man who had invented the story of a proposition in order to gain my interest and lay claim to my company.

How wrong I was!


I was on time for my appointment with Petitjean on Wednesday, but he was already in the foyer and suggested we should go into the dining room straightaway. Without asking me, he ordered champagne.

'On my expense account,' he said, smiling. 'You like champagne? But of course you do! Any diplomat – even an ex-diplomat – likes champagne.'

Aware that I had never told him I had worked in the Foreign Office, I smiled in return. But my smile was false, doubtless as false as his. I was wondering who was paying his expenses and what was to come. I didn't have long to wait. As soon as we had ordered and been served and were starting on our whitebait, he came to the point.

'I'm afraid it's a matter of blackmail, Monsieur Vermont.'

'You're being blackmailed, Monsieur Petitjean?' Deliberately I misunderstood him.

Surprisingly he assented. 'I was, yes. I suppose you might say that I still am.' He sighed, gave a sad smile, and lifted his glass to me. 'Join the club, Monsieur Vermont, as you English say.'

'I don't know what you're talking about.' I shook my head in feigned bewilderment. 'You must explain yourself.'

'That is what I intend to do. First, I must tell you that we have something else in common. We both go under names that are not our own by right. As a child I was smuggled out of Russia by a French couple during the revolution, when the Bolsheviks seized power in 1917. I am older than I look – I'm over eighty. They gave me their name and brought me up as their son. But when I grew up I discovered the truth about my birth and I was jealous of their own true son. One day we were fishing, the two of us. I pushed him out of the boat and let him drown. Unfortunately for me, I was seen. For my own sake, and for the sake of the other members of the family, I couldn't allow my guilt to be known, so – I was blackmailed.'

I remained silent. I don't remember eating the whitebait, but I found my plate was empty. Waiters bustled around the table, bringing the baby veal in its exotic sauce, the vegetables, the sauté potatoes, replenishing our glasses. At last we were alone again.

'An interesting story, Monsieur Petitjean,' I said at last, surprised at the calmness of my voice, 'but one no longer relevant, I would suppose.'

'On the contrary. Some actions that I did for the first time from necessity, I have continued to carry out. The process has been a most useful source of income. You see, when my adoptive parents died they left nothing, and by then I had acquired expensive tastes – like yourself, Monsieur Vermont. Nowadays, very little is asked of me, but I remain happy to oblige my masters, as I am now doing.'

'And who are these masters of yours?' I did my best to sound amused.

'The Soviet Union and the KGB, of course. At present, I suppose that Monsieur Khrushchev is my ultimate "master", though of course I have no personal dealings with him. In fact, my only contact is with my case officer.'

The phrase struck a chord – a chilling chord. 'You mean you're a Soviet spy, Monsieur Petitjean?' I did my best to laugh aloud, but I was shocked. 'What a preposterous idea! You don't expect me to believe you?'

Petitjean didn't smile. 'Yet you would be well advised to do so, Monsieur Vermont. Incidentally, the word "spy" is pejorative. I prefer agent.'

'As you wish.'

I shrugged my shoulders and continued to eat my veal. I am sure it was delicious, but to me it tasted dry and horrible, and I had difficulty in swallowing it, just as I was having difficulty in coping with the situation. I didn't want to believe that this elderly suave-looking gentleman sitting opposite me in this elegant dining room was a Soviet spy, agent – call it what you will – and, what was more, that his intention was to recruit me. Nevertheless, I knew I had to grasp it. His story about being rescued from the Bolsheviks and drowning his adoptive parents' son was almost certainly false, but I was sure that the similarities between it and my own past were not mere coincidence. The big question was, how much did Petitjean's masters know, or, to be more exact, how much could they prove?

'What now?' Petitjean asked as we finished our entrée. 'I can recommend the chocolate pudding. Or would you prefer a sorbet?'

'Just coffee,' I said. I was beginning to feel sick. When once again we had been served and the waiters had retired, Petitjean said quietly, 'Don't worry, Monsieur Vermont, it won't be as bad as you think.'

I made a gesture of exasperation. 'Monsieur Petitjean, if the proposition you intend to put to me is that I should join in enterprises similar to those you claim for yourself, I want no part of them.'

'But unfortunately you have little choice.'

I decided to force his hand. 'Perhaps you had better be more explicit. I'm not a fool. Obviously you believe you can blackmail me. Why?'

'Because you're vulnerable. And of course I'll explain.'

And explain Petitjean did. It was Pulent's revenge. Afraid that the evidence he had collected against me at the cost of Renata's life might be stolen, Pulent had made a parcel of it, which he had given to Steve Wade. Knowing what I knew then of Pulent I suspect he had some hold over the young man and could trust him – perhaps more than he could trust Moira, because he told Steve not to mention the transaction to his mother.

This would probably have had no consequences for me, except for a chance remark of Pulent's. If it had not been for that, after Pulent was dead Steve would have opened the parcel, found a copy of *Le Grand Meaulnes*, school prize of Nigel Hawker, and ten to one he would have thrown it away as not worth the few pence a second-hand book dealer might offer for it. But in order to impress on Steve the need to take care of the parcel, Pulent had said, 'Guard it well, son. The Russians would give a mint of money for this.'

I doubt if Pulent meant anything special by this remark. I don't believe he would have dreamed of trying to sell the information to the Russians himself. It wouldn't have occurred to him; he thought in terms of comparatively small-time blackmail, not of international intrigue. Of course, Steve was in a different position. The French book was meaningless to him. He had ruffled through the pages, but had found nothing, and he couldn't imagine why the Russians would want Nigel Hawker's old school prize. Nevertheless, he accepted Pulent's words at their face value. Doubtless short of cash, he saw an excellent chance of making some money for which he would not have to account to anyone.

Steve was streetwise, but in many ways he was an innocent, and here his innocence stood him in good stead. He rewrapped the book and took it directly to the Soviet Embassy in Kensington Palace Gardens. It doesn't seem to have occurred to him that this action might cause him to become an object of suspicion either to the British or to the Russians, and he got away with it.

According to Petitjean – and of course all this was second-hand as far as I was concerned – Steve was well received at the Embassy, and was soon explaining to an official that he had something valuable to sell. I don't believe it was as simple as that in reality; he would have had to do battle with Soviet bureaucracy. But the man who eventually interviewed him was no fool, and listened attentively to what Steve had to say.

'Inevitably he had heard about Chief Inspector Pulent's unusual death, and he was intrigued by Steve's story,' said Petitjean. 'Who wouldn't have been? He examined the book, *Le Grand Meaulnes*. At first it appeared innocuous, but he noticed something that Steve had missed. The blank pages at front and back had been stuck to the covers, and possibly something had been hidden between the sheets. He took the book to another room and set to work with a pocket knife. And, *mon cher Monsieur*, I do not have to tell you what he found. You know as well as I do. Irrefutable evidence that you had an excellent motive for killing Pulent.

'Poor Steve was given fifty pounds, a fraction of what he had asked, but he was not, I trust, too disappointed, and my colleague at the Embassy was delighted. Do I have to say more, Monsieur *Hawker*?'

No, he didn't have to say any more. They had the evidence that Pulent had obtained and, though they couldn't actually prove I had killed the blackmailing Chief Inspector, they could destroy me and Imogen and the children – all the family. Nevertheless . . .

Perhaps Petitjean read my thoughts, because he said, 'This must have been a dreadful shock for you, Monsieur Vermont, so please, please don't take any drastic action. You have a good life, an attractive wife, lovely children. Don't let some misguided idea of patriotism ruin everything for you – and them. It's not worth it. We won't ask too much of you, a little information from time to time, no more. Come, you have always been a practical man. You must accept the situation.'


There's an old saying about the man who knows which side his bread is buttered, a practical man, a man out for himself. As I lay on my bed after lunch with Petitjean in that cosmopolitan, expensive Swiss hotel, I thought about my past. Bitter at not being allowed my chance to go to Oxford, I had avoided becoming Tom Hawker's dogsbody in the grocer's shop by going into the Army. I had impersonated the Flight Lieutenant, first to save my life, then to get the best possible treatment for the ghastly maiming I had suffered, and finally to ensure for myself the kind of future for which I couldn't have hoped in my wildest dreams. And to preserve that future I had killed. Yes, I was a practical man.

But I hadn't always been purely selfish. Not knowing that the Flight Lieutenant was already dead, I had gone to his rescue, which was how I had been so badly wounded, and it was chance rather than intention that had caused me to be accepted as one of the Vermonts. Nor had I just used the family. Not one of them could say

174

that. On the contrary, each of them in his or her own way had learnt to depend on me. This they found a little surprising, for they had never thought that Simon was a totally dependable character. It was at least in some measure because of this, because I had come to love them, to feel that I belonged to them, that I had been prepared to kill Pulent – himself a murderer – instead of taking my diamonds and disappearing to South America. I felt no compunction at Pulent's death, only anger that because of him I was now in this appalling position. For as Monsieur Petitjean had said, I really had no choice. All the considerations I had taken into account when faced with Pulent's blackmail were equally valid now, except that garrotting Petitjean would achieve nothing.

So I lay and mused and, perhaps because of the amount of champagne I had drunk at lunch or because of mental exhaustion, after a while I fell asleep. I was woken by Imogen and the children, full of their day's activities. And there was more champagne at dinner, a farewell gift, the maître d' explained, from Monsieur Petitjean, who had left for Paris that afternoon.

I was relieved not to have to meet him again and, for the sake of Imogen and the children, I tried hard to relax and seemingly enjoy what remained of the holiday. Petitjean had said that I would be contacted when I got back to London, so all I could do until then was wait and, as I have said before, waiting is not something I find easy.

# Interlude

*1993*

By one o'clock on Friday morning, Peter had reached the end of the second part of the book, and knew that his hopes had been destroyed and his fears almost certainly realized. He sat back in his chair, mentally exhausted, and thrust the typescript back into its file. He could take no more. He was appalled at what he had learnt. If it was all to be believed, his father was not only an impostor, but also a murderer. After that loomed the possibility that he might have become some kind of spy, a traitor; this seemed almost insignificant, he thought as he tried to reassure himself. But of course none of it was true, and surely he could disprove it.

What he had been reading was not history, nor dependent upon the memories of old men. It was his own past. In 1960 he had been thirteen and he remembered the period clearly. It had been a memorable year, a year of change, an exciting year, though not altogether a happy one.

There had been the celebration of his father's fortieth birthday, but that had been swiftly followed by his grandfather's death. Then Uncle Martin, whom he and Edward had been expecting to marry his girlfriend, had departed to live in France, which had been a surprise; it was years before they appreciated that Martin was a homosexual. The family had seemed to be disintegrating – and was it his imagination, or had his father seemed rather distraught at this time? But soon there had been the arrival of Cousin Natalie from Scotland, the summer holidays, so many other distractions. Peter wondered how much he could rely on his own memory.

Certainly there were some things he had never known. Either they had been kept from him deliberately, or at the time he had been at school, encapsulated in his own life there. He couldn't remember ever hearing of a Renata Tamson, though he presumed his father had had at least one secretary. Nor could he remember his father ever having been mugged.

He supposed that Edward might remember, but Edward, now a Lieutenant-Colonel and married to Natalie, was with his regiment in Germany, and what reason could he give for phoning to make what would seem to them trivial but curious enquiries? To some extent the same applied to Noreen; he could take her to lunch and make the questions sound fairly casual, but she had been only eight in 1960.

The obvious people to ask were his Uncle Martin and Aunt Susan, both frequently mentioned by his father in the second part of the typescript. But did he want to confide in them? Anyway, Peter thought wearily, he had better wait until he had read the whole of the wretched book before he took any irrevocable action. He didn't think there could possibly be any more unpleasant surprises, but at this hour of the morning he was prepared to believe anything; there was a limit to how much he could absorb, mentally and emotionally.

He decided to go to bed; tomorrow was another day.

It was not until he was having breakfast that Peter took in the fact that what had been tomorrow was now Friday. Gussey would be picking him up at three o'clock to drive him down to Aubyn House for the weekend. The London house would be empty. Admittedly it had a burglar alarm system, but the police were often slow to appear and if thieves or vandals broke in they would probably force the desk. The typescript would mean nothing to them and the gunmetal watch was of no intrinsic value, but they might destroy them from malice – he recalled that a month ago his neighbours across the square had suffered an enormous amount of mindless damage – and he couldn't risk losing the book, or even the watch, though he had no idea what relevance, if any, it possessed.

As soon as he thought his clerk would have arrived Peter phoned to say he would not be coming into chambers that day. Then he called a friend, Terence O'Sullivan, whom he had known at Oxford and was now a senior executive at the *Telegraph*. While he had been reading the second part of the typescript the previous evening he had made notes of certain dates, specifically those of the murder of Renata Tamson and the garrotting of Chief Inspector Pulent. He wanted to read impersonal accounts of these events, so that he might judge how accurate the typescript had been, and the only place he could think of to search for such accounts dating from thirty-odd years back was a newspaper archive.

Carrying the typescript and the watch in his briefcase he took a taxi to the *Telegraph* offices, where he spent the morning, his way smoothed in advance by O'Sullivan. He found nothing in the initial stories about the two deaths, or in the follow-ups, that disagreed with what his father had written. On the contrary! If he had been trying to put together a jigsaw puzzle the pieces would have fitted perfectly.

Disgruntled rather than disappointed, for he had had no great hopes, he took O'Sullivan out to lunch, as some recompense for the latter's efforts on his behalf. However, Peter did not forget that O'Sullivan had originally been – and probably always would be – a journalist, who would instinctively smell a good story. He had prepared his own riposte, but he thought it best to let O'Sullivan take the initiative.

O'Sullivan didn't disappoint him. They had scarcely finished ordering when he said, 'Simon, I'm filled with curiosity. Why this sudden interest in old murders?'

'Not just any old murders, Terry; old unsolved murders, such as "The Garrotte Affair", for example. They're fascinating. One of these days when I have some spare time I propose to collect them into a book.'

Terry looked his disbelief, but Peter ignored it. He knew that a good lie should be kept simple and not elaborated. He tasted his lobster bisque and nodded his head in approval. 'Good,' he said. Then, resisting the temptation to change the subject he waited for O'Sullivan to comment.

'I've read about "The Garrotte Affair",' O'Sullivan said. 'It was a bizarre case. The police chap who was done turned out to be a blackmailer, didn't he?'

'Apparently. The theory is that one of his victims put an end to him. All kinds of individuals were questioned, including some quite well-known figures, such as Sir Dennis Cartwright. Ever heard of him?'

'Of course. The politician. Wasn't he Father of the House before he retired?'

'That's right. Unfortunately from my point of view the people who were questioned are mostly dead by now. I know that Cartwright is. I remember reading his obituary.'

'So you're largely dependent on newspapers and official records. Have you thought of biographies and memoirs? Politicians, retired or otherwise, love getting into print.'

'Good idea, Terry!'

And indeed it was. What was more, it hadn't occurred to Peter and proved well worth the price of the lunch in the little restaurant O'Sullivan had recommended.

Having said goodbye and agreed to meet again soon, Peter went straight to the London Library in St James's Square; luckily he was a member. Yes, Dennis Cartwright had written his memoirs and he had been considerate enough to provide an index. There were references to 'The Garrotte Affair' and, though in no way connected with it, to Sir Simon Vermont.

The comments on Simon Vermont were very flattering. Cartwright expressed great regret that ill health had forced him to retire before he had had the chance to reach his full potential and become Foreign Secretary, or even Prime Minister. It had been a considerable loss to the country.

Peter shook his head in self-disgust. Here was an impartial assessment of his father, the Simon Vermont that the public had known, that his friends and family had accepted. But was it a true picture of the man, or was it a myth? Simon's son, Peter thought bitterly, couldn't make up his mind.

He next looked up 'The Garrotte Affair'. Sir Dennis had nothing to add to the newspaper accounts of the crime, but he devoted several paragraphs to his questioning by the police as a possible victim of a blackmailer. He mentioned consulting a 'fellow MP', who had also been interviewed by Chief Inspector Pulent after having been attacked in the street. This was a clear reference to Simon Vermont, and yet another indication that Simon's book was fact, not fiction.


It was with a heavy heart that Peter went down to Aubyn House for the weekend, still carrying his briefcase. It was not unusual for him to have to study briefs at weekends, and no one would think it strange if he were to retire to his study. He had every intention of reading the final section of Simon's typescript before Monday.

THE BOOK

# Part Three

*1980–81*

# CHAPTER NINETEEN

'Hello, Simon. Happy New Year! Happy decade!'

The year was 1980, the speaker William Trevil. William was a mathematics don at Oxford. He was two years older than I, which meant that in a few months, when I was sixty, he would be sixty-two. He was not an attractive-looking man – short and thin, with sloping shoulders and a big head that appeared unbalanced on his small frame. In addition, he wore thick spectacles. It was this poor eyesight that had saved him from the services in the Second World War; instead, having obtained a brilliant First Class degree, he had gone to work on codes and ciphers at the so-called Government Communications Establishment at Bletchley Park, where Susan had also been employed.

I had known William for almost twenty years, and we got on well together. William was my Control. On my return from our family skiing holiday in Switzerland in the January of '61, I had waited to be contacted as Monsieur Petitjean had said I would be – and waited. My masters-to-be let me stew. It was not until the end of March, shortly before the Easter recess, that William had phoned me for the first time. He said that he would be in London the following week and would be delighted to give me lunch. I was slightly surprised until he mentioned that he was a colleague of Claude Petitjean. At once any hope I might have had that the KGB had decided not to use me disappeared.

In spite of his appearance, William had what is sometimes called charisma, and although he had never married, this, I am sure, was from choice. Unlike me he was a committed communist. He despised democracy, which he considered a sham, and he held the view that what was wrong with communism was not the system, but the people who would not co-operate with it. We had many an argument about this general subject, and about his extravagant lifestyle, which seemed to me to be contrary to his supposed principles. He always took such comments in good part.

We only met rarely, usually in London, but sometimes in Oxford. Our relationship was intended to appear casual, and I never invited him to Aubyn House. On the occasion of our first meeting when he took me to the Savoy, we came to a number of amicable arrangements. Most concerned meets and 'drops' and communications. He agreed that he would not telephone me at home unless he had failed to get me at my Westminster offices and the need to speak to me was urgent. If there was an emergency he would mention 'our mutual friend, Claude'. If Claude was ill, which Heaven forbid, it was a dire emergency.

In other circumstances I would have laughed, as one laughs at schoolboy antics, but William was serious, and Claude became a name that was to haunt me over the years. Not that we had many emergencies. After all, I was never asked to steal vital plans or commit an act of sabotage or even disclose murky secrets about any of my colleagues. Indeed, I sometimes thought that the information I provided could have been obtained more easily from an intelligent study of the daily press and periodicals such as *The Economist*.

William disagreed. He assured me that the material I produced was invaluable, providing a reliable rather than a merely journalistic insight into the Government's views on important matters, such as the Cabinet's reaction to the Americans' abortive attempt to overthrow Castro in the 'Bay of Pigs' disaster, and the subsequent crisis over the Soviet missiles intended for Cuba. Heaven knows if he was right, but I could see his point.

Those were early days. As China exploded its first atomic bomb and Harold Wilson became Prime Minister, I was retired to the Opposition Front Bench. But fortunes change rapidly in politics and I was a survivor. When Margaret Thatcher came to power in May 1979, I became one of her favourites, and by 1980 I was marked down as the next Foreign Secretary.

There's an old song I remember: 'Everything's Going My Way'. I am not sure if that was its title but that was its theme, and in 1980 when William phoned to wish me a Happy New Year and a happy decade, I believed it. Everything did seem to be going my way.

The children – except that they were no longer children – were all doing well. Peter, a rising young barrister, and his wife Julia had given us two healthy grandsons. Colonel and Mrs Edward Vermont had produced a pretty daughter, and Natalie was pregnant again. Noreen, now engaged to a literary agent, had just had her first book of children's stories accepted by a reputable house. Imogen and I were very proud of them all.

At Christmas and other occasions, Aubyn House overflowed with family, but it was never empty at other times. Guy had retired and he and Susan lived permanently in one wing. Imogen and I spent as much of our time in the country as we could, and even when the House was sitting we drove down at weekends; over the years Imogen and I had grown very close. And our children and grandchildren came and went, as did Martin. I often thought how lucky we, the Vermonts, all were, and if I had had to pay a high price for this happiness, I couldn't regret it.

On reflection, I suppose I knew it couldn't last for ever, and I had had a good run. Nevertheless, when the blow fell it came as an almighty shock. I had weathered crises before with William, but they had all been minor; Claude had been said to be 'not too well' or 'a bit infirm', and I must admit that these references to Monsieur Petitjean who, if he were not dead, would be over a hundred by now, no longer seemed to me absurd.

It was the spring of 1980. The Easter recess was over and the House was sitting again. I was extremely busy. When my secretary – a young girl straight from Cambridge University and a business school, who had aspirations towards becoming an MP – informed me the moment I arrived in my Ministry office that a Professor William Trevil had telephoned urgently; I accepted this information calmly. She liked to make the ordinary sound exceptional.

'He said he'd try you at home,' she continued, 'but I told him you'd probably be on your way here by now.'

'Did he leave any message?' I asked.

'Only to tell you that he needed to contact you urgently. Your mutual friend Claude – Claude – '

'Petitjean,' I prompted.

'Yes. Claude Petitjean is seriously ill. He's not expected to live.'

I turned my back on her and made a big show of looking for something I had dropped on the floor. I had never before received such an urgent, almost desperate, message from William. This must indeed be a crisis of some dimensions, but I couldn't imagine what it might be.

'Did he leave a phone number?'

'Yes.'

She picked a slip of paper from my in-tray and passed it to me. I recognized the number. It was that of William's club, the Oxford and Cambridge in Pall Mall, where he stayed when he was in London. At least this was normal, I thought. I was determined not to panic.

'Good. I'll call him now.'

I nodded my dismissal and she went. For a minute I sat motionless, then I dialled an outside line to the club. There was a pause while the porter fetched William.

'Simon, this is grave news. Very grave.' His voice was hoarse. 'You got my message? Claude is seriously ill. He's not expected to live. We should meet at once, though I'm damned if I know what we can do about it.'

'That is bad news, William. Yes, of course we must meet.' I was thinking quickly. I was due at Number Ten in half an hour, and I had no idea how long the meeting with the PM would last. 'William, I'm very busy this morning, but – '

'To hell with that! I need to talk to you, Simon. I must!'

William had never spoken to me in that tone of voice before, and I was taken aback. It was obvious that he was badly rattled, and that was unheard of, too. I felt the muscles of my stomach tighten in fear. What had happened? What might happen? I wanted to shout at him to tell me, but that was impossible on the phone.

'William, I will be with you at your club at one o'clock, if not before. Is that all right? You'll wait for me there?'

I could almost imagine the little man squaring his narrow shoulders and gritting his teeth. Then suddenly he cackled with laughter, startling me, and I wondered if he had been drinking, early in the day as it was.

'Sure, I'll wait for you, Simon. I don't suppose an hour or two matters a damn. I think poor old Claude has had it. The question is whether he's buried deep in the ground or gets cremated, with his ashes scattered all over. It could be important, old boy.'

To my relief at that point he put down his receiver. I was certain now that he had been drinking and I was horrified at the thought of what indiscretions he might commit. But there was nothing I could do about it. I couldn't cut the Downing Street meeting. Somehow I had to get through the rest of the morning.

★

It was ten past one when I reached the Oxford and Cambridge Club. William was waiting for me in the hall, and I was glad to see that at least he didn't look drunk. I was not a member, but he had already signed me in as his guest, and I at once agreed with his suggestion that we should go straight in to lunch.

The dining room at the Oxford and Cambridge is a huge, cavernous room that has always struck me as being unfriendly, not least because of the many single tables with their brass supports for books with which those taking a meal alone might entertain themselves. Anyway, today I was thankful for its cathedral-like atmosphere, which seemed to discourage conviviality, and as William had secured a table in a corner our privacy was ensured.

As soon as we were seated and William had written down our orders on the pads that many London clubs provide for this purpose, I said, 'William, there's obviously a crisis. What is it?'

'Ivan Sokalov.'

The name was vaguely familiar to me, but I couldn't place it. William gave me what I can only describe as a strange smile, and at that moment the waiter returned to verify what William had written, his cramped script being almost indecipherable. I waited impatiently until we were alone again.

'Who is this Sokalov, William, and what is he to us?'

'Our undoing. Yours and mine. We've never talked much about the organization we both work for; you haven't asked questions and I've avoided the subject. But Sokalov is – was – a senior officer of the KGB. He is – was – what you might call the big boss who oversaw operations in the UK, and possibly France and other countries, for all I know.'

William stopped and took a gulp of wine. He hadn't touched his soup. He was sweating badly and his hands were shaking.

'You corrected yourself twice – "is" to "was".'

'Yes. He has defected. That's the point. I had a phone call from a friend first thing this morning, warning me that Sokalov had apparently just come over to the British, and was on his way to London. It seems he was at an international conference in Paris, ostensibly as a delegate, but more probably to meet an important contact. At any rate he simply took a taxi to the rue St Honoré and presented himself at the British Embassy.'

'Do you know if he brought any papers with him?'

'A few, I'd guess. Probably not many, but his head will be stuffed

189

with names and dates and general information. He'll be greeted in London with open arms. He's a great catch for British Intelligence.'

A waiter hovered, and William waved away his untouched soup, and, while the entrée was being served, I had a moment to absorb what had been said. I could imagine the reactions in various Departments of the FCO and the Intelligence community here. Frantic activity. The implications were appalling. It seemed that once again my whole life and that of the Vermont family were being threatened. But I wasn't going under without a fight and the first essential was to calm William – for my own sake as much as his – since if he broke down he would certainly implicate me.

'How much would Sokalov know? He knows about you, of course, but would he know of the agents you've recruited or you're running? I imagine everything is pretty compartmentalized, in your own interest as much as anyone else's. Would he have heard of me, for example?'

'It varies, Simon. He'd know of some of my recruits, but your case is different. You weren't a recruit. You weren't set-up deliberately. You –'

'I know. I wasn't a volunteer. I'm neither a believer in the great cause, nor have I sought money. I was an accidental victim, a gift from the Gods to the KGB. Perhaps not quite a gift. I cost them a miserable fifty pounds, the sum they gave Steve Wade to whom Jim Pulent had entrusted the evidence against me. Anyway, if I wasn't unique, I was at least unusual.'

'Which means there'll be a pretty fat file on you in Moscow, I'm afraid,' said William. 'I think you must take it that you're compromised.'

'All right,' I said. 'It looks black, but let's not panic. There may not be that much of a hurry. Think of it from the British point of view. Even if this so-called KGB man – this "walk-in" to the Embassy – is now in England and has been escorted to a "safe house", his processing will take some time. For all MI5 know he might be a double agent; at least they've got to exclude the possibility. He certainly won't be trusted and believed immediately. It will take days to interrogate him in depth, and no one's going to take action against a Member of Parliament or a respected Oxford professor on the say-so of a defector, who might not be genuine. I guess that, even if he is accepted, it will take at least a week, possibly more, before either of us are approached. So we've got time to consider what we can do.'

By now William had become considerably calmer, and was listening intently. I went on.

'First you, because you and I are not in the same position, William. This chap – we'll call him Ivan, it's simpler – will name you. You're sure of that. So you'll be questioned. You could try denying everything. You could point out that as a mathematics don you have no secrets to sell, that the accusation is absurd.'

'Simon, I see your point, but Sokalov will be able to cite chapter and verse to prove I've been running agents in this country for years, that I've subverted and recruited undergraduates and – and – this may not be the Soviet Union, but MI5 are not kind, charitable chaps who give you the benefit of the doubt. Some say their interrogators are the best in the business. They may not torture you, as supposedly happens in Lubyanka, but they question you day and night, in relays, so you don't get any sleep. I – I couldn't stand up to that, Simon.'

I think that at that moment I understood William Trevil better than I had ever done before. I had met him originally as the man who was to control me, a committed communist, whom I had every reason to dislike. But he had won me over. He had been as considerate as could be. We found that we had much in common and could share the same jokes. Gradually I had become fond of him, but I had always been aware that our relationship was not that of equals.

Now, as I watched him blow his nose in order to hide the two large tears that had rolled down his cheeks from behind his thick spectacles, I realized that the situation had changed. William was as vulnerable as I was. Perhaps he might be said to have less to lose than I had, but being a spymaster had been his ultimate ambition. He had enjoyed his secret life and the power it had given him over individuals such as myself. Once this was taken from him, he was no more than an ageing don, unmarried, unattractive, and afraid of the very real possibility of a long prison sentence.

'William, there is an alternative,' I said gently, as if I had been reading his thoughts.

'What? Kill Sokalov before he has time to spill any beans?' William was bitter. 'We haven't a clue where he's been taken and he'll be well guarded. You don't think –'

'No!' I exclaimed. 'That's not a practical proposition, and it's not the alternative I meant. William, you've no wife or children or anyone dependent on you. Why don't you up sticks and make for Moscow yourself? There shouldn't be any difficulty if you act fairly quickly. A night ferry to France, hire a car, drive to Vienna, contact the Soviet Embassy there about a visa and take a plane. You've served the Party faithfully for years, and I'm sure you'd be made welcome in Moscow. The Russians have a reputation for being good to their own.'

'Yes – yes, I know, but – ' William pushed his food around his plate and absent-mindedly ate a mouthful. 'Simon, I'm almost sixty-two. I've lived in Oxford practically all my adult life. I don't think I could bear to live anywhere else.'

'William – '

'Yes, I know, Simon. It may be flight – or go to prison. You're right.' Suddenly he began to eat quickly. 'What about you?'

'As I said, we're not in the same position. I have a wife and family. I'm not and never have been a Communist. I've served the KGB because I had no choice, because I was blackmailed, because it was either that or ruin – even the possibility of being hanged. The death penalty wasn't abolished here until 1965, remember.' I managed to grin. 'Whatever happens now, William, I've gained twenty years of the good life and my children are grown up.'

'Yes, I suppose it was worth it from your point of view. I don't think I could have done it, sacrificed all my beliefs, but – '

'Oh, I'm not as highly principled as you are,' I said, and meant it; neither of us saw any humour in these remarks. 'I'm a practical man, William, like most politicians.'

'You're more than just a politician, Simon. You're a senior man, a Minister. As such you'd certainly be welcomed in Moscow, regardless of the – the pressure they brought to bear on you origi-nally, or your private beliefs. And, as you said, your family's grown up. Perhaps your wife would join you. It would be a practical solu-tion for you too, surely.'

I nodded agreement that I did not feel. I had no intention of going to Moscow. A plan which had lain dormant at the back of my mind – after all, there had always been the possibility that this or a similar situation might arise – was beginning to take positive shape. But it was not a plan I intended to share with William.

★

After lunch I took William to Paddington in a taxi and saw him on to the Oxford train. He wasn't drunk, but he wasn't quite sober either. However, our conversation seemed to have cured him of the worst of his panic, and I was pretty sure that by the time he arrived at his destination he would be able to cope.

Fortunately the train was half-empty. William found a corner seat in an empty carriage, but before he got into it he turned to me and held out his hand.

'Goodbye,' he said. 'This may be the last time – unless they catch up with us and interrogate us together.' He smiled. 'No hard feelings?'

'No hard feelings,' I replied.

# CHAPTER TWENTY

'Isn't this cosy?' Susan said. 'All us oldies having a nice quiet pre-lunch drink together on a Sunday, with not a child underfoot or a neighbour in sight.'

'Oldies be damned,' said Guy. 'I'm not seventy yet, and I'm the oldest of those present.'

'Middle-aged, then.' Susan corrected herself. 'Our own generation, and just family. Not the usual Sunday gathering.'

I knew what she meant. Much as I loved the children and the grand-children, it was pleasant not to have any of them around for once, or any neighbours, especially when I was so worried about the future.

It was the weekend after William Trevil had exploded his Sokalov bombshell; I knew nothing about what might have happened since then. We were in the morning room of Aubyn House. Susan, Martin, Imogen and I had been to church, in accordance with the Vermont tradition. Guy had stayed at home, pleading an incipient cold, though I suspect he wanted to get on with his current work, for he was still producing his abstruse books. And, during the service, I had taken the opportunity to pray wholeheartedly, if with little expectation that my prayer would be answered, that 'whatever gods may be' would save them, the innocent, if not me, the guilty.

'Another sherry?' Imogen asked. 'We might as well make the most of our peace and quiet. It doesn't happen often, which is probably good for all of us.'

I started to make a second round with the decanter, and came to Martin. He was busy reading the *Sunday Times*, but held out his glass to me.

I had just poured his drink when he turned to Guy. 'Guy,' he said, 'do you know a chap called William Trevil, a maths professor? You should. He's in your college.'

'Sure, Martin,' said Guy. 'A funny little man with a huge head that always threatens to unbalance him.' He laughed, but not unkindly and went on, 'Very bright, or so I'm told, but not in my line. We meet in the Senior Common Room, and I sat next to him at High Table not long ago. Why do you ask?'

Intent on what he was reading, Martin didn't answer immediately, and with great care I replaced the decanter on the side table. I had nearly dropped it when Martin mentioned William's name. I had at once assumed the news would concern William's detention, if not arrest. I had thought that the authorities would take no action for several days, not until MI5 were convinced that Sokalov was a genuine defector. But it seemed I had been wrong.

'What's happened to him?' I asked, hoping I sounded suitably casual.

'Ah, yes. You know him too, Simon, don't you?' said Guy.

'We had rooms on the same staircase my first year at Oxford,' I said. 'Then I bumped into him some years later, and we've had the occasional lunch together. Do you remember him, Susan? He was at Bletchley during the war.'

'Frankly, no,' she said. 'Anyway, what's he done? Why is he in the news? Don't keep us in suspense any longer, Martin.'

'He's hanged himself.'

'Hanged himself?' I repeated stupidly.

'Yes. Evidently he took a rope up to the college bell tower and attached it to a beam. He was found by a porter when the bell failed to ring properly.'

'My God! Poor devil!' Guy said.

'Poor man!' Imogen said. 'How very sad! Does it say why he did it? Did he leave a note?'

I felt the bile rise in my throat as I waited for Martin's answer. I swallowed hard. I blamed myself bitterly. It had never crossed my mind that William might commit suicide. I suppose it should have done, but I had thought that, when he got back to Oxford and had time to consider the situation soberly, he would accept that the only practical course for him was to go to Moscow. Once again, I had been wrong.

'Yes. Apparently he did leave a note,' Martin said, 'but it doesn't explain much. It merely said that he was sorry and that he couldn't go on. However, one of his colleagues said that he'd been depressed lately and complained of not feeling too well. Maybe he had an inoperable malignant tumour or something.'

'Really, Martin! What an idea,' Imogen protested.

'It happens,' said Guy.

195

It was an idea or the facsimile of one that was to occur to someone else.

A short time after supper that evening, while we were having coffee, I was called to the telephone. It wouldn't be right to say that I had forgotten about William, but he certainly wasn't uppermost in my mind at that moment.

'Hello,' I said. 'Simon Vermont here.'

'This is Claudia.'

It was a harsh voice, with a slight foreign accent that I couldn't place, and anyhow I didn't know any Claudias. 'Claudia?' I queried. 'Claudia?'

'Claudia Petitjean, a colleague of William's. Are you alone?'

'Yes.'

'Then we'll take it this line is safe – unless you want to go out and find a call box.'

I hesitated. 'That would be difficult. Let's take a chance.'

'All right. Well, you've heard about William?' She sounded impatient, as if I were a backward pupil.

'Yes. His death was reported in the newspapers,' I said carefully. 'I'm very sorry –'

'You should not be. It is most convenient. There is too much he could have spilt if he'd tried to save himself by turning Queen's evidence. For example, he would have been the chief witness against you, and there are others he could have involved.'

I decided to face the issue squarely. 'And would it be "most convenient" if I followed William's example?' I asked. 'Or will this be arranged for me – as it was arranged for William?'

'Don't be stupid, Mr Vermont!' was the immediate reply. 'You can do us no harm, but you can help yourself. Lie low and take no action. However, if you are questioned about William, which is likely, say that when you had lunch with him last week he was depressed, and he told you that he believed he had cancer. You assume that was why he killed himself.'

'Cancer?' I was thinking of Martin's suggestion of an inoperable tumour.

'Yes! Cancer! Do you understand?'

I hesitated. Then: 'Yes, I understand.'

'Right. You're on your own now. Goodbye – and good luck.'

The line went dead, and I put down my receiver. I had taken the call in my study and for several minutes I sat staring at the empty top of my desk. It was difficult to think logically, but I did my best to recall the exact words of the conversation I had just had with this woman who had called herself Claudia Petitjean. What had I learnt?

I had learnt what I was to do – lie low and take no action unless I were questioned, when I was to say William had cancer. That sounded simple, but would probably not be so simple in practice. And there was a great deal that I had not learnt, or that was ambiguous. I didn't know if William had taken his own life or been killed. I didn't know if Ivan Sokalov was a genuine defector, or when or even if he had defected to the British in Paris. I didn't know – and I would have given a lot to know – what the woman had meant by saying that I was on my own now, and wishing me goodbye and good luck.

Heaving a sigh, I returned to the drawing room where the family was gathered. I detested lying to them, but sometimes it was necessary.

'Nothing important,' I said. 'A meeting I have to chair tomorrow has been brought forward an hour. Incidentally, the secretary who phoned to tell me said her husband knew William Trevil and had heard he had cancer.'

'Cancer?' repeated Martin. 'That's what I suggested might be his reason for killing himself.'

'Yes,' I said. I didn't want to discuss William. 'Imogen, is there any more coffee?'

She lifted the pot as if to weigh it. 'Yes, of course. Lots more. What time will you be leaving tomorrow morning, Simon, now your meeting's been changed?'

'Nine o'clock approx,' I said, and blessed her. She was always very quick to sense my wishes, sometimes too quick. 'Are you coming with me?'

And we began to discuss the coming week.


I left Aubyn House the next morning soon after nine. I was feeling extremely despondent, and as I got into the car I had to resist a temptation to look back at the house. I knew that I might never see it again.

Imogen had decided not to come up to London until the middle of the week, but Martin was with me. I had promised to take him to Heathrow so that he could catch a flight to France, and we had no time to spare. I drove fast. In spite of my game leg, I enjoy driving. It would have been one of the disadvantages of being Foreign Secretary, I thought, always to have an official driver, and always to have a security officer in attendance. I smiled wryly as I realized I had relegated the possibility of my ever becoming Secretary of State for Foreign and Commonwealth Affairs to the area reserved for 'might have beens'. I no longer believed it was a reasonable possibility in the future.

'What's amusing you?' Martin asked.

'Nothing really,' I said. 'But it's a lovely day, isn't it?'

Martin agreed dubiously, though indeed it was a perfect spring day, grey-blue sky, white clouds, balmy breeze. We had reached the motorway by now and I concentrated on the road ahead and the traffic, which luckily was fairly light, but I was aware of Martin studying me. I guessed he was working himself up to say something that he thought important.

'Simon –' he began.

'Yes?' I said, hoping to encourage him. Martin had changed over the years. He was no longer the lean harassed army officer he used to be. He had grown plump on his partner's good French cooking, and had the air of a contented man. I envied him. 'What is it?' I said. 'Trouble?'

'That's just what I wanted to ask you, Simon, but you're not exactly easy to question. I know you cope with our problems, and always have, but you don't share your own – and never have. You're a very self-contained person. But – what I'm trying to say is: if you do have a problem and I can help in any way, I will.'

I tried to laugh, but the sound that emerged was more like a croak, and I had to clear my throat before I could speak. 'My dear Martin, that was a long speech,' I said, and hated myself for sounding patronizing. 'And I appreciate your offer, but what makes you think I've got a problem?'

'Because you've been terribly low-spirited and absent-minded this weekend – what Nanny Petticoat used to call "glumpy" when we were kids.'

'I'm sorry. I wasn't aware of it.' I spoke tightly.

When Martin didn't respond, I gritted my teeth and put my foot on the accelerator. I overtook a couple of lorries and then a car started to draw out in front of me. It had given reasonable warning, and if I had been paying more attention and not driving so fast I could have braked without any trouble. As it was, I had no choice if I were to avoid an accident that would have been my own silly fault. I hooted violently, accelerated again and slipped past with inches to spare. There was a squeal of brakes behind me and angry hooting. I didn't blame the drivers.

'Dear God!' Martin said. 'Are you trying to kill us?'

'Sorry,' I mumbled.

'It's not like you to try such a damn fool manoeuvre.' He was clearly shaken.

'No,' I agreed. 'I'm truly sorry, Martin.'

For a while we continued in silence. I had been shaken too, but the incident had sharpened my wits. It was clear that, so wrapped in my own worries as not to be aware of my mood, I had behaved badly during the weekend, in the sense that Martin had described. I had aroused curiosity, and I wondered if Martin had been delegated by the family to question me.

'Look, Martin,' I said at last. 'I haven't mentioned it because I didn't want to worry anyone, especially Imogen – as you know she's a little inclined to fuss over me – but my health's not been too good recently.'

'What do you mean by "not too good", Simon? For Heaven's sake, tell me. Is it serious?'

'I hope not, but I'm going to have a complete check-up to make sure. It's probably just overwork and general stress.'

I invented some symptoms, shortage of breath and dizzy spells, and asked Martin to promise to keep the information to himself – a promise he gave somewhat reluctantly. In return he made me promise that I would let him know when I had the results of the examination and any tests that were made, and he urged me to come and stay with him in France for a good rest as soon as I could get away. I was touched by his genuine concern. I only wished that my problem was of a kind that could be solved by a long, restful holiday.

I dropped Martin off at Heathrow and drove on to my house. I wanted to back up my lies to Martin and therefore telephoned my London doctor – one of the few remaining 'private' general practitioners – to ask for an appointment as soon as possible. His secretary said he had had a cancellation and could see me that afternoon. This was satisfactory for, Martin apart, it suited the plan I was formulating which demanded that doubts about my general health should be raised and substantiated.

Clement Brune was an excellent doctor and a highly successful one, but he was also something of a snob. I had rarely been ill over the years, and he hadn't often had occasion to treat me, but I was aware that he liked to have me as a patient. He was a dreadful name-dropper, and mine was more than acceptable – at least at present. I hoped it would continue to be.

With the prospect of some action to alleviate the waiting, my depression had lifted. I had a light lunch at my club, but drank a couple of large brandies in the hope that they would raise my blood pressure. My knowledge of medicine was modest, but I had learnt some tricks in the Army, and Brune wouldn't be expecting tricks. I had decided to counterfeit asthma. I had known a boy at school who had suffered from it, and before leaving for Brune's consulting rooms in Harley Street had had time to refresh my memory about the symptoms from a popular medical encyclopaedia in the club's library. It was a complaint that affected people in many different ways, and was not too difficult to simulate.

When I arrived at Brune's address I was pleased to find that the waiting room, which was shared by the several doctors who had suites of rooms in the building, was empty. I jogged hard on the spot, until Brune's nurse-cum-secretary came for me.

'My dear Simon, how nice to see you. I trust this isn't a serious visit?'

'That's what I'm hoping you'll tell me, Clement.'

He had come forward from behind his long mahogany desk to offer me his hand, but he withdrew it quickly. He was a fastidious man and I was sweating. He looked at me anxiously, and obligingly I drew a couple of deep breaths and made what I imagined were authentic wheezing sounds.

'Sit down, Simon, and tell me what the trouble is,' Brune said, becoming more professional.

I sat and regarded the elegant figure on the other side of the desk. I don't want to give a false impression. As I said before, Clement Brune was a good doctor, a very competent and conscientious general practitioner, which is all he claimed to be. Moreover, he always knew the right specialist to whom his patients should be referred if necessary. But I didn't want to see a consultant, so I was careful not to overdo my symptoms.

Brune pulled my file towards him, and took notes as I explained my 'trouble'.

'This dry cough you mention, does it bother you much?'

'No. I've had it for ages, but the breathlessness is increasing and as I was telling you I had a bad attack last weekend, when I found I was literally gasping for air. Quite frightening.'

'And you've no idea what brought it on?'

'No. I've never had anything like it in the country before. In fact, I've not been so bad before anywhere – at least not since the Sixties when we had that awful smog in London.'

There were more questions and more answers. I was asked to strip and was given a thorough examination. Brune frowned over my blood pressure, and his nurse took some blood samples. Then when I was dressed again Brune suggested I should have allergy tests, but he was not optimistic about them, and I said I'd prefer to wait for the moment.

We parted on good terms, Brune promising to let me know when he had the results of my blood tests, and I went straight from Harley Street to Westminster, where I found my secretary had left me a message.

A Mr Paul Quade of MI5 had telephoned and would I please return the call as soon as possible. It indeed appeared to be true that the security people were acting more quickly than I had expected, and I was glad that I too had taken some action.

# CHAPTER TWENTY-ONE

I arrived at the unmarked house in Belgravia at eleven o'clock the next morning. After the usual formalities at the security barrier – identification, issuing chits, and so on – I was escorted to Mr Quade's office. He rose from behind his desk to greet me, but didn't offer his hand.

'Good of you to come, sir,' he said, as if I'd had any kind of choice.

He waved me to a chair and it didn't escape my notice that while he had his back to the window, I was facing the light. Furthermore, my chair was a fraction too low, which made it impossible for me to sit in complete comfort, and was presumably intended to place me in a disadvantageous position. I thought all this was a mistake on Mr Quade's part, for it was an overt demonstration that in his opinion I was in fact not the highly respected Minister prepared to do him a favour, which was how he had treated me on the telephone, but someone to be regarded with suspicion.

I laid my stick on the carpet beside me and stretched out my game leg so that my built-up shoe was visible. I felt that somehow I had gained a small advantage by reminding him of my history.

'Well, now that I'm here, Mr Quade, what can I do for you?' I asked pleasantly. I had no wish to antagonize him. 'You wouldn't tell me what it was about on the phone, and I'm full of curiosity.'

Quade smiled. He was a small man, very upright, and I guessed that he had once been in the Army. I put his age at around fifty, not much younger than myself, and thought that probably his early background had not been dissimilar to mine, though he would have been too young for the war. But I didn't underrate him; I was sure he was dangerous.

'We're checking up on your friend, Professor William Trevil, or to be more exact, the late Professor.'

'Yes. Poor William!' I shook my head. I had no intention of denying William, which was probably what Quade had hoped I would do. 'But – but why, for Heaven's sake? What has William got to do with security? Or – ' I stared at Quade accusingly, ' – was he working for you?'

'He most certainly was not! In strict confidence, sir, we believe it's possible he was working for the KGB.'

'William? Oh, come, Mr Quade. I don't believe it. What on earth had he got to give or sell? He'd long stopped producing any original work.'

'Recruitment, Mr Vermont. He was in an excellent position to recruit members of his university to his cause, and he had friends in high places – yourself included, sir.'

'He never tried to recruit me, I assure you! Frankly, Mr Quade, I think this is a dreadful accusation to throw at a dead man. I can only suppose you have some evidence to support your claim.'

'All I said, sir, was that there was a *possibility*. I haven't actually accused Professor Trevil of working for the Soviet Union.'

'I'm glad to hear it!' I saw no reason to hide my annoyance.

'Perhaps you'd tell me when you first met Professor Trevil, and how well you knew him, sir.'

'With pleasure.'

I gave him the same story as I had given the family at the weekend. Quade didn't interrupt me. He played with a pencil on his desk and appeared uninterested, as if he had known what I was about to say.

'Professor Trevil came up to London to see you last Wednesday, sir,' he said as I finished.

'You seem pretty well informed about William Trevil's movements and intentions,' I remarked. 'Have you been keeping him under surveillance and tapping his phone? If so, I hope you had a warrant.' As a matter of fact, I thought it most unlikely that they had been able to act with such rapidity. Sokalov had defected in Paris early in the morning and we had met for lunch later that same day. Unless, of course, William had been under suspicion for some time . . . However, I thought I might as well try to assert my authority.

Then, when Quade didn't reply, I went on, 'And in any case you're quite wrong. Certainly William came up to London last Wednesday, but *not*, I am sure, expressly to see me.'

'Did he say what his other business might be?'

'Mr Quade, Professor Trevil had no *business*, as such, with me. Please don't put words in my mouth. He phoned and suggested we meet for lunch, as he sometimes did when he was in town. We lunched at his club, the Oxford and Cambridge. It was a casual social occasion and, to answer your question, I gathered that his reason for coming to London was to consult with a specialist. He was worried about his health.'

'What was the matter with him?'

'I think that's a question you should get his medical advisers to answer, but he told me he was afraid he might have cancer. I must say I assumed that was why he took his own life, but I could be wrong. As far as medical opinion is concerned, his College should know the name of his general practitioner; I'm afraid I don't. Nor the name of his consultant in London.'

Again, Quade made no direct comment. 'Was he upset that day, sir?' he enquired.

'What do you expect? His consultant's immediate verdict had not been entirely satisfying, and he was awaiting certain tests and their outcome. Yes, he *was* upset.' I thought it probable that Quade had already been to the Oxford and Cambridge, and knew of William's behaviour. 'He didn't eat much and he drank a lot. I was rather late in getting to the club – I'd been with the Prime Minister – and William had clearly had several drinks before I arrived, which is why after lunch I took him to Paddington and saw him on to his train.'

'That was kind of you, sir. And he never contacted you again?'

I shook my head, and Quade stood up. The interview was over. He thanked me for my help and expressed the hope that he hadn't inconvenienced me too much. I assured him he hadn't, but that his insinuations about Professor Trevil had worried me.

'Oh, I shouldn't worry, sir. There's probably nothing in it, but we do have to look into any suspicious circumstances that might affect the security of the State. That's our job, you know.'

'Yes, of course,' I said, and added, perhaps injudiciously. 'If you look into every suicide you must be kept busy.'

Quade laughed politely. 'Come along, sir. I'll see you out.'

I picked up my stick and got to my feet, and he waved me ahead of him. I expected him to take me to the lift, but he came right down to the front door and through the barrier with me. However, he again avoided shaking hands.

'Goodbye for now, sir,' he said.

And as I limped down the quiet Belgravia street in search of a cab,

I wondered if there was any significance in those four words. It was a common enough phrase, and didn't necessarily mean that you expected to meet again the individual you were addressing, but I wished that Quade hadn't used it.

I picked up a taxi and, relaxing in the back, went through the interview with Quade in my mind. I had kept very close to the truth, and I didn't think he could fault me on what I had said. There was one flaw, perhaps. If they had really been keeping William under surveillance, they would have known he had not been to see a specialist.

Of course, the fact that Quade had wanted to question me at all about William was extremely disconcerting. There could be no doubt now that Sokalov had tried to incriminate, presumably among others, not only William, but also myself, and, at the moment, there was no means of knowing how far he had succeeded. Unfortunately, even if Sokalov had merely started a hare, Quade didn't strike me as a man who would give up a case before he had solved it to his own satisfaction.

By now we had reached my house. I paid off the taxi, went up the steps and put my key in the lock. Then, hand outstretched towards the doorknob, I stopped.

I was back in Quade's office. He had come around his desk and was waving me to lead the way out. It had seemed a natural gesture at the time and I hadn't hesitated, but as I saw my own brass doorknob I realized that the knob on that office door had also been brightly polished metal, and I must have left an excellent set of my fingerprints on it.

Was this chance, or had the knob been especially polished in advance for my benefit? It was useless to guess. I had given my prints voluntarily to the CID after Renata's murder and had been told they had subsequently been destroyed. I had never been sure that I believed this, but the incident had happened in 1960, twenty years ago, before there was any question of computerizing fingerprint files, and it may have been true. Alternatively, Quade might have determined to gather any evidence for himself, and I told myself that whatever happened I must put no trust in Quade, but look for a hidden motive in everything he said or did. I was certain now that I would be meeting him again.

★

Quade was in no hurry to renew our acquaintance and it wasn't difficult to guess why. He believed he had me in a trap, a belief that William's suicide had helped to confirm, but he needed to build up the case against me. That Sokalov had denounced me was not enough. After all, I was a VIP, not a person to be accused, or even questioned – as I had been – too readily. Therefore it seemed probable that Sokalov had brought with him some proof of my activities, though I had no means of knowing what form this proof might have taken. Quade, given this, and with all the official records at his disposal, was doing his best to ensure that his case was watertight and that I wouldn't be able to escape from the trap.

Meanwhile he wanted me, guilty as he was pretty sure I was, to consider my situation and reconsider it, which of course I had to do. But if he hoped I would panic and try to make a run for it he was mistaken. I had my own plan, as I have said before, and I didn't intend to waste the time Quade was now allowing me.

First, I staged a realistic attack of asthma, gasping for breath and clutching my chest, so that I had to be helped out of a meeting. I made light of it, but I knew the story would spread and I reinforced it by coughing and wheezing at appropriate moments. When the Prime Minister expressed concern over my health I knew I had made my point, and I didn't overplay the part. I said I had had a complete check-up quite recently and my doctor had found nothing wrong with me. Naturally, this served to fuel, rather than allay, the rumour that Simon Vermont was not too well, which suited me.

Secondly, I set out to discover if I was being tailed. This was not easy without demonstrating the kind of suspicions which no innocent man would have. The tails would be experts and, if Quade seriously believed I might bolt, they would be instructed to act in twos and threes and change their cars regularly, however inconspicuous these might be.

I kept my eyes open but for several days saw no signs of followers. Then on Friday morning I went to Harrods to buy Susan a birthday present and, having accomplished this chore, was leaving the store, when I had a need to visit the men's cloakroom, which was down a flight of stairs leading off of the menswear department. I scarcely noticed the smartly dressed woman who had been a few yards behind me and who too had obviously been about to leave the store, but when I came up the stairs she was nearby, examining some men's shirts. It was too great a coincidence. By chance my question had been answered. After that I didn't bother. If Quade wanted to waste his staff's time and the taxpayers' money having me tailed I didn't care.

And so the days passed in a seemingly normal fashion. Still Quade didn't contact me. Nor was there any hint in the media about the defection of a high-powered KGB man. By the end of the third week I could feel the tension building up in me and the dry cough which I had affected had almost become a nervous mannerism, causing Imogen concern. I couldn't go on like this. Patience, never my strong suit, had grown thinner over the years.

I decided to put the cat among the pigeons, to force Quade's hand, to make life more difficult for him. I couldn't see that I had anything to lose, and at least it took the initiative away from him. As I had done many years ago to prevent any cover-up of Chief Inspector Pulent's blackmailing activities, I used a public telephone box to call a couple of leading dailies and a less reputable tabloid to ask if they had heard the rumour that a Soviet KGB officer called Ivan Sokalov had defected to the UK, and was even now being interrogated by British Intelligence.

The serious press, finding no confirmation of the story, ignored it, but the tabloid, perhaps short of material, blazoned it across the front page. It could have died there, at least until it suited Quade, but the Russians, bless them, admitted that Sokalov had disappeared while staying at their Embassy in Paris, and accused the British of kidnapping him. The story had broken and I had the satisfaction, which I recognized as being childish, of knowing that Quade must be annoyed.

But he continued his policy of inaction as far as I was concerned, raising my hopes that he might have nothing against me except Sokalov's word that William had been my controller. In my heart I knew this wasn't true, that I was only fooling myself, but I couldn't help it. It meant so very much to me and, though they were unaware of the danger, to all the Vermonts.

And I thought of the ace that I held, of which no one was aware, and the plan I had been maturing in case I was compelled to play it. I didn't want to make this move, partly because I was afraid that it might somehow be trumped and partly because I had always looked upon it as a last resort. But realistically I accepted that it was likely to become necessary.

# CHAPTER TWENTY-TWO

It was Thursday, I remember, and I was in the Members' Dining Room at the House, having a meal with a couple of my colleagues. We were discussing the case of the Libyan diplomat who had shot a policewoman from the window of his embassy in St James's Square, when the Chief Whip came across to our table.

'Simon, when it's convenient, would you mind coming along to my office? I'd like a word with you,' he said in his customary polite manner.

'Of course,' I said, accepting as we all did that the request was in fact an order.

'What have you been up to, Simon?' one of my companions asked as the Chief Whip departed. 'Don't tell me you abstained on last night's vote?'

'Certainly not!' I feigned horror. 'I wouldn't have dreamt of it. What an idea!'

I was not as amused as I sounded. My parliamentary record was good, and I didn't expect a reprimand from the Chief Whip on that score. However, he had been looking particularly solemn, as if he had weighty matters on his mind, and I wondered if he had heard a whisper connecting me with Ivan Sokalov; he was renowned for his private intelligence service, and there might have been a leak – intentional or unintentional – from MI5.

But he greeted me pleasantly, almost solicitously, when I went to his office after coffee. My fears had been unjustified. On the contrary, he wanted to ask me a favour.

'It's about poor Stapleton,' he said; Vernon Stapleton was my opposite number on the Opposition front bench. 'He's going into hospital tomorrow for a hernia operation, so he'll be off all next week and he needs a pair. That wouldn't present any problem, except that he seems to think his pair should be a Minister. I was hoping you might be prepared to oblige.'

I thought rapidly. There was always plenty of work to be done in

Committees, and there was never a convenient time to take off a whole week while the House was sitting. But the debates scheduled were not of particular interest, and it would do no harm to have the Chief Whip indebted to me.

'I could do it, yes,' I agreed, seemingly with some reluctance. 'If the Secretary of State says it's all right.'

'Thanks, Simon. I'm grateful. And a week off won't do you any harm either. You've been looking far from well recently. Why don't you go away somewhere and have a real rest. Take your wife. Enjoy yourself. Forget Westminster and Whitehall.'

'Excellent advice,' I said, and decided to take part of it. Here, with the blessing of the Chief Whip, was my opportunity to go to Switzerland.


I telephoned Imogen, who was at Aubyn House, immediately. I said I was sorry, but 'something had come up' and I wouldn't be home this weekend. I was flying to Paris the next day, and possibly on to Geneva. I'd be away several days, but would phone her.

'Public or private business?' she asked.

The question startled me. Over the years I had often had occasion to pay sudden visits to various parts of the world, usually for meetings of one kind or another, and Imogen had accepted these absences without expecting any detailed explanations. Today seemed to be different.

'With luck a little of both,' I said. 'Why do you ask?'

'Oh, I don't know.' She sounded embarrassed. 'I suppose because you've been so distrait lately, Simon. I was afraid you might be unwell.'

'I'm fine, darling. A bit of a wheezy chest, that's all. You fuss too much.'

'I can't help it. You know, Simon, you're – you're very important to me.'

'I do know. But please don't worry. There's no need,' I lied. 'I must go now, darling. I'll phone Sunday evening. Goodbye and God bless.'

'Goodbye, darling. Take care of yourself.'

I let her put her receiver down first. She had meant it when she said I was important to her and I knew that was true. If the worst happened and I was disgraced and imprisoned, she would suffer more than the rest of the family, but she would never desert me.

I had made no secret of the fact that I was going to Paris. My secretary had booked my flight and had arranged for my driver to pick me up at my house in good time to get to Heathrow. I had personally called the hotel where I wished to stay, but I had told her the name and address. It was a small but excellent hotel near the Bois de Boulogne, which I had often patronized before when not on a large Ministerial expense account, such as might warrant the George V or the Prince de Galles. Personally I preferred the less ostentatious place.

I had also mentioned my trip to several of my colleagues, as well as seeking the Secretary of State's permission. There was no question but that I had given Quade every opportunity to stop me if he wished to do so.

So it was with some trepidation that I checked in at Heathrow, collected my boarding card and passed through the various controls. Even when I had reached airside and was waiting in the VIP lounge I felt nervous, in case Quade was playing some cat-and-mouse game, and intended to embarrass me in public. Indeed, I didn't relax until the aircraft doors had closed and we were backing away from the loading bay. At least for the moment I was safe. My first glass of champagne tasted wonderful.

My trepidation returned when we landed at Charles de Gaulle, but there was no trouble entering France. I then took a taxi to the hotel, where I remained until Monday, though I was not idle during that period. After dinner on the Friday of my arrival in Paris I telephoned Jean-Paul Le Rossignol at his home. I said I would be in Geneva the following week, and hoped to see him. He at once invited me to dinner, an invitation I gladly accepted, but I added that I also needed to consult him on a business matter and we made an appointment for Monday morning.

'And I have a favour to ask of you, Jean-Paul,' I said.

'It is yours, Simon, providing it doesn't contravene the law.' He laughed. 'The law of Switzerland, I mean.'

'Nothing like that,' I assured him. 'I wish to consult a doctor, someone on whose discretion I can count absolutely, and who would perhaps take me into his *clinique* for a few days of observation.'

'You are ill?'

'No, not ill, but –' I hesitated. 'Jean-Paul, I will explain when I see you. Meanwhile, if you would be kind enough –'

'*Bien sûr, Simon, bien sûr.*' Somehow it sounded less supportive in French. 'I understand and I will do my best. Until Monday, then.'

He said goodbye somewhat abruptly, and I was shaken by doubt. The favour I had asked of him was minor. There was a much bigger one I hoped to ask, one which might not contravene the law, but would possibly strain the Swiss banking regulations, and now I was uncertain how he would respond. But I had to trust him. No one else was in his position to help me. I refused to consider what I would do if he declined; it would be the end of our long relationship, which would be sad, but most importantly it would make my situation even more precarious.

The next morning I got up late. I went to the Air France office on the Champs Elysées, where I booked a seat on an early flight to Geneva on Monday. I did a little desultory window shopping, and bought Imogen a brooch in the form of a small silver rose. I spent part of the afternoon at the races at Longchamp, where I won the equivalent of twenty pounds. I dined in the hotel and didn't go out again that day.

On Sunday I went for a walk in the Bois, and lunched with some French friends whom I had telephoned earlier. Again I dined in the hotel, afterwards spending five minutes on the phone talking to Imogen. I did not go out. I flattered myself that I was behaving normally, a man relaxing in a city he knew well, enjoying himself quietly and taking things easy. I had no business to do there. My only reason for coming to Paris was to distract Quade by drawing attention away from my need to visit Geneva. I assumed he was having me watched, though I had seen no sign of any such activity. After all, why else had he allowed me to leave Britain, if not to see where I went and whom I visited? He had taken a risk that I wouldn't run for it, but in the circumstances I supposed it was a fair gamble.

Early on Monday morning I flew to Geneva, and passed through the formalities at Cointrin Airport without difficulty. I stayed at the pleasant but modest Hôtel d'Estève by the Parc de la Grange. It had been in the Fleurie family for three generations, and was excellent of its kind. I told Monsieur Charles Fleurie that I would be leaving at the end of the week. I said I would retain my room until then, but I had had some breathing problems and might be absent from the hotel for two or three nights as I intended to go into a *clinique* for some tests on my lungs, but I would let him know. And at once I was overwhelmed by the questions and commiserations of this kind man, who assured me that he and Madame and their entire staff were at my disposal and ready to care for me. Feeling an awful hypocrite I thanked him profusely.

I had coffee with the Fleuries, then took a taxi across the Rhône via the wide Pont du Mont Blanc to the Banque St-Pierre de Genève for my appointment with Jean-Paul Le Rossignol. I was nervous. I hoped it didn't show, but so much depended – or might depend – on the banker's co-operation.

Jean-Paul greeted me warmly and said, 'Which first, business or pleasure, Simon?'

'Business, please. The banking side.'

I explained what I wanted and he listened carefully. When I had finished speaking he didn't reply immediately, but kept me waiting in suspense. His face, disturbingly serious, gave nothing away, and he was silent for so long that I began to lose hope. Then suddenly he smiled.

'You are in trouble, Simon.' It was a statement, not a question. 'I will do what I can to help.'

'Thank you,' I said. 'I am in no trouble at the moment, but it's more than likely that I will be in the course of the next month or two, if an old scandal catches up with me – which is why, though I am not ill, I am paving the way towards retiring on health grounds, should it become necessary. But please treat that as confidential.'

'Of course. No need to say more, Simon. Let us go down to the vault and deal with that matter. It may take a little time. Afterwards I'll take the opportunity to tell you what I have done about your medical "problem". Then we'll discuss when you can dine with us. Does this suit you?'

'It does indeed, and I thank you, Jean-Paul. I am extremely grateful to you.' As I said this it occurred to me that I would probably have cause to be even more grateful to him in the future.


Jean-Paul Le Rossignol was really the most tactful of men. He had sensed how tense I was, and how important our transactions were to me, and refused the invitation to lunch which I had felt bound to offer him. Thankfully I went back to my hotel, glad to be able to relax and consider the achievements of the morning, knowing that I would be dining that evening in the friendly atmosphere of the Le Rossignols' home.

My affairs couldn't have gone better, thanks to Jean-Paul, who, while keeping his distance, had co-operated fully and without asking questions. I was more than content. Of course, the circumstances weren't ideal. I was still in deep trouble. Nevertheless, I had put myself in a position where I was ready to fight Paul Quade – ironic that he should share a first name with Le Rossignol – and, if the worst came to the worst, due to Roy Gunther whom I remembered with affection, I had been able to arrange for Peter to have access to a small nest-egg, which I was certain he would use for the advantage of the family.

I had chosen Peter, partly because he was my elder son, and partly because I considered him an intelligent, practical, hard-headed man, who would accept the responsibility and deal with the situation as I would have wished. For there was no doubt it would be a responsibility involving a good deal of ingenuity. I couldn't impose on Imogen or Susan; Martin was too occupied in France, Guy too absorbed in his academic work. None of them would have been able to cope, however willing they might be. Besides, they would need all their emotional strength, without being bothered by strange requests.

Anyway, Jean-Paul had somehow imbued me with confidence and I couldn't believe that the worst was going to happen. I patted my pocket, feeling the thickness of my wallet through the cloth, and was doubly reassured.

When Monsieur Fleurie came to my table to enquire if I had enjoyed my lunch I took the opportunity to tell him that I would be out for dinner that evening, and that the next day I was entering the Clinique de la Rocque, probably for three nights, but would be returning to the hotel on Friday and flying home that night. My wife, I added, would be happy to see me for the weekend.

Monsieur Fleurie acknowledged my plans with a small bow, and said, 'It is a fine *clinique*, Monsieur, and the air is wonderful up there in the hills. Even three days will help your breathing, and I sincerely hope that all your tests prove negative.'

I thanked him, and made enquiries about transport, as it would be a long trip for a taxi. But he said there was no difficulty; he had a cousin who would be happy to drive me and he promised that there would be a car at the door the next morning at nine. So it was with a comparatively contented mind that I spent a lazy afternoon and later an enjoyable evening with the Le Rossignols.

In the morning Monsieur Fleurie's cousin, a Monsieur Roger Fleurie, arrived punctually in a large Renault, and I was installed in the back as if I were an invalid, an unnecessary rug laid over my legs. We crossed the Rhône again, and headed along the Quais towards the autoroute to Lausanne. Traffic was heavy, but we proceeded at a steady, sedate pace, my driver taking care not to cause his precious passenger any discomfort.

Beyond Nyon we left the autoroute and began to climb the winding roads into the foothills of the Jura north of Lac Léman. The day was fine and warm, with a hazy blue sky. I didn't like to reject the rug, but I wound down the window and took great gulps of the clear pure air, as if I really did have breathing problems.

Rounding a bend we came on a neat signboard at the roadside indicating the turn off for Clinique de la Rocque. A private drive about a thousand metres long brought us to a cluster of low white buildings. Monsieur Roger Fleurie drew up in front of what was obviously the main entrance and helped me out of the car.

'If you will telephone my cousin Charles when you wish to return, Monsieur Vermont, I shall be pleased to fetch you.'

I thanked him, and was reaching for my wallet when he stopped me. Any payment due, he said, would be put on my hotel account. And not for the first time I thought how much I liked the Swiss; they had all the virtues and none of the vices of the French and the Germans. I could be very happy if I were allowed to retire here, though I would miss England, especially Aubyn House. But I was looking too far ahead. I needed to concentrate on the present.

A nurse, who must have been waiting for the arrival of my car, had come out to meet me. She took my bag, and said that Dr Demourant was expecting me, but perhaps I would like to see my room first. When I agreed, I was taken up to a small suite, comfortable but impersonal, with a glorious view over the lake far below. She waited while I went to the bathroom, then led me down and along several corridors to a door with Demourant's name on it. We passed through an office where a secretary smiled a greeting, and into another, larger room.

Demourant rose from his desk and offered me his hand. He was a man of medium height, with dark hair and bright brown eyes, probably a few years younger than I was. I liked him at once and, as we exchanged pleasantries, I decided that had I really been worried about my health I would have been happy to consult him.

'Monsieur Vermont,' he said after a few minutes, 'perhaps you would tell me something about yourself. Usually, as I'm sure you realize, you would be referred to me by a doctor who would have given me a certain amount of information about your case. As it is, I know only that you are a senior politician in your country, and were commended to me by Jean-Paul Le Rossignol, who is a very old friend of mine. To be frank, it is for his sake that I agreed to have you here.'

'I understand and, believe me, I appreciate Monsieur Le Rossignol's advocacy on my behalf.' I hesitated, then took the plunge. 'I asked Jean-Paul if he could arrange for me to see a doctor who would treat what I have to say with complete confidentiality, whosoever might question him on the subject. I make myself clear?'

He nodded. 'Perfectly. For my part, I can assure you that whatever I might learn about your medical history I would treat in the same absolute confidence as a priest would treat a confession. I wouldn't lie for you. I would merely refuse to answer.'

'I accept that, and thank you,' I said, and went on to explain my visit to Dr Clement Brune in Harley Street about my breathing problems. I hesitated, then added, 'Dr Brune ordered various tests and X-rays, but said that on examination he could find nothing wrong with me except a certain amount of tension and a slightly elevated blood pressure.' I paused once more. 'This was hardly surprising because in fact I had faked my symptoms.'

Demourant raised an eyebrow. 'May I ask why?'

'In the next reshuffle of the British Cabinet I had hoped that the Prime Minister would offer me the prestigious post of Foreign Secretary, which I have coveted for some time. Unfortunately, this is not to be. A scandal in my past has caught up with me. I now hope to retire from politics on health grounds, and in order to scotch rumours which would be intolerable, not only for me but also for my wife and family, I wish it to be known in advance of my retirement that I am suffering from poor health.' I paused and looked him in the eye. 'That is the truth. Now will you accept me as your patient?'

Demourant grinned at me. 'I have already done so,' he said.

'Whatever your breathing difficulties, Monsieur Vermont, you are certainly very tense. A few days rest will do you a power of good.'


He was right. By Friday, after a regimen which included gentle exercise, massage, jacuzzi baths and light but excellent meals, I did feel far more relaxed in body and in mind. It was not to last.

Monsieur Roger Fleurie, who had come to collect me from the Clinique de la Rocque as arranged, had scarcely reached the end of the drive when he cast an anxious glance at me over his shoulder.

'Monsieur,' he said, 'I do not wish to worry you. Perhaps there is a simple explanation, but – '

I leant forward so that I could hear what he was saying more easily. 'What's the trouble?'

'No trouble, Monsieur, but I think perhaps you should know. When I brought you to the *clinique* on Tuesday there was a blue BMW behind us for much of the way. When I left you it was parked a little further up the hill, and it followed me back to the city, where it disappeared.'

I laughed. 'It must have been chance. Who would want to follow me? But thank you for telling me, Monsieur Fleurie.' I made light of the matter, but I had been painfully reminded of Paul Quade and his minions, and what would probably await me on my return to England.

# CHAPTER TWENTY-THREE

The weekend at Aubyn House, otherwise enjoyable, was marred by two small incidents.

The first occurred soon after I arrived home on Friday evening. I had caught a later flight from Geneva than I had originally intended, in order to lunch with Jean-Paul Le Rossignol and tell him about my stay at the *clinique*. The family, consisting this evening of Imogen, Peter and Julia and the Sinclairs, had already had dinner; my two grandsons were in bed and asleep. I refused the offer of food, having eaten on the plane, and suggested we should all have a nightcap.

'Are you sure you should, Dad?' Peter asked.

'Why ever not?' I stared at him in amazement; he had never before queried my drinking habits.

'It can't be good for your health at this time of night.'

I opened my mouth to say there was nothing wrong with me, and shut it again, thinking that perhaps this was as good a moment as any to suggest that all was not well with me. It wasn't the moment I would have chosen, but at least it would give them time to get used to the idea.

'Who told you there was anything wrong with my health, Peter? Was it Martin?'

'No. It was one of the barristers in chambers. He said how sorry he was to hear your health was poor, and he hoped it was just over-work and you wouldn't have to resign.'

'Well, I'm damned!' I said. 'How rumours grow and spread!'

'What rumours?' Imogen demanded. 'Simon, what is this? Are you ill? Is it something you haven't told me about? I've noticed you coughing a bit, but –'

'Darling, please don't fuss,' I said. 'I am in my sixtieth year. I have some trouble with breathing occasionally, but it isn't serious. I went to see Clement Brune in London. He gave me a thorough overhaul and I've just spent three days in a *clinique* near Geneva. The verdict is that I'll probably live to be a hundred, but I must take things more easily and try to avoid stress. That's all.'

'But how can you do that in your present work?' Peter persisted. 'And if you become Foreign –'

'Let's wait and see, shall we?' I glared at Peter, willing him to shut up. 'Whatever the rumours you may have heard, I am *not* seriously ill. There is no need for anyone to be anxious about me. Like most people of my age, I have a minor ailment. Nothing more. Now, having made that clear, I hope someone will get me a very large scotch.'

'I'll get it, and another for myself,' Guy said surprisingly. 'We old men must stick together, Simon.'

I blessed him for lightening the atmosphere, though I knew this wouldn't be the end of the matter. Separately, in the course of the weekend, each of them would question me about my health, but I could easily deal with them individually.

The other incident was more worrying. It arose from the Sunday papers. A journalist had got hold of the story that the defector, Ivan Sokalov, who had been in the news for several days, had in fact accused several important people in political, business and academic life of treachery. No actual names were mentioned, but in two newspapers a photograph of William Trevil, with a brief couple of paragraphs on the fact that the inquest on his death had been adjourned *sine die*, had been juxtaposed to a picture of Sokalov and a follow-up piece on him. The reader could draw his own conclusion. Certainly Guy had done so.

I found him in the morning room with Peter after we had all come back from church. Imogen was in the kitchen talking to Cook, Julia was in the nursery with the children, Susan was writing letters. Even before I opened the door I could hear Guy's raised voice as he argued fiercely with Peter.

'I don't care a damn what you say, Peter. It may be legal, as you maintain, but it's morally wrong.'

'There's nothing one can do about it.'

'Yes, there is. Write to the wretched paper and complain that they've made accusations – or at least insinuations – against a man unable to defend himself, and have also thrown suspicion on his colleagues and practically anyone who knew him.'

'But they haven't!'

'What's the trouble?' I enquired mildly.

I wanted to stop the argument before it became bitter. Usually Guy and Peter got on very well together. Guy was an easy-going man, prepared to shrug off any of Peter's didactic statements with which he disagreed and, except on legal matters, Peter was not obdurate. But clearly the matter under discussion was one about which they both felt strongly, and tempers had flared.

'*That's* the trouble, Simon!'

Guy thrust the newspaper he had been reading under my nose, and I found myself staring at the photographs of Sokalov and William Trevil. At a quick glance the screaming headline SOKALOV NAMES TRAITORS appeared to encompass the note on William, and I could see why Guy was annoyed. It was an old trick. And, after all, William had been a fellow don, a member of the College, and Guy had no reason to suspect him.

'Peter seems to imagine it's perfectly legal, and therefore perfectly fine, to imply that an innocent man was a traitor – a man who can no longer speak up in his own defence.'

'I did not say it was perfectly fine. I said the editor had done nothing illegal,' Peter protested.

Guy ignored him. 'And it's not only poor Trevil. It impugns his colleagues, his friends, almost anyone he knew. We're all liable to be thought guilty by association.' Suddenly he turned on Peter. 'I hope you realize that includes me and your father? Personally I don't relish the idea of having a finger pointed at me as a possible traitor of some kind.'

While Guy nattered on I had been skimming through the two articles. Except for their position, the photograph and paragraphs on William were of no significance. Had they been on another page, next to an advertisement, say, few would have bothered to read them. However, the juxtapositioning of the two pieces lent colour to both, and I was afraid there might have been a leak, either accidental or purposeful. I didn't like the mention of 'important people in politics'. Quade apart, the media were clearly closing in, and I knew how gossip could start and spread. It only needed someone to throw a pebble in the water for the ripples to begin.

'I still think it's a disgrace that editors can do this kind of thing,' Guy said. 'Whether or not the law allows it.'

But it was apparent from his tone of voice that his anger had subsided, and shortly afterwards Julia came in with the little boys, to be joined by Imogen and Susan, and we gave them our attention.

On Monday morning I drove up to London and once again I caught myself wondering if this would be the last time I'd see Aubyn House. Imogen came with me. She had been very good. She hadn't fussed or asked a lot of questions about my health since my admission that I had been consulting doctors, but I knew that she was worried.

I dropped her off at the house, and instructed my driver to take me on to my London bank, where I left in the safety of my deposit box certain photocopies I had made in the Banque St-Pierre de Genève. Then I went on to Westminster. I had been absent for a week, a week in which there would have been plenty of rumours and gossip about Sokalov and especially, since yesterday, his alleged disclosures. I was eager to test the temperature.

Several people stopped to ask how I was and say they were glad that I was back, which was encouraging and gave me a chance to spread the news that I had been in a Swiss *clinique* for a few days. But one of my Conservative colleagues, who would happily have got rid of me as I was blocking his path to promotion, asked if I had heard that my 'friend Trevil' was suspected of being a spy. I laughed the idea off as nonsense, but it was a warning that I had enemies who would be busy sharpening their knives.

It was a warning I might not have taken too seriously if my old friend, Dennis Cartwright, hadn't underlined it. Meeting me in a corridor shortly before lunch, he suggested we should have a drink in the Members' Bar. As soon as we were ensconced in a quiet corner and he had asked after my health, he too broached the subject of Sokalov.

'You've been away for a week, Simon, and you probably haven't seen many British newspapers during that time, but you can imagine the names that are being whispered here, and the stories that are spreading, some of them quite extraordinary, just as in the Profumo affair.'

'And probably just as inaccurate.'

'Most of them, I expect – but it makes life extremely distasteful. At least I find it does.'

'They don't affect you personally.'

'That's where you're wrong, Simon. Do you remember that police officer who was garrotted, years ago now? Pulent was his name. It turned out he was a blackmailer. He left a sort of account book identifying his victims only by initials, and many people, such as myself, with initials similar to those mentioned were questioned. You must remember. Well, the story goes that he wasn't black-mailing them merely for money. He was recruiting them.'

'But that's absurd, Dennis.'

'No more absurd than implying that William Trevil, that harm-less old don, was controlled by the KGB, which is what the news-papers now suggest this man Sokalov has been claiming. You saw the Sundays?'

'Yes. My brother-in-law, who was in Trevil's college, said they not only cast suspicion on William, but on all his associates. He was very indignant about them.'

'I don't blame him. You know the old adage: there's no smoke without fire. It's not easy to prove innocence.' Dennis finished his drink and stood up. 'I'd suggest we lunch together, but I'm enter-taining a couple of constituents. We must dine soon.'

Waving a hand in farewell, Dennis left me. I got myself a second drink. The bar was filling up but no one offered to join me, and I wondered if I was beginning to smell.


I grew more and more worried. Dennis Cartwright's mention of Jim Pulent and a possible connection between someone he was blackmailing and the Russian defector had greatly disturbed me. As far as I knew I was the only connection between the two, or rather Nigel Hawker was. If the merest hint of this reached the public domain and was taken up by the media, my plan – on which so much depended – would be rendered almost worthless; a dark shadow on my name would make retirement on health grounds unbelievable. I now yearned for Paul Quade to take his finger out and confront me, the reverse of what I had once hoped.

Of course, in spite of her apparent calm and sensitivity, the fact that I had been worried and under stress during the last few weeks had not gone unnoticed by Imogen, and my casual explanation of my visits to Clement Brune and the Swiss *clinique* had merely tended to sharpen her fears. I was stupid to have imagined other-wise. Apart from the symptoms which I had faked and which had caused her some concern I had been losing weight and was not looking well. That this gave verisimilitude to my supposed ill-health, and support to my plan, was ironic.

Imogen had come up to London with me the previous Monday on the pretext of shopping, but I suspected that her half-expressed intention had been to have a serious talk with me, uninterrupted by any of the family. And what must have seemed my increased depression as the week progressed made her determined not to put it off any longer. On Wednesday things came to a head.

There was never going to be a perfect moment for this conversation. Imogen chose late at night. I had left the House immediately after the ten o'clock Division, and was home by ten-thirty. I was tired and would have gone straight to bed, but she suggested a nightcap. I couldn't argue; it was clear that she was determined.

'Simon darling,' she began, as we sat down with our drinks in the comfort of our sitting room. 'I know it sounds trite, but we've got to talk. Either you're seriously ill, or there's something very wrong. What is it?'

I tried to prevaricate, but it was useless. She persisted until I lost my temper and shouted at her, something I had never done before. For a moment we stared at each other in silence. Then I apologized abjectly, and she came and knelt beside me and put her arms around me.

'Simon, I don't care what it is. I love you, I always will. Nothing could ever change that. Nothing.'

I don't know what made me say it, but I replied, 'Enough to give up Aubyn House and the family and come and live abroad with me?'

'Of course,' she said simply and at once. 'You're more important to me than any place or any person, even the children.'

'I don't deserve it,' I said.

And she smiled at me. 'Probably not. But it's lucky we don't all get our deserts or there would be a lot of unhappy people about. Darling, please tell me the truth.'

'I – I can't,' I said. 'It concerns something that happened ages ago, before – '

'Before you met me?'

I tried to laugh, but it came out as a croak. 'I'd only have been a kid, Imogen.'

She shook her head. 'Oh no, you wouldn't, darling. Simon would have been, but not you. We didn't meet until I visited you in that hospital, did we?'

I was astounded. 'What – what do you mean?'

I told myself that she didn't know, she couldn't know, but she did. She had suspected I wasn't Simon Vermont since the first night of our honeymoon. She explained that Simon would have had no opportunity to become the experienced lover I had proved to be in between the one occasion he had made clumsy love to her and when he had crashed his plane in France, a mere twenty-four hours later. She had wondered why Simon – as she then thought I was – had made no further overtures in the interval between his recuperation and their marriage, and now she believed she knew why. After that night she had watched me, and in various little ways – such as my fluent French – I had betrayed my secret and confirmed her suspicion.

I was amazed, bemused, shattered. I couldn't believe it. 'Why – why – ' I stammered. 'For Heaven's sake, Imogen, once you were sure why didn't you speak out, accuse me? You could easily have done that.'

'For two excellent reasons, darling. First, I was truly in love with you. I had been fond of Simon, admittedly. I would have married him, but he never excited me as you did. Secondly, it would have been an appalling blow to the family, especially to the General and Aunt Antonia. They were so happy when the news came that Simon was alive, though very badly wounded, and so delighted when you reached England. Think what it would have meant to them, to have their son safe, and then to lose him again. I couldn't tell them. I suppose I could have faced you with it but I didn't know how you'd react and by that time – after we were married – I was afraid to lose you. It was easier to pretend I didn't know, to accept the situation.'

'But weren't you curious as to who I was and how – how I had become Simon?'

'Of course. I still am. Tell me.'

So I told her. I didn't lie. I didn't distort the facts. I didn't try to excuse what I had done. But I didn't make myself out a villain either. I was as truthful as a man can be, describing after forty-odd years his motives and his emotions. Imogen, being Imogen, whom I had so often undervalued, was more understanding and compassionate than I had any right to hope.

'Now someone has discovered this secret, and is blackmailing you?'

'No! I was blackmailed a long time ago, in the Sixties.'

I had spoken involuntarily, and at once regretted it. Taking Simon Vermont's place had been an extraordinary act, or rather a series of acts and passive acceptances, but in the circumstances I didn't believe that General Vermont, whose judgement I had respected, would have considered it totally dishonourable, any more than I had. To kill a man, however, was a different matter, and as for Sokalov's presumed accusations . . .

But I had gone too far to stop now, and I told her the rest – or most of it, including the present hideous position in which I found myself. Probably it was no more than a minute before she spoke, but, waiting for her verdict, it seemed to me an age, and during that time I reached a decision. I would do whatever she wished.

At last she said slowly, as if she had been giving the matter careful consideration over a long period: 'First of all, forget the murder. The man was a murderer himself and a blackmailer. You've nothing to reproach yourself for there. As for the rest, if there's a reasonable chance that you'll be allowed to resign on grounds of ill-health and can go to live somewhere like Switzerland, as you say there might be since the Government won't want a scandal any more than we do, I think you should take the opportunity, for the family's sake. But, Simon, it must be what you believe would be a reasonable chance. Better than evens. Otherwise pack some bags, go and buy a couple of airline tickets for South America and – '

'A couple of tickets?'

'Of course, my dearest Simon. You wouldn't leave me behind, would you?'

For a moment I stared at her in disbelief. Then we were in each other's arms laughing and crying.

'Darling,' I said after a while, 'I'm not going to run away to South America, either with or without you. I believe I have a reasonable chance to strike a bargain, and I intend to take it. So, with that decided, let's go to bed and make love.'

We did.

# CHAPTER TWENTY-FOUR

They arrived at eight-thirty the next morning, Paul Quade and his sidekick whom I was to know as Mike Pellman. Imogen and I, still in our nightclothes, had just finished having breakfast in the kitchen. She was startled by the doorbell, but I guessed at once from its authoritative ring that this was an official call; the British equivalent of the Gestapo had come for me.

'You remember me, Mr Vermont, sir, I'm sure. Paul Quade, Security,' he announced when I opened the front door; he didn't introduce the tall dark-haired man who stood behind him.

'Of course,' I said. 'It's not long since we met. This is an early call, but come in.' I took them into the sitting room.

'You helped us with our inquiries into Professor William Trevil,' said Quade. 'Since then the scope of those inquiries has expanded, and we need your further co-operation. Would you please come with us, sir? The matter is urgent and important.'

'Come with you! Right now! You realize who I am – a Minister of the Crown. I have commitments and meetings and work to do. I'll help you if I can, but I can't ignore my obligations merely to suit you.'

I spoke angrily, but quite calmly. I was trying to strike the right balance between the citizen ready to help the police and the senior politician who felt that this abrupt request was absurd, especially without warning at this hour of the morning.

'I don't want to insist but, as I said, it is important and urgent, sir,' Quade said evenly.

'Very well,' I said at length, 'but it had better be. First, where are you taking me? I have to let my office know.'

Quade didn't answer my question. Instead, he said, 'It's all arranged, sir. The Secretary of State is fully aware of the situation.'

'What situation?'

'That you may be able to help us with some important inquiries, sir.' He hesitated, then added, 'Mr Pellman and I will wait in the car while you shave and dress.'

I could see that there was nothing for it but to capitulate. 'Okay, I'll come with you, but under pressure. And I'll be half an hour – perhaps more. I intend to check up on this outrageous demand, then phone my secretary with instructions and make some other arrangements.' I didn't intend to hurry.

'I said it was all arranged, sir,' Quade said, and added as I was seeing them out. 'Mr Vermont, it might be a good idea if you packed an overnight bag. This business may take a while.'

I raised my eyebrows in surprise, but made no reply, and banged the front door on them.

Imogen had left the debris of our breakfast for Mrs Curwen to clear, and had gone upstairs to dress. I found her in our bedroom. I told her exactly what had passed between Quade and myself. I didn't comment that Quade must be pretty sure of himself to suggest that I bring an overnight bag with me.

'But where are they taking you?' Imogen asked. 'Not some police station?'

'Not these boys, no. I don't know, and they won't say. To a so-called "safe house" somewhere, I imagine. Imogen, they won't do more than try to interrogate me. They're not going to pull out my finger-nails, so don't worry.' I kissed her gently on the lips. 'I'll phone you as soon as I can, if they'll let me – as I expect they will. But, remember, they'll probably be listening to the call. Be careful what you say.'

'I understand. But supposing you don't phone, and I hear nothing from you?'

'That won't happen,' I said with assurance. 'Ministers, even suspect ones, don't just disappear, at least not in this country. I expect to be back within thirty-six hours. I don't believe they can keep me longer than that without all kinds of formalities. After all, I'm going with them voluntarily.'


Pellman drove. Quade sat in the back of the car with me. There was very little conversation, and what there was confined itself to matters of a practical, general nature. Surprisingly the traffic was not too bad, and within an hour, during which I spent my time wondering how much they guessed, how much they knew and how much they could prove, we reached our destination, a medium-sized house in a couple of acres of land outside a Buckinghamshire village.

Pellman opened the car door for me. A houseman appeared and took my bag. I might have been a weekend guest rather than a suspected traitor. Quade told the man to bring coffee, then asked me if I wished to wash my hands, an offer I refused. He led me into what appeared to be a small sitting room.

There were several comfortable armchairs, tables conveniently beside them, what looked like a well-stocked drinks bar, a bookcase containing leather-bound and probably unread books. The four pictures on the walls were the typical prints often found in mediumly-expensive hotels. An ornamental mirror made me suspect that it was two-way, and that a third person would be watching my every blink and every twitch throughout the interrogation. I nearly laughed when Quade pointed out to me the tape recorder sitting on one of the tables and asked if I minded our interview being recorded.

'Not if it will be of any use to you,' I said. 'But I still fail to see what all this fuss is about.'

The coffee came. Pellman poured and put my cup on the table next to me. Then he served Quade and himself, and went to sit in an armchair beside Quade and opposite me, so that the situation suddenly became adverse, even hostile. Quade turned on the tape recorder, and made a few routine remarks stating the date and the time and the names of those present.

Then, 'Mr Vermont,' he began. 'The last time we talked you admitted you were a friend of Professor William Trevil.'

I agreed, though I remarked that I would hardly have used the word 'friend' – 'casual acquaintance' would perhaps have been more accurate. The interrogation had commenced and for a while it was a mere repeat of our previous encounter, the questions mainly concerning William.

'There is little doubt now that William Trevil was working for the KGB,' Quade said. 'Ivan Sokalov has produced irrefutable evidence. I'm sure you are aware of Sokalov's defection, Mr Vermont – from your work if not from the media.' He paused, then asked. 'How well did you know him, Mr Vermont?'

'Who? Sokalov? I don't know him at all. I've never met the man.'

'Strange. Trevil answered to him, and as you were a friend – even acquaintance, as you maintain – of Trevil's I'd have supposed you might –'

'Then your supposition would have been quite inaccurate, Mr Quade,' I snapped. 'I find it difficult enough to believe your statement that Professor Trevil was some kind of Soviet agent but, even if you're right and aren't being tricked by this defector, it's absurd to suggest that everyone who knew William Trevil was also involved in a conspiracy – which seems to be precisely what you're doing. Or is one presumed guilty by association in England these days? Because if so, I strongly object.'

Quade ignored the question and my objection. 'What about Monsieur Claude Petitjean?'

'Claude Petitjean?' I frowned. 'The name's vaguely familiar, but I can't place him. Who is he?'

'He is – or rather was, since he's dead – a Frenchman who worked for the Soviets. Let me refresh your memory, Mr Vermont. You met him in January 1961 in Geneva, where you were on holiday with your family.'

'Claude Petitjean?' I repeated. 'Yes, I do remember now. An elderly man. I met him literally by accident. I tripped over his legs in the foyer of the hotel we were staying at and he insisted on buying me a drink. And I think we lunched together once. My family used to drive over to Villars for the skiing, but with my old war wound it was not a sport I could take part in.'

'Go on, Mr Vermont. This is interesting.'

'I can't think why. That's all there was to it, anyway. Or are you suggesting that Monsieur Petitjean recruited me or something? A while ago it was William Trevil who was the recruiter.' I let my temper show. 'Really, Mr Quade, if you've made all these intricate arrangements merely to produce laughable innuendoes, I consider your conduct insufferable, and I won't stand for it. This bloody Russian comes to England and starts accusing people right, left and centre, and you and your people appear to swallow everything he says just like that.'

'Mr Vermont, please!' Quade held up his hand.

'You did come with us voluntarily, Mr Vermont,' Pellman reminded me.

'Is that what you call it? If so, I'm beginning to think it was a mistake,' I replied. 'For the first and last time I state categorically that I have never been recruited into, nor have I volunteered for, the service of the Soviet Union.'

'We believe you, Mr Vermont.' This was Pellman again.

'But were you blackmailed into it, Mr Vermont? That's really what we'd like to know,' Quade said gently.

'Blackmailed?'

I heard my voice as if from a long distance. The constant use of my name – the name of Vermont – should have warned me. Nevertheless, the accusation that I had succumbed to blackmail came as a shock. They weren't guessing. They knew. But how much did they know?

As they waited, letting the silence lengthen, I debated with myself whether or not it was worth trying to bluff.

'Blackmailed?' I repeated. 'Are you talking about my former secretary – and mistress, I admit – Renata Tamson?'

'No, Mr Vermont. If knowledge of that had become public it might have grieved your wife, but it wouldn't have ruined your career irrevocably. It's generally accepted that political responsibility is hard on marriage, and you wouldn't be the first MP or Minister to have an affair with his secretary. No, it was a much more serious matter than that. Can't you guess what it was, Mr Vermont?'

'I'm not exactly in a guessing mood.'

'Ah well, let's leave it for the moment, shall we?' Quade looked at his watch. 'It's almost time for lunch. I think we'll take a break now.'


I lunched alone – that is, apart from the watchful presence I assumed was behind the two-way mirror. My food was brought in by the houseman on a trolley such as hotels use for room service. It consisted of homemade soup, cold chicken, a mixed salad, cheese and biscuits, and coffee. If my interrogators expected me to pick at the food and sit wringing my hands and refusing to eat, they were mistaken. I ate well and enjoyed my meal.

When the houseman came to collect the trolley I asked him for the cloakroom. He showed me the way and left me. There seemed to be no attempt at surveillance, nothing to prevent me, had I wished, from walking out of the house. But I returned to the sitting room, having seen no one on my foray to the cloakroom, and soon afterwards I was joined once again by Quade and Pellman.

'I hope the lunch was to your liking?' Quade said.

'Splendid,' I said cheerfully, 'though it would have been improved by a half-bottle of Chablis.'

Quade's smile was sour. 'We'll try to do better for dinner,' he said, indicating that he intended to keep me there overnight. 'Meanwhile, shall we get down to business?'

229

So the afternoon session began. It was short, interrupted by tea at four, and as far as I could see was more or less a repetition of the morning's effort, achieving nothing further. I was becoming impatient, and even though I realized their intention was to rile me, my answers to their questions became increasingly abrasive.

Maybe they were getting impatient too, because in the three hours after tea the pace of the interrogation increased. I was shown photographs of William Trevil, Claude Petitjean, Ivan Sokalov, a member of the Opposition, a trade union leader, the wife of a Cabinet Minister and several other individuals, mostly unknown to me. I assumed that many of them were perfectly innocent of any crime, but I was asked if I had ever met any of them. If so, when? Where? How well did I know them? What were their politics? There must have been at least thirty prints, and the portrait shots were intermingled with photographs of buildings, one of which was the Soviet Embassy in Kensington. I took this to be some kind of psychological ploy; if so, it didn't work.

Nor did it matter that often the questions were repetitive and that I had already answered them. If I was slow the photographs would be removed, but would reappear in a different order. It was a sort of cat-and-mouse game, the object being to catch me out, and it was bad for the nerves.

There was another break at seven-thirty for supper, which once again I ate alone. Again, it was a perfectly good meal – avocado vinaigrette, I remember, lamb cutlets with appropriate vegetables, chocolate mousse – but by this time I had no appetite. I had to make an effort to eat the food, in spite of the fact that a half-bottle of wine accompanied it. The truth was that my interrogators were getting me down.

I knew I had to fight back, and when Quade and Pellman reappeared I immediately demanded that I should be able to telephone my wife. There was no objection. Indeed, I sensed they were pleased with the request, and might have offered me the opportunity during the evening, even if I hadn't asked for it. I was glad I had warned Imogen to be careful what she said.

Pellman fetched a phone and plugged it in for me. 'Just dial whatever number you wish, Mr Vermont. You have an outside line,' he added gratuitously.

'Thanks,' I said, and waited for them to leave, which they did at once.

Imogen and I had agreed that it would be best if she returned to Aubyn House, so I knew where she would be and I pictured her sitting beside the phone, metaphorically if not literally, willing it to ring. Perhaps that was how Quade and Pellman also pictured her, except that to my knowledge they had never met her. We were all wrong, though she admitted to me later that that was what she had yearned to do. But purposely, as if she wasn't worried about me and waiting anxiously for my call, she let Susan answer.

When Imogen came to the phone she said, 'Hello, darling. I suppose this means you won't be coming down tonight.'

'I'm afraid so. It's too late now and I've not finished here. But I'll be down tomorrow afternoon, or early evening at worst.'

It was the sort of casual conversation that a trusting wife would have with a husband who often worked irregular hours. It was warm and affectionate. It included some gossip about the grandchildren and the news that there was a long letter from Martin. It gave my listeners no information whatsoever, and they betrayed the fact they had been listening by returning to the room almost immediately after I had put down the receiver.

They settled themselves in a businesslike fashion and Quade said, 'Mr Vermont, I propose to try a different tack this evening, and see if we can make some headway.'

'Right,' I said. 'That's fine with me. I've just told my wife to expect me home – that is, at our country house – tomorrow afternoon.'

Quade didn't comment. He said, 'Earlier we mentioned the subject of blackmail, but we didn't pursue it. However, I think it's time we considered it in detail.'

I could only nod, and brace myself. He had warned me, and I knew what was coming. I wasn't altogether sorry, but I resented the timing. I had passed a stressful day, as my interrogators knew damn well – they had laid it on – and now they were about to take advantage of it. They were ready and waiting to spring their trap on me. It was not what General Sir Patrick Vermont would have called cricket, but they weren't playing by his rules. Nor was I.

It was not Quade, but Pellman who fired the first shot. 'Mr Vermont,' he said, smiling at me. 'You remember Nigel Hawker, I'm sure.'

'No-o,' I said. 'I don't think so. Remind me.'

'Certainly. Nigel Hawker is the son of Thomas and the late Maria

231

Hawker. They kept a grocer's shop in Islington in London. Nigel was their only child. He was a clever boy, ambitious and not over scrupulous. He thought himself too good for the grocery business. He went into the Army, becoming a sergeant in the Intelligence Corps during the war, and was dropped into France on several special missions. It was there in 1944 that his big chance came. The small aircraft in which he was to travel crashed on attempting a landing at a remote airstrip. The pilot was killed, or at any rate he died – we'll give Nigel the benefit of the doubt over that – and Nigel took this officer's place, deceived his family and inherited all the property and wealth and position that should have gone to the second son. Not a nice character!'

'What a preposterous story!' I said. 'I'm not sure I believe a word of it. And in any case, what the hell's it got to do with me?'

'It may sound preposterous,' Quade intervened, 'but it's perfectly true.'

He was wrong. It was a distorted version of the truth. I hadn't expected them to understand or show any sympathy, but I was shocked to see myself through their eyes as a mercenary figure who had taken everything and given nothing. There had even been a suggestion that I had deliberately killed Simon Vermont, which was the complete reverse of what had happened. And I was disgusted. I had had enough.

'Personally, as I say, I find this tale hard to believe, even though you insist it's true. Would the family – whoever they were – really have been so easy to deceive? What about appearance, voice, the difficulty of meeting friends and relations, sharing reminiscences? For that matter, what about little things? For example, when he went "home" he would have to have known the way to – his bedroom, say.' I shook my head. 'No, it doesn't make sense. It's not practical. And I can't imagine why you're wasting your time and mine over it. Anyway, I can't help you. Hawker means nothing to me. I can't recall anyone of that name.'

They explained about the rebuilding of the face, which also changed the voice, the supposed loss of memory, the circumstantial evidence that had laid the groundwork for the family's acceptance. All this was reasonably accurate. They had done their homework thoroughly, which presumably accounted for the long delay before my present interrogation. And what could I say? I shrugged, again denying any relevance to myself.

232

'All right,' Quade said. 'Let's assume for the moment that you accept this story, Mr Vermont. Here is Nigel Hawker, fifteen years after he took the other man's identity. He's married with children, respected, rich, successful in his career and with a great future ahead of him. Then out of the blue the blow falls. He's confronted with proof of his shameful past. He could lose everything, possibly go to prison. But he's given a choice. This catastrophe doesn't have to happen. His secret can be kept, but only if he agrees to betray his country – actually he's half a foreigner; his mother's part French, part German – and work for the KGB. What do you think he would do – sir?'

I had my answer ready. 'Obviously you believe he would have made, and did make, a bargain with the Soviets,' I said, remembering how at school I had been called Frog and Hun by Jim Pulent and his chums; I was sure Quade and Pellman would have approved of that attitude. 'But what proof of this bizarre story do you have, apart from Sokalov's word?'

'Hawker's fingerprints in a book he won at school as a prize for French are identical with those of the man he now claims to be, and, as you know, we have some more sophisticated tests nowadays. Old Thomas Hawker is still alive, and it would probably be possible to confirm a relationship between father and son, but none between supposed brothers. And, of course, this is all backed up by circumstantial evidence.'

So the trap shut. To my surprise, Quade decided at this point to call it a day. He summoned the houseman to show me to my room, saying they would see me in the morning, and I left them to replay the tapes. As the houseman closed the sitting-room door behind us I heard Pellman say, 'With luck that bastard should get thirty years for this,' and I wanted to spit in his eye.

# CHAPTER TWENTY-FIVE

I slept better than I had expected, thanks to a hot bath and the nightcap I had asked the houseman to bring me. But I woke early and lay in bed, thinking of the day to come and how I should approach the various problems that were certain to arise.

The houseman arrived with morning tea and biscuits at seven forty-five. Breakfast, he informed me, would be served in the sitting room when I came down, and Mr Quade and Mr Pellman would hope to join me at nine-fifteen. It was all very gentlemanly, but for how much longer? So far no one had directly accused me of being Nigel Hawker, but playing around the edges of the crux of the matter couldn't continue.

After all, they *knew* I was Nigel Hawker. It was not a question of suspicion. They had real evidence, and more could be produced if necessary. Given that evidence, my friendship with William Trevil and Ivan Sokalov's accusation would add up sufficiently for any jury to find me guilty of treason. But I couldn't allow it to come to that. As I drank my tea, washed, shaved and dressed, I reviewed my plan.

I went downstairs and into the sitting room. I saw no one, but I had scarcely seated myself when the houseman wheeled in the trolley with my breakfast. His immediate appearance showed that, whatever appearances might suggest, I was being watched closely, and I made a point of obviously enjoying my food. It was important that I should seem confident.

Quade and Pellman arrived punctually. The tape recorder was switched on and we got down to business. Quade asked me if I had given any thought to the story of Nigel Hawker, and whether I now recalled him. The blankness of their faces was a poor cover for their surprise when I at once assented.

'Yes, indeed,' I agreed. 'But you haven't been looking up the right records, or else the – er – authorities weren't prepared to make them available to you. In fact, Hawker was a British agent during the

Second World War, spending a great deal of time in occupied France, and making occasional trips back to the UK. Many people would consider that what he did required more courage than was needed by the Flight Lieutenant who went to pick him up, but of course Hawker was only a sergeant. Had they both lived, the pilot, who had made several such trips, would have received a DFC, and Hawker merely an MM. However, if your theory is correct, Mr Quade, he managed to acquire the higher honour after all. But you know about all this, don't you? You're an expert on Nigel Hawker.'

'Not such an expert as you, it would appear, sir.' Quade had quickly regained his composure. 'I'm glad your memory has been refreshed.'

'Ah, that might be your mistake,' I said. 'Perhaps you should have done more research on Hawker – especially on his last mission to France. But, as I commented earlier, maybe they wouldn't give you access.'

'What do you mean by that?'

'You told me a story about Nigel Hawker, which I agreed to assume was true, at least for the moment. Now I'm going to tell you a story about him, and I expect you to do me the same courtesy and assume it's true, at least for the moment.' I looked enquiringly from one to the other of my interrogators.

Quade answered. 'Yes, of course. Why not?'

'Good!'

I knew what Quade was thinking, that the more I talked the more likely I was to give myself away. To some extent he was right, but I had no choice. The time was ripe, I had decided, to play my ace and hope they wouldn't trump it.

'It was the early autumn of 1944,' I began. 'On this occasion Hawker had been in occupied France for over a year. I won't make him out to be a hero – you wouldn't buy it – but he hadn't been having a picnic, and before you say that neither had the men in the services, I would agree. Nevertheless, apart from the constant fear of capture and torture and death, you must know that there is an appalling loneliness in being an agent in an enemy-occupied country in wartime, and this wasn't Hawker's first stint by any means.'

To my surprise Quade nodded in genuine sympathy. I can't say I liked the man but I definitely preferred him to Pellman, whose face had disbelief written across it from the moment I started to speak.

'Anyway, at this point in the war the Allies, after their initial

235

success, were meeting a lot of resistance as they fought their way across Europe. Hitler hadn't given up hope, but one of his generals had. This general had a son, still in his teens, whom he was eager to protect, and he arranged for him to be taken by car to the Normandy coast and then by boat across the Channel to England. At least, that was the idea, but the plan failed. The boy and the man to whom he had been entrusted were caught in a Resistance ambush. The boy was killed. The man died later.'

'An interesting story,' Pellman sneered as I paused for breath. 'What's its relevance?'

'The general hadn't sent off his son empty-handed. In earlier, happier days for the Nazis, Hitler had written a letter to Rudolph Hess in his own hand with a list of English people who were pro-German, and who would give him every support and assistance when he landed in the UK. You remember his 1940 solo flight in a Messerschmidt fighter, apparently with the idea of contacting the Duke of Hamilton and arranging a peace settlement? Well, Hamilton was one of the names on Hitler's list.

'Why Hess didn't bring the letter with him when he came here and how the general acquired it I have no idea, but clearly he passed it on to his son in the hope that it might enable the boy to start a new life in England among influential friends, who would do their best to pull strings for him.'

'Are you suggesting Hawker saw this letter?' Quade asked.

'Oh yes. It was in German, of course, but he could read it and he understood its significance.'

I didn't say that I had been part of the ambush and had myself searched the Germans. And, even had I wished, I couldn't have explained why I had taken the youth's gunmetal watch and chain, the secret of which I discovered later and in private. Perhaps it was instinct. Perhaps it was the fact that the watch was so large and clumsy for a boy to be wearing. Whatever the reason for my act, I blessed it now.

'Go on, sir,' Quade said.

I had scarcely realized I had stopped speaking. I continued: 'Now, let us assume that Hawker not only read the letter but brought it back to the UK with him. The people for whom he had been working showed no great interest in his presumed fate or in what he might have achieved, so he kept the letter – as an insurance policy, you could say. Which means, gentlemen, that if your story is true and my story is true, Hawker is in an excellent position to make a bargain with the – er – authorities, which at present means you.'

'A bargain? With a traitor?' Pellman practically spat out the words.

'Why not, Mr Pellman? It's been done before, as you well know, and almost certainly will be done again.'

'Wait a minute!' Quade interrupted. 'Such a bargain – and remember we're still talking in terms of assumptions – would have to be a fair exchange. This letter would be out of date by now, wouldn't it, with most of the people dead?'

'Some,' I admitted, 'but not all. For that matter, you tell me that Nigel Hawker's father is still alive. And those of the Führer's British chums who are dead had families. Some of them must have known – and possibly shared – their parents' feelings and quite a few of them have become eminent people.'

'Blackmail!' Pellman muttered.

'You could call it that,' I said. 'You could also call it self-preservation. There would of course be a *quid pro quo*. Complete immunity against prosecution. Guaranteed secrecy. No sudden denunciation afterwards, as happened with poor old Blunt, who had thought himself safe. Retirement with honour.'

'Honour!' Pellman snorted.

'We're going too fast again,' Quade said. 'It's really impossible to discuss the matter until we've had a chance to evaluate the letter. Have you any idea how that might be brought about, Mr Vermont?'

This was my Rubicon. After it there could be no turning back, no denial of the story I had told them, no depending on a brilliant barrister to shred their case against me. I would have convicted myself. But it was the course I had decided on, and I was sure it was the best.

'Yes, Mr Quade,' I heard myself say. 'I happen to have in my London bank a photocopy that should convince you. If we drove up to town now I could fetch it and give it to you. I promised my wife I'd be arriving at Aubyn House this afternoon or early evening – I have a surgery for my constituents tomorrow morning – so it would be most convenient.'

'What about the original?' Pellman asked.

I looked at him, but didn't answer. Quade was obviously weighing up the situation. He knew that to begin with he would have to see a photocopy and form some judgement about it. He daren't call my bluff, in case I wasn't bluffing, but he didn't want me catching the next flight out of Heathrow either.

'Very well, Mr Vermont,' he said. 'If you'll pack your overnight bag we can leave at once.'

'My bag's already packed,' I said.

It was a small point to score, but it gave me some pleasure.


The return journey to London was even more taciturn than had been the trip to the 'safe house'. We drove straight to the bank and Pellman stopped directly outside the main entrance, regardless of the double yellow line. They let me go into the building alone, and it only took a few minutes to complete the formalities and collect the envelope I had brought back from Geneva and put in the London safe-deposit box. But there had been time for a traffic warden to spot an illegally parked car, and she was busy arguing with Pellman.

I handed Quade the envelope. He and Pellman must have agreed on their next move, but the traffic warden had upset their plans. She banged on the roof when I got in and Pellman, faced with mini-bureaucracy, didn't have the nerve to drive away immediately. In the end, Pellman acquiesced and accepted a ticket. It then took him a full five minutes to find a legal parking space, and meanwhile Quade, unable to contain his curiosity, had opened the envelope and studied its contents.

His face expressionless, he passed the document to Pellman and said to me, 'Two questions, Mr Vermont. Obviously there are some lines missing from the middle of the list. Why? And how are we to know the whole thing isn't a fake?'

'I cut the lines out myself, in order that whoever read the photo-copy wouldn't learn all the names at once,' I said truthfully, giving Quade full marks. 'But the complete document does exist. As to whether or not the whole thing is a fake – that's up to you and your experts to decide. After all, there is such a thing as handwriting analysis, for example, and when and if you get the original you'll be able to check the paper. However, I assure you that if you take the risk of having this letter made public you'll rival Nigel Hawker for unpopularity.'

Quade regarded me seriously, and I was pretty sure he was convinced that I was telling the truth, though he wasn't going to admit it – not yet. 'Of course we'd need the original before any, er, agreement could be reached – supposing such a thing could be possible,' he said.

'Of course,' I agreed, 'and, as you pointed out, Mr Quade, these matters can't be hurried. They need consultation and consideration. Therefore, what I suggest is this. It's now Friday. If you would drop me off at my London house I can make myself a quick lunch and then drive down to Oxfordshire for the weekend, which is my normal habit. I'll return to London on Monday. I have meetings in the House in the morning, but if you'd call on me at my home at – say, two o'clock in the afternoon, we can discuss this matter of Nigel Hawker further. By then you will have had plenty of time to assess the situation, and consult your superiors. I hope for everyone's sake that we can come to a civilized agreement.'

'Bloody cheek!' Pellman muttered, just loudly enough for me to hear. 'If I had my way –'

I was never to know what he would have done with me if he had had his way. Quade, who was a much more experienced operator, cut him short. But I could guess.

'Very well, Mr Vermont. It is agreed. You spend the weekend in Oxfordshire and we meet again on Monday. Let's go then.'

Pellman started the car with an unnecessary jerk to show his disapproval, and when we reached my house he stayed behind the wheel. Quade got out of the car.

'Until Monday, Mr Vermont.' He looked me straight in the eye.

'Until Monday, Mr Quade.' It must have sounded like a double act at some old-time music hall, but it was in deadly earnest. 'I shall be there,' I said. 'I want the matter settled as much as you do. So no dirty tricks and – ' I glanced towards Pellman who was staring straight in front of him. 'No leaks, accidental or otherwise.'

Quade's smile was sardonic. 'A temporary truce,' he said.

I nodded. We didn't trust each other completely. How could we? But we were at least communicating. He waited until I had gone into the house and I watched from an upstairs window as they drove away. I had no doubt they would put up a full team to keep an eye on me.


The weekend passed too quickly. By chance all the Vermonts were there. Aubyn House was full of our children and grandchildren. Even Edward and Natalie had flown in from Germany on a few days' leave. It was a great family reunion, and I scarcely had time to worry about the future. I did, however, achieve three things.

Most importantly, on Friday night after we had gone to bed, I had a serious talk with Imogen. I told her about the letter that had been folded and concealed in the back of the gunmetal watch and the use to which I was putting it; I now had no more secrets from her. But we discussed what I should ask for in return, if Quade was empowered to make a bargain with me, and we considered some contingency plans. Once more I was grateful for Imogen's commonsense approach and her unfailing support. Looking back, I don't believe I could have got through this immediate period and what followed without her.

Then on Saturday morning, after my surgery, I warned my agent that I would possibly be forced to retire from politics on health grounds at the end of the present parliamentary session. I hadn't expected him to whoop with joy, but the dear man was frightfully upset and nearly wept. He assured me that the constituency would never find another Member who would serve them as well and as faithfully as I had done. He was obviously sincere, and I was touched.

Finally, on Sunday evening, as I had agreed with Imogen, I broke the news to the family. Once I had assured them that I was not about to die in the near future, they took the news calmly. My simulated asthma, which I had not forgotten over the weekend, and my visit to the Swiss *clinique* had given them some warning, even though I had made light of my supposed ill-health. Guy and Susan extolled the merits of retirement. Edward pointed out that I was sixty, and as a serving officer he expected to retire with a reasonably high rank a while before that age; there was a general nodding of heads. Only Peter and, to my surprise, Martin showed any real appreciation of my position. They alone – apart from Imogen – seemed to realize that I was giving up a life I loved and renouncing all ambition at the very moment when the top prizes were within my grasp.

Perhaps it was for the best. For all their sakes I hoped they wouldn't have to know the true reason for my resignation.


On Monday morning I drove up to London. I hadn't found it easy to say goodbye to Imogen and the rest of the family, but I was reasonably optimistic. I went straight to the House of Commons, where I dealt with my correspondence and then attended a meeting from which, after a lot of wheezing and seeming difficulty in breathing, I withdrew, gasping an apology.

By now it was nearly lunchtime and, having duly recovered from my 'attack', for which I received much undeserved sympathy from my colleagues, I drove to my house, garaged the car and ate the excellent light lunch that Mrs Curwen had prepared for me. As I finished my coffee the front doorbell rang. The guardians of the State's security had arrived.

# CHAPTER TWENTY-SIX

Mrs Curwen showed Quade into the sitting room. I saw him glance around and curl his lips in contempt. I could read his thoughts. He was thinking how richly I had done for myself and, while he despised me for what I was, he also envied me – and that made him angry. I don't believe it ever occurred to him that in spite of my crimes, I had probably worked as hard as he had and served the country as well.

I waved him to a chair. 'Sit down, Mr Quade. You're alone?'

'Yes. On purpose, Mr Vermont, so that we can talk frankly. Of course I shall report back, but there will be no witness to our conversation and you can always deny it afterwards.'

'No concealed tape recorder, or anything of that kind?' I was wondering if they had bugged the house in my absence.

'No, definitely not,' Quade said. 'It wouldn't be in anyone's interest to have a record of this meeting.'

With difficulty I managed not to give a sigh of relief. I had apparently won the first round. My offer to bargain hadn't been turned down out of hand, as I had secretly feared it might. Quade's masters were prepared to do a deal.

'The same goes for you – denying our words I mean,' I said amicably. 'But let's start with the supposition that we hope to reach an agreement acceptable to both sides.'

'Why not?' Quade was ready to be amicable too. 'But you must realize that I am not in a position to make firm commitments. This could be considered to be a preliminary sortie – if you want to think in army terms.'

I yearned to say, 'Let's forget all this stupid fencing and get down to essentials,' but I knew this wasn't feasible. While I was the main – indeed, the only – protagonist on my side, Quade had others to whom he was answerable, and beyond them rose a whole hierarchy, several of whom might be affected as much as me by the decisions that were ultimately taken. This business couldn't be hurried.

'Before we can offer any – er – terms,' Quade continued, 'we would have to be convinced of the validity of the document in question.'

The words were not his. He was obviously quoting someone else, and I had an insane desire to laugh. But my situation was far too serious for that.

'We've been through all this before,' I said. 'I realize you'll have to make your own tests. However, the original letter that Adolf Hitler wrote is in my safe-deposit box in Switzerland and, as you know, Swiss banks are sacrosanct. But if you care to accompany me there, I'll get it for you.'

He stared at me in disbelief. 'You'd hand it over to me – just like that?'

'If you believe it's possible to meet my conditions, yes.'

'You mentioned immunity, and a guarantee that there would be no breach of the secrecy of the – er – arrangements.'

'As happened with Blunt, yes. I don't propose to be tricked, Mr Quade. Nor do I want there to be an accidental leak. You and Pellman, and your superiors, can presumably be trusted to keep Nigel Hawker's secret. But does anyone else know about it? For instance, what of the Russians? How did they get hold of the story in the first place?'

I knew the answer to my last question, thanks to Claude Petitjean, but I wanted to know if Quade did. There had been no reference to Chief Inspector James Pulent during my interrogations.

'That's a difficult question to answer,' said Quade slowly. 'Our source, as you're aware, is Sokalov, but he's dependent on us for his future and we can control him. He told us, and he had no reason to lie, that he had taken over from a colleague who had been disgraced, and merely accepted what he was given. When pressed, he said he believed William Trevil might have been responsible originally for – er – unmasking Hawker. But that was a long time ago, and anyway, Mr Vermont, I see no reason why the Russians should wish to denounce him now – do you?'

'Not really,' I agreed, thankful that there seemed to be no known connection with Jim Pulent, because this simplified the situation. 'Right, Mr Quade. You offer immunity and secrecy, which is fine. No one wants a scandal – and I emphasize no one – for that includes the Government.'

'Which is to your advantage in the present circumstances.'

243

'I appreciate that. However, Mr Quade, that won't be enough to buy that letter. I have other conditions.'

'We imagined you would.' Quade showed no emotion. 'You may discover that we too have conditions. For instance, you must hand over all photocopies as well as the original, and, if from the safety of a foreign country you ever cast any doubt on the integrity of the people named in the letter or their families, our agreement would immediately become null and void.'

'Okay,' I said, irritated by the portentous language, which didn't come naturally to him. 'Whether we like it or not, there has to be mutual trust in this matter, so let's try to be businesslike. At the end of the present Parliamentary session, which is in a matter of weeks, I will resign on grounds of health. The Prime Minister will express great regret. I will go to Geneva with whomsoever you wish, collect the letter and hand it over. Soon after I will go into the *clinique* where I stayed earlier in the year, and in due course I will settle permanently in Switzerland. I shall expect to receive there my RAF invalidity pension and my full Parliamentary pension, and no restrictions must be imposed on any private money I wish to take out of the country; this should present no difficulty since Exchange Control Regulations have been abolished since the end of 1979.'

I stopped. Quade had made an impromptu sound. He looked at me and slowly shook his head. He thought I was asking too much.

'Oh yes, Mr Quade,' I said. 'I've earned that Parliamentary pension. You ask my constituents. Even firm Labour supporters, who wouldn't dream of voting for me, wouldn't begrudge it. As for private money, I don't intend that my wife and I should have to scrimp in our old age.'

'Your wife?'

I had surprised him. 'Certainly, I hope and trust she'll come with me.'

'I see.' He gave me a cynical glance; he didn't believe it, but then he didn't know Imogen. 'Well, the life you're visualizing for yourself doesn't sound too bad, Mr Vermont. Any other requests?'

I hesitated. There was one. Imogen had suggested it, and I had laughed thinking it a joke, but she had been serious, and I had promised to consider the idea. But now, I was sure, was not the moment to mention it. I had pressed Quade enough. It was my turn to give a little. So I didn't answer his question directly.

'I don't think we can go any further at present,' I said. 'But once you have informed me that the arrangement I have sketched out is acceptable in broad outline, I will offer the Prime Minister my resignation immediately. Any further details can be fixed later. I will then be at your service to go to Geneva to collect the letter. Would you consider this reasonable, Mr Quade?'

He nodded. 'Fair enough,' he said.


There were no difficulties. My resignation caused a certain amount of flutter in the media, but most of the comments were sympathetic, and I received a good deal of unexpected praise for what I had accomplished during my political career. In the House commiserations came from both sides, and the Prime Minister – I was not sure, and I certainly didn't enquire about the extent to which she was aware of all the facts of the case – sounded perfectly sincere when expressing the deepest regret at my departure. Personally I put a higher value on the many letters that poured in from my constituents telling me how much I would be missed, the telephone calls and the friendly reassurances from those whose opinions I prized – friends and colleagues in and out of Parliament and the Ministry. But it was a trying time.

Apart from the constant worry that something might go wrong, I had a heavy workload, both in the House and the constituency – heavier than usual because I was retiring – and there were innumerable decisions to be made and problems to be solved in connection with the family. It was a relief to go to Switzerland for a couple of days, even attended by Quade and Pellman. I had refused to go for a shorter period and I had refused to seem to be accompanied by them, but they sat behind me on the aircraft and kept me in their sights until we reached the hotel; it was one in which I had not stayed before and where I was not known. We ate at separate tables and directly after lunch went in separate taxis to the Banque St-Pierre de Genève. What a farce! Nevertheless, I was nervous.

Before leaving England I'd had a long telephone conversation with Jean-Paul and had warned him of my intentions and the line I wished him to take, so he was expecting us. When we were shown into his office he greeted me distantly and without warmth, as we had agreed. I introduced Quade and Pellman as officials from the British Government, to whom I had agreed to make available my safe-deposit box – I had already made it clear to Jean-Paul which one was to be opened – so I would be grateful if Monsieur Le Rossignol would co-operate.

'It is more than a little unusual, but if it is your wish, Monsieur Vermont,' said Jean-Paul, showing disapproval, as befitted a Swiss banker who believed in the sanctity of his bank.

Jean-Paul shrugged his shoulders and took us down to the vaults. Although I would have bet that it was a new experience for Quade and Pellman, neither showed any emotion. Jean-Paul used his key and I used mine, and he left us as I slid the box out of its compartment in the wall of the vault.

This particular safe-deposit box contained only one item, a sealed envelope. I gestured to Quade to take it and, carefully, as if he thought he might damage it, he removed it. I slid the box back and locked it, but left my key in the lock; I wouldn't be needing that box again.

'Let's go!'

'What about the watch?' Pellman asked. 'Where is it?'

I looked at him in feigned surprise. 'I've no idea. The last time I saw it was in France. I gave it to one of the Resistance chaps,' I lied. 'What does it matter? The letter is what's important.'

'And that's in here?' Quade tapped the envelope.

'Yes. Plus the other photocopy I made.'

'Good!' Quade seemed satisfied. 'As Mr Vermont said, then, let's go.'

I called to Jean-Paul, who rejoined us. For a moment he looked at me anxiously, and I was afraid Quade might sense the close relationship between us.

'All is well, Monsieur Le Rossignol,' I said. 'Isn't that so, Mr Quade?'

'Yes, most certainly. We are quite satisfied,' Quade hastened to say.

'*Ah, c'est bon*! I was worried,' Jean-Paul said, covering his anxiety by admitting it. 'I am sure you understand that a bank does not like trouble, especially a Swiss bank that prides itself on its reputation for confidentiality, which can so easily be dented by a scandal.'

Quade reassured him again and at the door of the bank we thanked Jean-Paul for his co-operation, shook hands and said goodbye.

I was sweating with relief. All was indeed well – so far.

★

We assembled in Quade's room at the hotel for what amounted to a ceremonial opening of the envelope. The bedside table was small, and there was no other. Pellman cleared the dressing table of the oddments that seem to collect even during the shortest of stays in a strange place. Quade slit the envelope with a pocket knife, extracted its contents and laid them out carefully. I watched from the comparative comfort of the one armchair in the room; after all, it was only weeks since I had prepared the envelope, so I had no reason to be curious. I knew exactly what they would find – the two pieces of the letter and a photocopy of them.

'Toilet paper,' Pellman said.

He wasn't far wrong. Hitler's letter had been written on the thin flimsy paper which the British tended to despise, but the Continentals favoured at that period. This had made it possible for the sheet to be folded small enough to be inserted into the watch, but it also meant that the pieces were badly creased. Quade smoothed them out with gentle fingers.

The letter was brief, scarcely more than a note. It contained a greeting, plus two columns of names of individuals said to be sympathetic to the Nazi cause and ready to welcome anyone the Führer commended. Its importance lay in the fact that it was addressed to Rudolph Hess and signed by Adolf Hitler. If it were authentic, it damned those who were mentioned in it.

'Satisfied?' I asked.

'No. Why is the original in two pieces, like the photocopy? There must be a strip missing. Where is it?'

'Mr Quade, you must know enough about me by now to accept that I am not a fool. Surely you can't believe that I'd be so stupidly trusting as to hand the whole letter to you – intact. If I did, what would prevent you – or one of your paid lackeys – from pushing me under the nearest bus or causing me to have some other unfortunate accident as soon as we got back to England. In that case you would have achieved your objective with no scandal, and I would have achieved nothing. You could even start a nasty rumour about my being an impostor and a traitor. I wouldn't want that for my family's sake.'

There was a long silence. Either the possibility I had outlined had genuinely not occurred to them, or they hadn't expected me to be so suspicious.

'Nevertheless, you've broken the agreement you made, Vermont,'

Pellman said, adding 'Hawker' under his breath. 'You undertook to hand over the original authentic letter.'

'And I have done precisely that, Pellman. The small strip I have removed contains four additional names, two in each column; and two of these are particularly eminent persons, and as long as I have this evidence I'm confident that, because the handwriting is Hitler's and the strip can be authenticated since it fits exactly into the letter, I shall remain safe and you will honour your side of the bargain. Incidentally, I might point out that I have given you the letter, but until now *you* have done nothing except allow me to offer my resignation to the PM. When your people have studied the letter I reckon it will be up to you to commit yourselves. With this in mind, I have one final request.'

Pellman shook his head in disbelief that I was still making demands. He would have preferred to see me on my knees, begging for mercy. I could sense his antagonism. Quade was more reasonable.

'And what's this final request?' he asked mildly.

'I wish to be awarded a knighthood.'

For a moment they were stunned. Whatever they had expected it was not that I should ask for an honour. Then Pellman gave a raucous laugh and doubled up with pseudo-amusement. Even Quade was grinning broadly.

'A knighthood,' Pellman spluttered.

'You must be joking,' Quade said.

They were over-reacting. They were pretending to be amused. Basically they were angry at the mere idea that I might – just might – and they never would . . . It was insulting to them and what they stood for. They couldn't believe I was serious, but I was – now. When Imogen had first suggested the idea I too had been disbelieving, but she had persuaded me of the desirability – indeed the need for such recognition; it would make it impossible for them to go back on their word.

'I am not joking,' I said firmly. 'I've done my best to prepare the way for my departure from public life on health grounds, and in ordinary circumstances, though the resignation of a Minister always causes interest and some gossip, that would be fine. But the circumstances aren't normal. Thanks to the defection of Sokalov there are many rumours going around, and my resignation is bound to arouse some suspicion. The award of a knighthood would do more than anything to quash these rumours and therefore I've begun to look on it as a necessity.' I paused and then added frankly, 'In addition, of course, it helps to tie your hands.'

'I see,' Quade said. 'I appreciate your difficulty, Mr Vermont, but you must realize you're asking the impossible. You really can't expect Her Majesty to confer on you –'

'Why not? If it hadn't been for Sokalov's accusation I would be going to the House of Lords. I'm prepared to bet there's many a man or woman on those red benches who's served the country worse than I have. But who's to judge? At any rate, Mr Quade, it's what I want and when I think of the names of Hitler's chums missing from that letter I don't consider it unreasonable. If I tell you that three of them are alive and one of them has Royal connections, perhaps a lovely "K" won't seem a high price to pay for my silence. Therefore I ask you to put my request to your masters.'

I marched out of the room and neither of them tried to stop me but, alone, I wondered if I had gone too far, if indeed I had been too greedy and asked for the impossible. I should, of course, have trusted Imogen's judgement.

# CHAPTER TWENTY-SEVEN

It was difficult to make plans or take important decisions while I was still unsure of my future, and on my return to England I was kept waiting for ten days before I heard anything from the authorities. As far as the House and the Ministry were concerned I was understandably taking sick leave; in fact, I lounged around Aubyn House, coping as best I could with the delay.

Then early one morning Quade telephoned me. He said a car would pick me up at two o'clock that afternoon to take me to a meeting; he hoped that would be convenient.

I assured him that it would be. Though worded as a request we both knew it was a command I couldn't refuse. Not that I would have wanted to refuse, for I have never liked waiting for someone else to take the initiative. And if there was concern it arose from Quade's failure to mention whom I was to meet and whether the car would be bringing me home again.

At two o'clock precisely the car arrived. Imogen kissed me good-bye and wished me luck; we knew how much could be at stake. The driver opened the rear door of the car, and my spirits rose. I found myself alone. No one had been deputed to 'escort' me to this meeting. I settled down with my thoughts.

It was a lovely bright afternoon, and in other circumstances I would have enjoyed the drive across country, but today it was hard to relax and I was glad when we arrived at the 'safe house' where I had first been interrogated. Quade came out to meet me.

'Good afternoon, Mr Vermont. Will you come along to the sitting room. The Director-General's waiting for you.'

I followed him into the house. He opened the sitting-room door, waved me in and shut the door behind me, leaving me to go forward into the room alone. A large heavy man in his late fifties rose slowly from an armchair. I recognized him at once, for it was not the first time I had met the Director-General of the Security Service – MI5 – the man who was ultimately responsible for the safety of the country and the preservation of its secrets.

'Afternoon!' he boomed in his deep voice, and gestured to a chair opposite the one in which he had been sitting.

'Good afternoon.'

I sat, stretching out my game leg and making myself comfortable. I waited. It was up to the DG to open the proceedings. I hadn't been brought here, I was sure, for further interrogation, but to be told what decisions had been reached, though there was always a chance that some options might remain open to me.

The DG seated himself. He didn't speak for a moment, but regarded me solemnly. It was a strange situation. The previous occasions on which we had met had been purely social. We both belonged to two of the same London clubs, and we had mutual friends. None of this would have made any difference to what had been decided, but it couldn't help but colour our approach to each other.

'Mr Vermont,' the DG began formally, 'as you must have guessed, a great deal of consideration has been given to your present position, and how it could affect others. I am not speaking only of the great and the good; the dislodgement of a small rock can cause an almighty avalanche, carrying all before it, even a Government.'

I looked at him doubtfully and he continued.

'Let me make myself clear. I heartily dislike what you have done. I think it despicable for any man or woman to betray his or her country's secrets to a foreign power. During your interrogations I believe you implied that you had given away nothing of great importance, but you know as well as I do that even a general description of a private meeting on a vital subject can contain a nugget of value to an enemy. A great deal of intelligence work consists of collecting seemingly non-essentials which, when analyzed, may make up a vital whole.'

I didn't contradict him, although I thought he was going a little too far. To me it seemed that most useful intelligence nowadays came either from technical sources or from an intelligent reading of the world's press. Nor did I say that on several occasions, when the opportunity arose, I had supplied misinformation; God knows I never had any love for the Soviet Union. But I refused to grovel or offer excuses for what I had done. As I studied this man, who was to

251

once more the three major choices I had had to face during my life –
to usurp or not to usurp Simon Vermont's place, to kill or not to kill
Jim Pulent, and to become or not to become a reluctant Soviet agent
– I would make exactly the same decisions.

'While it appears,' the DG continued, 'that you did not receive
any money for your services, and indeed acted under duress, the
fact remains that over a period of years you were a traitor, and that is
abhorrent to any decent citizen. How the devil someone like you,
with all the – '

He stopped abruptly. He had just remembered that I was not
Simon Vermont, with all his privileges. I was Nigel Hawker, who
had had few advantages. I smiled cynically. He didn't miss my reaction, but to my surprise he apologized.

'I'm sorry. I have no right to make personal comments, and for
two reasons. First, I have never been in your position so I don't
know how I might have acted. Secondly, whatever my feelings, officially I have to condone what you have done. In other words, I hope
to come to an agreement with you which will be acceptable to both
of us.'

I nodded. I felt almost sick with relief, but my voice was quite
steady, almost indifferent, as I said, 'Good, I'm glad of that,
Director-General. What do you propose?'

'In return for that letter from Adolf Hitler which you have
provided, you will be given a guarantee of immunity and complete
confidentiality, which was what you requested. You will, of course,
undertake never to name any of the persons mentioned in the letter
to anyone. It will be accepted that you have retired on health
grounds, with honour, if one can use such a word in the circumstances. Both the RAF pension and your Parliamentary pension will
be paid in full, and what you do with your private money is your
affair. However, as you are not really entitled to own either your
country estate or your town house, you must not sell them.'

'I have no intention of selling either, though to be frank I don't
think it's any of your business. However, I've already consulted my
lawyer on the matter. I am making over both properties to my elder
son, Peter, with the understanding that there will always be a home
in either place for Martin Vermont and his sister Susan and her
husband, as indeed there is now.'

'Good. That sounds a reasonable arrangement.'

'I have made some other arrangements, too – with your approval, naturally.' I couldn't resist the sarcasm. 'I propose to make my home in Geneva. I shall go there shortly and will stay at the Clinique de la Rocque as before. This will give additional credibility to my excuse of poor health. My wife, to whom I've given a Power of Attorney, will follow as soon as our affairs in England are settled. Except perhaps for brief special occasions such as my daughter's wedding next year, I shall not return to this green and pleasant land.'

The DG gave me a hard look. He suspected that I was taking the mickey. In his heart, try as he might, he wanted me to pay for the wrongs I had done. The many good things – and there were quite a few to my credit – he ignored. He was bound by his prejudices.

'That's acceptable,' he said curtly. 'But, as I see it, there are just two more issues to be considered. First, the idea that you should be awarded a knighthood as a sort of underwriting of your innocence is out.'

'Why?'

'Because I say so. It's a ludicrous idea.'

'I'm not so sure of that. I believe I've earned an honour. As I told your man Quade, if it hadn't been for the untimely defection of Sokalov I would in due course almost certainly have been offered a peerage.'

'That's different.'

I shrugged. 'What's the other issue?'

'I want the slip of paper you cut out of the letter.'

'No. Definitely not, and for a very good reason – because I don't want to die an early death.'

'I give you my word –'

'No. That's not good enough, Director-General. I'm sorry.'

'Then the deal's off. You'll be disgraced, you and your wife, your children. You'll go to prison for years.'

'Perhaps not for all that long. A clever barrister could win me a lot of sympathy. Imagine me limping into the dock and him drawing a picture of the poor but clever boy who served his country coura- geously, but was tempted – and one thing led to another. And, as for the disgrace, I wouldn't be alone, would I? He could point out how over quite a period I had risked my life for my country, had been badly wounded and indeed very nearly died. I hadn't been a secret Nazi, hoping that the enemy would win the war.'

'You've kept a photocopy of the letter,' he snapped accusingly.

'No. But I'd challenge you to produce it in court. Would you lie on oath to save some of your upper-class chums and their families from disgrace?'

He pushed himself out of his chair and started to walk up and down the room. He was very angry. He would have loved to tell me to go to hell, and the fact that he couldn't made him the more furious. It was an impasse, and we both knew it.

'Supposing – just supposing – you got your knighthood,' he said at last. 'You would then give me that missing piece of the letter.'

It wasn't a question. It was an offer to exchange, tentative only because he resented having to make it. It didn't occur to him that I might refuse, but I did.

'Then what the devil do you want?' he demanded.

'Nothing beyond what I've already mentioned. If you promise me a knighthood, I will give you a photocopy of the missing strip of the letter, but I will *not* part with the original. Your experts can confirm that the photocopy is really of the missing strip.'

'Very well, I agree,' he said heavily. 'You have my word. I won't go back on it.'

Oddly enough, I believed him, and anyway as long as I had the original strip of paper I was relatively safe. It was time for me to make a gesture. I took out my wallet, extracted a piece of paper and held it out to him.

'Four names,' I said. 'I'm afraid you'll find two of them unpleasant, and one –'

'I need to know,' he muttered.

He took the paper and turned away from me so that I couldn't see his expression, but I watched his shoulders slump. As I had warned him, of the four people mentioned, two were important. The minor member of the Royal Family who was named would bring the DG no joy as there would certainly be complications and pressure for secrecy would be brought to bear. Nevertheless, he could accept it with some phlegm; after all, the man had been known to be a friend of the late Oswald Mosley, and luckily he was now dead. Moreover, it didn't affect the DG personally. The other name was a different matter. It was that of a respected member of the aristocracy, the present head of an ancient family and the eldest brother of the DG's wife. It must have been a blow to him, but he recovered quickly.

'All right,' he said finally. 'I'm satisfied. What about you? Is there anything else you want to ask or tell me?'

'No,' I said. 'I am satisfied too.'

'Then we have an agreement, Mr Vermont? We understand each other, and we understand that nothing can be put in writing?'

'Yes, we have an agreement, Director-General.'

I suppose this was the point at which we should have shaken hands to seal the bargain, but the DG showed no inclination to do so. He went to the sitting-room door and called to Quade, who appeared at once; obviously he had been waiting for the summons.

'Mr Vermont is leaving,' said the DG. 'Perhaps you'd see him to the car and then come back. We have many details to arrange.'

'Yes, sir.'

'Right, then. Goodbye, Mr Vermont.'

'Goodbye, Director-General.'

And five minutes later I was in the car that had brought me to the safe house, and on my way home to Imogen. I felt exhausted, but I had won for myself and the family more than I had ever hoped for since poor William Trevil had first warned me that Sokalov was on his way to London and that all I held dear was in danger.


By the end of the year Imogen and I were established in Geneva. It had not been an altogether happy period. How could it have been? On the one hand the DG had kept his word. I was now Sir Simon Vermont and, while my supposed ill-health had precluded too many farewell parties, much praise had been showered on me by a wide section of people from the PM down to the most lowly of my constituents, and much regret had been expressed at my departure from public life. More importantly, the media publicity given to me had been wholly without snide hints of involvement on my part with Ivan Sokalov or any kind of scandal. All this had been most satisfactory.

However, there had been many problems that required personal and practical solutions. Innumerable questions had arisen, such as who would be responsible for the day-to-day running of Aubyn House – Peter was much too busy – and how the estate and the London house should be financed if my support and Imogen's were withdrawn. But eventually, thanks to the co-operation of every member of the family, these and other such problems were also dealt with satisfactorily.

There remained the important question of where in Geneva Imogen and I were to live, and here Jean-Paul Le Rossignol's help proved invaluable, as it did with the various formalities concerning residence in that country. It was Jean-Paul who found the delightful villa for us on the north side of Lac Léman which we were able to rent. But it required much work and money – and here my Swiss numbered account and my precious hoard of diamonds proved essential – to redecorate and furnish it to our taste, since all we brought with us were a few books, some pictures, silver and one or two favourite pieces of furniture to make us feel at home.

Home is an emotional word and for both of us it meant and always would mean Aubyn House, so that our first Christmas in Geneva was a rather sad affair. However, in the New Year Peter and Julia came to stay, bringing the boys, followed one after another by the rest of the family, and gradually the whole atmosphere of the villa seemed to change. We never again felt lonely there, as we had that first Christmas.

Of course we continued to miss Aubyn House and the family, London, the political scene, watching the grandchildren grow up. We missed a very great deal. Nevertheless, we were never troubled by the British authorities, and when Imogen died some months ago we had had ten good years in Geneva, which was doubtless more than I deserved.

And, except to say that inside the gunmetal watch is the original sliver from Hitler's letter, that is the end of my story.

God bless you all.

# Postlude

*1993–94*

Peter Vermont stared out of his study window at the garden of Aubyn House, which now legally belonged to him – or perhaps it didn't. It was a view he had known all his life. Spread out on the desk in front of him lay his father's manuscript which he had just finished reading, the dismantled pieces of the gunmetal watch and the sliver of paper containing four names in what he presumed to be Hitler's handwriting.

Peter was not particularly interested in the individuals themselves, none of them now alive, though he appreciated that their families would be appalled if the names were published in such a context. This applied especially to a certain eminent politician, known for his right-wing views and his bullying tactics in the House, for whom the revelation could prove disastrous if the tabloids got to work on it. But Peter had no desire to ruin anyone or cause anyone distress. He was only concerned about his own father, himself and his family.

What was he to do, if anything? Was there some wrong to be righted? Financially Martin had suffered most. With his elder brother dead, Martin should have inherited Aubyn House and the responsibilities that went with it. And how he would have hated the prospect; he would have felt bound to marry that girl who had wanted him, Audrey Dreisland – Peter was surprised that he should remember her name – and the marriage would have been a disaster, probably childless. As it was, Martin had enjoyed a happy life in France with his man friend, always aware that there was security for him in England.

There had been security for Susan too, for all of them. His father had seen to that. Even when the old man had gone to live in Geneva – a notoriously expensive city – there had been no drain on the Vermont resources, though he and Imogen had lived comfortably and had provided a wonderful holiday home for the whole family. Clearly, the diamonds and the numbered account had made this possible. They had all benefited from his foresight and care for them.

Peter hated to think what might have happened to the Vermonts if it hadn't been for his father, for Martin could never have coped – and it was not only the family who had gained. The Right Honourable Sir Simon Vermont had been a conscientious Member of Parliament and Junior Minister. He had done his best for his constituency, and had applied his skills to whatever office had been given to him. The many regrets expressed at the time of his retirement, the praise given to him in the obituary columns at the time of his death and the grief of each member of the family, young or old – all this had been genuine. Yet, Simon Vermont had been a myth. In reality, he had been an impostor, a murderer, a traitor. Peter groaned aloud. He had loved the man. He couldn't stop loving him now.

A while later Peter's troubled thoughts were interrupted by a knock on the study door, and a small head poked around the side.

'Dad, it *is* Sunday, and Mummy says it's time for drinks before lunch.'

'Thank you, Antonia darling. I'll be right there.'

The door shut. Peter drew a deep breath and exhaled it through his teeth. Drinks before lunch had always been something of a ceremony on Sundays at Aubyn House, and he couldn't ignore it. He had already disappointed the family by refusing to go to church, but this had been his first opportunity that weekend to complete the manuscript, so he had said he must work and was not to be disturbed.

It was the last injunction that had caused Antonia to be sent to fetch him. Everyone knew that however irate he might be at the interruption, he would never swear at his beloved daughter. He was devoted to his last-born, Antonia, who had been named after her great-grandmother, as the child was fond of declaring. But that was untrue, as he now realized – a kind of black joke. Antonia Vermont, the late Lady Vermont, wife of Sir Patrick Vermont, was not Antonia's great-grandmother. At best, because of Imogen, his own mother, she was a distant cousin.

Suddenly aware that he was wasting time, Peter collected the pieces of the gunmetal watch into an envelope which, together with the manuscript, he locked up in his briefcase. The slip from the letter he put in his wallet. He would have to decide what to do about them later.

He hurried from the study. From the sound of voices he could tell that everyone was in the drawing room, and there he found Susan and Guy, his sister Noreen with her husband John and their two girls, and Julia with his own three children – the boys home for half-term. In addition to the family there were a couple of neighbours and the Reverend David Carmichael and Mrs Carmichael. Patrick and Hugh were carefully pouring sherry and the girls were passing titbits around. It was a typical Sunday morning gathering, and everything was distressingly normal.

'Sherry, Dad?' asked Patrick, the elder son.

'Please,' said Peter, though he would have preferred a strong whisky. To Carmichael he added, 'Sorry I couldn't come to church this morning, David. I really did have to work – a terribly complicated brief.'

'Even on the Sabbath, Peter?' Carmichael shook his head in mock reproof.

'Unfortunately, yes. What's more, I regret to say I've also got to work this afternoon.'

This last remark met with a chorus of protests, cries that he had promised and he must come with them. For a moment his mind was blank. Then he remembered.

'Of course, the Sandersons' garden party for some charity or other. I'd forgotten. I'm sorry. I'll be with you.'

'That's the spirit, Peter,' said Carmichael. 'Always put your family before all else.'

The words came back to Peter as he lay in bed that night trying to sleep. They had been lightly spoken, and Peter wondered if the parson really believed them. Certainly the man whom the world had known as Simon Vermont had acted on that principle. In a sense, he had betrayed his country rather than the Vermonts; he had killed a man to protect the Vermonts; he had loved the Vermonts more than his own honour. And he had asked not to be judged too harshly.

Anyway, who was his son to judge him? Would he have taken the same actions in Simon's place? Peter asked himself. Could he have done the same? Would he have had the courage? As he thought of Julia and the children, Edward and Noreen and their families,

Martin and Susan and Guy, he hoped and prayed that he would never be put in any such position.

In the weeks that followed Peter more or less came to terms with the situation into which he had been plunged. With difficulty he reconstructed the gunmetal watch, inserting the slip from the letter and, having made a small parcel of it, deposited it in his bank. The manuscript he kept in a safe at his chambers where, by treating it as a brief, he managed to reread and study it. As a result he concluded that there was no further action he needed to take, and in due course the script joined the watch in the bank.

Slowly the apprehension he had felt on learning the truth about his father faded. For long periods of time he never thought of it. Then, suddenly, something would remind him – a chance remark of Susan's about the war, perhaps, or a reference by his son Hugh, who liked statistics, to the number of generations of Vermonts who had been at Eton. But for the most part he was happy, enjoying his work and his family, with nothing worse than minor worries to disturb him – a man apparently to be envied.

So the traumatic year ended, and in the following January, since the villa in Geneva was no longer available to them, Peter decided to take Julia and the three children to Canada for their winter holiday. Though he had no means of knowing it, the choice was ironic.

While the Vermonts were skiing in the Laurentians north of Montreal, an old man was dying of cancer in North York, a suburb of Toronto. He was an obstinate character. He had refused to go to a hospice. He was determined to die in the house which had been his home for over ten years, looked after by his housekeeper, who was also his common-law wife. He died the day the Vermonts flew back to London from Mirabelle Airport.

A week later there appeared under 'Deaths' in the Personal Column of *The Times* the following notice: 'GREEN. On 9th January, at his home in North York, Ontario, Canada, John Michael, after a long illness.' Peter Vermont didn't read it and, if he had, it would have meant nothing to him; he had never heard of a Canadian called John Michael Green. Indeed, few people had, for John Green had lived a very quiet life and, apart from Eva Koenig, his housekeeper, there was no one to grieve for him. Not that Eva grieved for very long, not after she discovered that the house, which

262

she had expected to inherit, was merely rented, and that the lease would come to an end with the old man's death. His income, too, had ceased on his death, leaving Eva homeless and with only her own savings.

Fortunately, Eva Koenig, now in her late forties, had always been able to look after herself, and the post of housekeeper to an unsuspecting and relatively well-off John Green had enabled her to supplement the generous wages he paid her, so that her savings were not inconsiderable. But they wouldn't last for ever, and she had no desire to work for anyone else. She wanted a home of her own and a steady income for independence. And she thought she knew how she could achieve these ambitions, though the project would need a certain amount of research first. She had to be sure of her facts.


It was one evening three months later that Peter Vermont received a telephone call at his London house. The caller was a woman who gave her name as Eva Green. He knew no Eva Green, and he was tired; he had spent a hard day in court with recalcitrant witnesses and a judge who seemed purposely to misunderstand his submissions. He was not in the best of tempers.

'Yes, Miss Green, this is Peter Vermont, but I don't believe I know you. Are you sure it's me you want?'

'Mrs Green,' she corrected him. 'And yes, Mr Vermont, I'm sure it's you I want. You're the son of the late Sir Simon Vermont, aren't you? You see, I'm hoping to write a biography of your father and I need your help.'

'A – a biography of my father?' Peter heard himself repeat. 'Why should you want to do that? He never rose to any of the highest offices.'

'No, but he might have done if he'd not been forced to retire, and he was an interesting man – ever so interesting. Surely you could spare me half an hour of your time, so that I can explain my intentions?'

'I'm extremely busy at present. Perhaps next week –'

'I shall be returning to Canada next week. Fit me into your schedule before then, Mr Vermont. It'll be worth your while. You wouldn't want me to write a book about your father that might cause distress to you and your family, would you?'

'Wait a minute!'

Peter put down the receiver. He was frowning. There had been something vaguely menacing about the woman. He would have to see her, find out what she was hinting at. She could be dangerous. Her last words had sounded like something approaching a threat. Hurriedly he referred to his engagement book.

'Hello, Mrs Green. I am free in the early part of tomorrow evening. Would that suit you? Say between six and six-thirty.'

'That would be fine. I'll come to your house. I know where it is. Until tomorrow, then – '


The following evening Peter sat in his study and waited for the doorbell to ring. Somehow he had coped with the routine of his day, glancing through briefs, consulting with his clerk, conferring with solicitors, and appearing in court. But his thoughts kept on shifting to Eva Green, who had spoken of 'returning' to Canada as if this point had some significance, and who, in spite of that and her use of the occasional Canadian idiom, had a guttural – probably a German – accent.

Eva Green arrived at six twenty-five, when Peter had begun to wonder if she was not coming. She apologized for being late. As he showed her into the sitting room they exchanged pleasantries about the traffic and the English weather. Then Peter decided to take the initiative.

'You're a Canadian, Mrs Green?' he asked suddenly.

'I have Canadian citizenship, but I was born in Dresden. My parents took me to Toronto when I was a child. At first we were very poor. I wore second-hand clothes, and didn't always have enough to eat.'

As she talked, Peter studied her. She was a short, square woman with bright blue eyes and gold hair that owed more to her hairdresser than to nature; she was smartly dressed and self-possessed. She fiddled with her wedding ring which looked new to Peter. He wondered how much of what he was hearing he should believe.

'You say that for some while you've been earning your living as a housekeeper, Mrs Green. Frankly I don't understand why you believe this qualifies you to write a biography of my father or anyone else.'

'That's where you're wrong, Mr Vermont. For the last ten years I have worked for John Green, or that was what he called himself. He was always very secretive about his past. It wasn't until he was dying of cancer that I learnt who he was – and a lot more.'

'You're talking about your late husband?' Peter asked as she paused.

'We were not actually married, and I didn't get a cent when he died, though I'd nursed him for months.' Her resentment was obvious. 'But at least I wasn't left quite empty-handed.'

Deliberately Peter looked at his watch. 'Mrs Green, please come to the point. What is the connection with my father?'

'Okay. I'm coming to it. John Green was an ex-KGB man. His real name was Ivan Sokalov. He defected to the Brits in 1980, and when they'd finished interrogating him they gave him a new personality and a pension and arranged with the Canadian Government for him to settle in Toronto. Of course the money stopped when he died, and the house was reclaimed, but think what the newspapers would pay for his story.'

'Mrs Green, aren't you becoming confused? At one moment you talk of writing a biography of my father and the next of selling this man Sokalov's story to the press. I'm afraid I fail to appreciate the connection,' Peter lied, his mouth dry.

Eva Green nodded sagely, and Peter felt a surge of anger. He hated this woman who had it seemed by chance discovered his father's secret, or part of it. He wished her dead, but there she sat opposite him, smiling smugly, and he had to continue the pretence of not knowing what she was talking about.

'I guess I didn't tell you the exact truth,' she said. 'I never intended to write a biography of Sir Simon Vermont, but I needed to see you. It's John Green's – Ivan Sokalov's – story I intend to tell. I reckon it'll be worth a million dollars, more with luck. But while I'm writing it I need to live, and live comfortably. That's where you come in – and your late Pa. You see, there is a connection. When Sokalov came to Britain he confessed that Simon Vermont had been working for him for years. In fact, the highly esteemed Simon was a traitor!'

'That's nonsense!' Peter did his best to sound surprised and shocked.

'Oh no, Mr Vermont. For some reason, I don't know why, except I suppose he was part of the British Establishment, the authorities covered for your father. Sokalov was not to mention Simon

Vermont's name. In return for that, and all the other information he provided, he would be given a new life.'

'That's a dreadful accusation to make. What proof have you of all this?'

'No actual proof. But I've got Sokalov's dying words, and there's circumstantial evidence. Everything hangs together.'

'I still say it's nonsense. Libellous nonsense!'

'Maybe nonsense, but certainly not libellous. As a lawyer you must know you can't libel the dead.'

'But you can go to prison for blackmail.'

'What blackmail? All I'm asking is a loan of a hundred thousand English pounds to enable me to write the book. I'll get much more than that from advances and serial rights, and I'll pay you back in a year's time. In return for the loan I'll swear not to mention any member of the Vermont family, or even hint at your father's treachery.'

'No!' Peter said at once.

He knew the woman was lying. He would never see the money again whether or not she wrote the book, and there would probably be demands for more. And anyway she didn't need to write a word. All she needed was to get hold of some enterprising investigative journalist and tell him her story. Whatever denials were made, a lot of mud would stick.

'I realize this has been a shock to you, Mr Vermont.' She was standing up, collecting her handbag. 'I'll go now, give you time to consider my proposition. I'm sure you'll come to the conclusion that this is the best solution for everyone. I'll phone you tomorrow or the next day, and we can make arrangements.'

She was moving out of the sitting room and Peter, stumbling to his feet, followed her. He opened the front door and let her out. He didn't respond to her 'good night'. All he could think of was that history was repeating itself, and that what he had hoped would never be had come about. He now found himself in the same position as his father had been in years ago. And what was he to do?

It was now late at night. Peter sat at the desk in his study, his head in his hands. He had drunk too much whisky. He would have a hangover in the morning. And he had reached no conclusion. He felt shattered, devastated, incapable of dealing with the situation. He was too close to the problem for his legal training to be of any help at the moment.

He supposed his father had suffered similar emotions when faced with Jim Pulent's attempt at blackmail. Somehow the book didn't suggest that Simon Vermont, though he had admitted to being shaken, had been completely overwhelmed by the catastrophe that threatened himself and the family. But Simon Vermont had been a man not unused to crises and prepared to take risks, a man who was both physically and mentally capable of killing.

I am not like that, Peter thought. I can wish that damned Green woman dead, but I couldn't kill her, not in cold blood. If I tried I'd probably bungle it, and God knows what the consequences would be. He wondered what Simon Vermont would have done if he had been able to foresee the repercussions of his act. Peter shrugged. There was no knowing, and the past was dead. It was the future that mattered.

However, thoughts of the future were less than encouraging. To acquiesce to blackmail was out of the question; the wretched woman would bleed him and the whole family white. So she must be told to go to hell, to do her worst and the Vermonts must face up to the disgrace and scandal and probing of their private lives that would ensue; even Martin's relationship with his French friend would become part of the story. But could they face up to it? It was a reflection of his state of mind that, no sooner had he made the decision than, picturing the headlines in the tabloids, Peter reversed it.


Eva Green telephoned Peter the next morning at eight o'clock, taking him by surprise. His head ached, his stomach felt uncertain and he cursed himself for having drunk so much the previous night.

'Have you considered my proposition, Mr Vermont?' she asked.

In spite of his condition, Peter's mind reacted reasonably rapidly. 'I am considering it, and I'm inclined to – to accept it, but I must have more time, Mrs Green. For one thing there's the problem of raising such a large sum of money unexpectedly. I think I'll need to consult my brother Edward. Would you object to that?'

'No, providing you're quick about it. I'll be around this evening at the same time to tell you how I want the money paid.'

Damn the woman, Peter thought as she cut the connection. She was crowding him, sure of herself, sure he would pay rather than accept the consequences; either way she would gain, and there was nothing much he could do about it. He had no intention of consulting Edward. The decision had to be his.

And by the evening, as he waited for the doorbell to ring, he had reverted to his first decision, which in his heart he had known was inevitable. He would tell her to get out and do her worst. As a last resort he switched on the recorder, which was out of sight, in the hope of getting evidence of blackmail that might conceivably prove useful later.

When Mrs Green didn't arrive and he didn't hear from her, he didn't know what to think. He spent a sleepless night and an anxious morning. It was not until he read an early edition of the *Evening Standard* that he learned what had happened.

Chance, which Simon Vermont said had played such a large part in his life, had once more intervened. Eva Koenig Green had been knocked down by a bus the previous evening. A foreigner, she had been looking in the wrong direction before crossing a busy street, and no blame was attributed to the driver. She had died before reaching hospital.

And so the Vermont myth was safe for now, perhaps for ever, but the thought of what might have been was to haunt Peter Vermont for a very long time.